DEFIANT EMBRACE

"I'm staying, Quint," Holly said quietly. "Silver Creek is my home now."

"It's too dangerous for you to stay here," he whispered, feeling his good intentions dwindling fast under her tantalizing stare. "You'd best go back to Tennessee."

Caught up in the caressing tone of his voice, she didn't hear his words at first. When she realized what he'd said, her eyes flashed in defiance. "I will stay and see that Tom Farrell pays for what he did to Papa. Then I'll run that land exactly as Papa intended." Her chin trembled. "No matter who tries to get rid of me. Whether you want me here or not!"

Quint stared at her, horror-stricken. How could she think he didn't want her here? How could she possibly think that? "Lord, Holly, I want you here." Taking her in his arms, he buried his face in her soft mass of black curls. "I want you here."

Holly clasped her arms about him tightly, as though she feared someone might tear them apart. She pressed closer to Quint's hard, lean body, feeling his fingers massaging her shoulders, her back. They felt like fingers of fire traveling down her spine, exploding in tiny bursts of fireworks inside her brain.

Quint lowered his lips to hers fiercely and lost himself in the moist fullness of her kiss . . .

ZEBRA BOOKS
KENSINGTON PUBLISHING CORP.

ZEBRA BOOKS

are published by

Kensington Publishing Corp.
475 Park Avenue South
New York, NY 10016

First printing: May 1987

Printed in the United States of America

To my mother
who taught me to dream,
And to my husband
who never gave up on me.

Chapter One

Holly Campbell crushed the telegram from her sister in her gloved fist and stabbed a straggling black curl beneath her dusty gray silk bonnet.

"Come to Texas," Papa's letters had urged. So here she was, two months from her home in Tennessee, weary and bedraggled from hours of jostling in stagecoaches, miles of trudging through muddied roadbeds, headed for a remote place on the edge of civilization—clutching the message she had received in New Orleans:

"Papa dead. Suicide. Return home immediately. Caroline."

Suicide! Holly thought of his enthusiastic letters, his plans to buy land, his commitment to the community. He was needed in Silver Creek, Texas, and he knew it; he was happy in Silver Creek. She was sure Papa did not commit suicide.

And she did not return home. Instead, she wired Caroline to forward any future communications to her in Silver Creek, then boarded the next steamer for Galveston Bay, intent upon her mission: to retrieve his belongings and place a marker on his grave *after* she discovered the truth about his death.

Suddenly the rhythmic jouncing of the stagecoach hesitated, then the coach lurched forward, spilling its occupants into and on top of one another.

Her grief turned to fear as a hand pushed her small frame to the floor, a knee jammed into her back, and, through the rumble and clatter, the voice of the lawyer, Ezra Hinson, echoed, "Rifle shots! Keep your head down, Miss Campbell!"

Holly coughed, strangling from the acrid mixture of gunpowder and dust, smothered by feet trampling her body as the men maneuvered themselves into better shooting positions.

The stagecoach paused again, and Holly slid violently to the left; then after an instant of wild swaying, the vehicle poised on two wheels and slammed to earth on its side, and Holly's head hit the door.

Her slender arms trembled as she tried to push herself away from the side of the coach. Had Papa gone mad to love such a country?

The thought startled her. Her father, Dr. Holbart X. Campbell, had resettled in Silver Creek after the Confederate surrender, and for four years he wrote Holly eloquent accounts of his new homeland, encouraging her to move to the frontier where she could escape not only the loneliness of reconstruction Tennessee, but also its dangers. Never a word about stagecoach holdups. Or worse, she thought, clutching the telegram in her now damp, steel-gray leather glove.

"Are you all right, Miss Campbell?"

Holly mumbled an assent while tugging at the pearl gray skirt of her alpaca traveling suit, which was caught beneath portly Mr. Rich's knee. As the passengers silently tried to dislodge awkwardly tangled limbs, she cleared her thoughts. "Was anyone shot?" she asked.

"Don't know yet, ma'am," Mr. Hinson answered.

At that instant the door flew open, and two black eyes glared down at her from a bandana-covered face. A burly arm reached in and jerked her upward through the door.

"Easy with the lady," Mr. Rich called.

"Shut up in there and throw out your weapons." The voice was rough, like the arm that hauled Holly onto the top of the coach.

As she pulled her shaking legs up behind her, they became ensnarled in her heavy, mud-caked skirts, and she stumbled over the edge of the vehicle, landing in a heap upon the rocky ground. Lifting herself up, she gasped at seeing the driver prostrate alongside the coach.

"Mr. Monk!" Holly rushed to his aid.

"It ain't nothing, ma'am." Monk hobbled to his feet and wrapped a filthy bandana around his arm.

"Get on back here." The first outlaw jerked her toward the side of the coach. "Line 'em up," he ordered his men.

Then she noticed the other bandits, three of them, with guns trained on the driver and passengers. All wore bandanas over their faces and long yellow slickers. Their eyes, the only identifying features visible between their felt hats and the tops of their bandanas, were all alike—harsh, cold, and leveled on their targets.

When the passengers were positioned to the leader's liking, the shorter of the outlaws removed his sweat-stained hat, revealing a nondescript mop of dirty brown hair. He passed the hat along the line, taking coins and a watch from one man and jerking Mr. Rich's gold pocket watch and fob from his pocket, tearing his beige brocade vest. As he approached Holly, he reached for the amethyst breastpin adorning her lace cravat. She tilted her chin at him, defiantly slapping his hand away.

"Don't touch me!" With quivering fingers she removed the pin herself and slammed it into his palm, point first.

The man yelped in surprise, jumped back a step, then, flushing with embarrassment, he struck Holly across the face. She fell to the ground.

"You brute!" Ezra Hinson delivered a quick punch to her attacker's midsection, and the outlaw immediately slammed the barrel of his pistol to the lawyer's head, knocking him to the ground beside Holly.

Holly reached toward Mr. Hinson, but before she could speak, the outlaw leader took her by the arm, dragged her to her feet, and pulled her behind the stagecoach.

"Where are you taking the lady?" Mr. Rich shouted.

The other thieves kept their guns aimed at the passengers. "Shut your trap, or you'll get worse'n him," the short one said, jerking his head toward Mr. Hinson, who had risen and now looked dazedly around the back of the overturned coach.

"Bother the lady, and I'll see you hang," Rich hollered.

"Keep 'em quiet," the leader called from behind the stagecoach. He shoved Holly toward the rear boot, ripping it open. "Which one's yours?"

"What?"

"The baggage?" he demanded. "Which one's yours, Miss Campbell?"

Holly drew a sharp breath at the mention of her name. He prodded her with his gun. "Point it out. We ain't got all day."

She pointed to a small rose-colored tapestry valise which he rummaged through, then cast aside. "You expect me to believe you come all the way from Tennessee with no more'n that?"

Her stomach churned violently, and her knees started to buckle. She wanted to scream at him through her terror: Who are you? How do you know me? But she had learned from the Yankee soldiers quartered in her home during the war that any form of weakness always drew more violence. So she steadied her voice as best she could, silently cursing the soft Southern accent which she greatly feared would make her sound conciliatory. "My trunk is on top."

The outlaw dragged her a few steps to the rear, and they found her Moroccan leather trunk where it had tumbled into a thicket when the stage turned over.

"That all you have?"

"Yes," she answered, praying this ordeal was now over, but suddenly he jerked her silk bonnet from her head and began pulling her loosely pinned black curls.

She screamed in pain. "What do you think you're doing?"

"During the war," the outlaw told her, "female spies carried secrets to the Yankees in their false hair." He gave her black locks a couple more pulls.

"I am *not* a spy!" she protested. "And I don't wear false hair!"

He loosened his grip on her head, then, evidently satisfied that the mass of black curls was indeed growing on her head. But as she began to relax, she felt his rough hand run down her slender, trembling body.

"Take your hands off me." She jumped as far away from him as his hold would permit. "What do you want?"

He tried to lift her bulky skirts, and she fiercely struck out with her foot, catching his shin with the point of her scuffed gray leather shoe.

He wrenched her arm behind her. "Straighten up, lady, or those big brown eyes are gonna be black and ugly."

Then, swinging her body around forcibly, he held her with one arm across her heaving bosom and the pistol barrel pointing up her quivering chin, as he fumbled among her lace-trimmed white petticoats with his other hand.

"Take off your bustle." Exasperation tinged his demand.

"What?"

"Them lady spies," he said, "they carried papers in their bustles, too. Take it off."

She glared daggers at him from the depths of her smoldering brown eyes, her loathing now almost as great as her fear. "I will not," she answered firmly.

"You're a mighty troublesome woman, Miss Campbell." He stared straight back at her while he jerked up the back of her dress, found the bustle, and ripped it off, breaking the ties.

"You're a beast!" she cried, watching him tear apart her ruffled crinoline bustle. "The Yankees never treated me this indecently!"

As the outlaw shoved her ahead of him toward the front of the stagecoach, her mind whirled. What could he possibly think she was hiding?

Apparently satisfied, he called to his men. "All right, boys, let's get movin'." He motioned toward the trees where Holly, for the first time, noticed horses calmly cropping grass in a mesquite thicket a few yards from the road, waiting for their riders.

The leader addressed the passengers. "Everybody down, face on the ground. And stay put till Monk here counts to a hundred." As he disappeared behind the stagecoach, he called back, "Sing it out loud, Whip."

In a voice crackling with hatred, Monk recited the numbers, and Holly rushed to his side, forgetting for the moment her own ordeal as she urged Monk to let her look at his wound.

She gently unwound the dirty bandana and threw it aside. The bullet had shattered his thin arm above the wrist. Holly looked around at the desolate countryside, then called to the men to find her two smooth boards.

"Now, Mr. Monk," she said as though she were tending a patient in the best equipped hospital, "your arm has been broken by the bullet. I will use a portion of my petticoat, which is somewhat cleaner than your handkerchief, to staunch the blood; then we'll splint and wrap it, and you'll make it to our next stop just fine."

Ezra Hinson brought her two rough pieces of wood which were caked with mud. "These are the best I can find, ma'am. They're used for staking horses, but I reckon they'll do for splints."

Holly took the two sticks and began brushing the mud away. "They'll do nicely, thank you. Now, would you see if, by chance, Mr. Monk has a bottle of spirits stashed in the boot?"

The driver's blue eyes came alive. "Yes, sirree, break out that jug! It's almost worth gettin' gunshot to have a pretty young thing tie up my wound and feed me likker."

Mr. Rich fetched a brown jug and handed it to the driver, who took a couple of long pulls before Holly doused his wound with its amber liquid contents.

"Where'd you learn this doctorin' stuff?" Monk asked.

"From Papa mostly."

"That's right," he recalled. "I plumb forgot. Holbart Campbell was your pa. Doc Holly we called him out here." Monk grinned at her. "Just like you."

Holly smiled, "He was known as Doc Holly back home, too. I always loved sharing that name with him." Her smile dimmed. "I also spent a number of years working in a field hospital near my home in Tennessee, where our brave boys suffered more gunshot wounds and broken bones than I ever hope to see again."

Monk looked at her through wizened eyes. "You do mighty fine work, ma'am. An' I've been shot up enough to know when a job's done proper."

As Holly gave the wrapping a last tug, she heard a loud crash and turned to see the coach land upright on all fours. The men groaned, slumping against the cab.

Monk held out his bottle. "Here you are, boys. Come an' get it. You deserve to wet your whistles as surely as this ol' reprobate."

Mr. Hinson passed the bottle around, and Holly noted how carefully each man measured his swig. They were leaving something to ease Monk's pain on the ride into Silver Creek, she supposed, smiling at their thoughtfulness.

Holly helped Monk to his feet, and he reached for the brake stick to steady himself before climbing onto the driver's box.

"Mr. Monk! You cannot drive this stagecoach!"

Monk looked down at Holly with a twinkle in his blue eyes. "That's news to me, ma'am, sure enough it is." He settled himself on the driver's seat, calling below, "All aboard!"

The passengers climbed back into the coach, while the young shotgun guard crawled onto the driver's box beside Monk.

Holly held back protesting, but Ezra Hinson guided her into the coach. "Rink will do the driving, ma'am," he assured her quietly, "but nobody can take away Monk's right to ride on the box and call the shots. He's in command here."

"He's in terrible pain," Holly objected.

"Beggin' your pardon, Miss Campbell," Mr. Hinson said, "most folks out here tend to their own affairs. Oftentimes it don't pay to do otherwise."

"But I am doctoring him," Holly replied, trying to hold her ground.

"As he said, ma'am, he's had a caution of gunshot wounds in his lifetime, and likely none of them has laid him up. Don't worry none about him, he's a crusty old dog."

Holly sighed. "Papa wrote that people in Texas live by different rules."

The lawyer nodded. "Born of necessity, ma'am."

At that the air was pierced by the call of Monk to his team, and the coach pitched forward, forcing the occupants to scramble for secure positions.

Mr. Rich felt inside his vest pocket, and his face took on a wistful look. "I reckon it to be around four o'clock," he said, indicating that even though he had been relieved of his gold watch, he had in no way relinquished his self-appointed task of advising the passengers on the time of day. "Couple more hours and we should be pullin' into Silver Creek."

Holly pushed her tousled black hair from her eyes. Two more hours and this wretched journey would be over.

Her shoes cut into the flesh of her swollen feet, every joint in her body throbbed, and the stays in her confining corset were wreaking havoc with her ribs and the tender flesh of her bosom. She was so exhausted from lack of proper sleep that she fought delirium.

And being a female on a trip like this made matters worse. Inside the cramped quarters of the coach every move bumped one or more passengers, sometimes in the most awkward places. Each shift in position pushed the next person, causing him to move as well, so that the cab was in a constant state of reshuffling.

Two hours. Holly squeezed her eyes closed, shutting out the countryside Papa had loved so well, holding in the tears which threatened to flow.

Her confidence and anticipation of two months ago had been erased. Today, nearing the place he called home, she was filled with misgivings and fear. As the desolate, alien land rocked by her window, her thoughts were on Papa, his life and death, the holdup, the telegram. What did it all mean?

She recalled her bitter tears of four years ago when he rode away from Hedgerow Plantation, a torn and broken man. He had returned from the War Between the States to find Mama dead of yellow fever, their farm destroyed, and his line of thoroughbred bays dispersed as mounts for Yankee soldiers. In desperation he turned Hedgerow over to his elder daughter Caroline and her husband, William Bedman, and headed West.

Through the ensuing years, he wrote to his family often, and Holly kept every precious letter. Sometimes late at night, when the big old house seemed unusually lonely, she would reread the whole stack.

Through his candid dialogue and witty descriptions she came to know his new friends, and after he pleaded in six consecutive letters for her to join him and start a new life, she made her bold decision to come to Texas.

When she announced her plans to Caroline and William, her sister was stunned. "You always were a willful sort, Holly Louise! Ladies simply do not travel about the country alone—especially not to an uncivilized place like the frontier. And even if no physical harm comes to you, you will be dreadfully lonely for everything you have ever known—books, music, friends."

"Perhaps," Holly had agreed. "But I'm lonely here, too." She looked around the once-elegant room that a few years before had been alive with the laughter and dancing of her friends. "You have William," she cried, desperately trying to communicate her lonely predicament to her married sister. "No matter how miserable things get, you won't be alone. But there is no one here for me, Caroline. No one. The single men who were lucky enough to come home from the war have been forced to leave again by the dastardly carpetbaggers."

Tears and wrangling followed, but two days later, a day after her twenty-fourth birthday, Holly left to join her father. Now, with her destination in sight, fear prickled from every pore in her body.

What had lured Papa into this arid country to meet his death? And what could she have in her possession that caused the outlaws to take her trunk and to search her in so indecorous a manner? She repeated the question aloud.

"Can't rightly say, ma'am," Ezra Hinson replied, "but like as not, when they found the cash box nigh onto empty, they decided to take a chance on finding valuables in your trunk." He looked around the coach. "The rest of our baggage likely did not look as promising."

"Don't forget they took my gold watch," responded Mr. Rich. "And my carpetbag full of tobacco samples, too. Now I have nothing to sell."

"That's a fact," Mr. Hinson recalled. "You see . . ."

Holly pursed her quivering lips, hoping to contain the fear which threatened to explode within her. "That does not account for them knowing my name and where I'm from, or searching my person."

The men diverted their eyes, and she knew the attack had been an attack on them, as well. They had been within earshot of her outcries, yet were prevented from protecting her.

"They'll pay for this," Mr. Hinson vowed. "Believe me, ma'am, they won't get by with such indecent behavior towards a lady."

The other men mumbled their assent, but no one

asked the delicate questions which she sensed were on all their minds. What had really occurred behind the stagecoach?

Holly accepted their regrets. "That trunk was the last thing I had in the world, so it really doesn't matter. The war taught me exactly how little value material things hold . . . but I was so looking forward . . ." Tears welled up in her eyes, and she was unable to continue.

"You're a mighty brave woman, ma'am," Mr. Rich said. "Not many women venture this far from civilization alone. Mostly it's men running from something—or from someone—or hunting adventure."

"That's right," Ezra Hinson agreed. "Why, you'd be real surprised at the number of men who come to these parts looking for all that gold and silver the Spaniards are rumored to have found. Did your pa ever write about the legends of Silver Creek?"

She shook her head. "Papa was a gentleman, not a vagabond treasure hunter. He believed a man should make his way by using his God-given talents."

Mr. Rich grinned broadly. "Not everybody sees things thataway. Matter of fact, just the other day, I ran into a man in Austin who claimed to have discovered the location of those twenty muleloads of silver bars."

Mr. Hinson nodded. "And I once met a man in San Antone who would sell you the authentic plat to the Lost Bowie Mine for fifty dollars gold. No telling how much that old gent made off unsuspectin' treasure hunters, till someone came upon him in the act of creating a brand-new batch of those antique plats."

Tensed against her uncertain future, Holly listened to the men with only half an ear. She appreciated their obvious attempt to take her mind off her troubles, but right now she needed a solution to her very real problems. What was it the gambler, Troy Grant, had been saying just before the holdup?

She sat bolt upright. "Where's Mr. Grant?"

The other passengers simultaneously shifted their startled glances toward the cracked black leather seat where Troy Grant had been sitting.

"I'll be a monkey's uncle!" exclaimed Mr. Rich. "He ain't along!"

Ezra Hinson nodded his head in agreement with the obvious. "We were so taken up with our . . ."

"We must go back," Holly insisted. She leaned her head out the window. "Driver!"

"Ma'am, we're more than an hour away," Mr. Rich said.

"But he may be injured."

"Doubtful, I think," responded Mr. Hinson. "As you recall, he had his horse hitched to the back of the stage. It likely broke loose when we turned over, and Mr. Grant has gone to catch him up."

"Poor Mr. Grant," Holly pleaded. "We must go back."

"Now don't you worry yourself, Miss Campbell," Mr. Hinson said. "Mr. Grant struck me as a man who is quite capable of taking care of himself."

Mr. Rich agreed. "He'll probably meet the stage when we roll into Silver Creek."

"I'm sure he's fine, ma'am," Mr. Hinson began, "but if it'll make you feel better, we'll let the new sheriff know all about it when we get to Silver Creek. I hear he's a fine young man. Name's Jarvis . . . Quintan Jarvis."

Holly raised her stricken brown eyes to meet those of the lawyer from El Paso, and her usually soft voice sounded a strident note to her own ears. "Quintan Jarvis?" she asked. "Foreman of the TF Ranch?"

"You're familiar with him?"

"Through Papa's letters," she answered dismally.

"He wrote a lot about the TF's owner, Tom Farrell, and his . . . his hired hands."

"As I heard it, ma'am," Mr. Hinson continued, "Jarvis and Farrell had a falling out a while back, and Jarvis up and quit the TF. He's running a small spread of his own and filling in as sheriff till Governor Davis approves an election for a new one."

"According to Papa's letters," Holly said, "the whole country knows that Farrell hired nothing but cut-throats and thieves, and Quintan Jarvis was his foreman—that speaks plainly enough, wouldn't you say?"

Ezra Hinson shook his head. "Maybe regarding Farrell's son—now there's a ringtail-tooter. But not Jarvis. With all due respects, ma'am, you pa likely didn't know Jarvis himself. I'll say it again, you won't be finding a better man than Quint Jarvis. I knew his pa, and I've known him most of his life. He's a man you can ride the river with."

Holly gripped the leather handle on the side of the stagecoach with all the terror inside her. As the coach dipped with the road, she stared out the window at the cottonwood trees which rimmed the bank of a creek, their new growth shading scattered patches of tender grass. The coach ran beneath the trees for a few hundred yards, then made an abrupt turn and followed a trail up the side of a hill. Clumps of prickly pear and bear grass sprouted from the numerous outcroppings of sandstone blanketing the hillside. How she longed for the safe, rolling hills of Tennessee.

Loneliness. She had come West to escape the prospect of a life spent alone. Yet, how much lonelier could she be now that the sheriff—the one person she had hoped to rely on—turned out to be nothing more than a known ruffian?

Painfully she realized that the only plan she had been

able to come up with since receiving that dastardly telegram back in New Orleans had been foiled even before she reached Silver Creek. She had decided to take Papa's letters and her suspicions directly to the sheriff upon arriving in town. Now . . .

Through her daze, Holly gradually became aware of the bugle sounding their approach to a settlement.

"Silver Creek!" the crusty driver intoned, and she watched terror-stricken as weathered buildings took shape along a rutted main street.

It could have been any one of the dozen or so small, dusty towns she had traveled through these last weeks, and she wished desperately that it were any of the others—any place except Silver Creek, Texas.

The stage rolled into town with barely enough daylight remaining to see clearly. A number of people had gathered on the boardwalk to welcome the stage, and suddenly her attention was drawn to the building looming behind them.

Ornate green letters spelling Hotel O'Keefe stood out against a background of white lacelike tracery. A spindaled, two-tiered porch ran across the front and wrapped around each side. She immediately saw the accuracy of Papa's description of this mail-order hotel as a giant white swan among the traditional false-fronted buildings which faded into the landscape like gray doves.

Her curiosity piqued, she looked around the crowd for the hotel's proprietress, whom Papa had described as equally flamboyant.

Suddenly her search was interrupted as her gaze was caught and held by an amused pair of honey-gold eyes. Her senses wobbled disjointedly, and her first thought was that he must be extremely tall, since he appeared to be standing in the street, while meeting her eyes directly.

When Quintan Jarvis heard the stagecoach thunder into town, he stepped from the sheriff's office and walked across the street to stand with the crowd in front of the Hotel O'Keefe, his mind on the trail drive leaving Silver Creek in two days.

Every drive this year had been hit by rustlers, and this time he vowed to protect the good folks of his community. The question was what could an ordinary cowhand like himself do against a group of organized rustlers?

He hadn't gone looking for this sheriff's job, he reminded himself, but the town was left high and dry when Sheriff Fryer took off for California. He couldn't very well sit out at the ranch singing to his cattle and watch every lawless element around take over. These particular rustlers, though, were shaping up to be somewhat akin to hell with the hide off.

And for the time being, he was sheriff in Silver Creek. Once the rustlers were behind bars and reconstruction ended, he could, he promised himself, leave town life behind and return to his small but growing spread of untamed land.

Not that Silver Creek was much of a town. Not like Kansas City or Dodge or even San Antone. Those were the only towns Quint had ever visited, but at least they provided diversions to help a man out while he tended to other, graver duties.

Silver Creek didn't have a first-rate gaming hall or even a whorehouse. For that matter, there were no single women in town, if you didn't count Mavis or Aggie Westfield. Aggie was old as his own ma would be had she been alive still, and Mavis . . . Mavis was indeed a diversion, but . . .

Quint squinted through the afternoon haze at the approaching stagecoach, wishing Monk would be bringing something to liven up the town a bit and help him deal with the weighty matters of the rustlers a bit easier. The stage came closer, and he frowned, seeing Rink holding the ribbons instead of Monk. What in blazes had gone wrong now?

At that moment the stage rolled in, and Quint had time to blink but twice before his eyes locked in a visual embrace that sent a quiver through his towering body.

Her eyes were brown, like velvet, the darkest brown eyes he had ever seen. And they flowed into his with the intensity of hot molten ore, which seemed suddenly to pulsate through his veins.

In his confusion his only coherent thought was a mocking one—an old Irish adage Aunt Jen used to quote to him whenever he wanted something really farfetched. "Be careful what you wish for," Aunt Jen used to say to him. "You might get it." Then he grinned.

Holly stared transfixed. Rays from the setting sun illuminated the man from behind and ignited golden sparks in the warmth of his eyes, as their brown depths engulfed her. After what seemed like an eternity, she was finally able to shift part of her attention to the man himself.

He was tanned and rugged, and wisps of blond hair straggled from beneath his hat, which was one of those terrible misshapen things she had seen cowboys wearing. Highlighted by the golden sun, his high cheekbones and the fine straight nose radiated a sense of strength. He was clean-shaven, except for a mustache—not the sweeping handlebar style often seen today, but rather a smaller, well-trimmed brush of glistening honey-colored hair that turned up in a slight, almost amused arch at the corners of his mouth . . .

Unconsciously, Holly sucked in her breath at the sight of his full lips, which, just as she looked at them, parted in a disarming smile that bared two rows of gleaming white teeth.

Holly awkwardly pushed a lock of hair from her face, and Quint swallowed the lump in his throat at the thought of running his hands through the tumbling curls of black silk that fell in an arousing disarray about her doll-like face.

He took her all in then, as if breathing in a draught of wildflower-scented spring air. With her delicately pointed chin and pert, slightly upturned nose, she reminded him of the china figure Aunt Jen had kept on the mantel in her bedroom.

The color on her cheeks brightened as he watched, echoing the moist rosiness of her full lips, and he blushed, too, knowing that she was giving him an equally thorough inspection, yet unable and unwilling to discontinue his tour of this tantalizing creature.

Dropping his eyes boldly, he encountered a lacy barrier just below her chin which extended in a vee to the top of where her small breasts were tightly trapped by the jacket of her traveling suit.

Quint watched, seduced, as Holly's hands began to fidget with her bodice. Then he suddenly became aware of her disheveled appearance—her bonnetless head and disarranged clothing. A mental message of the hardships of stagecoach travel passed through his mind with a pang of sympathy, and he was immediately conscious of being in the presence of a lady.

He quickly removed his hat, holding it awkwardly across his chest, and Holly stared at the sun-lightened hair, the damp brow.

She returned his smile unselfconsciously, aware of no one else around them, taking in his broad, yet relaxed shoulders. The humorous, devil-may-care attitude he exuded was at once arrogant and confident—the same quality she had felt in the young men who had called on her before that dreadful war which destroyed everyone's dreams—a breathtaking air which seemed to promise that love was still something to believe in.

Quint ran a hand through his hair, and, as the stage halted, he pulled open the door, extending his hand. When she put her small hand into his large callused one, he felt her tremble, and in the depths of his being, he knew one thing with certainty—he had to have her.

A warning voice whispered inside his head, "Be careful, this female's apt to cost you more'n one night's tumble in the sheets."

But the growing need for her already burned inside his body, and he recklessly swore to himself that whatever the price, he'd gladly pay it.

As she stepped onto the boardwalk, Holly took his hand, and a sense of completeness washed over her at his touch. She tilted her head to look into his face; then her eyes stopped, riveted on the star pinned to his vest. A sheriff's star.

"Welcome to Silver Creek, ma'am. I'm . . ."

"I know well enough who you are," Holly retorted, her words tumbling out an instant before the shock reached her eyes, turning their warm invitation to cold rejection. She wheeled quickly on her heel, and with a very heavy weight settling over her small shoulders, she walked proudly into the Hotel O'Keefe.

Quint Jarvis stiffened as the persnickety young woman left him standing startled and red-faced on the boardwalk. He clamped his hat on his head and turned abruptly, bumping into Monk.

"Doc Holly's daughter," Monk explained with a twinkle in his eyes.

Quint cleared his throat as embarrassment gave way

to disgust. "She must have been raised on sour milk."

"Give her time. She's had a passel of trouble." Monk glanced at his own arm. "We run into some road agents a ways back."

With a brief vow that such a haughty creature as Miss Campbell would not be getting any of his time, Quint assumed the duties at hand. "A holdup?" he asked. "Was it the State Police?"

Monk shook his head. "Not to my reckoning."

"They're everywhere," Quint said. "Governor Davis would set them on you in a minute, if he wanted something you're carrying."

"Or somebody."

Quint cocked a blond eyebrow at the wizened driver. "Spell it out."

"It was the dangedest holdup I ever seen," Monk said. "Oh, they made a show of robbin' the passengers, but what they was really after was the girl's trunk. And, by gum, that's all they took."

Quint's gaze followed Monk's through the hotel doors where Holly had disappeared, and he clenched his jaws tight against the returning embarrassment. "She was likely carrying a king's ransom in jewels," he said, bitterly aware that he would, after all, have to give the uppity Miss Campbell some of his time, while the ache in his loins taunted him with the knowledge that he still desperately wanted this woman.

Chapter Two

Holly Campbell awoke struggling, wrestling with the dream, unsure for a moment that it wasn't real. She pulled the covers up to her chin, her uneasiness soothed somewhat by the cool crispness of the first sheets she had slept between in two months.

But they were not the sheets on her bed at Hedgerow Plantation—that had been in the dream. And the voices outside the window were not the soldiers who had taken Hedgerow as their command post; nor was the smoke she smelled smoke from their burning slaves' quarters. Those were the sounds and smells of her dream—her nighttime return to memories from which she could not escape.

A commotion outside the bedroom window stirred her, and she pushed back the colorful patchwork quilt and sat up, slowly flexing the muscles in her back. Every move exposed another ache. At least she had finally reached Silver Creek, the end of her journey. She studied the intricately crocheted counterpane as an image suddenly floated unbidden across her mind: the handsome, smiling face of Silver Creek's sheriff, Quintan Jarvis. Fiery tingles coursed her spine at the unwanted sense of pleasure this image ignited within her. Sighing deeply, she dreaded what lay ahead; it looked like the beginning of a real-life nightmare.

Slipping into the buff linen wrapper which lay across the foot of her bed, she moved to the window and looked down from the second floor of the hotel onto the scene of activity she had previously only heard.

A group of men were gathered in the middle of a pecan grove cooking huge slabs of meat over a large pit in the ground, while other men nailed boards between the trees, and ladies in homespun dresses spread many-hued quilts, much like the one on Holly's bed, over the boards, all the time laughing and nodding their heads in high-spirited conversation.

Through the noise a knock came at the door, and she turned as a frail, elderly woman entered the room. The stooped woman, whom Holly guessed to be in her sixties, was encased from head to toe in black linsey-woolsey, and her sharp features were accented by the severity with which her thin gray hair was braided and twined about her head. But her voice carried a soft, grandmotherly welcome.

"What are you doing out of bed so soon, dearie?" The woman placed a silver tray on the marble-topped table. "Miss Mavis sent you some hot tea and toast. She'll be up herself directly."

Holly sat on the canopied bed and poured tea from a delicate handpainted china pot into a cup with matching pink rosebuds. "What's the occasion?"

"A real shindig," the woman confided. "The last trail drive of the year leaves Silver Creek in the morning, and folks've come from all around to send the boys off with barbeque, dancin', and other doings." She hung several black garments inside the wardrobe. Holly recognized none of them as the gray traveling suit she wore in last night.

"Won't you join me for a cup of tea, Mrs.—ah, it is

Mrs. Westerfield, isn't it?"

"Lordy, me!" The woman turned wide eyes toward the bed. "That's me, all right. But you just call me Aggie like everybody else." She peered over the wire rims of her spectacles. "How did you know my name?"

"Papa wrote wonderful letters about all of you. Even about this elegant hotel!" She gestured widely around the elaborately furnished room with its heavy walnut appointments. The walls and even the ceiling were papered with pink roses, and topping the intricately carved spindles of the canopied bed was a draping of fine crochet to match the counterpane. Lacy curtains at the two windows added to the very feminine aura one had of basking in a fragrant English garden.

"Imagine," Holly mused. "A mail-order house! I've never been inside one before. Tell me, how did they ever get it out here?" She recalled the dreadful time the stagecoach had had crossing the rugged hills north of Austin and the miles of muddy roads before that from Galveston to beyond Houston.

"That's a tale, all right, but I'd best leave it for Miss Mavis to tell. It's one of her favorites."

Holly sipped the hot tea, enjoying its minty flavor. "Doesn't Mavis get terribly lonely out here, being a widow and all?"

"Lonely?" Aggie shook her gray head slowly. "That's what life's all about, dearie. Loneliness. Leastways for us womenfolk. Now, you take me, for instance. I was widowed nigh onto thirty years ago. A while back I come out here with my only living son and his family, and—well, there was an Injun raid, and me and my poor little grandson, Davy—we're all that's left."

"I'm sorry . . ." Holly began.

"No need. It's the way of things." Aggie started making the bed, and Holly jumped up to help, pulling the soft muslin sheets smoothly over the plump feather mattress.

"But gettin' back to Miss Mavis," Aggie confided, "I don't figure her to be single much longer, what with all the suitors she has."

"Really?" Holly's interest picked up. Papa hadn't supplied much in the way of female gossip.

Aggie nodded, fluffing a feather pillow. "There's Tom Farrell, of course. He would be the front-runner, if he had his way. Why, he's been courtin' Miss Mavis since shortly after Mr. Sean's passin'—too shortly if you ask me. But she won't marry him. Refuses to give up this place and move to the ranch."

Holly's heart leaped in her breast at the mention of Tom Farrell. Farrell was the person in Silver Creek Papa had written about most unfavorably—the only person she knew of who might have played a part in his death.

"Who is Tom Farrell?" she asked quietly, trying to keep the urgency she felt from showing in her voice.

Aggie winked at Holly. "Dearie, Tom Farrell is the best catch in this whole country. He has enough ranchland and money to set a widow woman up in style for the rest of her life."

Holly shrugged offhandedly. "Papa wrote that Mr. Farrell has a . . . ah, a rather unsavory reputation."

Aggie snorted. "Tsk! Tsk! You're young yet, dearie, that you are. But don't you fret none. For my money it's a younger man who's going to win Miss Mavis's hand . . ."

Giving Aggie a sharp look, Holly busied herself straightening the already smooth counterpane. The handsome face of Silver Creek's sheriff warmed her thoughts for the second time in this still-new spring day, followed by the cold realization of who he was, and who his employer was.

Handsome? Well, so what? she asked herself, turning

the old saying around in her mind: handsome is as handsome does. Mavis could have him!

"Shame on you, Aggie. Gossiping about me behind my back!"

At the sound of the lilting, feminine voice, Holly looked up to see an elegantly dressed Mavis O'Keefe standing in the doorway, her obvious good nature echoing in her welcoming smile. Papa's description of the hotel's proprietress had, if anything, she noted, been modest. Her eyes were so green they should be shaped like shamrocks, and a mass of red-gold hair, which, although wrapped conservatively about her small head, still rebelled here and there with an escaping curl.

What strange country this was, she thought suddenly. Already her images were proving false. Even with Papa's lavish descriptions, she was not prepared for Mavis O'Keefe. In her white muslin apron and green bows (Papa must be wrong about her thirty-five years!), Mavis was hardly the coarse Western woman Holly had imagined a woman living alone in these wilds would be.

"Holly!" Mavis swept forward, enfolding Holly in scents of lavender. "How lovely to have you with us at last. Did you sleep well?"

"Oh, yes, and thank you for the hot bath last night. It was wonderful." She recalled with longing the sitz tub full of steaming water and the scented soap which Mavis had sent up for her the evening before.

"That's what we're here for, darling." Mavis smiled and turned to Aggie. "Did you bring the clothing?"

Aggie indicated the wardrobe, and Mavis continued. "Be a dear, then, and run help Rosie. You know she never puts enough salt in the mop sauce."

Aggie left, and Mavis began taking articles of clothing from the wardrobe and spreading them on the bed. "Did Aggie tell you about the festivities?" she asked, then rushed on without waiting for an answer. "We have less than an hour before dinner, and the folks are all anxious to meet you."

Holly watched Mavis in amazement. "I can't attend a party, Mavis, what with Papa just gone. Besides, I'm still exhausted from . . ."

"Nonsense." Mavis spoke without stopping work. "I know you're tired, Holly. We've all made that dastardly trip. But these people were your father's patients, people he cared for . . ."

"But . . ."

"You don't have to join in the dancing later this evening, but you can have dinner with us and meet his patients. They're looking forward to extending their condolences."

"I have no clothes," Holly said, then realizing the meaning of Mavis's activity, quickly added, "of my own." She thought of her missing trunk and her valise lying forgotten along the desolate roadside. She and Caroline had agonized over her selection of clothing, choosing only garments they believed would fit in with her life on the frontier. Scanning Mavis's airy green and white outfit, she sighed. Nothing she brought had been as fancy as what Mavis wore today.

Except one costume. Caroline's wedding dress with its veil and train. Holly recalled the tears in her sister's eyes as she insisted they make room in the trunk for this one extravagance.

"When you find your handsome prince, " Caroline had said, "you must wear my dress. Then I will feel as if I am with you."

So much for that! The dress was lost. And what use would it be here anyway? Of one thing she was dead sure—no prince charming awaited her in Silver Creek.

It really didn't matter, she scolded herself. As soon as

she discovered what had happened to Papa, she would return to Hedgerow and become a half-reconciled maiden aunt to Caroline's children.

Mavis's voice was definite. "You have no excuse not to attend the barbeque, Holly. Aggie measured one of my mourning costumes by your traveling suit, and would you believe it?" She looked Holly up and down with a nod of approval. "I'm only a wee bit shorter than you, and . . ." She pursed her lips, staring from Holly's small bustline to her own more ample endowments. "Of course, we could have added some padding . . ." Mavis paused at Holly's affronted gasp, then continued. "But Aggie is a wizard with a needle. I'm sure she has taken in quite enough."

Holly considered her hostess, unable to believe what she saw and heard. "You're kind, Mavis," she said finally. "But I won't be needing your clothes. I'm only here for a short time."

Mavis flashed her green eyes. "You must be clothed during that short time, mustn't you?" She picked up two garments from the bed. "I didn't know whether you prefer the bustle, or this smaller crinoline tournure."

"Mavis, I'm not going to the party," Holly said. "Your clothes are lovely, but I will wear my own dress, if you'll tell me where to find it."

Mavis stood her ground. "You cannot wear that dirty old thing." She dropped the garments on the bed and walked to the door. Her voice lost its amusement. "I will leave you to dress, Holly. I am sure with your upbringing, you will not disappoint your father's friends."

Angry at Mavis's domineering attitude, Holly tilted her chin and stared across the room. "I am not here to visit my father's friends, Mavis." Her eyes narrowed. "I have come to discover the truth about his death."

Mavis stood stock-still for a moment, then quickly stepped back inside the room and closed the door. Her voice softened. "Didn't you know, darling?"

Apprehensive at discussing Papa's death with someone she barely knew, Holly hesitated. But Mavis was a trusted friend of Papa's; surely *she* could trust Mavis, too. "Papa didn't kill himself," she said. "I don't care who says so."

Mavis took a step toward her. "He said so, Holly. He left a message—in his own handwriting."

Holly blinked, unsure for a moment what she had heard. Then she pursed her lips tightly together, as if forbidding such perfidious thoughts entrance into her determined mind. "It isn't true," she whispered.

"I know you don't want it to be true," Mavis said. "But I've seen the letter. It is authentic."

"But . . ."

"Now, you get hold of yourself and come on downstairs. Our guests are waiting. Tomorrow the sheriff will show you the letter." Mavis took Holly by the shoulders and smiled into her eyes. "Will you be all right?"

Holly took a deep breath. "I'll be down soon."

She dressed mechanically, picking up the black cambric petticoats, the black grosgrain skirt, and wasit with numb fingers, putting them on an unfeeling body. She brushed her black hair, then loosely looped and pinned it, and tied on the small black tulle and grosgrain bonnet without seeing the image before her in the looking glass.

Holding up the tulle and lace fichu which Mavis had provided as a cover against the still cool April air, she studied it a moment, then tossed it back on the bed. Too frivolous. A sob escaped her constricted throat. Would she ever be ready for parties again? With all the death she had seen during the war, with burying

Mama, and now Papa's death, she had no room in her heart for revelry.

After a moment, she straightened her shoulders, took up the black fan and parasol, then smiled in spite of herself. Mavis surely had a way about her. Papa had failed to mention her forceful nature.

At the door she almost backed out, but finally goaded herself onward. She would go downstairs, meet Papa's friends—or enemies—then return to her room.

She could handle a brief encounter; of course, she could. Besides, this gathering might be a stroke of good fortune, she thought. If everyone in the country was to be there, mightn't that include whoever was responsible for Papa's death?

As with past fears, Holly found the party very unlike what she had imagined.

Passing through the parlor and dining room, she discovered them as beautifully furnished as her bedroom. Heavy wine-colored draperies hung over lacy white casements at the windows, and the floors glistened around the edges of finely woven woolen rugs. As neither room was in use, she followed a savory aroma to the kitchen where she saw a middle-aged Mexican woman stirring a pot of bubbling red sauce over a modern wood-burning cookstove. Loaves of fresh-baked bread cooled in the window.

In a flurry of white muslin and glorious auburn hair, Mavis burst through the kitchen door from outside. "Hurry, Rosie, we are ready for more sauce." Her quick glance about the room took in Holly. "Oh, here you are," she said, refraining from adding the "and it's about time" Holly heard in her tone. She steered Holly through the door, calling over her shoulder, "Bring the sauce, Rosie. The men are waiting."

Outside Holly blinked against the midday sun. Finding herself in the midst of a gathering similar to the barbeques and family parties she had loved at Hedgerow before the war, she was suddenly overcome with a desperate feeling of homesickness. Ahead of her the river rippled over limestone stepping-stones. Nearby, men lounged about the pit, turning meat and slapping one another on the back in easy conversation. Children of varying ages chased each other around and under the tables, while their mothers, immersed in their own chattering, made half-hearted efforts to calm them down.

Peaceful. Serene. Civilized. How could Papa have been murdered in such a tranquil place?

Mavis waved her arms, signaling the group to join them beneath a massive pecan tree. The women hesitated, then shyly beckoned their husbands, gathered their children, and the families timidly presented themselves to Holly. Mavis performed the introductions in her predictably grand manner.

"Sophie and Jeremiah Benford and their little daughter, Katie."

Jeremiah removed his hat, the now-familiar, sweat-stained felt. Sophie was frail and weathered, dressed simply in a straight homespun garment. Her hollow eyes shone brightly from beneath a faded blue checked gingham bonnet as she hugged her daughter. "Little Katie was the first babe your pa delivered here in Silver Creek."

"Your pa was a good one," Jeremiah put in. "We shore miss him."

"Thank you." Holly smiled into the spunky eyes of the little girl who wore the same homespun dress as her mother, with her own miniature blue bonnet.

Next came the Sperrys, a family of nine. "Your pa surely helped us through the measles. We didn't lose a single one of our brood," Maggie Sperry announced. Although her dress was a coarse, colorless cotton,

Maggie, like the other women, had obviously worn her Sunday-best bonnet, hers a lovely white muslin with multiple rows of stitching on the brim and a tiny crocheted edging.

And the McPhersons, whose son Joel looked to be about ten years old. "Lookee here at this leg," Anna McPherson said, pulling up the pant leg of a struggling Joel. "It broke clean through when Ol' Buck fell on this youngun, but Doc Holly fixed it up good as new. Why, it don't even have no knot on it."

"Yes'm," said her husband Mac. "We're sure gonna miss your pa."

Then the Jefferies with Mose, Hank, and little Suzanne, followed by Jed and Anne Varner, Anne swollen with the last weeks of pregnancy.

"We're mighty worried, ma'am," Jed confided. "Anne has lost two babes already, and Doc Holly was all set to help save this one."

Holly looked sympathetically at the young woman who was nearer her own age than any of the other women. Anne was dressed in a homespun wrapper which had been dyed with indigo and over which she wore a coarse white bibbed apron. Her sheer blue cambric bonnet was gathered fully onto the crown and had a ruffle around its sturdy brim. The bavolet fell over her shoulders to near elbow length and afforded her more protection from sun and wind than the shorter bavolets on the other ladies' bonnets.

Anne spoke anxiously. "Doc Holly told us how you know so much about medical things, and we were wondering . . ." She broke off, diverting her gaze in obvious embarrassment.

Her husband finished quickly. "We was hopin' you'd agree to see to the delivery."

Holly grasped Anne's hands in her own. "I'll do what I can to help. You send Mr. Varner to fetch me as soon as the pains start." She quizzed Anne about her previous confinements and suggested she stay in bed as much as possible.

"Jed's real good about helping out," Anne said, losing some of her shyness. "And he's a right fine cook, too."

"Aw," Jed blushed. "I wouldn't go so far as that. 'Bout all I do is boil up a pot of beans and fix a mess of ash cakes."

Mavis left and returned with two plates of food, and the others drifted off to fix their own plates and tend to their children.

Holly marveled at the heaping plate which Mavis handed her. Juicy meat with an almost blackened crust, covered with Rosie's steaming red sauce; Mexican beans she had learned to call frijoles, which were plump and tender to the fork, not cooked to muck as the ones she had been served at a few of the stage stops had been; something she did not recognize which looked like little rolled cornmeal cakes filled with meat; Rosie's sourdough bread; and a slice each of sweet potato pie and pecan pie.

"This is more food than I saw on the entire trip," she told Mavis. "Where did it all come from?"

"Cookie made the beans at the cow camp," Mavis answered. "And Tom Farrell donated the beef, as he does every year."

"Tom Farrell?" There was that name again, and as Aggie's respect for the man had been clear earlier, Mavis's admiration for Tom Farrell was now revealed in her voice.

Mavis nodded toward a group of men standing near the river. Their backs were to the women, and they appeared to be caught up in a serious conversation.

Holly had barely taken in the older, more distinguished looking of them to whom Mavis pointed when she gasped as her eyes automatically focused on the broad shoulders of the tallest man in the group. Even though she had never seen Quint Jarvis from the rear, she knew him instantly. A disturbing sensation coursed her body, and the warmth of a blush rose along her neck. Pressing her lips together tightly, she prayed that her emotions were not as evident as she felt they must be.

"That's our sheriff standing next to Tom . . ."

Nervously Holly gritted her teeth together in a concentrated effort to attend to Mavis's conversation, but a strange feeling took hold of her. The moment she looked at Quint Jarvis, she knew she had been unconsciously searching for him all day. Now that she saw him standing before her, her heart beat fast in her breast, and her body felt weakened by something she did not understand.

"Come." Mavis took Holly's arm, attempting to pull her to her feet. "Let me introduce you to the men you haven't met."

"No," Holly whispered. Then, feeling Mavis's eyes on her, she somehow managed to get a grip on herself. "I'm . . . I'm a little weary at the moment, Mavis. Later."

Mavis looked at her quickly, then they both turned back to their overfilled plates, eating silently, Holly's mind abuzz with thoughts of Tom Farrell and Papa and . . . Quint Jarvis.

Later, looking about the gathering, Mavis explained that many of the families had arrived the day before. She pointed to wagons parked in the distance. "Most of them cannot afford rooms in the hotel, so they camp under their wagons. The women prepare their dishes over their own campfires, then bring them here to add to what we have." She repeated what Papa had written, that these women were hungry for news of life back East.

"Give them time to get over their shyness, and believe me, they will besiege you with questions," she said.

Holly watched the men wander away from the gathering, while the women finished their meals and set the younger children off to nap under the care of the older ones.

Then, true to Mavis's prediction, the women made their way back to the tree where Holly visited with Aggie Westfield.

Frail Sophie Benford, stout Anna McPherson, stooping Maggie Sperry, all weathered beyond their years. But curiosity, and yes, she thought, hunger sparked their eyes.

And their questions surprised her. Sophie, who obviously could afford only the most modest of garments, longed for a look at *Godey's Lady's Book* or the new *Harper's Bazaar*. Anna talked about asparagus, and Maggie about Georgia peaches.

She heard again that her father had spread word of her medical experiences, and learned that the women expected her to take over his work.

"I'm not a doctor," she protested to the women who had seated themselves around her like a homespun fan spread upon the grass.

"You would do us fine," Sophie said.

Anna and Maggie nodded their heads.

"I only came to Silver Creek to discover how my father died."

The women exchanged looks.

"I mean," Holly began, realizing she shouldn't voice her suspicions to these strange women. "I mean, the telegram wasn't specific, and I . . . I need to understand what could have driven him to such a desperate act as suicide."

The women's eyes met again, and Anna spoke solemnly, simply. "Life out here can be mighty trying sometimes, Miss Campbell."

Holly looked at each of the sincere women, their faces lined and haggard, their work-worn hands rough and reddened, their daily burdens of a magnitude she knew she could scarcely imagine. "Please call me Holly," she said. "And don't worry yourselves over this. I'm sure there is a simple explanation."

Suddenly loud whoops and yells broke loose from in front of the hotel, and the women got to their feet, pulling Holly with them.

"The horse races are starting," Maggie said. "My William had better not lose his trail money before they even set out."

"Rather to neighbors, than to those rustlers up the trail," Anna replied.

Sophie nodded. "I tried to get Jeremiah to leave our cattle home this drive. We can't afford to lose them to rustlers. But he said we can't afford not to try to sell them, either."

Holly followed the women around the building where a crowd had gathered along either side of the street. Dust boiled as three spirited horses sprinted past them, nose to nose, their riders urging them on with quirts and curses.

Men yelled and slapped their legs with their hats, and the unlucky ones dug into their pockets. Holly made her way to the spindled porch where she saw Monk talking with young Hank Jefferies.

"Mr. Monk, how is your arm?" she inquired.

Monk grinned through grizzled whiskers. "Now, here's a pert woman for you," he told Hank. "Knows when a man needs his likker."

Holly blushed. "It was for medicinal purposes, Mr. Monk. Let me look at your arm."

"Aw, it's all right, ma'am," he said. "Hank here is trying to get my fiddlin' job."

"You can't play a fiddle with a broken wrist," Hank insisted, looking to Holly for encouragement.

Monk winked. "Bring your fiddle along, son, and when I tire, you can spell me."

"All right!" Hank whooped and ran off toward the parked wagons.

"Why do you torture yourself, Mr. Monk?" Holly asked.

"Lawdy, Miss Holly, my fiddlin' ain't no torture—'cept maybe to untrained ears."

Inside, Holly found the parlor cleared of furniture, the lovely patterned rugs rolled up, and a scattering of chairs placed around the walls. Monk took his place on the makeshift stage between two velvet-draped windows, and as he tuned up his fiddle, people drifted into the room, husbands and wives pairing off.

Holly had intended to retire to her room when the dancing started, but now, worried about Monk's arm, she took a seat between the stage and the punch bowl.

Looking around the festive crowd, she recognized almost all of them as people she had met earlier this afternoon. The few cowboys she didn't know were probably from the trail herd bedded down outside town, she decided, and . . . Suddenly she tensed, frozen with the realization that she was searching for one man, and one man only. Quint Jarvis.

Stop it, she scolded herself. Stop it right now. She couldn't spend what time she had here in Silver Creek pining over a man she would obviously be better off without. Matters of much greater significance demanded her attention, such as finding out who killed Papa. And why.

Aggie Westfield found a chair beside her. "Land sakes!" she exclaimed. "If it isn't old Tom Farrell his ownself comin' to the dance!"

Holly followed Aggie's gaze and studied the man she had seen only from behind this afternoon. Recalling Papa's dramatic description of the county's biggest rancher, she was surprised to see, instead of the devil himself, a compact, handsome man in his early fifties, conservatively dressed in twill pants, cambric shirt, and an unstained felt hat, which he promptly removed upon stepping inside.

He surveyed the room, his glance brushing the top of her head, and strode toward the punch table. His stride, every step of it, exuded power—not the swaggering, overconfident power of youth, but power born of years of command.

Holly turned to ask Aggie if Farrell had served in the Army; then her gaze met that of the young man in the rancher's wake, and she shivered.

"Do you need a wrap?" Aggie asked.

Holly quickly diverted her eyes. "Who is the man directly behind Mr. Farrell?"

Aggie snorted. "His son."

Jim Tom Farrell, she thought, glancing back at the young man who appeared to be around her own age. Papa had written about him, too, and here was the swagger, the overconfidence, the threatening demeanor she had expected to find in the father. Here, in the leering black eyes, the unruly hair with hat still . . .

As if reading her thoughts, Tom Farrell turned, directed a cold stare toward Jim Tom's offending head cover, and, after a contemptuous glare at his father, the son removed his hat and found space for it on the rack alongside those of the other men.

Holly watched Tom Farrell guide Mavis onto the floor, and she stared a bit longer, wondering which of these two strong-willed individuals would take the lead. No, Mavis definitely knew how to handle a man,

Holly decided, as Farrell glided her to and fro smoothly and at will.

Strains of "Wildwood Flower" faded and the couples broke, clapped, and parted. Holly turned toward the stage to check on Monk, and her breath caught in a gasp at finding herself face to face with Quint Jarvis. He was every bit as handsome as she recalled, and just the sight of him quickened her blood in a way she had never before experienced.

Having successfully avoided her all day, Quint was taken aback by suddenly coming into contact with those wistful brown eyes. Damn! She was a sight to behold—ebony curls framing her slender face, and a natural smile which faded into . . . What? he wondered—expectancy? . . . a touch of fear?—at the sight of him. Rejection, most likely, he thought, as a flush of the embarrassment she caused him last night on the boardwalk pierced through his taut body. He started to turn away, telling himself that the world was full of lovely creatures.

Before he could escape into the crowd of dancers, however, Aggie took command. "Holly, let me introduce our sheriff, Mr. Jarvis."

Holly hesitated, pushed a curl from her face, then offered her hand reluctantly, and his touch reverberated up her arm like lightning traveling across a blackened sky.

"I'm sorry about your pa, ma'am," he managed, determined not to let her play him for the fool again today, yet unable to look away from her delicately alluring features.

She flinched at the hardness in his honey-brown eyes—eyes which had held such a warm welcome yesterday, but which now pinned her to her chair with a defiant stare. Giving him a curt nod to acknowledge his condolence, she withdrew her hand from his lingering grasp.

Her brain felt like a bowl of hot gruel, but she could not tear her attention from his very masculine stature. He was younger than Tom Farrell, she observed, closer to Mavis's age, and the idea again came to her that he could be Mavis's younger suitor to whom Aggie had referred earlier, a thought which brought both relief and a sick feeling to her stomach.

When he neither moved on down the line nor initiated further conversation, she became angry at his rudeness and awkwardly endeavored to gain some control over her own spinning senses. "Have you investigated the holdup, Sheriff?" she demanded, wondering at the unintentionally harsh tone in her voice.

"Yes'm, but about your trunk . . ." he began, still unable to shift his stare from her face.

"My concern at present, Sheriff, is for Mr. Grant. You are aware that he was abducted during the robbery?"

Quint ran a hand through his hair and thought how a good night's sleep surely hadn't improved her attitude. "Tracks show the man caught up his horse and headed out behind the robbers," he answered.

"Are you suggesting that poor Mr. Grant was in league with the highwaymen?" Her anger puzzled her, yet she was grateful for it, knowing somehow that it hid the deep yearning which stirred inside her at the nearness of this man.

"No, ma'am." He spoke slowly, keeping his voice steady, all the while telling himself that the lady was new to this country, had just lost her pa, and would be out of his hair before he knew it. "Mr. Grant, or whatever he called himself, likely did not know that the robbers were ahead of him. I mean, by the time he caught up his horse, they were long gone, and he headed out in the same direction, accidental-like. I found no sign of foul play."

Aghast at his apparent indifference to the matter, Holly's mouth dropped open, then her chin jerked upward in a gesture of contempt. "No sign of foul play?" She raised her voice above the din. "The stagecoach is held up at gunpoint, Mr. Monk is shot, Mr. Grant disappears, all my worldly possessions are stolen, and *you* find no sign of foul play! Obviously, Sheriff . . ."

At that moment Mavis glided between them, taking the sheriff by the arm. "Quint, darling, you haven't danced with me all evening. And this is my favorite waltz."

Holly saw relief reflected in Quint's eyes, and he had barely uttered his "Excuse me, ma'am," to her, before he swung Mavis onto the floor with such vengeance that Holly heard her shriek, "Quint, darling!"

Hot with the anger that had built inside her, Holly excused herself to Aggie and stood up. Time to retire, she thought, before she lost her composure completely. As she stepped away from her chair, however, a hand grabbed her arm and pulled her toward the dance floor.

"You can't leave before you take a twirl with ol' Jim Tom."

Holly jerked her arm free and fought to control herself. She had seen enough drunkenness among the soldiers to know that an intoxicated man was easily provoked.

"I am in mourning," she said.

Jim Tom leaned into her face. His breath was strong with liquor. Her rage turned to fear, and she shrank backward, trying to avoid his eyes which were not languid with drink, but mad from some fire within.

Behind him a couple of paces and eagerly backing him up were the two men who had followed him into the parlor. Their hair wanted combing and their shirttails needed tucking, but their eyes relished the excitement.

"Aw, come on. It won't hurt to give the poor ol' feller one little dance."

Jim Tom smirked at this help from his cronies. "You heard 'em . . ."

"And you heard the lady." Quint Jarvis suddenly stood beside her, and his deep, rich voice settled over her like a warm blanket filled with soft goose down. Although he towered above her, she noticed curiously that he and Jim Tom were fairly well matched, both in height and weight.

Uneasily, she observed that, instead of backing off, Jim Tom had turned his full attention to Quint. Glaring at the sheriff, the drunken young man looked from side to side, rallying his men behind him.

Quint motioned toward the door. "Wilt. Luther. You've had too much to drink to be around the ladies. Get on outside and take Jim Tom with you."

Wilt and Luther moved to take Jim Tom's arms, and young Farrell erupted into wild action, throwing the two men aside and swinging at Quint, who caught his arm by the wrist and held it. "Time to go home, Jim Tom."

Jim Tom struggled. "I aim to dance with the lady."

"The lady is not dancing. Now, get out of here before you get yourself in trouble."

"You want trouble, I'll give you some." Jim Tom jerked his arm vigorously, freeing it, while striking Quint with his other fist.

Quint staggered, kept his footing, and Jim Tom swung again. But Quint was ready. He grabbed Jim Tom's arm with his left hand and landed a punch to his midsection with a powerful right.

Jim Tom sputtered. Hatred shot from his eyes. "You'll be sorry." His threat was veiled by the whine in his voice.

Quint turned Jim Tom's arm behind him and caught the other one. "Let's sleep it off in jail."

Tom Farrell stepped in front of them. "No need for that, Quint. Wilt, get his hat." His voice was firm but moderate, and he bowed formally to Holly.

"Forgive the intrusion, ma'am." Then studying her seriously, he added, "Miss Campbell, I will say good-bye. You no doubt will have gone home to Tennessee by the time I return from the trail drive."

Holly measured the rancher's words. Were they merely social pleasantries, or the command they sounded? "Indeed, I hope so, Mr. Farrell," she answered. "But I must remain in Silver Creek a while longer to settle my father's affairs." And to solve his murder, she thought angrily.

Farrell gave her one brief nod, then turned toward the door. "Be sure you show her that message, Quint," he commanded. His tanned, tightly muscled face betrayed no emotion; his voice remained steady and strong; and Holly saw her only lead to Papa's death evaporate before her very eyes.

She watched Farrell make his way through the crowded room. Men here and there slapped him on the shoulder, calling, "Take care of my cattle, Tom," and "Careful of those rustlers along the Concho, Farrell," and "We can't afford to lose any stock this trip."

Tom Farrell waved them off with an aplomb that said, "I am in charge here. Rest assured that wherever I head to with those cattle is where they will end up."

Shaken, Holly stepped through the French doors onto the front porch. The air inside was stifling, not to mention her latest encounter with the men of Silver Creek. What heathens they all were! How could Papa have imagined she could find happiness here?

At the far end of the porch, she sat down in a white, ladder-back swing and rocked slowly, closing her eyes and mind to the people and voices inside.

She followed a practice of relaxation she had learned years ago from her father, concentrating on a peaceful, beautiful image, this time her mother's long-vanished rose garden with its vivid pinks, yellows, and reds. If she worked at it really hard, she could even smell the sweet fragrance of the roses her mother had tended herself.

Suddenly the swing rocked against her own rhythm, and she opened her eyes, bewildered to find Quint Jarvis looming over her with hat in hand. A shock of blond hair had tumbled over his forehead, and he reached up to push it out of his eyes, but even then his masculine features were concealed by the shadows of the night.

"Excuse me, ma'am . . ." He stopped, thinking how tiny and fragile she looked, like one of Mavis's china cups. Maybe Monk was right about her. Maybe she just needed time to get over her hurt. He motioned to the swing. "Could I . . . ?" His voice was rich and mellow and sent a quiver along her spine.

Her heart beat so hard in her breast, that she was sure he could hear it pound against her ribs, and although she intended to refuse his request, she found herself moving her skirts aside.

When he sat down, his arm brushed hers, and she pulled away from his touch as from a burning ember. Moments passed while they rocked back and forth. The moon illuminated the street in front of them and the saloon and sheriff's office across the way with near daylight brightness. In the shadow of the porch, they sat enveloped in a pocket of darkness, lighted only by a soft glow from the parlor windows behind the swing.

She had begun to wonder why he chose to sit beside

her instead of taking the empty swing at the opposite end of the porch, when he finally spoke.

"I'm sorry about the ruckus, ma'am." He twirled his hat in his hands. "Hope you don't go judging all of us by Jim Tom—he's a rare one."

Quint turned toward her then, but she stared straight ahead, giving no indication that she had even heard him. The golden lamplight lay on her hair like a halo and glistened on the lacy porch railing he could see beyond her. All else was lost in the deep blackness of her hair and shrouded body. "I . . . ah, I want to apologize for implying that you did not suffer an injustice at the holdup," he continued. "Fact is, what they did to you was a hateful thing, and I intend to do whatever it takes to get your belongings back."

Holly heard the intensity in his voice grow as he spoke, and she felt weak and vulnerable and suddenly frightened that she might surrender to the powerful attraction this herculean man seemed to hold for her. But she could not let herself succumb to such base physical desires, she warned, and her determination steeled against him. "Thank you, Sheriff," she responded with perfunctory politeness.

Quint stared at her a moment longer, then followed her gaze toward the empty street. "Doc Holly was a fine man." With effort he was able to maintain what he hoped sounded like a casual conversational tone to his voice. That he would sit here trying to make peace with this difficult woman surprised him, but he didn't move, and, although she was busy ignoring him, he felt his body grow warm with longing, just from her nearness. "Everyone hereabouts thought real highly of your pa."

"I appreciate that, Sheriff," Holly replied.

Quint rocked, and they both kept their silence. Finally he asked, "You really believe your pa met with foul play?"

"Yes."

"They found a message beside the body," he said, turning toward her once more and laying his arm along the back of the swing behind her. She sat as still as death with her white hands clasped in the lap of her black, black skirt. Only her breathing betrayed any life, and he watched, mesmerized, as her small breasts rose and fell beneath their casement of black. His stare fastened to the line of shiny ebony buttons which drew a string of light down the center of her tight-fitting bodice, and his hands . . .

Desperately he tore his mind back to reality. "Best we can tell, the message is in Doc's own handwriting. I'll show it to you tomorrow."

"Thank you," she answered, feeling herself quiver once more at the huskiness in his voice, knowing she should stand up and walk inside the hotel this very minute, while she was still able to leave him.

"Folks act in strange ways," he said. "Never can tell when a feller is going to up and do something contrary to what you would expect."

As his words registered, she turned to him angrily, and again this less dangerous emotion came to her aid, dousing her desire as with a splash of cold water. "My father did not take his own life," she insisted.

"You sound mighty sure, ma'am, for one who wasn't even around these parts when he died."

"I am positive, Sheriff." Her words were firm and filled with fury. "If you will find my trunk, which I presume is part of your job, I will show you letters I received from Papa which prove that he didn't take his own life. That is, letters which would prove it to any fair-minded person."

Quint squinted at her from under a furrowed brow. "Who are you accusing of not being fair-minded?"

Holly grimaced at the sharpness in his voice, and

looking at him quickly, she saw the lampglow glisten in the golden highlights in his eyes. She hesitated. "No one, only . . ."

He returned her stare, hearing the anger in her response, seeing something much different in the velvet of her eyes. Blood pounded through his veins at a quickened rate as he realized that two separate battles raged here: the war of anger and words without, covering only partially the passion and desire they both fought to contain within themselves. "Only what?" he asked.

She tore her attention away from him. "I'm . . . I'm afraid your loyalties might prevent you from seeing the truth," she said, intently studying the mud-rutted street.

"What's that supposed to mean?"

She shrugged. "Papa wrote that Mr. Farrell hired nothing but rascals and rabble—tobacco-chewing, whiskey-drinkers, all."

His eyes widened, and he grinned at her with new awareness. "Your pa wrote that?"

She nodded, pleased somehow at the tone of incredulity in his voice.

He laughed then, a laugh which rumbled in deep resonance to the pit of his stomach, bringing relief and understanding about this confusing bundle of femininity beside him. It wasn't him she was so busy rejecting, but an image of who she believed he was. No wonder she was so riled up. "And I was Farrell's foreman, so that makes me the worst of the lot?" he asked, chuckling to himself.

His laugh resounded along her already quaking nerves like Monk's bow across the strings of his fiddle. She braced herself against a weakening resolve. "That really does not concern me, Sheriff. Except if you had anything to do with Papa's death."

Quint bristled. How dare she accuse him of being

involved in what she, and only she, he reminded himself, had cooked up to be a murder. He bit his tongue and answered with a firmness in his voice she had not heard before. "I am not employed by Tom Farrell or by any other man in this county."

"If that were true . . ." Her words drifted off, and she allowed herself to imagine how wonderful it would be to truly confide in him—to trust him.

He looked at her, exasperated. He'd heard that women could be an aggravation, but this one took the prize. "It's up to you whether you believe me or not." He spit out the words and wondered why he was wasting time with her, but he continued. "I have a ranch west of town, and after Sheriff Fryer left for California, someone had to take over his job, so the town chose me."

Anxious for her to believe him, he looked over at her, and finding her staring at the moon, devoid of any expression, any emotion, the lid suddenly flew off his temper. She doesn't believe a word of this, he thought desperately, and, roughly taking her face in his hand, he turned her head so she had to look into his eyes.

She was startled by his sudden action, and her heart pounded at the fierceness of his touch—at the fervor in his voice. Her eyes looked deeply into his . . .

"Not Farrell," he repeated, his voice near a whisper. "The *town* chose me." Her face felt soft under the roughness of his skin, and her chin trembled in his hand. Their faces were very close, and when her full lips parted slightly, he pulled her toward him, and their lips brushed, then met eagerly.

Suddenly the hotel door slammed, and they both jumped. He dropped his hand and stared at her, wondering what kind of demon had taken hold of him. This was a lady, not some dance hall floozy to be kissed on the front porch of any public place. But his breath came in short gasps, and the flame she kindled within him continued to grow. Somehow he knew that, lady or not, she was the only woman who could bring a wildfire such as this under control.

The revelers began to depart, a few of the young men ribbing Quint about the new lady in town as they passed, the couples going quietly to their homes or wagons.

"I'll look into your pa's death, if you like," he said gruffly.

She nodded. Her heart pounded furiously, and she didn't trust her voice enough to speak.

"I can't promise anything, so don't go getting your hopes up," he cautioned. "I'll try to get a word with Tom before the trail drive pulls out. You say he and your pa had words?"

"Yes," she mumbled, feeling yet the silkiness of his mustache against her face.

"What about?"

"He didn't say."

Quint sighed. "I'll nose around, see what I can come up with. What brought him to Silver Creek?"

"The same thing that brings a lot of people, I suppose. He had nothing left after the war, so he came out here to start over." She stared at the sky, the stars shining in their patterns, and a sob caught in her throat. Rival emotions struggled within her. If only things . . . She shook the cobwebs loose. "Maybe that's why we all come," she said, thinking of her own futile attempt to escape loneliness by running away from it.

He disagreed. "Some of us just love the land," he said. "And there are lots of other reasons, too. Men running from things—the law, family, you name it. Some of these old geezers are here for the gold and silver."

At the familiar topic, she relaxed a little. He was interesting and easy to be with, she thought, as long as she didn't have to look into those disarming, honey-gold eyes. "Do they ever find any?" she asked.

"Enough to keep the stories alive," he said, feeling the tension drain from his body, leaving him with only a dull, unfulfilled ache. "But I figure I'll come out ahead by steady work."

"Papa thought that way, too."

He looked at her quickly and thought how life had dealt her an unfair hand of cards—grief, fear, loneliness. And he had been too hard on her. "I'm sorry things didn't work out for your pa."

The lights dimmed behind them unexpectedly, and Holly turned to see Mavis extinguishing the lamps in the parlor.

Quint jumped to his feet as though he had been snake-bit. "Mercy, Miss Holly!" he exclaimed. "I've been running off at the mouth something fierce. I sure enough beg your pardon." He made for the steps and looked back over his shoulder. "See you at breakfast."

Holly caught her breath as they stared at each other. "Breakfast?"

"Mavis feeds us bachelors here at the hotel along with the visiting folks." Quint headed down the street, and Holly ran into Mavis at the door.

"Whatever did you do to Quint Jarvis, darling? I've hardly heard him string two sentences together before now, and he's been sitting out here talking to you for an hour."

Holly smiled, feeling a blush rise to her cheeks. Sighing deeply, she knew she would dream of the way moonbeams had danced in the golden depths of Quint's eyes. Why did everything have to be so complicated?

Quint walked through the sheriff's office to his

small, sparsely furnished room at the rear. The disgust he had felt earlier for the haughty Miss Campbell was gone, replaced by an uncomfortable light-headedness. Lordy, he thought, for such a small bundle, she surely can get a man's dander up.

The lamp he lighted cast a dismal pall over the room, which had never looked quite so shabby to him before: a cracked washbasin and pitcher perched on a crate he had salvaged from Mavis's trash heap, one chair, and a rickety bed. His cabin at the ranch wasn't much better, he thought grimly.

Angrily tossing his hat at a peg on the wall, he wondered what kind of fool he was, anyhow. What did he have to offer a lady?

Undressing for bed, Quint studied the situation. Holly Campbell was definitely a lady, no doubt about that. And how in hell did a man make love to a lady?

A lady in Quint's book was strictly separated from other forms of womenfolk. A lady was someone like Ma, who had died when he was only five years old. Or Aunt Jen, who never . . . he blushed . . . but she must have, he thought. She had to have to have produced children, but . . . A lady didn't enjoy it. Only whores enjoyed it. Why, every married man he knew—even Uncle Tom—frequented whorehouses.

At that moment, Quint Jarvis had an uneasy feeling that something in his upbringing was amiss. These old-fangled ideas of his didn't hold much water after the fire he'd seen in Holly Campbell's velvet brown eyes.

Her need, her hunger for him was every bit as great as his was for her. He grinned and hopped into bed. And who was he to disappoint a lady?

Chapter Three

Holly awoke the following morning filled with a sweet flush from her dream. Idly watching a slight breeze stir the lacy white curtains at her window, she smiled. True to her prediction, she had dreamed of Quint Jarvis, but not, she thought, of his gleaming, honey-brown eyes.

With a quiver of delight she relived the last part of that dream when his lips had brushed, then claimed hers in such passionate possession that her breath caught merely at recalling it.

Alarmed, she sat bolt up in bed, shaking herself loose from this latest reverie—a sweet dream which she knew posed more of a threat to her than any of her frightening wartime nightmares.

Quintan Jarvis had no place in her life, she insisted to herself, as she searched the room for whatever dress Mavis had left for her. Why, he was one of the very ruffians Papa had warned her about, and, even though he professed innocence in Papa's death, still he was associated with the only person in Silver Creek Papa had had trouble with.

Holly relaxed a bit at the sight of her own pearl gray traveling suit hanging, sponged and pressed, on a hook behind the door. She dressed quickly, fired with renewed determination to get on with the business at hand so she could return to Tennessee when the stagecoach came back through town in two weeks.

Winding and looping her hair, she pinned it up and put on the jacket of her suit. At the sound of Rosie's breakfast bell, she took a quick last glance in the looking glass. No. She looked too severe. She tugged a black curl loose here and there around her face, as she had done yesterday. Then, still not satisfied, she removed her jacket and decided to wear only the skirt and matching silk blouse with its lace cravat. At the sight of that unadorned cravat, she sighed forlornly, wishing for the amethyst pin which had belonged to Mama and which had added such an elegant touch to her costume yesterday.

Sucking in her breath, she stepped back once more and took a quick turn, admiring her trim waist; even after that long trip, it was still eighteen inches. The skirt hung well, she decided, with its rows of steel gray banding . . .

Stop primping for him! she scolded herself, aware that Rosie's dinner bell had called to mind Quint's parting promise last night that he would see her at breakfast.

With a last tug at her corset, she vowed to banish Quint Jarvis from her thoughts and to turn her attention to more important matters. After breakfast she would visit Papa's grave; her guilty conscience reminded her that she had intended to do that yesterday. Then she would find his house, where she planned to stay for the remainder of her time here. She could think more clearly there, she was sure, and perhaps among the things he left behind, she would find some clue to his death.

Downstairs the diners were already seated at the

breakfast table, and Holly paused in the doorway, unsure where to sit. Although he had not seen her yet, Quint Jarvis sat facing her, engaged in an animated conversation.

A flush of excitement washed over her at the sight of his unruly blond hair and his handsome face. When, sensing her presence, he raised his head to meet her gaze, she returned his welcoming smile, and her admonishments to herself that he had no place in her life were momentarily forgotten.

In the middle of Slim Samples's tale about a broken-down nag over at the livery stable, Quint was suddenly seized by a strange feeling that Holly was near, and looking up, he saw her standing in the doorway. His heart flip-flopped in his chest. God, what a woman, he thought, smiling at her across the room.

Mavis saw her then, also, and quickly ushered her to a place beside Aggie Westfield's grandson, Davy, while introducing those at table she had not met the day before.

Woody Woodson, heavyset and friendly, owner of the Woodcock Saloon down the street; Slim Samples, shaggy and thin and equally friendly, hostler at the livery stable; and Herman Crump, a thick, red-faced, and pleasant German merchant.

Each of the men rose in his chair and mumbled, "Ma'am," as his name was called, and Mavis proceeded around the table.

"You know Aggie and Davy, and, of course . . ." she paused dramatically, "our sheriff, Quint Jarvis."

An unwelcome blush warmed Holly's face, and she nodded feebly and took her seat at the opposite end of the table from Quint. Spreading her white linen napkin over her skirt, she struggled to control an almost irresistible urge to raise her eyes and closely examine, here in the broad daylight, the man whose stare was burning into the top of her bowed head. At least, she had her own clothes to wear, she thought, grateful that she wasn't decked out in Mavis's frivol-fravle again today.

Studiously attending to her own business, Holly accepted the platters of steak, biscuits, and gravy as they were passed to her, and Mavis continued her soliloquy.

"This empty chair belongs to Possum Burrus, a young man who runs errands for us, and who is very late for breakfast."

Rosie came from the kitchen at Mavis's ring, bringing a pot of coffee, one sip of which told Holly that if the meal were not strong enough for her empty stomach, the coffee would finish her off for sure.

Talk resumed around her with Aggie asking the merchant about his upcoming trip to San Antonio.

"I need a new needle, Mr. Crump, and if you have time, would you pick up some peppermint sticks for Davy?"

Holly looked at the silent boy. He didn't appear to be sick, but he hadn't attended the barbeque yesterday. Once she had seen him sitting at the window of an upstairs room, looking past the gathering into the wilderness beyond the town. Unusual behavior for a ten-year-old boy, as was his lack of reaction to a treat like peppermint sticks. He was very pale, yet . . .

Her attention was drawn back to the conversation by the sound of her name.

"Holly," Mavis said, "Mr. Crump can pick up anything you need while he is in San Antone. You will have room, won't you, Herman?"

"Yah," Herman Crump answered in his heavy German accent. "For a few things. This will be final trip for a while. I am bringing back lumber enough to build my new store."

Everyone at table congratulated Herman Crump, and Aggie explained to Holly. "Mr. Crump has been our local merchant going on two years now. He hauls supplies from San Antone and sells them from his wagon. All this time he has been saving up to build a store."

Mr. Crump beamed. "It will be real nice to sleep inside a building, too," he said, "instead of in that drafty tent."

"You'll have drummers callin' on you now," Woody Woodson, the saloonkeeper, said.

"Yah," Mr. Crump agreed. "I hope this is my last trip to that city for a long, long time."

"All those drummers comin' through," Woody continued, "they'll be bringing new folks to Silver Creek."

"Looks like you picked the right time to settle here, Miss Campbell," Slim Samples said. "We'll be a-needin' medical services for sure."

Holly raised her head to protest, wondering how often she would have to tell these kindly people that she did not intend to make Silver Creek her home, and she looked directly into Quint Jarvis's amused honey-brown eyes—eyes she had successfully avoided until now.

She grimaced, then instantly regretted it, for his smile broadened to a grin, which set her heart to pounding so hard she was sure everyone could see the rise and swell of her bosom. The challenge in his gaze only added to her discomfiture, but she could not break the stare between them.

Fortunately, at that moment a tow-headed young man burst into the silence of the room.

"Sorry to be late, Mavis," he said, removing his cap and sitting on it. Mavis introduced him to Holly, who had already guessed him to be the very late

Possum Burrus.

"Howdy, ma'am," he said, and rushed on without taking a breath. "Say, did you see that old trunk out back?"

"What trunk?" Mavis asked.

"There's an old brown leather trunk out by the shed. Looks real beat up, like it's seen better days. It wasn't there last night when I fetched wood for Rosie."

Quint forgotten, Holly swallowed the last of her biscuit and wiped her mouth with her napkin. Dared she hope? "Did you see the initials on it?" she asked.

Understanding her meaning, Quint suddenly moved his chair back, looked at her, and they rose together. "Excuse me, Mavis. I'd best see to this," he said.

Holly followed him out the back door as fast as her shaking knees would allow, and the others trailed behind, breakfast and San Antonio forgotten.

The trunk was in such a wretched state that she wasn't sure at first, then she gasped, seeing her very own initials in brass above the latch.

"It is mine!" Questions raced through her mind like a runaway team of horses. She fell to her knees, pulled the trunk apart, and pawed through its contents, oblivious to the men standing nearby.

Nothing appeared to be missing. Her mother's emerald and diamond parure, the string of pearls which had belonged to Grandmother Campbell, and several other pieces of jewelry, including Grandfather Easton's gold watch. All were here.

Mavis knelt beside her, then suddenly moaned and stood up, holding a torn piece of beribboned lace.

"Oh, you poor darling. A wedding veil. And it's in shreds."

Holly felt another blush rise to her cheeks. Quickly she grabbed the veil from Mavis's hands and stuffed it back inside the trunk, hiding the matching wedding dress from view.

"It was my sister's," she mumbled, uncomfortably aware that Mavis's remarks had drawn the attention of the group. What would they think? That she had come out here to catch a husband? That she was no better than those mail-order brides she had read about?

"But it's ruined," Mavis insisted.

"Really, Mavis!" Holly regained a hold on her composure when she saw that Quint Jarvis was engaged in studying tracks, instead of standing over her with that mocking grin of his. "It was merely a veil," she said, "to be used as bits and pieces for other garments. It's of no consequence. None at all."

Wistfully, though, she stuffed her jumbled belongings back into the trunk, closed, and tried to latch it. Then turning to Possum, she said, "If you would deliver this trunk to my father's house sometime today, I would appreciate it."

"Your father's house?" Mavis's voice rose an octave, as if in protest.

Holly sighed, assuring herself that Mavis truly meant well. But why hadn't Papa warned her that she would have to get up early to keep this busy lady from running her life? "I've decided to move to Papa's house so I can begin straightening out his affairs," she answered firmly.

"But you're welcome here," Mavis insisted. "And you will be ever so much more comfortable in the hotel."

Holly put her arm around Mavis's waist. "I know," she said, guiding them toward the hotel. "And I thank you. You will have me for every meal, I promise."

The three businessmen drifted off toward the street, leaving Quint to study the area around the shed.

At the back steps, Holly stopped. "I'm going up to the graveyard."

"Let me get my wrap, and I'll come with you," Mavis offered.

Holly shook her head. "I need to go alone this time. Later, if you like, we can go together."

The cemetery was a good three hundred yards east of town along the stage road, and Holly hoped the walk would relieve some of the anxiety she felt building within her, anxiety stemming from the increasingly perplexing questions which faced her here in Silver Creek.

She shivered at the thought of her trunk, returned with nothing missing. But her brief investigation indicated that every one of her dresses had been torn to shreds. Who would do such a dastardly thing? And why?

Immersed in the terror of her private thoughts, she had barely reached the edge of town when a loud whoop erupted behind her, causing her to jump around. The two men who had backed up Jim Tom Rainey at the dance last night dismounted and began hitching their mounts in front of the saloon . . . Wilt and Luther she thought Quint called them.

A piercing chill coursed her body, and she shuddered, wondering for the second time in three days if her sister was to be proved right so soon.

Perhaps she was headstrong, Holly thought, as Caroline had always delighted in telling her. Well, now she would pay for it—in loneliness, as Caroline had predicted, and in fear, she realized, feeling the stares of Wilt and Luther sear into her retreating back.

The cemetery was on a slight hill, and she leaned against the rough cedar gatepost, catching her breath while absorbing the beauty which surrounded her. Although the usual multitude of rocks and patches of bear grass and cactus sprinkled the area, she also saw stands of wildflowers and a number of fine oak trees.

The thirty or forty graves lay scattered under the trees, most of them marked with simple wooden crosses. She passed four together with the name "Westfield." Aggie's family, she thought. The only distinctive marker in the tiny graveyard was of red granite and bore the inscription which Holly expected even before she drew close enough to read it: "Sean O'Keefe, Beloved Husband."

Tensed against the reality that she desperately wished was only a dream, she walked hesitatingly to the summit, as Mavis had instructed, and found his grave. Papa's grave.

The rough wooden cross was not unlike the others, except for being newer with still-fresh scars from the chisel. A sob caught in her throat and unheralded tears flowed down her cheeks at the finality of the simple words: "Doc Holly—1818–1871." So it was true. Papa was really gone.

Her strength drained from her body as she knelt beside the grave, clutching her arms about her trembling body. Finally her tears subsided, and she stared out over the hill to the pastoral setting below—a creek running in a thin, broken stream over the endless rocks, a few longhorn cattle grazing in the distance.

Peaceful. For the first time since arriving in Silver Creek, she felt true warmth return to her soul. This was the country Papa had spoken of in his letters, the land he had come to love.

But bitterness suddenly chilled the warmth, and she threw herself sobbing upon his grave as she faced the truth—this was the land in which he had been murdered. Harbored somewhere within this rocky, broken terrain, his killers roamed as free as the longhorns and rattlesnakes.

Leaves crackled and Holly jumped, terrified of the deadly snakes she had heard so many stories about since coming to Texas. Quickly swinging her body around to face the clump of dusty green shinoak at her left, she gasped. A Mexican woman about her own age stood at the edge of the thicket, fidgeting, anguish haunting her large brown eyes.

"Excuse me, Miss Campbell, I did not mean to startle you."

Holly smiled broadly, knowing this slight, toast-brown girl must be Papa's beloved housekeeper and student. "Elena Salinas?" she asked.

"You know me?" Surprise followed by relief sounded in the young woman's voice.

"Of course!" Holly reached to embrace the woman whose beautiful brown eyes were filled with fear. "Papa wrote about you so often that I feel as if I've known you forever."

"Your papá was special. He treated us kind, not as other gringos treat my people."

Relieved to have found someone who had been so close to Papa, Holly studied Elena excitedly. The girl was dressed as simply as the ranch women she met at the barbeque yesterday, but in a different style. Elena's faded red skirt was fulled onto a band, and with it she wore a coarsely woven white blouse which gathered around the low neckline and had no collar. Her shining black hair was draped about her head in much the same style as Aggie's, but, because of her youth and the delicate oval shape to her face, the style was becomingly soft rather than severe. Only the agitated, fearful expression in her large almond-shaped eyes betrayed her emotions.

"Papa hoped we could be friends," Holly said.

"Here it is not possible for gringos and Mexicans to be friends," Elena said. "Once Texas was a part of Mexico, but now . . ." She shrugged as if not understanding. "My grandfather fought for the Texians, and besides, the war was not even in my lifetime."

"We have a greater bond than I realized," Holly said. "The carpetbaggers who have taken over my home treat us as outsiders, too. The wrench has been awful."

"I understand," Elena answered.

"Come, let's . . ." Holly guided Elena toward a fallen log, thinking to sit together awhile and become acquainted.

But Elena pulled away and spoke quickly. "There is no time. I have come to warn you, but I must hurry before they suspect what I am about."

Holly tried to interrupt, but Elena rushed on.

"Shh . . . I have not time for the whole story." Her brown eyes flashed. "Your life is in danger. There are people who believe that you have something from your papá. I do not know what it is they want, but they are willing to do anything to get it."

Holly's eyes widened in astonishment. "The holdup?"

Elena nodded. "They did not find what they wanted," she said. "They are very angry. Please return to your home before harm comes to you." Elena turned toward the shinoak thicket.

"Where are you going?"

"Back to the ranch," she answered. "Since the death of my husband, I have worked for Tom Farrell. I am not allowed to come to town, but today is the anniversary of my husband's death, and I told them I had to go to the grave to pray for his soul, or people would become suspicious. They think our customs strange anyway, so they did not refuse. But I am being watched, and I must go now."

"Stay with me, Elena," Holly pleaded. "We'll go to Papa's house."

Elena smiled and her voice carried a note of great sadness. "Tom Farrell would never allow that. He is a man who must always be in charge."

"Did he kill my father?" Holly demanded.

"I cannot prove that," Elena said. "I have never heard them speak of it."

"Did he kill your husband?"

Elena shook her head. "No. Jim Tom shot Raphael, and the court ruled the shooting was fair. There were no witnesses."

"Do you believe it was a fair shooting?" Holly persisted.

"Leave Silver Creek, Holly Campbell, leave now or you will be killed." She crossed herself and turned once more.

"Wait . . . Elena." A feeling of panic swept over Holly at the thought of Elena leaving her alone, Elena who would be able to help her solve Papa's death. "Please help me. I can help you, too. We can get to the bottom of this. I know we can."

"Two women?" Elena questioned. "No, the only way you can help me is to leave here at once."

Holly stared wide-eyed at Elena, feeling the woman's rejection sting into her growing feeling of helplessness. "I will not leave," she said finally. "I can't go until whoever killed Papa is brought to justice. And if you won't help me, I will do it alone."

Elena's look was a plea for understanding. After a moment she said, "I should have no part in this." She paused, then added, "Go to the house of your papá. The bottom right stone in the fireplace is loose. His journal is behind it. Perhaps he wrote the answer in his book." She seemed finished, then added almost as an afterthought, "Find Sancho. I heard them say he had disappeared. He was all the time with your papá, so he may know something." She parted the shinoak, and Holly saw a faint trail.

"I will set you free, Elena," Holly whispered after her.

Elena turned, her eyes shining brighter than ever in her suddenly pale face. "Tell no one I was here. My life depends on that." Then she was gone.

After Elena disappeared down the trail, Holly sank to her knees beside her father's grave once more, her head a whirlwind of confusion. Then she noticed the freshly picked red and blue wildflowers beside his marker. Thank you, Elena, she whispered.

Bewildered, Holly thought how the situation became more complicated with each unfolding event. She had wanted to find Elena and Sancho. Elena, who had kept house for Papa in exchange for English lessons. Papa was so proud of her, writing that he was sure she would be able to open a school with his help.

And Sancho, the orphaned boy who had come down from the hills and into Papa's heart. Papa named him Sancho, and they became sidekicks, inseparable. From the sound of Papa's letters, Sancho deserved much of the credit for putting life back into his dying soul.

Elena and Sancho. The two people closest to Papa, yet Sancho had disappeared, and now that she had found Elena, she was bound to secrecy, lest she endanger the woman's life.

Shivering suddenly, Holly thought of Wilt and Luther arriving at the saloon at such an early hour. Were they the watchdogs Farrell had set on Elena's trail?

Finally she arose and started back down the hill, still thinking about Elena. Papa had written something in one of his letters which might explain Elena's actions. What was it?

She tried to recall what he wrote about Raphael Salinas's death. He had mentioned it, but, as best she could remember, he hadn't elaborated on the shooting. And he wrote nothing at all about the trial. She shrugged. Perhaps the trial was held somewhere else.

She neared the edge of town thinking about the journal, and her spirits rose. Papa had been a prolific writer; whatever he failed to write in his letters he would surely have included in the journal. The journal would set things straight.

Deep in thought, Holly approached the saloon before she realized it; then, crossing the street, she stopped short at the sight of Quint Jarvis's towering body. Yesterday, even this morning in the presence of others, she had been too self-conscious to study his powerful form. But here on the street alone, she allowed herself to appreciate his well-muscled shoulders which bulged beneath the soft gathers of his cambric shirt. His rugged cotton twill pants fit snugly over small hips and fastened with three buttons at his small, low waistline. The heavy fabric stretched tautly over powerful muscles in his thighs and gathered slightly before disappearing into the tops of over-the-calf black Wellington boots.

He stood at the corner of the building, and, although his body faced her, he was obviously lost in earnest conversation with two roughly dressed men. Stepping nearer, she frowned at recognizing Wilt and Luther. But she had just started past them, when Quint raised startled eyes to hers.

Sensing movement in the street before him, Quint looked up into Holly's suspicious brown eyes. Heat traveled quickly down the tightened muscles of his neck to his lower body, and he struggled to dispel the trance her beauty cast over him. Yesterday, dressed all in black, her skin had been the color of a lazy summer cloud and her brown eyes were almost black. But today her gray silk blouse shimmered beneath the morning sun, her ebony hair glistened, and her face took on the transparency of clear bubbling spring water. Her eyes were rimmed with red and puffy, and he knew she had been crying. He swallowed hard against the weakness her unguarded sensuality brought to his limbs.

Was she really this beautiful? he wondered. Or did he want her so badly that she seemed beautiful? Or did he want her because she was . . . ?

Becoming more confused by the moment, he quickly removed his hat and grinned at her. "Mornin', ma'am."

"Sheriff," she called, and her musical voice strummed along his already taut spine. "May I have a word with you?"

Without taking his eyes from her face, he spoke to the men beside him. "That about wraps things up, boys. I don't need to tell you what's at stake if we're found out."

Wilt and Luther turned toward their horses, and Quint stepped into the street toward Holly, his heart racing. "What's on your mind?" he asked in the most casual tone he could muster.

Holly waited until the two men mounted and rode out of earshot. "What did you find out about my trunk?"

"Hardly anything at all, ma'am," he said. "There are a couple of smudged tracks behind the shed that I'll keep an eye out for."

She cocked her head in the pert manner he was coming to recognize as her way of starting an inquisition.

"Those men you were just talking to," she began, wondering how to phrase her question without revealing what she had just learned from Elena. "They work for Tom Farrell, don't they?"

"Yes'm," he agreed, unsure what she was accusing him of this time.

They stood across from each other in the rutted street, and his closeness excited her. Yet, the memory of Elena's terrified eyes haunted her, and, at the sight of

Quint speaking seriously with Wilt and Luther, fear began to suppress the romantic longings she felt for him. In her mind, his actions were proof of the pudding, as Mama used to say, and confirmed his affiliation with Tom Farrell's cutthroats.

"What did they know about my trunk?" she demanded.

"They just rode into town, ma'am. I doubt . . ."

"They could have brought my trunk in earlier, then returned to town after daylight," she insisted.

"Now hold on a minute, Miss Holly. You're barking up the wrong tree there. Wilt and Luther have been friends of mine for a long time."

"Exactly, Sheriff." She smiled indulgently, considering her point made. "Don't you think it likely that when you apprehend the desperadoes who robbed the stage—and who murdered my father—they will be friends of yours?"

He stiffened. "I thought we whipped that dog last night."

"The only thing we settled last night was that I am looking for my father's murderer, and I think those men should be questioned about it—or at least about the holdup." She wanted to tell him about Elena Salinas then, but she dared not. Not after the girl's terrified warning.

Quint ran a hand through his sun-streaked hair and stared at her in disbelief, disgusted with himself for acting the fool last night. He hadn't been wrong about her; she was the same uppity female who stepped off the stagecoach, except that now she was telling him how to do his job. "Are you saying you recognize Wilt and Luther from the holdup?" he demanded.

She turned her head away from the coldness in his eyes. Even filled with anger as they were, the honey-gold depths of those eyes sent tremors through her being—unwanted sensations, she assured herself firmly. "No, but I know . . ."

"I take it you have evidence against them. I can't go around the country arresting folks without evidence."

"I realize that, Sheriff, but you've had two months to find Papa's murderers, and . . ." She clamped her jaws tight against a sob.

He grasped her arm roughly, ushering her across the street to the hotel. "Miss Campbell, last night was the first I'd heard that your pa's death might have been murder. Far as I know, you're the only person in these parts who thinks that way. I will look into it, like I said I would, but all my evidence points to suicide."

She stopped at the hotel steps, and suddenly all her warring emotions jelled into one—an overwhelming feeling that she was totally alone. Surely someone could help her, she thought. Surely Quint Jarvis . . ." "You said you would show me Papa's message."

"I'll bring it to the hotel when I come for dinner," he said, and immediately turned on his heel and strode away, swearing to himself for letting this little bit of woman rile him so.

Holly stared after him a moment, then walked into the hotel, tears of disappointment brimming in her eyes. She had actually begun to think she could trust him—and heaven only knew how she needed someone to trust—now here he was in conference with Tom Farrell's men.

Elena's warning still rang in her ears as she passed the parlor, where Mavis, clad in cleaning apron and cap, put aside her duster and rushed into the hall.

"Holly, since you've returned so early, come with me." She led the way to a large room at the back of the house, where Aggie stood amidst stacks and stacks of trunks. Some were open, and from them clothing poured onto the floor.

"Here she is, Aggie," Mavis announced. "Ready for your pins and needles."

"What?" Holly asked.

"Aggie is going to fit the rest of my mourning costumes on you, darling. The clothes in your trunk looked hopeless, and you must have something to wear."

"Oh, no," Holly protested. "I'll make do."

"Nonsense!" Mavis dragged several garments from an open trunk. "You need clothes, and these old things are just lying around, doing nobody the least bit of good." She handed Aggie the dresses she held in her hand and climbed on top of a couple of trunks, reaching for something near the top. "Some have been cut and sewn into other costumes, but I think we can find enough to do you." Evidently finding the box she searched for, she slowly eased it to the floor, where she began pulling out everything from bustles to hoops to traveling suits and paletots.

"Where did all these things come from?" Holly asked, astonished at the array of finery.

Mavis surveyed the crowded room proudly. "I brought them all with me. When we decided to come West, I knew I would never have a chance to shop for pretty things again, so I bought everything I could find. Aggie is a genius at remaking all this into the latest styles."

Aggie beamed at the praise and filled her mouth with pins. "Now, you stand right up here on this stool, dearie, so I can get to work."

"Please, Mavis," Holly insisted. "I really shouldn't. I have no way to repay you."

"That's all taken care of," Mavis assured her. "For myself, I only want to see you well dressed." She handed Holly a black alpaca skirt and waist. "Now, off with your clothes."

Holly removed her gray silk blouse and skirt, complying with Mavis's commands merely because she could think of no graceful way to resist at the moment. And Mavis was right about one thing, she thought—she did need something to wear.

"As for repaying Aggie," Mavis continued, "she can use your medical expertise. Can't you, Aggie?"

The older lady nodded. "It's my grandson, Davy," she said. "He's such a sickly boy, and lately all he does is sit in his window and pine."

Holly recalled her own suspicions about the pale, listless child at breakfast. "What brought this on?"

"Can't rightly say," Aggie replied. "He was doing right well for a while after his folks passed on, but of late he won't eat enough to keep a grasshopper alive. Nor play outside, neither. Just sits by the window staring out at the creek."

"What did Papa say about him?"

"Davy wasn't ailin' when your pa was alive," Aggie said.

Holly fastened the alpaca skirt and stepped dutifully onto the stool. "What are you doing for him now?"

"Calomel, that's all," Aggie replied through teeth clenched around a mouthful of pins. She adjusted the hem and started pinning the garment. "Been giving him as much as he'll take going on a month."

Holly shook her head, knowing Papa wouldn't approve of calomel in such large doses. He believed too much calomel caused soreness and inflammation in the gums, and on the tongue, too. No wonder Davy couldn't eat. "I'll be happy to look in on him, Aggie," she said.

Holly moved, and Aggie snapped at her. "Hold still now. You're the squirmingest thing ever I set a pin to."

"I'm sorry," Holly apologized. Having clothes fitted had never been her favorite pastime. Caroline had been content to stand still for what seemed like an eternity, so she would have elegant clothes for the balls at Hedgerow and neighboring plantations, but Holly preferred to wear last season's dresses rather than spend her time having someone pin and tuck all around her.

Aggie patiently marked the outfits, one after the other, and Holly put her foot down after one or two, labeling them too fashionable for this Western country. Some of the others she thought she might be comfortable in, but they were all such elegant costumes.

Mavis bustled around pulling shoes from one trunk and pockets and fans and parasols from others. Truly, Holly thought, one would think they were in the heart of Atlanta society.

"Let's fix only the simpler ones," she suggested to Aggie. "I don't want to be overdressed around the other women."

Mavis frowned. "Wherever did you get such a silly notion, darling? The women like to see us dressed up. It lifts their spirits, gives them something to dream about. You noticed how many of them asked about the fashion magazines."

Holly nodded, then objected. "But they will never be able to afford clothes like these."

"Holly! Shame on you!" Mavis's impatience crept into her voice. "You haven't given up dreaming, surely."

"Of course not," Holly answered, but she wondered if Mavis was even aware of the world of difference which existed between dreams and reality, living, as she did, like a fairy princess here in this most real of all worlds.

"We must put color into our drab existence," Mavis cautioned, her green eyes dark with earnestness, and

Holly was inclined to see her point. Certainly her lodgings here at the Hotel O'Keefe improved her whole outlook on life.

And the women had such a good time yesterday. They seemed not to mind the contrast between their homespun and Mavis's silks.

Still, Holly hesitated, not sure she would have the nerve to wear some of these costumes. Alpaca, faille, silk. Not exactly the stuff of functional frontier garments.

But a prick of Aggie's pin called forth the pain and terror in Elena's troubled eyes, and Holly knew it would take more than fine clothes and a fairy godmother like Mavis to transport her out of the nightmare she found herself in this time.

Aggie finished, and Holly dressed once more in her own clothing and started upstairs to check on Davy. Since they had found no obvious malady, she wanted to get to know the boy and gain his confidence. Perhaps in that way she could discover what troubled him.

Mavis had resumed dusting in the parlor, and Aggie had decided to go to Davy's room with Holly, when the front door burst open, and Possum rushed in, panting for breath.

If only Possum's spunk could be shared with Davy, Holly thought . . .

"Whatever is the rush, Possum?" Mavis reprimanded.

"Doc's house," he began, then took a deep breath. "Doc's house has been ransacked real good!"

Chapter Four

Holly fell to her knees before the fireplace, oblivious to the smut-covered hearth. At Possum's startling announcement, she had raced from the hotel, only to find herself standing in the middle of the street, her mind whirling inside her head, lost. Mavis, Aggie, and Possum followed, then led the way to her father's house, where they found the interior of the small stone structure in shambles.

Not a chair or table stood upright—belongings had been strewn about, furniture smashed against the wall like kindling. The sofa and mattress were slashed; horsehair stuffing and feathers covered the floor, stirring along with the dust at each step.

She picked up a crumpled photograph and studied it dry-eyed, but with a deep sadness growing inside her—a photograph of herself, her mother, and Caroline, decked out in Sunday best standing in front of Hedgerow. How many lifetimes ago had that been?

Hands trembling, she placed the picture on the wooden mantel and brought her full attention back to the present—to the fireplace stones. Which one had Elena said concealed Papa's journal? The bottom right?

The bottom right stone dislodged easily, but she stared in disbelief at the empty place she found behind it.

Empty. Tears pressed against her tightly closed eyelids, and she leaned back on her heels, hugging her knees to her quivering body. No journal. No answers.

"Don't worry, darling." Mavis patted her shoulder. "We'll fix everything good as new."

"It's just that . . ." She stood up, dejected, and Mavis cradled her in an aura of lavender.

"I know darling," Mavis crooned. "Such a waste. Why anyone would get pleasure from destroying perfectly fine furnishings, I . . ."

Holly drew back. "This was done on purpose, Mavis."

"Whatever do you mean?"

"They were looking for something. Like in my trunk." And they probably found it this time, she thought, as sharp fingers of fear began to displace her sense of loss.

"Holly, darling, you're distraught. Come back to the hotel and lie down. I'll send Rosie's girls to clean up this mess."

"No!" Alarm raced through Holly's mind, reason temporarily conquering emotion. "I don't want a single thing touched until I have a chance to examine it all myself."

She looked around the demolished cottage. But where to begin? The house contained only three rooms: kitchen, bedroom, and a parlor where Papa had seen patients and received guests.

The ruffians were no better than heathens, she thought angrily, stooping to pick up Papa's copy of the *Physician's Visiting List* which had been torn cover from cover, page from page. A large oak desk stood in the corner of the parlor, and she rifled through its strewn-about contents.

What she found was not that for which she searched—nothing to indicate a grudge against her father, no broken agreements or outstanding debts, no problems with anyone.

Yet everything to stir memories—memories long since handled and put to rest. Letters Mama had written Papa while he was at war. Letters from herself since he had been in Silver Creek.

And the vandals had not even had the sensitivity to leave these innocent keepsakes untouched.

Where they had obviously been tied with string and bits of ribbon and stashed in neat stacks in the cubbyholes of the desk, they were now torn and scattered and would not serve as pleasant reminders of the past any longer, but as a grim proclamation of reality.

Reality. Cold ashes shoveled from the fireplace and cast about the kitchen. Precious photographs torn from their frames. Dishes raked from cupboards, lying broken upon the floor.

Reality. Papa had something someone wanted. Wanted badly enough to hold up a stagecoach and steal her trunk. Enough to do what man rarely dared do in this country, accost a lady. Enough to destroy everything a man had left in the world.

Enough to kill?

Fear descended around her like a glass dome, isolating, yet not protecting her from those without, while Elena Salinas's warning reverberated through her head like a steeple bell tolling a death.

Almost reverently she closed the desk over a stack of her father's papers, knowing she must go through them later and salvage as many of his writings as she could.

In the bedroom Mavis had done a quick job of sweeping feathers into a pile. "Look what I found." She held up a black leather bag. "It was way back under the bed where they must not have taken time to look."

Holly's eyes blurred with tears as she took Papa's beat-up old medical bag—the same one he had used when she went on calls with him when she was a little girl. How many times she had watched him refill the contents the moment they arrived back home, then tuck the bag under his bed just within reach of his long arms, so he could get it in the middle of the night without waking her mother.

"Habits," he had told Holly so often that she could hear the sound of his voice even now. "You must form habits. Then when the unexpected comes along, you can act instinctively without losing precious time."

Habits. One thing here had been saved by a good habit. She sighed, wishing it had been the journal. The journal, which, if Elena were right, would lead her to Papa's killers.

"Mavis?" Holly asked suddenly. "What do you know about Elena Salinas?"

Mavis thought a moment. "Oh, yes, your father's housekeeper. Tragic, tragic about her husband."

"What exactly happened to him?"

"If I recall correctly, he confronted Jim Tom Farrell. A foolish thing to do. That Farrell boy has a hair-trigger temper."

"Where is Elena now?"

"I wouldn't know," Mavis answered. "I suppose she went back to Mexico to her own people."

"Her own people?" Holly questioned. "Her people are from right here in Texas."

"Well, wherever she is from, I'm sure she went back there. Most widows do, if they have a family. Some of us are not so fortunate."

Holly ignored the note of self-sacrifice which sounded in Mavis's choice of words, as well as in the tone of her voice. "Could she be working for Tom Farrell?"

"I suppose," Mavis said. "Tom never mentioned it, but that would be a good position for her." Mavis looked at the little gold watch she wore pinned to her bodice. "Gracious! It's nearing noon. Come along, darling." She reached for Holly's hand. "We'll let Rosie's girls finish here. You must have seen all there is to see."

"Not yet." Holly turned away, stepping into the kitchen where she began picking up pieces of pottery. Very little could be saved.

As she worked, replacing a few metal plates and tin cups in the cupboard and sorting out the cooking utensils, Mavis followed and started sweeping ashes into a pile.

"What about Sancho?" Holly asked.

"Sancho? Another of your father's urchins. I'm not sure where he came up with that boy. He said the child turned up at his house one evening, half starved to death."

"Where did he go after Papa's death?"

Mavis shrugged. "Who knows? Back to where he came from, I suppose—or traveled on. You never can tell about folks out here."

Holly drew a deep breath, and when she spoke, her voice was filled with exasperation at this addlebrained woman. "But he was only a boy—nine or ten, Papa said. And he had no place to go. He must be around here somewhere."

Mavis leaned on her broom, oblivious to Holly's feelings or ignoring them, Holly wasn't sure which. "I haven't seen him. In fact, I'd forgotten all about him." She resumed sweeping, then stopped again. "That might explain what's been happening to those hams in my smokehouse."

Holly stopped in her movement to pick up a tarnished metal plate. "What do you mean?"

"Several times during the last couple of months," Mavis began, "hams have disappeared from the smokehouse. Not all of them at once, just a ham now and then. And I've seen small footprints around."

"When did it happen last?"

"About a week ago," Mavis answered. "I decided the footprints belonged to Davy."

Holly shook her head. "Aggie said Davy doesn't go outside at all."

"You know children," Mavis replied. "He might tell us that to get attention, and then go outside unobserved." She swept the last of the ashes into a pan. "But thinking back on it, Sancho and Davy were about the same size."

"Were they friends?"

"Oh my, yes," Mavis said. "When Sancho was around, we had no trouble with Davy. They were together constantly. Whenever Sancho wasn't out with your father, that is."

Holly stared out the back door transfixed, seeing nothing but a possibility of finding Sancho. "I must find him," she murmured half aloud.

Mavis rested her broom in the corner and turned back to Holly. "You really believe something sinister happened to your father, don't you?"

"Yes."

Mavis spoke softly. "He left the note, Holly. You have no facts to refute a suicide note which was written by his own hand and found on his body."

"One fact," Holly insisted. "Papa would not kill himself."

Mavis shook her head. "That is not a fact, Holly. A daughter's wish, a hope. But not a fact."

Holly pursed her lips. "Papa wrote that he and Mr.

Farrell had had words."

Mavis laughed. "Everyone in this country has had words with Tom. He's ornery and self-righteous and extremely land-hungry. He would even go so far as murder, I have no doubt. But he isn't crazy. Tom does not kill people indiscriminately—without any reason."

The front door creaked, then slammed, and both women jumped at the jingle of spurs in the front room.

"Mavis is right, ma'am. Tom had no quarrel with your pa." Quint Jarvis removed his hat and stepped into the disarray. "Someone surely had himself a party in this room."

Holly tilted her chin angrily. "Your flippancy is not appreciated, Sheriff. I know exactly who ransacked this house—and why. Even if you choose not to believe ill of your employer." She wished she were free to tell him of her meeting with Elena, of her suspicions that Wilt and Luther were sent to town to keep watch on Elena and probably to ransack this house while they waited, looking for Papa's journal.

Quint tensed at her heated accusation. "You do mighty little listening, ma'am. I don't work for Farrell. I quit him over a year back . . . for reasons of my own."

"That doesn't necessarily change your colors," Holly retorted.

"This does." He pointed to the badge he wore on his leather vest. "When I took this job, I swore an oath to uphold the law in Silver Creek, and I intend to do just that. It makes me no nevermind what you or anybody else thinks."

Quint returned Holly's stare spark for spark, until Mavis interrupted, announcing, "Time for dinner" in a lilting voice which befitted one who had without design dropped into this fracas from the moon. "Let's all go back to the hotel and eat." She took Holly by the arm, but Holly pulled away.

"Go ahead without me, Mavis. I haven't finished here, and I . . . ah, I want to be alone."

Mavis hesitated, shrugged, and started for the door, then stopped to put a hand on Quint's shoulder.

"Come on up to the hotel with me, Quint." Her green eyes sparkled. "There's no need for you to miss dinner."

Holly's mouth dropped open, and she turned abruptly toward the fireplace. Her heart beat up in her ears, shutting out their conversation. Stooping to study the empty hole where Papa's journal should have been, she saw only the faces behind her, and she screamed inside.

What was the matter with her? Why did she lash out at these people with such bitterness? She didn't even know them, and here she was treating them all like enemies.

"Are you all right, ma'am?" Quint stood above her, wondering why she knelt on the dirty hearth. She looked so small and vulnerable—like a child playing in the ashes. "I brought your pa's message." When she looked up at him he saw tears glistening in her dusky eyes, and he knew that the paper he held would bring her more sorrow.

Suddenly overcome with emotion, he reached to help her up. Crazily he hoped the message he brought would convince her of his friend's innocence, and at the same time, he wondered why that was so important to him.

Holly stood up and dusted her hands. "I'm sorry, Sheriff . . ."

Quint held out a hand to stop her. He wanted to take her in his arms and comfort her, but he held back, recalling how instantly she could reject him. "No need to be sorry, Miss Holly. You've been under a bit of strain lately, and for my part, I think you're holding up most respectable."

She started to object, her eyes dark and round and very large.

"Tell you what." He handed her a smudged piece of paper. "Take this letter and read it by yourself. I'll take a look around outside and see if the characters who ramrodded this free-for-all left their mark. When you finish, I'll be here, in case you want to talk."

The letter felt cool to her touch, foreign, and she stared at it without moving. She was not conscious of Quint leaving, of the screeching door, of anything except the paper in her hand. The last letter Papa wrote. The letter in which he explained why he took his life. She tensed. Or a forgery that someone expected her to accept as Papa's last letter.

She unfolded it slowly. Suddenly her legs became wobbly, and she had to sit on the floor and support her arms on her knees to steady herself. For a moment his graceful, familiar handwriting masked the horror of the words.

"Life has become too painful to bear.
Forgive my weakness. Holbart X. Campbell"

Simple. Final. None of his usual flourishes, his philosophizing. But if he had truly been in the state of mind to kill himself, he would have been, she knew, a changed man from the father she remembered.

She sat for a while, empty and dry-eyed, numbed by this latest collision with reality. Then, her hands trembling, she tucked the letter inside her sleeve and proceeded to straighten the small house. Later she would question. Later she would study the message. Later.

Like the greedy power-driven lady from the past, she knew that tomorrow would creep toward tomorrow, in ad infinitum. Tomorrow she would have time to think.

Then she would decide what to do, how to discover the author of that message, how to cope with the reality that Papa—her last support—was gone forever.

She fought back tears as she surveyed the room and planned what to do about the mess. Everything must be hauled to the dump, so she might as well get started.

Carrying an armload of splintered chair rungs to the back porch, she stopped short at the sight of Quint sitting on the steps, long legs outstretched, elbows resting on his knees. Suddenly her tears gushed forth, and the wood in her arms clattered to the floor.

Quint jumped to his feet, startled. He stooped to pick up the chair rungs, but at the sight of the tears, he hesitated, then quickly stepped forward and took her in his arms.

She wept uncontrollably, her tears soaking the front of his coarse shirt, while he stroked her silken mass of black curls and patted her slender shoulders.

Gradually her tears subsided, and she became aware of his strong masculine body molding to her own. Swiftly drawing back in shame, she looked up.

But as she did so, his intense honey-gold stare flowed into her wilted soul, filling her with the force of his strength. Then she felt his body quake. Their eyes held a second, and their lips met fiercely, searchingly, releasing a hunger she had not known was growing inside her.

Her soft lips melted beneath his, and he tasted the salitness of her tears; her unexpectedly eager response set his body on fire. When she had first drawn back, he had looked down at her, shaken by a sudden fear of losing this moment. Then their lips met, pulled together by a magnetism he felt flowing from her as well as from himself.

His mouth slid over hers in moist entrapment, his tongue found passage into her yielding sweetness, and his senses quickened at the delight of her small tongue reciprocating—touching, curling, exploring his own waiting mouth. He had known other lips as soft, but none as sweet; others as willing, but none as quick to give.

Enraptured by the softness of Quint's lips on hers, Holly eagerly returned his kisses, opening her mouth to his, as in her dream, and feeling the rhythm of his suckling kiss pulsate through her throbbing veins. With a thrill of passion, she stroked her fingers over the nape of his long neck and across the sinewy muscles of his shoulders in a fiery caress.

Moaning with the glorious sweetness of this assault on her senses, she felt light-headed and weakened, yet strangely overcome by a desperate craving for more of this wanton pleasure—pleasure such as she had never experienced, never imagined, never . . .

Kissing her with all the need that had built up inside him since he first saw her on the stagecoach, Quint watched her face, her creamy, closed eyelids, while his fingers fumbled over the silky fabric of her blouse, among the heavy folds of her skirt as it draped over her padded petticoats and bustle. His hands slid to her tiny span of waistline, but everywhere they were hampered, frustrated by stays and structures.

Desperately, the wanting in him about to explode, he placed his hands on either side of her head and pulled their faces apart.

"Holly . . . Holly . . ."

The huskiness of his voice almost took her breath away. She opened her eyes to look at him from the protective restraint of his viselike grip on her head. Golden streaks of light glistened over his face. If eyes could speak instead of merely see, she thought, his would echo the cry she felt within her brain—more, more, more. Never before had she known such intense pleasure and such a piercing need at the same time.

When he rubbed a thumb lightly over her flushed cheek, Quint felt her body tremble, and, as he slowly lowered his lips to hers, he whispered, "Look at me, Holly. Don't close your eyes."

Her soft lips opened to receive him, and he groaned, quickly claiming her with a kiss as fierce as the first one had been, her obvious desire filling him with a greater need than he had ever felt before.

Holly stared at him entranced as their lips met; their tongues found each other's once more—giving, giving, taking, giving. Her mind reeled and swirled in heady sweetness . . .

Quint clasped her to him tightly, his lips pulling urgently at hers. His breath came in short gasps, as he felt her body press seductively against his, and his roaming hand finally slipped between them to encircle a firm breast. A thought suddenly filtered through his erotic reverie—the thought that this lady was damned pleasing to make love to, after all; that is, she would be if he could figure out how to get rid of all the paraphernalia that protected her chastity.

A lovely release washed over Holly when Quint grasped her swollen breast, but then at his gentle kneading, it hardened and filled her with an even greater, more wanton desire. Frightened, she stared into his languid eyes, and reality hit her suddenly like a bucket of cold spring water.

What was she doing? What was he doing? How could she have . . . ? Shame crept up her neck like fingers of evil, coloring her face with streaks of red. She pulled away from his embrace, turning from him, from her own shamelessness.

Quint stared helplessly at Holly's back, confused. One minute she had returned his kisses eagerly, the next . . . He ran a hand through his tousled hair.

Damn, he thought. He'd rushed her. He hadn't meant to . . . She seemed so ready, so willing . . . He should have been more careful, taken more time. After all, she was a lady, not some damned fancy woman of easy virtue.

Hobbled by a feeling of clumsiness, he stepped toward her and put his hands gently on her shoulders. He sighed deeply at the quivering he felt beneath his palms. "Holly, I'm sorry. I didn't mean to . . ."

His arms felt warm and strong, and she bit her lip to keep from crying again. What was happening to her? She didn't even know this man, and here she was . . .

He turned her around to face him, staring into the top of her down-turned head. "Holly, listen to me. I didn't mean to take advantage of you like that. I . . . *we* got carried away, but there'll be time . . . We'll take our time, get to know each other better, then . . ."

From somewhere deep within she summoned enough control to lift her head and look him straight in the eye. "No," she said. "There'll be no time . . ." But she could not finish for the sob which caught in her throat and forced tears to brim in her eyes.

Pulling away from his move to help, she took a handkerchief from her sleeve and wiped her eyes. "I'm sorry . . ." Again tears rolled down her face, and she was unable to continue.

He watched her, feeling as useless as he'd ever felt in all his grown days. Surely there was something he could do to stop her crying, but he had no idea what that might be. His heart throbbed in his chest. "God, Holly, I didn't mean . . . I had no right . . ."

She swallowed, regaining some of her composure. "I was as much to blame as you. I don't know what came over me." She dabbed furiously at a new flow of tears. "Lately all I do is cry."

"There is nothing wrong with crying," he said,

relieved to have a new topic to distract them both from his still-raging passion. "Seems to me you've had a passel of trouble to cry over lately." He pulled her gently forward until her head rested against his chest. "Way I see it, a lot of ladies cry over a pail of spilt milk. But that won't do in these parts where our troubles come a mite stronger than in most places, and about as regular as nightfall." He tightened his arms around her, conscious of a need to keep his hunger for her under control. "No ma'am, you're cut out for this country. You surely are."

His philosophizing brought her back to the present, to why she was here, to Papa's death. She stepped back. "Well, I'm not staying in Silver Creek. At least, not any longer than it takes to find Papa's murderers." She turned toward the living room, and Quint followed.

"The message . . . ?" he asked.

"No," she replied. "The letter did not convince me. It was clever, but misguided. Whoever contrived this scheme did not know Papa or me or my relationship with him."

She patted her hair in place and straightened her skirt around from the twisted position it had traveled during their embrace. Even the thought of that sublime encounter caused her head to spin and brought hot spots to her cheeks and the back of her neck.

Looking after her, Quint felt a sudden urge to protect her. She reminded him of a caged animal, skittish of all who came near. She couldn't fight this thing alone; he couldn't let her. "You loved him an awful lot," he said.

Holly sucked in her breath, struck by his simple words, the honesty of his perception. Surely, this man would live up to her trust . . . to her . . . But she must get her mind back to the business she was here for, she admonished herself. Back to Papa.

"It was much more than love," she replied. "He was my anchor. He was steady and sure and dependable. The only time he ever faltered was when he returned to Hedgerow after the surrender and found the shambles the war had made of our lives. All the buildings the Yankees could not use, they burned. Our freed slaves who wanted to stay, couldn't, because they had no place to live. Papa couldn't work the fields alone, just himself and Caroline's husband. His horses—the horses he loved so much—had been distributed to every Yankee soldier who passed by unmounted. None were left after the war."

Quint stood silently beside the fireplace, listening to her reminisce. "And worst of all," she choked, "Mama died while he was gone."

He watched her small trembling body and listened to the hurt in her voice, painfully aware that he could do nothing to take that hurt away. Not right this moment, anyhow. He wanted to take her in his arms, but he was afraid she would misunderstand his intentions. Damn, he thought, she was wrong. There would be time for them later. There had to be.

When she turned toward him, Quint saw fire in her smoldering eyes. "Even then," she said. "Even when he left Hedgerow broken and alone, he did not leave to end his life. He left that torn-up life behind and came out here to start another one. To start over, not to give up."

"With all respect, Holly, maybe that wasn't possible." He hated to add to her hurt, but he knew she must start seeing things as they were. "After losing all he had, maybe he couldn't find it in himself to start over."

"I know better," she insisted. "And I have letters in my trunk at the hotel which will prove that he had not given up. I'll show them to you." She stopped suddenly and caught her breath. "Oh, what's the use? You don't believe me. No one believes me."

"I want to believe you, Holly." The fury in his voice surprised him, and he slowed down and continued. "I must have facts before I can call it anything but suicide. The facts I have now say he killed himself."

"But he . . ."

"Hold it," he demanded. "I said I want to believe you, and I do. Show me the letters. Show me anything you have, and I'll help you. But you can't expect me to start accusing folks of a crime that might not have been committed."

"I understand."

"So show me your letters," he repeated. "I want to help you."

"I will." She nodded. "I'll bring them to you first thing in the morning."

Quint looked out the window and realized with a start that daylight was fast fading. "We'd best be getting back to the hotel. If I know Mavis, she's standing on her ear worrying about you already."

Holly smiled. "All right." She took up her father's medical bag and the photograph from the mantel.

Quint glanced at the picture. "What's that?"

She held it out for him. "It's Mama, Caroline, and myself."

Taking the photograph in his hands, he examined it closely. "Where was it made?"

"In front of our home at Hedgerow." She shrugged. "That's the way it used to look." Engrossed in the picture, she stood close beside him as memories leaped from the small paper likeness—the red brick house with its white pillars and shutters, and the white rocking chairs across the porch. Papa and Mama had spent many happy afternoons on that porch, finishing off the day with a julep or cherry brandy.

Quint whistled through his teeth. "It's bigger than

Mavis's hotel."

Holly smiled. "Yes, it is. And in those days the rooms were always filled with guests. Mama loved to entertain, and Papa knew people from everywhere. Looking back, it seems that our biggest problem was deciding which gown to wear to what ball."

"I've never seen a house like that," Quint admitted. "Fact of the matter, I've never even been curious about such a place before." He handed the photograph to her, telling himself to back off real quick. A girl raised up like that would surely not take to courting a plain, everyday, bow-legged wrangler like himself. If he had a lick of sense, he knew he'd get her pa's death cleared up and her on that stagecoach and out of his life pronto.

"The war changed everything," she told him. "There are no places like Hedgerow anymore, no people like we were then. Even though some of them don't realize it yet, we're all different now."

"It must have been terrible."

When she thought of the war her images were of rows and rows of dying men in the hospital where she worked. And the funeral march playing endlessly in the street. "Yes," she said, and put the photograph inside the medical bag for safekeeping.

Later, at the hotel, Holly freshened up and decided to resume where she had been interrupted earlier in the day by visiting Davy Westfield. Perhaps that would take her mind off her disgraceful behavior with Quint Jarvis. The shameful thing about it, she blushed thinking on it, was that she wasn't sorry. She knew she would have to work hard to keep herself in line around this irresistible man. He was definitely the most stimulatingly masculine man she had ever known.

She found Davy sitting in the window of his bedroom, where Aggie had said she would. When he showed no reaction to her greeting, she walked over to him.

"Do you mind if I sit with you?"

He shrugged his shoulders, so she sat down beside him and followed his gaze.

The window looked out onto the river fifty yards beyond the hotel. A soothing scene, with clear water trickling over rocks where they formed a natural barrier, like a dam. Below that the water was deeper and swirled into a blue-green pool. Moss grew along the edge among the rocks.

She pointed to a patch of deep green leaves which flourished in a few of the more stagnant places. "What is that plant?"

"Watercress," the boy answered in his thin voice, almost to himself.

"Oh, that's why I recognized it," she said. "We had some with dinner yesterday."

"I don't like it," Davy said. "It's bitter."

Holly recalled the pungent, sharp taste of the cress, as Rosie had called it, and agreed. "You must see a lot of interesting things from here," she said, thinking of the picnic which was held on the grounds directly below them. Then she caught sight of the stone building by the edge of the river and heard again Mavis's idea that Sancho might be the thief who was stealing hams from the smokehouse.

"What is that building?" she asked.

"The springhouse," Davy answered.

"Where's the smokehouse?"

Davy directed his mute gaze out the opposite side of the window, to another stone building, similar to the springhouse, except that it stood back from the water so that the front was nearly parallel to the back of the hotel, making it impossible to see anything except this one side of it.

"Where is the door?"

"On the other side," Davy answered.

Holly thought about it. If the thief were indeed Sancho, he surely wouldn't walk across the backyard, in full view of anyone who might be looking out a window.

Not knowing how to approach the topic of Sancho, Holly turned her attention to Davy's own problem. He was a slight boy, small-boned, dark-headed, and frail, with skin that had a transparency to it, even in this late afternoon haze.

"Did you know that Doc Holly was my father?"

He nodded and a tiny spark enlivened his eyes. "Are you going to be Doc Holly, now?"

She laughed. "No, I'm just Holly. But if you will let me, I'd like to help you get some strength back. Would you mind if I looked inside your mouth?"

He raised his eyebrows and drew a breath, leaving his mouth slightly open.

"If you'll open real wide, I'll look without even touching you."

He drew back from her, but opened his mouth quickly, giving her just enough time to see his inflamed gums.

"Is your tongue sore?" she asked.

He nodded slightly.

"That calomel tastes awful, doesn't it?"

He nodded again.

She smiled. "I think you're well enough to quit taking it. How would you like that?"

He grinned.

"I'll tell your granny at supper, then. But you will start eating more of Rosie's good cooking, won't you?"

He nodded, and they sat silently for a while, looking out at the river.

"I came out here to live with my father," she told him. "But he died before I got here."

From the corner of her eye, she watched him steal a quick look at her, then resume his vigil.

"My mother died during the war," she said without emotion, letting him know that he could relate to her if he chose.

Although he didn't speak, Holly sensed no discomfort on Davy's part. She hoped she had gained more with him than he showed.

Suddenly the silence was pierced by the clanging of Rosie's supper bell, and Holly jumped to her feet, extending her hands to him. "Let's go get something to eat. I'm starved."

He stared at her, not responding, yet not quite closing her out, either. She dropped her arms to her side. "I won't push you, Davy, but I would like to be your friend. I'll come back to see you tomorrow."

Turning at the door, she was startled by moisture glistening in the boy's eyes as he watched her leave, but he jerked his head away quickly. Was he thinking of his own mother and father? she wondered. Or perhaps his lost friend? Hadn't Mavis implied that Davy's problems began after Sancho disappeared?

She closed the door and started down the hall with her heart pounding against her ribs. Would she be able to find Sancho through Davy? Or was she chasing shadows? And how would she ever find out if he knew anything? Davy's delicate grasp on life demanded that she put his problem before her own. Her job was to put Humpty Dumpty together again, not break him into smaller pieces.

When she reached the landing, Holly took several deep breaths to settle herself, but in spite of all her efforts, she became completely unnerved once more upon entering the dining room. Everyone else was there, seated in the usual places, and she exchanged a brief glance with Quint as she slid into her own chair.

For a moment, during which she self-consciously spread her napkin over her gray skirt, she was sure everyone at table had taken to staring at her—seeing the telltale puffiness Quint's kisses had left on her lips. But finally, after a couple more deep breaths, she atuned herself to the conversation around her and wound up eating two bowls of stew and three biscuits before Mavis admonished her.

"That's what you get for skipping a meal. And you, a doctor's daughter, should know better."

A conversation on Doc Holly's attention to the community diet followed, with Mavis telling how he had instructed her to plant the kitchen garden out back and teach folks to eat vegetables.

Holly laughed. "That sounds like Papa. He always insisted we have more vegetables than meat. I enjoyed eating at my friends' homes, where I could gorge myself on fried meat and potatoes."

"The vegetables are fine with me," Aggie said, "but it's the garden itself that's a travail."

Quint had little to say during the meal. In fact, except for that one brief glance, Holly felt like he was intentionally ignoring her. And that one look, she thought, had chilled her with its indifference.

She sighed. Quintan Jarvis was certainly not like other men she had known. The men back home had vied for a lady's favors with clever conversation and attentiveness. But not Quint.

Disappointment began to take hold within her as she recalled his gentle embrace, his passionate kisses. This afternoon she had seen a kindness in him. She blinked back a tear—the truth was that any gentleman would have shown her sympathy as Quint had this afternoon, more than likely even Tom Farrell.

But they had been comfortable together, easy. Several times during the day, she found herself on the verge of confiding in him about Elena. How simple it would be to get him to ride out to the TF and set the girl free, if she were indeed a prisoner.

Each time, however, Holly had seen again Elena's frightened eyes, heard her plea for Holly to tell no one. And she could not be that sure of Quintan Jarvis.

When the other diners retired to the parlor for a bit of after-dinner reading, Holly excused herself and went to her room.

But no sooner had she closed the door than a knock came, and she opened it to admit Rosie, carrying a pitcher of hot water.

"Miz Mavis says it would refresh you to bathe off with some warm water." She exchanged the pitcher and basin for Holly's empty one and closed the door behind her.

Holly smiled to herself at Mavis's thoughtfulness. She might be bossy but there was definitely a kind side to her nature, Holly thought, removing the silk blouse and soiled gray skirt with a grimace. If Mavis thought them beyond repair before, she would certainly consider them ready for the trash heap now.

Untying her corset, she then unhooked it, and with a great sigh of pent-up air, she tossed it on a chair. Her chemise still clung to her form in damp pleats, creased in place by the corset. Crossing her arms in front of her, she grasped the wilted cotton and pulled it over her head, casting it aside as well.

Facing herself now in the looking glass, she scanned her nude body with new awareness. Before today she had paid little attention to her body. It was merely a body like any other, capable of feeling pain, sadness, and happiness.

Tears had flowed from her eyes—tears of anger at the war; tears of sadness over the destruction of her home; tears of grief at the deaths of her parents.

Her heart had ached, and she had known the exhilaration of joy. But never before had she experienced the emotions she had felt this day. Never before today had she thought of this body—her body—as a living instrument for giving and receiving such unbelievable pleasure.

Releasing the drawstring, she stepped out of her white cotton bloomers and gazed at her creamy white body as though it were some strange, new invention. Slowly, she took up the washcloth, wrung it out in the warm water, and began to bathe the day's soil from her fair skin.

She screwed up her nose at the sight of her small breasts. Were they too small? she wondered. Watching the rosy points of her nipples stiffen beneath the roughness of the cloth, she stared at the rise and fall of their fleshy mounds, while the erotic sensations she had experienced when Quint caressed her breast washed over her once again.

Bathing downward, she studied her black triangle of curly hair, mystified at the throbbing, pulsating ache she had felt there when Quint kissed her lips. She ran her small tongue gingerly around her parted lips, then, the memory of his moist, possessive kiss, his large, thrusting tongue, brought a weakness to her thighs once more, and she felt a stirring of desire begin within her.

After today she would never view this body as simply flesh and blood again. After today this body was only one part of a whole, capable of joyous pleasure in companionship with that other, sensuously masculine body.

Her gaze traveled to her face, with its parted lips full and expectant, cheeks rosy with a comely blush, eyes soft and dreamy. Then suddenly, as she held her own stare in the looking glass, an accusing voice screamed within her, pronouncing her a wanton slut who had lost any sense of decorum.

Shaken by this new, wicked knowledge of herself, Holly turned quickly from her reflections, clothing her nakedness in one of Mavis's chaste linen nightdresses, covering that with the buff linen wrapper.

Tears of sadness rolled down her flushed cheeks—sadness for her lost innocence. Today a demon had been released within her, and she knew she would have to battle it for the rest of her stay in Silver Creek.

Quint Jarvis was probably the kind of man Papa said he was, and if her body didn't know that, her mind must always remember it. How could she have disgraced herself and Papa's memory with such behavior today? With such sinful reveries now?

Determined to keep Quint Jarvis out of her thoughts and out of her life, she squared her shoulders, took the pins from her hair, and gave it its daily one hundred strokes with her own brush, salvaged from the trunk. With her upbringing, as Mavis had so firmly reminded her yesterday, she could surely keep her social life in order for the short time it should take to discover the truth about her father's death and return to Tennessee.

So she turned down the bed, plumped the feather pillows, and checked the wardrobe to see what Mavis intended her to wear tomorrow. Then she looked around the room for something else to occupy her time, all the while ignoring the finger-smudged message she had removed from her sleeve and placed on the marble-topped washstand.

Finally deciding to get it over with without further dallying, she plucked up her courage, settled herself in the cozy, green velvet wing chair, and took up the letter.

It bore the same message. And as desperately as she wished otherwise, the handwriting was Papa's.

But for the same reasons she had given Quint earlier, she knew Papa could not have written such a letter—not willingly. Someone had forced him to write it, she was sure of that, perhaps even dictated it.

To Papa writing a letter was as personal, and as easy, as a spoken conversation. She could not believe that, in what was to be his last communication here on earth, no matter how depressed he had become, he would have been so abrupt—so impersonal.

Holly recalled her promise to take the letters she brought with her to Quint first thing tomorrow, so she set aside the soiled message and opened the trunk, all the while admonishing herself for the sudden thrill she felt at the thought of seeing Quint again. From now on, she promised, their relationship would be strictly business, nothing, but nothing more.

Lecturing herself in this manner, she searched the contents of the trunk, once, then again. Not until everything was out and carefully arranged on the bed did she grasp the situation.

The letters were missing.

With quivering hands she repacked, trying to put it all back in its original place. The top drawer first, lingerie and nightwear. Next her jewelry—the emeralds and diamonds, pearls, and gold watch. The ruby ring Papa gave her for her eighteenth birthday, and Mama's magnificent diamond solitaire earrings that Caroline had insisted she bring.

In and around the jewels she packed her handkerchiefs, bonnets, and fans. The next drawer held petticoats and bustles, and the bottom drawer was reserved exclusively for books.

Papa had written of the scarcity of books, and she could not begin to bring all she wanted, so hours of decision had gone into the final selection—which ones to bring, which ones Caroline could send later, and which she would never see again. Fortunately, Papa already had a respectable collection of Shakespeare, Milton, and Pope, along with his other favorites in English poetry. And she would leave the family Bible for Caroline's children.

So she settled on Longfellow's *Evangeline,* one of Morier's *Hajji Baba* books, Seneca's *Medea,* and a translation of *Arabian Nights.* With Papa's books this should be a broad enough selection for a while, and it certainly filled the drawer, but then she could not resist stuffing in two French plays, *Le Mariage de Figaro* and *Le Barbier de Seville.* Her French had never been good, but wouldn't she have plenty of time ahead to polish it?

The other side of the trunk held the ragged remains of her dresses, and a faintness passed over her as she stared at them. Her skin turned suddenly cold and damp. Goose bumps rose against her nightdress, and she pulled the wrapper more tightly about her, feeling vulnerable and alarmingly naked.

Trembling uncontrollably, she pressed her fingers against her throbbing temples. Her dresses shredded! Papa's letters stolen! What did it all mean?

She knelt beside the trunk to examine again the box the letters had been stored in. It was still there, just beneath the one holding her shoes, and wedged in as tightly as when she had packed back at Hedgerow. The box was probably too hard to dislodge, she thought, so they left it—proof to her way of thinking that the letters had not simply fallen out of the trunk.

Caroline had been dismayed that Holly would take up trunk space with the letters. "They are nothing but old news, Holly Louise, and they should be thrown away."

Holly and Caroline had always been different. Caroline loved the here and now; Holly loved things with a history—memories and experiences. So she knew that if she left the letters behind, Caroline would carry out her own wishes by burning them.

But why would anyone except she herself want Papa's letters? She could think of nothing he had written which would be damaging to anyone. His remark about having words with Farrell could not be important as she had supposed, since Mavis insisted that everyone had words with Farrell. And everything else he'd written was positive. He admired the courage of the men and the stamina and persistence of the women. He loved the country and planned to make it his permanent home. Had he not asked her to share it with him?

Papa would not have asked her to come into a situation where he was in danger. She knew that. He would not have wanted her anywhere around trouble. So that could only mean that he didn't know of the danger himself.

But if the letters were important enough to steal, they must contain something which neither he nor she recognized as dangerous. The thought sent shivers up her back, and she cradled her arms about her. Was this problem too big for a mere girl of twenty-four years?

The war had strengthened her, and she was confident that she could stand her own against a known enemy. But she knew no one here. Papa had written of them all, and she trusted his perceptions, but . . .

Her heart beat wildly, and noise rose up in her ears like a wagon rattling over stones. She and Papa had confided their souls to each other, so she knew his killer if he did, perhaps even if he did not. And she knew how to find out who it was.

Taking pen and ink from the walnut ladies' desk and stationery from her trunk, she began to re-create Papa's letters.

The whole stack would be impossible, she knew, but

if he had been in danger long, it stood to reason that he would have been killed sooner. So she began with the last letter she received before leaving home and worked backward.

At first her arm shook, and her fingers held the pen so tightly that her writing was jerky and hardly legible. But soon she got into her task, and her tension vanished before his fluent prose. In places his writing approached poetry. His description of the landscape was beautiful; where some people saw only rocks and cactus, he had found strength and determination to withstand the frequent dry spells, Indian raids, and isolation.

She remembered him calling Mavis "that lovely Irish mist," and as she wrote the things he said about Tom Farrell and his men, she thought Quint might be too angry to help her once he'd read the unflattering words.

She could not re-create everything, but she worked at it as diligently as she had ever worked in her life. For she knew very well that her life might depend upon her recalling one innocent-sounding detail.

He wrote many truths and ideas about life, and as she recalled them she became aware once more of the reason she had insisted on keeping these very special letters. They had kept her going, given her courage and the will to continue. In a life filled with negatives at every turn, Papa had been able to write—and she knew to believe—"My darling daughter, do not despair. The lady called Tomorrow holds in her hand a promise just for you."

Some promise it had turned out to be, she thought bitterly. One of loneliness and fear. Perhaps even a promise of death.

Unable to involve himself in the conversation at

Mavis's table, Quint had swallowed his tasteless supper, excused himself quietly, and left by the kitchen door. The wide range of emotions he had felt this day had left him with one feeling he could not recall ever experiencing before—a sense of helplessness?

Or was it hopelessness? he questioned, shooting angry looks about the unpainted walls of this shack he called home.

Undressing with angry motions, he tried desperately to shake these new and unwelcome feelings. Why did she have to come to Silver Creek, anyhow? He had been perfectly happy—a bit aimless, he admitted—but happy, until this tiny bit of . . .

He breathed deeply, fighting to erase the image of Holly's seductive femininity from his aching brain. Why the hell couldn't he get her off his mind? Think about his ranch? His difficulties with the rustlers?

Unmindful of the mess he made, Quint carelessly splashed cold, stale water from the cracked basin onto his feverish skin, hoping to cool the rising fire this woman had set inside him. The thumping palpitations of his heart struck hard beneath the soft covering of blond hair on his chest, and he imagined suddenly how her skin would feel against his.

Swearing aloud, he wondered why in God's Holy Name, when he finally found the one woman he desired above all others, she had to be Holly Campbell. Beautiful, seductive . . . completely beyond the reach of a lowly cowhand.

Images of that fancy plantation in Tennessee burned into his mind, and he warned himself not to forget them. Those images were his protection; they would bring him back to earth every time her intoxicating beauty sent his brain soaring with the eagles.

Quint stripped and settled himself on the rough, straw-filled mattress he had once thought of as a bed and tried to imagine Holly Campbell sleeping on such a bed—in such a room. Even though she had returned his kisses with a passion to equal his own, he had no doubt that from a lady like Holly, a kiss or two was all he would ever get.

And a kiss or two was not what he ached for most of the night as he tossed and turned on the crude mattress. Of all the emotions that had jangled his nerves since he met Holly—from anger, to sympathy, to a fierce greedy passion, he was left now with a hollow hunger and longing he had no hope of ever satisfying. Not after seeing that photograph.

A shudder wracked his taut, muscled body, and he wondered how many sleepless nights it would take to get Holly Campbell out of his system.

Chapter Five

Holly slept little and with the first cock's crow arose, dressed, and headed to the kitchen for coffee.

She had sat long into the night with pen in hand, re-creating Papa's letters, but as the rosy glow of morning pierced the delicate fabric of her curtains, her memory lagged, and she fell exhausted into the bed she had turned down hours before.

Her sleep was troubled, however, and the crowing rooster aroused her, so she slipped into the least fussy of the dresses Aggie had altered—a black sateen fulled-onto-the-waist skirt and tight-fitting basque which buttoned up the front to a small collar of black crocheted lace. In spite of its gathered sleeves, the entire outfit left her feeling even more depressed, as though, she thought, she were actually garbed in sackcloth and ashes.

Leaving the bonnet aside for the moment, she went downstairs, her stomach queasy with apprehension over the day ahead of her.

"Buenas días, señorita," Rosie greeted her.

"Good morning," Holly returned. "Is the coffee ready?"

"It has been ready for hours, señorita," Rosie

replied, handing Holly a cup of the steaming black liquid which Slim Samples claimed was strong enough to float a horseshoe.

Mavis sashayed into the room then, looking fresh and elegant in an apricot muslin morning dress with matching flowers in her russet hair.

"My, my, Holly, you're up early." She cut a healthy-sized chunk of Rosie's hot sourdough bread, and handed Holly part of it. "Sorry, Rosie, you know I can't resist bread fresh from the oven." She turned to Holly. "Be sure to use plenty of sweet butter. Except for the fort's, we have the only milk cow within a hundred miles."

"Mavis," Holly said, trying to conceal the tremors she got even thinking about the missing letters. "I went through my trunk again last night. You won't believe what's missing."

Mavis whirled around, almost spilling her coffee. "It can't be jewels; you found those undisturbed."

"Not jewels."

Mavis sighed. "What a relief." She spread her bread with a good portion of wild grape jelly and offered some to Holly. "What did they take, darling?"

Holly stifled her irritation at Mavis's implication that anything other than the aforementioned jewels wouldn't be much of a loss. "Papa's letters," she replied.

"What?"

"The letters Papa wrote me after he came out here."

"Oh, well . . ." Mavis began. "I'm sure they hold sentimental value for you, but they're hardly something you can't live without." She moved into the dining room, where she started setting the table for breakfast. Holly took up the stack of china plates—they were using blue Dresden today, in keeping with her mood, she thought—and followed Mavis.

"What about your clothing, Holly? Did they shred

everything the way it appeared?"

"Just about," Holly answered, her irritation turning now to aggravation. Why was Mavis always so materialistic?

"Fortunately, Aggie is about finished with the rest of the alterations. Aren't we lucky?" Mavis looked into Holly's face for the first time this morning. "You look ghastly, darling. Did you not sleep well?"

"I rewrote most of the letters last night," Holly answered quietly.

Mavis stopped, put her hands on her hips, and stared at Holly. "You what?"

Holly repeated her statement, adding, "Don't you see, Mavis, they think Papa told me something in a letter. I don't know what it could be."

Mavis shook her head. "Holly, Holly. Why would anyone think a father wrote his daughter anything sinister? Your letters simply fell out of the trunk. Surely you don't think highwaymen take time to put everything back in its proper place."

"Mavis," Holly said sternly. "The box the letters were in is still in the trunk. They couldn't dislodge it, so they removed the letters." She added a white napkin at each place. "And, yes, I do think these thieves put everything they didn't want back in the trunk."

Holly stood at the end of the table, looking down its length at Mavis. "They weren't careless, Mavis. They were very deliberate." She hesitated, swallowing back a sob. "And it frightens me."

"I'm sure it does, darling," Mavis said. "I really don't see your point, but I'm sure if I felt the way you do, I would be frightened, too." She paused, holding a fork in the air. "Why did you rewrite the letters?"

Desperate to convince someone to help her, to believe in her, Holly pleaded. "I know they hold the answer, Mavis. They must. Sheriff Jarvis agreed to go over them, and since they were gone, I rewrote them." She looked doubtful. "He probably won't believe me, either."

"Hey, don't I get a jury trial before I'm strung up?" Quint stepped through the door, and Holly's heart missed a beat.

He was clean-shaven, except for his neatly trimmed honey-colored mustache, and he smelled of bay rum. The yellow stripes of his gingham shirt enhanced his golden tan, and when he saw her, his eyes lit up, telling her, as if they could speak, all she needed to know about being desired. At his broad smile, the fatigue of her sleepless night fell like a heavy mantle from her shoulders.

Mavis broke into the moment with a twitter. "Well, Sheriff, what brings you to our table so spruced up?"

Quint blushed and retreated to the hall, where he hung his hat on the rack, all the while reminding himself that he was a damned fool if he treated Holly Campbell in anything but a businesslike manner. But the warm flush which coursed his body at the sight of her loveliness told him that he'd likely have as hard a time convincing his body of such an arrangement as he seemed to be having with his mind. Coming back into the room, he asked Holly, "What's this about the letters?"

"They were stolen from my trunk," she said, telling him then her reasons for believing that this proved her theory her father met with something evil here in Silver Creek. She was painfully aware of the harm she could be putting herself in by admitting her suspicions, however vague they might be, to anyone here. But she had to trust someone, she told herself. She had to. And Quint . . .

"I said I would look over the letters, and I will," he told her. "But you remember you promised to keep an open mind."

"I do have an open mind," Holly insisted. "Do you think I want Papa to have been murdered?"

Quint and Mavis exchanged glances, and the sudden deadening of their expressions alarmed her. "What are you thinking?"

"Nothing," Quint said.

"Yes, you are," Holly retorted. "You looked at each other like you know something you aren't telling me."

"Well, Holly . . ." Mavis began, then stopped.

"Tell me," Holly demanded. "He was my father. I deserve to know what's going on."

"Holly, you won't want to hear this," Mavis said.

"Tell me, anyway. Go ahead, tell me."

Mavis shrugged. "Very well, Holly. As you say, he was your father, and you loved him very much." Mavis drew in her breath, as if inhaling courage to continue. "No daughter wants her father murdered, of course, but . . . well, murder is preferable to suicide."

Holly looked from one to the other of them, stunned. "You think I'm making this all up to protect the family name?"

"Now, Holly . . ." Quint stopped, conscious of dropping the proper form of addressing a lady one hardly knew. But he knew her well enough, he thought, to feel the agony that filled her eyes to overflowing and tore at his heart.

Mavis nodded. "It seems likely that that is exactly what you're doing, Holly." She held up a hand to stop another outburst. "I didn't say you're doing it deliberately. It's a natural reaction from a loving daughter."

The breakfast bell clanged, and the others drifted in. Everyone seated himself in his usual place. Aggie and Davy, Possum Burrus, Woody and Slim. Herman Crump had gone to San Antonio, she recalled numbly.

Mavis looked into the kitchen, then took her seat, and Rosie began placing heaping platters of food on the table.

After a couple of attempts at conversation, Aggie spoke to the table at large. "Did a norther blow in over night unbeknownst to me? All this frigid air is likely to give me a case of the pleurisy."

Mavis gathered her wits then, and led the others in conversation, but Holly remained silent and excused herself early.

As she reached the foot of the stairs, Quint touched her arm. His touch thrilled her, but she pulled away; he jerked her arm roughly then. "Hold up a minute."

Surprised by his brutality, she stiffened, tilted her chin, and looked down at him, seeing in his sparkling eyes not the desire of an hour ago, but the painful reflection of her own fury.

The instant Quint saw that haughty tilt to her chin, he warned himself to prepare for a tongue-lashing. He ought to turn her loose and say to hell with her, he thought. But he didn't.

Something in her highfalutin manner, in those feisty brown eyes, challenged and excited him as no woman had ever done before.

"Release me," she demanded, and the harshness in her voice brought him back to reality.

Breaking the angry glare between them, he cleared his throat and tried to keep his voice low and steady. "Mavis came down on you a little hard back there, but she didn't mean any harm. We want to help you, Holly."

Angry tears pressed inside her eyelids. "You've done quite enough, Sheriff." She pulled away from his grip and took another step up the staircase, but he grabbed her arm again.

"Wait up, now," he said. "I want to go over the

letters. Will you bring them to me?"

With a deep sigh, she fought to hold back her tears, knowing she had no other choice. "Very well." She climbed the stairs, enraged, but determined to keep her temper. By the time she reached her room, though, melancholy overtook her, and she threw herself onto the bed, sobbing to break her heart.

Why did she care if they believed her? She hadn't expected help from the sheriff when she arrived, so why did it matter so much now?

And she did not need Mavis! The lady was as harebrained as any Tennessee belle she had ever known, and out here in the wilderness, where a woman should have a head on her shoulders. How she survived . . . Holly collapsed again in a fit of weeping, recalling the tender manner in which Quint and the other men treated Mavis.

Mavis would survive, she thought. At this point, she wouldn't bet on herself.

But enough of this. Still sniffling, she sat up, pulled a handkerchief from her sleeve, and dried her eyes. She couldn't lie here black and blue with melancholy. She must find Papa's killers so she could get back to Hedgerow. She would sooner live in Sodom and Gomorrah than in Silver Creek, Texas.

Splashing her eyes with cold water from the washbasin, she rearranged her hair, and, pinning on the good black velvet and satin bonnet, she tied it pertly under her chin. No use flaunting her wretched state to an uncaring world.

Finally she plucked up her courage and took the packet of letters across the street to the sheriff's office. She could leave them on his desk, she assured herself. She wouldn't have to exchange more than a simple greeting with him.

A tremor of expectancy gripped the back of her neck

when Quint stepped around his desk to greet her, but he took the letters without touching her hand and avoided meeting her eyes. He wouldn't press his attentions on her; he figured neither one of them would like that in the long run. He'd look into her pa's death, then she'd be gone. She wasn't his type of woman, anyhow, and he surely wasn't her kind of man.

"I'll go over these right away." He spoke more gruffly than he intended. "I might need to talk to you about them later."

She nodded abruptly. "I'll be at Papa's house."

Doc Holly's house lay a hundred yards down the street and around the corner past the livery stable. She walked slowly, taking time to examine the house from a distance. Yesterday she had been in such a rush she hadn't even noticed the picket fence around the yard or the building to the side which must have served as a primitive carriage house.

As she approached the house, an intense sense of loss overcame her, and she stopped beside the fence, thinking of the lovely way things could have been if Papa were still alive. He wrote that he had the perfect yard for some of their roses and cannas, and she imagined them there now, surrounding the stone house, all in bloom.

So deep in thought was she that it took the familiar squeaking of the front door to draw her attention to the man leaving the house.

Tom Farrell strode confidently down the path; he showed no discomfiture at being caught red-handed at the ransacked house. "I'm surprised to find you still in Silver Creek, Miss Campbell," he said.

Holly regained a measure of her own composure. She tucked a stray curl casually behind her ear and steadied her voice. "You have taken me by surprise, also, Mr. Farrell. What were you doing in Papa's house?"

Without answering, he walked quickly toward the gate, forcing her to step aside to keep from being run down.

She rephrased her question. "What were you doing in *my* house, Mr. Farrell?"

Farrell paused, then gave her a scornful look from head to toe. "You've no business here, Miss Campbell. Best leave the law to our sheriff."

"I would never take the law into my own hands, Mr. Farrell. But . . . well, Papa found a good life here, and I thought . . ." She shrugged, looking from the agitated man in front of her to the sturdy stone house, then back at Tom Farrell. "The climate's so healthful, and the people are so friendly . . ."

Tom Farrell started to speak, pursed his lips, then finally found words. "Silver Creek is no place for a young lady of your upbringing. You'd do well to return to your home on the next stage."

Holly raised her eyebrows in defiance. "Silver Creek *is* my home, Mr. Farrell." The shock on Tom Farrell's face reflected the surprise Holly felt at hearing her own words.

Anger rose in splotches of white across Farrell's sun-weathered face. "Don't you go rushing into the Florence Nightingale business," he thundered. "We don't need another midwife."

Holly narrowed her eyes. "According to the people in this community, Mr. Farrell, I am needed here. And my experience far exceeds that of a midwife."

He glared at her as she continued. "By the by, what takes you away from your trail herd?"

Her question seemed to anger him further, for he took a step backward and shifted his gaze. "Didn't anyone ever teach you any manners?" he demanded. "In this country it's taken as an offense to question a man's actions."

"Even if that man is coming out of my house just after it has been ransacked?" she asked. She wanted to ask him about Elena then, and about her trunk, and about Papa. Especially about Papa. But she knew he wouldn't answer any of her questions. Watching him stride toward his mount, which was tethered at the far side of the yard, she knew there was one more reason she couldn't ask Tom Farrell any of these questions. Fear. She had never been as afraid of anyone before in in her life.

Upon reaching his horse, he turned and pointed a finger at her. "For your own good, young lady, you get on the next eastbound stagecoach that comes through here."

"My father's dead, Mr. Farrell. I am my own keeper now. And I've decided to make my home in Silver Creek."

Farrell stared at her a moment longer before mounting his horse. "You are a stubborn woman, Miss Campbell. A mighty stubborn woman."

Holly stood immobile watching him ride away. Her heart beat a staccato every bit as loud as Rosie's dinner bell, and she had red marks on the back of one hand where her nails had dug. She wondered if Farrell noticed her terror, and hoped he hadn't, because she had sensed his deep need for power and control.

Especially over women, she guessed. His commands were neither noisy bluster nor gentle warnings. Tom Farrell had spoken, and he was, she knew without doubt, a man prepared to enforce his demands.

Suddenly her anxiety turned to panic. What had he wanted in Papa's house? She could think of nothing which hadn't already been destroyed—nothing worth taking. Except the journal.

But didn't he already have the journal? Surely whoever ransacked the house took the journal. And if that wasn't Farrell's men, she wondered, who was it? Where was Papa's journal?

She held her head in trembling hands, while questions raced about inside. Oh, to be a man! she thought. She wouldn't sit around drinking and driveling! A duel, at least, or whatever they called it out here—a showdown?

Inside, the house looked as if the showdown had already taken place. The chaos from yesterday lingered untouched—the disemboweled sofa, bed, and chairs, the fragments of paper, china, and clothing. Once the furniture was hauled to the dumping grounds, she would be left on bare boards.

In the kitchen she paused, wondering again what Tom Farrell had done here. Poison in the coffee Papa ground before he was killed? No, the coffee, along with everything else, had been dashed to the floor. She need not be afraid of poisoning.

She stumbled to the back porch and sat on the steps, holding her quaking body with wrapped-about arms. Noise roared in her head, pounding against her eardrums. This kind of violence was more than she could handle. She must admit it and go home. Papa would not want her to take such chances with her life.

But as she sat staring at the pecan trees which lined the bank of the river in the distance, she knew that it wasn't in her to give up. It never had been. She considered her stance with the Yankees at Hedgerow. Wasn't Caroline forever warning her to remember her place? And at the hospital. Hadn't the doctors been exasperated with her refusal to accept the poor conditions and lack of equipment and medicine?

No, giving up was not in her, and yet she had never

faced such odds before. Was Mavis right? Was her family pride so strong that she could not let herself face reality?

Surely she didn't have a chance to win against Tom Farrell. Not alone.

Quint found her on the back porch—sitting on the steps with her little black bonnet in her hands, staring out at the silent river.

Standing behind her unobserved like this, his heart pounded so hard he was sure it would startle her, and he was suddenly gripped by a desperate urge to drop the basket he carried, scoop her up in his arms, and make love to her right here—fierce, beastly, satisfying love.

Struggling with himself, he began to hate this desire he felt for Holly Campbell, feeling himself weak for not being able to concentrate on her obviously depressing situation with her pa's death instead of on his own carnal appetite.

Quint shifted his weight, and Holly turned to find his rugged masculine body hovering above her.

He cleared his throat. "Mavis sent over some food. Says you are not to go another day without dinner."

In his silent, open face she read instantly the passion glowing in his honey-brown eyes—passion which sent heat up her neck and set her head to reeling. She smiled. "Mavis could mother a girl to death if she set her mind to it."

Quint put the basket on the floor. "And this telegram came for you." Without lowering his gaze from the glow of expectancy he saw in her face, he handed Holly a folded piece of paper.

She stared at the telegram. It must be from Caroline. No one else knew to contact her in Silver Creek. News from home would be so welcome.

Tearing open the message, she studied it intently. It

was from Caroline, but not news about the family. As she read, her heart leaped in her breast, and her decision took form.

"Papa bought some land here," she said. "Caroline received the deed in a letter from him, and she is posting it back to me. She gives the metes and bounds, though." Holly handed the telegram to Quint and stood beside him. "Do you recognize the place?"

Quint studied the telegram silently, as she watched with newfound zeal. Then his sun-weathered face gradually turned pale. She looked at him in alarm.

Still staring at the paper in his hand, he whistled through his teeth. "Looks like we've found your motive."

Holly drew a sharp breath. "What do you mean?" She peered over his arm at the telegram, but all she could see were numbers and directions.

"This is a piece of the TF." He tapped the paper with a long, slender finger. "Reason I recognize the boundaries is that they border my property on the north."

Her eyes grew misty, and she relaxed. "So Papa did find some land where he could raise his spanking thoroughbred bays."

Quint cocked his head. "That land isn't fit to raise blooded horses on."

"Fiddlesticks!" Her excitement grew. "Papa knows . . . he knew what kind of land is required for thoroughbreds. He raised prize-winning bays in Tennessee before the war."

"He didn't buy that piece of land to raise horses on," Quint repeated.

"How do you know?" she demanded, furious with his continual pigheadedness.

"It's nothing more than a box canyon," he answered calmly. "Pretty country, but a man'd have a hard time raising horses on it. The entrance opens smack-dab into the middle of Tom's best ranchland. And Tom Farrell is mighty cautious about who uses the spring coming out of that canyon."

Holly tilted her chin toward him and spoke in a commanding tone. "You're mistaken, Sheriff." He knew nothing about raising blooded horses, she reasoned. Nothing.

He looked her straight in the eyes, reading her hurt and despair. "No, Holly, I'm not. That piece of property is for sure a box canyon. My place runs right up to the edge of it."

Holly walked away from him, trembling, confused.

"What I'm wondering," Quint spoke as much to himself as aloud, "is how Doc Holly came by that land in the first place."

She whirled around with fiery eyes. "What do you mean, Sheriff?" She asked the question slowly, speaking in measured syllables, intending him to understand how very much damage he had done with that unthinkable, unpardonable question.

Quint bit his tongue. He instantly regretted his choice of words, but, at the same time, he wondered how a society accomplished a damned thing by pussy-footing around every hurtful issue. Out here a man spoke his mind.

"I don't rightly know what I mean," he answered quietly. "Except that Tom Farrell doesn't sell land, especially not a piece as valuable as Mustang Canyon."

She glared at him. How could she ever have imagined he would be open-minded enough to help her? "First you tell me the land isn't fit to raise horses on," she said bitterly. "Now you say it's valuable."

Quint stood his ground. "It's only valuable if you own the land outside the canyon. Tom depends on that spring to water a fair amount of livestock. He wouldn't up and sell it."

"It appears he did exactly that." Her finger quivered when she pointed to the telegram.

Quint shook his head. "Sure doesn't make sense, though, no way you cut it. Tom Farrell doesn't sell land."

Tears welled in her eyes. "My father was an honorable man, Quintan Jarvis, and don't you suggest otherwise. He bought that land to raise horses on." She folded the telegram and put it in her sleeve. "I'm going to the TF Ranch today, and I insist that you come along and arrest Tom Farrell for the murder of my father."

Quint held up his hands. "Now, hold on a minute, Holly," he said. "Claiming a parcel of Tom's land is one thing, being murdered by him is a whole different animal."

"He's guilty," she insisted. "You said as much yourself when you read the telegram. You said, 'Here's your motive.' "

He nodded his head in agreement. "But that's all it is—a motive. We don't have any fact tying Tom to your pa's death." Damn, he thought, how could any one female be so hardheaded?

After a moment, she said tentatively, "The hold-up . . . and this ransacked house. Farrell was here today, just before you came. That's evidence that he's involved."

"Tom was here? What did he want?"

"He refused to answer that question for me."

Taken aback by this information, Quint looked at her with new understanding. "That is curious behavior," he admitted, "but hardly evidence that he ransacked the place, either. You didn't come right out and see the folks who did the dirty work, did you?"

She shook her head despondently.

"I can't storm out there and arrest him without any evidence. Do you understand that?"

"Of course I do," she sighed. "It's true, though. How am I going to prove it?" She buried her face in her hands. "Dear God, how am I going to prove it?"

"We," he corrected her. "How are *we* going to prove it?" Suddenly a need to comfort her, to protect her, rose within him in a powerful surge of heat, and along with these new feelings, the old ones returned—a yearning so strong that he knew if he didn't get out of this house and busy doing something else real quick, he would be hard put to resist his earlier temptations.

Picking up the picnic basket, he headed for the back door. A breath of fresh air, he thought, that should cool him down. "Tell you what," he called to her over his shoulder, "let's take this food and go down by the river and eat it before it ruins and Mavis gets mad. Have you ever had Mavis mad at you?"

"Disgusted, maybe," she answered, wondering at the abruptness of his actions.

"Well, you ain't seen nothing yet," he said, laughing. "Her Irish eyes can flame hotter than a branding iron."

Quint led the way and Holly followed him. He looked about a bit, finally deciding on a grassy place under one of the large pecan trees where they could watch the river, protected from the sun by the massive, overhanging limbs. Wildflowers in hues from yellow to orange to red and blue blanketed the area and filled the air with sweet fragrance.

Inside the basket Holly discovered a lovely blue cloth, which she spread over the tender spring grass growing around the tree. Tucked beneath the cloth, she found some crisp fried chicken, wedges of apple pie, and two jars of tea with mint leaves floating in them.

Quint studied the river intently, and they ate in silence. Holly felt light-headed, weak, and not at all hungry from the sudden taffy-pull her life had become. A thought, like a fragile thread, reeled through her mind, repeating itself over and over: He said he would help me! Quint said he would help me!

She took a small bite of crisp chicken leg. "Fried chicken must be a delicacy out here," she said, recalling how, by the end of the war, this food which had once been a staple had become a rare treat.

"Everything's mighty scarce out here," Quint answered.

She watched him as he ate, feeling her heart flutter at his nearness. "Did you find anything in Papa's letters?"

He looked up, rather sheepishly, she thought. Finally he grinned. "I know now where your opinion of me came from."

His grin lightened her mood, and she smiled, but pressed on. "Was he right about Farrell?"

"Mostly," he admitted. "I'd say he knew Tom better than I suspected." He finished a large piece of salmon pie and took a couple of swallows from one of the jars of mint-flavored tea. "The only puzzle in the letters is why he didn't mention the Salinas trial. That trial was the talk of the country, and your pa's testimony saved Jim Tom's bacon. It's curious that he didn't see fit to mention it."

She shrugged, their eyes met, and his need for her spread like wildfire through his body.

"After reading what your pa wrote, I can see that I'll have to start from scratch to earn your respect."

His husky voice blended with the fragrant spring air, leaving her breathless. "Find Papa's killers," she whispered.

"I intend to." He resumed his examination of the purple and white thistles on the opposite bank.

Holly drank some of the refreshing tea and gazed at the cool water rippling past them. "It takes a tough skin to live in this country," she said. "I wonder why Papa loved it so?"

Quint raised an eyebrow, struggling to appear unaffected by her presence, all the while trying desperately to steady his rapid pulse. "Each man has his own reasons for coming, and his own reasons for staying. What draws one man, drives the next one away. That's the best part, I reckon—everyone has a chance to be different. To be his own self. Of course, he has to pull his freight, too. But there's always a neighbor ready to help out in times of trouble." They sat across the blanket from each other, watching the river.

Quint continued. "It's a hard life, no denying that. Too hard for many." He looked quickly at Holly, then back to the river. "You won't find luxuries and nice homes, like back East."

She recalled his reaction to the photograph of Hedgerow. "There's not much luxury left there, either. At least, not where I come from."

He thought of the red brick house, of the ladies in fine dresses. "It must be a lot different there."

"Different, yes. And maybe life is harder out here, but Mavis has made it."

He nodded. "Mavis didn't come from the same kind of home you came from, though."

She looked at the side of his face and imagined her fingers stroking his silken mustache. "What do you mean?"

Feeling her eyes on him, he turned toward her, and his gaze held hers. Suddenly she felt as though they were involved in two separate conversations at the same time—one with words, the other with only eyes and senses.

"Mavis told me about her childhood once," he said, unsure how much longer he could sit here beside her without doing something he'd likely regret—later, after it was over. But instead of leaving, he turned his eyes back to the river and continued. "Mavis had it pretty tough up until she married O'Keefe. He was a rich Boston lawyer, and they put all their money into the hotel. Now, it's all she has. She stays on, because, as she tells it, out here she's a big fish in a little pond, but back in Boston she'd be just another little fish in a big pond."

Holly sat quietly, trying to contain her racing heart, thinking of Mavis, Aggie, and the others she had met these last few days. Mostly of Quint Jarvis. "Tom Farrell ordered me to return to my home," she said. "Do you know what I told him?"

He shook his head, smiling at the ease with which she could unleash her anger. Old Tom must have really caught an earful.

"I told him that Silver Creek *is* my home."

He looked up, astonished, and, as their eyes met, he held his breath. Every emotion he had ever experienced—desire, hope, longing—flowed between them in a mesmerizing stream of passion.

Finally he found his voice and a measure of reason. "It's too dangerous for you to stay here." That telegram had convinced him that somehow the TF was mixed up in all this. Maybe not in Doc Holly's death. But he knew Tom, and if Tom sold that land to Doc Holly, now that the doc was gone, Tom would try to get it back. And Tom Farrell could be downright mean when it came to land. "You aren't safe here, Holly," he whispered, feeling his good intentions dwindling fast under her tantalizing stare. "You'd best go back to Tennessee."

Caught up in the caressing tone of his voice, she didn't hear his words at first. When she realized what he had said, her eyes flared in defiance. "And let him take Papa's land? Certainly not!"

"I'll handle it," he told her quietly. He was afraid for

her now, and he knew she must leave Silver Creek. How could he protect such a headstrong female? If she stayed all hell could break loose. And if she left . . . He clenched his jaws firmly against the pounding in his heart.

Holly rose to her knees, facing him. "No, Quint . . ." She stopped suddenly, momentarily taken aback by the sound of his name coming from her lips. The first time she had spoken his name aloud. Quint. His name.

Steeling herself, she brought her thoughts back to the problem at hand. "I will stay in Silver Creek and see that Tom Farrell pays for what he did to Papa. Then I'll run that land exactly as Papa intended. He bought it to raise horses on, and I'm going to raise horses on it." Their eyes met, and her chin trembled. "No matter who tries to get rid of me. Whether you want me here or not!" She collapsed with her head in her hands, her tears quickly intensifying to sobs.

Quint watched her, horror-stricken. How could she think he didn't want her here? How could she possibly think that? "God, Holly, I want you here." Taking her in his arms, he buried his face in her soft mass of black curls. "I want you here."

Holly clasped her arms about him tightly, as though she feared someone might tear them apart. Her breath came in great heaves, causing her breasts to quake against the firm muscles of his chest. As her tears subsided, she felt the fierce rhythm of his heart throbbing against hers, and her fears were somehow calmed.

Quint slowly lowered them to the ground as one. He clung to her for a moment, assuring himself that she was really in his arms again, like before, like in his dream, and this time . . .

Holly's breathing slowed, and she pressed herself to Quint's hard body, feeling his fingers in her hair . . .

massaging her back. They felt like fingers of fire traveling up her spine, exploding in tiny bursts of fireworks inside her brain.

He gently pulled her head back, and she gasped at the sudden passion that washed over her when he looked into her eyes. The golden highlights she had always found so sensual were now molten and flowed into hers with an intensity which seemed to melt her to her very core with sweet, liquid heat.

The eagerness reflected in the depths of her soft brown eyes surged through Quint, and he lowered his lips to hers fiercely. He wondered briefly if all their lovemaking would be as intense; then all thoughts were lost in the moist fullness of her kiss, the minty flavor of the tea he tasted within the inviting sweetness of her mouth, the saltiness of her drying tears. He groaned aloud with the intense pleasure she gave so freely.

His groan awakened in Holly a yearning that surged into her breasts, swelling them against the confines of her clothing. She arched her supple body against his, desiring, craving, searching . . .

"Sweet Holly," Quint murmured. The seductiveness of her slender body moving against him was almost more than he could stand. His need for her had grown from that first moment when he saw her through the stagecoach window, until now his entire body and soul seemed filled to the bursting point with a passion so great he knew it must be satisfied.

Calling on strength he didn't know he possessed, Quint controlled his frantic desire, and gently, slowly stroked her hair, loosening the pins and pulling the long black curls around her face. At the sight of her beauty, a new wave of passion swept over him, and he kissed her hungrily.

When her sweet mouth opened even wider, and her small, inviting tongue urged him to greater delights, his own large tongue explored the depths of her offering. Suppressing a tremor, his lips slid over hers in a rhythmic suckling which she returned, entwining her fingers in his tousled hair, pulling his face closer to her own.

Breathlessly he moved his hand to caress her flushed cheek, her delicately angled jawline, finding at last the buttons on the black bodice of her mourning dress.

His touch excited her to longings she had never dreamed of, and when she felt the cool air gently brush her bare chest, she opened her eyes. Quint's gaze spoke to her of desire with such intensity that it took her breath away.

Without saying a word, he kissed her pert nose, her chin, and propping himself on an elbow, he studied her exquisite loveliness with a calm he did not feel inside. His eyes traveled downward from her graceful neck and shoulders to the sensual mounds of her small breasts which were trapped inside her stiff, tightly fitted corset. He watched them heave beneath the snowy-white lace of her chemise.

With trembling fingers, he pulled back the edge of the corset and gently lifted one creamy breast from its confinement. Entranced, he flicked a thumb across the delicate rose petal and saw its color deepen and the tiny nipple harden with expectancy.

Holly watched Quint's face, mesmerized. A weak cry of resistance rose in her throat when she felt him pull her breast from her corset and cup his hand around its firmness. But then he moved his thumb across her nipple, sending piercing, sweet pains throughout her body. She saw his jaw clench, his features take on an almost animallike fierceness, and instead of drawing away, with a deep gasp she arched herself toward him, at the same time, pulling his head to her waiting breast.

As he nuzzled and suckled at her breast, Holly was

filled with such sweet, agonizing desire that her mind reeled. She urged him on, pressing him to her in a desperate attempt to satisfy the increasingly unbearable urgency she felt—a hungering for some height she was not even sure existed.

Then he rolled her throbbing nipple between his teeth, and the force of her yearning spread to a sweet, burning pain between her legs, and she whimpered.

At her sound, Quint raised his head to see her writhing beneath him, and he reclaimed her lips, leaving her breast cooling and burning from the moist assault of his mouth. As his tongue found entrance to her mouth again, he felt her hand travel between them over his chest, pulling at his shirt, lifting it up, leaving him breathless with intolerable pleasures. She pressed her body to his, her taut little nipples shooting flames all the way to his manhood.

Tightening his arms around her, his lips released her mouth and showered kisses over her face, into her hair. Tracing the delicate curve of her ear with his tongue, he caught her earlobe tenderly between his teeth and felt her shudder.

Suddenly the enormity of what was happening to them struck him, and he drew back, looking down at her. "Sweet Holly." His breath came in ragged spurts he was unable to control. "I need you, sweet Holly. God, how I need you."

Trembling with the pleasure of his words, she raised her head to kiss his chin, then ran her small tongue around the tight skin at the top of his neck.

With a quiver of delight, he tightened his arms about her, drawing her head to his chest. Reluctantly, he spoke with great resolve—not the words he wanted to say, but words he knew he must say to this woman who somehow meant so much more to him than the pleasure of this one moment.

"I can wait, sweet Holly," he said. "*We* can wait . . . for a better time . . . for a private place where we can love slowly, gently."

He lifted her face to his, and she looked intensely into his eyes, seeing beyond their mutual carnal desire, to the fear that she felt herself . . . fear that this might be the only time they would ever have.

If she were forced to leave Silver Creek . . . if something happened to her like had happened to Papa . . . At that moment she knew deep within her soul, more surely than she had ever known anything in her life, that she wanted this man, Quintan Jarvis, to be the man who brought her to womanhood. Then no matter what happened, she would have this one small bit of joy to cling to.

Breathless from the driving passion that clamored within her, Holly moved so that her lips brushed against his when she spoke. "Please don't stop, Quint. Please." Then she covered his mouth with her own small one, trying desperately to convey the depth of her need for him.

With a great sigh he returned her kiss, knowing her thoughts as surely as he knew his own. In order to keep her safe from Farrell, he should send her away. But he knew that this desire he felt for her would haunt him forevermore if he did not savor it now while he could.

Conscious of her reputation, even though they were protected by the sweeping pecan branches, he resigned himself to accomplishing his goal—and hers—with her clothing intact. Since she seemed to be wearing enough clothes to set up storekeeping, he had no doubt they would be, at the least, an encumbrance.

Driven by the promise of finally making love to her, he took possession of her waiting mouth once more, anxiously thrusting, exploring, devouring the sweetness of her lips, while moving one hand to her naked breast to fondle and caress its still-taut nipple. Then with a slowness which belied the quickness of his heartbeat, he planted kisses in a trail down her creamy neck and shoulders, until with a surge of blood through his veins, he recaptured her breast in his mouth. She responded by arching up to fill his mouth with her tender, sweet gift.

Deftly, then, he lifted her skirts and traced the outline of her slender hips through her bloomers. Knowingly, his hand moved gently inside the open crotch of the garment, caressing her with whisper-soft motions.

Holly flinched as Quint's hand touched her skin beneath her bloomers; then she held her breath at the intense pleasure that washed over her—the sudden, acute awareness that this was what her body had been longing for, craving. Her head throbbed in waves of unbearable delight when his hand stroked her firmly. Then she gasped breathlessly, feeling his fingers slip into the wetness between her folded flesh. Urgently she pulled his face from her breast to her lips.

When their eyes met, Quint groaned with unfulfilled passion. He held her stare in a weakening trance, while his fingers found entrance to her inner core and were suddenly seized by her intense response, as she lifted her hips to meet his probing fingers in erotic undulations.

Inflamed by the delight which showed in her face, Quint lowered his lips and kissed her softly at first, then, as her hips moved more rapidly against his thrusting fingers, his kiss became fierce, and when she began to seductively suckle his probing tongue, he knew he could wait no longer.

Reaching to his breeches to free his fevered manhood, Quint suddenly stopped all movement and looked closely at her flushed face.

"Holly, sweet Holly, is this the first time?"

His husky voice resounded seductively through her addled brain, but his words alarmed her. She pursed her lips together, afraid to answer, afraid he would stop if he knew the truth.

But he guessed the answer by her reactions, and with his free hand, he smoothed the damp ringlets of black curls away from her face, tenderly stroking her skin. "It may hurt for just a minute," he said. "But it won't hurt long—and it won't be bad."

Relieved at his words, at knowing that he would not stop this terrible, delightful assault on her senses, she moved her hips against his stilled hand once more and raised her parted lips to receive his kiss.

Instead of kissing her, though, Quint held her gaze, while he removed one of her hands from around his neck and guided it downward until he had curled her fingers around his swollen manhood.

She gasped, and he grinned lovingly at her. Then in a voice weak with the final throes of passion, he spoke quietly. "See what you do to me, sweet Holly?"

Intoxicated by the desire she felt was about to explode within her at any moment, Holly moved her hips urgently toward him. "Hurry, Quint. Please."

Quint shifted his body between her thighs then, and, as she helped, he guided his manhood to its place, never taking his eyes from her face. Thrusting himself gently within her, he stopped, and, before she could urge him to go on, he brought his mouth to hers with a caressing, sensual kiss which further tantalized her senses.

Frantic for relief from the pressures raging within her, Holly moved both her hands to his buttocks, attempting to urge him deeper within her, while her hips encouraged him from below. With tormenting slowness he moved inside her, gradually working himself deeper and deeper, until she felt herself ready to explode from the unrelenting torture.

Then suddenly the sweetness was pierced by a tiny sharp pain, and she felt his powerful manhood plunge to her depths, filling her emptiness like a hand in a glove.

Slowly he began to rhythmically move within her, sending shimmering sparks of fire through her already sensitized body. As he moved faster and faster, she raised her hips to meet him over and over again. Her arms clung to his shoulders; her fingers dug into the corded muscles of his back; her eyes clenched tight against wave after wave of passion—passion which at last surged through her entire body, breaking suddenly in a great crescendo of light and power, racking her small body, her mind, her soul.

Quint felt her shudder of release, heard her cry of delight, and a second later, he released his own passion inside her in a spew of pent-up pleasure.

As his carnal spasms subsided, he dropped beside her and clasped her to him in a tender embrace. Her heart beat against his chest, echoing his own slow return to normalcy.

After a while he tilted her face up and looked lovingly into her dream eyes. "How was it?" he asked, his voice still hoarse with left-over passion.

She studied his gold sparked honey-brown eyes, the way his tousled blond hair fell over his sun-bronzed skin, his taut, chiseled features. "It was . . ." A sob caught in her throat at the wondrous pleasure they had shared. "It was perfect."

He ran his thumb lazily over her sculptured black eyebrows, bent to kiss first one eyelid, then the other.

“Someday, sweet Holly,” he promised her, “someday we’ll make love all day and all night.” He kissed her lips lightly, then added with a grin, “without any clothes on.”

She smiled at the wicked delight in his eyes and snuggled her head in the hollow of his shoulder. Please, Dear God, she thought, make that promise come true.

Chapter Six

After that day, life in Silver Creek took on a glorious new meaning for Holly. She belonged now, and she was loved. Of course, Quint hadn't actually *said* he loved her, she reminded herself. But the desperate yet caring manner in which he had made love to her said as much as words. Words could come later. She drew in a deep breath of sweet spring air. It was as though by telling Tom Farrell that Silver Creek was her home, she had somehow made it true.

She pushed aside the questions that plagued her, refusing to delve into the factors which had made her decide to stay, or into the implications of her growing relationship with Quint.

Hadn't Papa always warned that undue probing was like spilling a pail of worms? Questions could come later. For now she was content to enjoy her newfound home. Not that she had forgotten her mission: nor that that mission had lost its intensity.

To the contrary, her determination to discover the truth about Papa's death burned even brighter. Silver Creek was her town now, and she felt a responsibility to see justice and law and order shape its growth.

More urgent matters took precedence, however, and

she knew that if she were to remain in Silver Creek much longer, she would have to bolster her dwindling finances. She had come prepared to live with Papa, not to set up housekeeping for herself.

So the morning following the picnic with Quint, Holly spread her jewelry on the bed—the same jewels which she herself had buried in the garden under the cover of darkness to keep the Yankees from finding. Studying the jewels, she was aware that she had no idea of their actual value. They would certainly be worth less here than in a city like Boston or New York. In fact, Mavis was probably the only person in Silver Creek who would be the least bit interested in jewels, but Holly refused to impose further upon Mavis's generosity.

Surely the banker would be willing to take a piece or two as collateral for a small loan, she thought, putting the emerald and diamond parure into the black velvet bag. She then replaced the other jewels in her trunk and spent the remainder of the morning deciding how much money to request.

The matching set of earrings, bracelet, and necklace should bring her a tidy sum, yet she must not appear greedy or frivolous. Now that she was in charge of her own life, as it were, she was determined to proceed in this man's world in a businesslike manner.

The Bank of Silver Creek stood off to itself on the eastern edge of town, and Holly ranked it alongside the Hotel O'Keefe in its appearance of prosperity—the bank being the only establishment in town built of native white limestone.

She stepped onto the boardwalk and, turning the polished brass doorknob in her gloved hand, entered through one side of the double front doors.

The interior was small, but gave the feeling of spaciousness, due, she supposed, to the complete absence of clutter. The Bank of Silver Creek not only looked and smelled new, but it appeared virtually unused, as well.

A sinking feeling gripped her stomach as she thought that this whole ostentatious bank seemed nothing but a charade—a set for a theatrical play with no customers and no money.

A play in which the teller turned out to be the cleaning lady, she noted, for the sole occupant of the room, a gaunt young woman with an unsmiling countenance and a pair of wire-rimmed glasses was engaged, not in counting and sorting money, but in studiously polishing the already gleaming brass teller's cage.

Holly clasped the black velvet bag to the bosom of her white muslin blouse. She had chosen this ensemble—a simple white blouse with stand-up collar and a black wool skirt with polonaise—for its casual comfort, but now she wondered if she wouldn't feel more businesslike with a jacket, instead of the soft black crocheted shawl.

She swallowed the lump in her throat. "May I please see Mr. Norton?" she asked.

The young woman looked Holly up and down a moment, then recognition lighted her otherwise dull eyes. "Miss Campbell?" And without waiting for a reply, she took the necessary four or five steps to a closed door and tapped gently.

The door was, if anything, more elaborate than the entrance doors, its frosted pane etched in an intricate pattern that completely eliminated visibility from either side and from the center of which gleamed a giant gold-leaf "N."

The young woman beckoned formally, and Holly stepped inside the banker's office, followed by a chill of foreboding.

She had not met banker R. J. Norton, but his secretary's deference was inhibiting, and Holly ran her tongue around suddenly dry lips.

The interior of his office stunned her by its continued show of splendor—gleaming brass, polished wood, and, here also, the uncluttered desk.

Mr. Norton stood, extinguished his large cigar, and motioned her to one of the two green leather wing-backed chairs. When he smiled, she half expected to see a set of brass teeth flash between his flaccid jowls.

"Miss Campbell, an unexpected pleasure. How might the Bank of Silver Creek serve you?" He hooked a thumb in the pocket of his brick red vest, as the garment strained further in its attempt to cover his portly figure.

"I'm here to see to my father's affairs." She took the offered chair, and Mr. Norton seated himself opposite her. "Did Papa have an account with your bank?"

Banker Norton shook his head. "No, I'm sorry to say, your father did not use our services. However," he rushed on, "we've been open only a short while, and no doubt he would have come to trust us in time."

She tucked back a damp, straggling curl and wondered how to proceed. "In that case, I must talk with you about a . . . ah, a loan."

He nodded, stroking his walrus mustache. "Stage fare for your return to Tennessee. A dreadful mess you find yourself in. Dreadful."

"Actually, Mr. Norton, I've decided to stay in Silver Creek. You must be aware of the area's need for medical services, and with my experience, I can be of use until a doctor is found. I will need funds, however . . ."

"Now, Miss . . ."

Holly rushed on, not trusting her nerve to stand up to any protestations the banker might voice. "I wouldn't think of asking you to loan money without collateral, so I brought these." She opened the velvet bag as she spoke and now spread the jewels across the gleaming expanse of the walnut desktop. "I'm sure you will find them adequate to secure a small loan of . . . say, one hundred dollars."

Norton's mouth dropped open when he saw the flawless emeralds and diamonds before him. She thought for a moment he might drool on the jewels, but then he pursed his lips and nodded his head. "Mighty fine. Mighty fine, indeed."

Seconds later, however, his mustache twitched on one side, and he shoved himself away from the desk as though from temptation, raising his eyes to meet hers. "But I cannot help you."

Her heart skipped in its rhythmic pattern. She stared at him with incredulity.

"You don't belong in this country, miss. I should think you would have figured that out by now. So you bundle yourself and these little jewels up and head on back to your home, like your dear, departed father, rest his soul, would have wanted his little girl to do."

Her astonishment turned to disbelief. Who was this man to refuse her a loan on the grounds of what Papa would have wanted? "You did not know my father very well, sir, if you think he would want me to leave so many people unattended when I am able to be of service."

The banker drew a slow breath and released it, studying her all the while. "Be that as it may, I advise you to return to Tennessee. You do not belong out here amidst these western ruffians."

Holly was taken back momentarily, unsure how to respond. She had not envisioned being instructed to leave Silver Creek, but Mr. Norton appeared well intentioned, and . . .

"Mr. Norton, I've made up my mind to stay, and I'm sure you agree that these jewels are valuable enough to secure the piddling amount I'm asking to borrow."

"Yes, yes, quite adequate," he said, eyeing the jewels with a decided degree of lust.

She tilted her chin in challenge. "Then what do you have to lose?"

"I'm merely thinking of your welfare, miss. These jewels belong to a lady—a lady who has no business on the frontier."

Holly surveyed the banker's office, wanting to scream at him, what about you and your gaudy bank? But she answered quietly, trying to control her voice. "Perhaps, as you say, I'm not suited for this country. But that's for me to decide, Mr. Norton. What do you have to lose by loaning me such a small sum?"

"You're forcing me to be blunt, Miss Campbell." He rose from his chair, staring down at her. "We all know that a woman's pretty head is not made to hold enough brains for serious things like doctoring."

Holly sprang from her seat. "Mr. Norton!" She put her hands on her hips and returned his condescending stare with one of anger. "It really doesn't matter whether men's or women's heads hold more brains, Mr. Norton. What is important is that we each use all the brains we have." She scooped the jewelry into the velvet bag. "And if you will excuse *my* bluntness, you are passing up a very good business arrangement. Especially if things turn out as you predict, and I fail."

The banker stiffened at her words. "Be that as it may, I feel it is in your best interest to return to Tennessee. The stage company will undoubtedly exchange one of those lovelies for passage." He walked to the door and opened it, concluding the matter. "Why don't you make it a point to be on the next stage out?"

Holly stepped through the doorway, her mind in a

dither. Then, as in a game of chance, her whirling brain stopped on a new idea.

"By the by, Mr. Norton, this message came for me yesterday." She took Caroline's telegram from her sleeve and handed it to the banker. "Perhaps land would be more acceptable collateral."

He read the message quickly, then again, pursing his lips. The flesh of his jowls turned white, leaving a small island of red on his chin. He sat down slowly and unconsciously reached for a cigar, lighted it, and studied the cryptic message. After a long while he spoke.

"What makes you think this property is valuable? Why, land around here isn't even worth the nickle an acre folks are paying." His voice sounded casual, showing none of the tension which revealed itself in his mechanical motions.

"Sheriff Jarvis said this piece of property is a box canyon in the middle of Tom Farrell's best ranchland."

Norton sputtered, shaking his head. "Can't be. Jarvis is . . . ah, he's mistaken. Must be thinking about another place."

"The sheriff said that canyon borders his own land, so I'm certain he knows." She smiled at him, noting his suddenly flushed face. "If, as you believe, my venture fails, you should have no trouble selling the deed to Mr. Farrell. The sheriff thinks he would be extremely anxious to get that property back."

The banker's agitation grew. "You are a foolish young woman. This is a telegram." He shook the paper in her face. "A telegram, not a deed. You expect me to loan money on a telegram?"

"The deed will be forthcoming, sir," she replied between clenched teeth. "And should it get lost en route, you can be sure it is recorded at the capitol in Austin. Papa would have seen to that."

She saw his eyes blink, and he jumped to his feet, paced to the window and back, seated himself once more, and, removing a handkerchief, mopped his beading brow.

"What do you say, Mr. Norton?" she prodded. "You won't find a better risk."

He nodded slowly, as if his mind were somewhere outside this room, and began writing. "Mind you now, I expect that deed as soon as it arrives."

"Of course."

"And you must sign this contract." He slid the sheet of paper across the polished desktop, urging her to sign immediately.

His flourishes were hard to decipher, but she studied the contract carefully. "It says that you can call in the loan at any time. I prefer to set a specific date upon which the principal is due."

He glowered at her. "Around here a man never knows when he might need that money."

She wondered how much land he had already taken from the area's small ranchers in this very manner. "Nevertheless, I prefer an arrangement that would give me a chance to repay the loan." She stared straight at him. "You see, Mr. Norton, I do not intend to fail. I will not lose Papa's property."

He returned her stare with such contempt that she expected him to order her out of the room without the money, but instead he hastily scratched through a line of writing.

"Three months would be fair to both of us, don't you agree, Mr. Norton?"

His hand stiffened on the pen, but he made the necessary changes. "Remember you are to bring me that deed the instant you receive it. Otherwise, I will call in this loan immediately."

She nodded. "Of course. However, by that time I

shall have the cash to repay you."

But where would she get cash? Papa had written of the shortage of money here on the frontier. Patients paid for his services in everything *but* cash, trading what they raised or services of their own. Like Aggie exchanging dressmaking for medical attention for little Davy.

Norton followed her to the front of the bank, where he handed her five twenty-dollar gold pieces from the vault.

She stepped outside, closing the door behind her, feeling the noonday sun warm the chill that had penetrated her shaking body. Her head whirled with anger and resentment, and she turned to stare back at the pretentious facade. So, Banker Norton purported to value land over brains—and jewels. What an unconvincing actor he was! Unable to conceal his appetite for the diamonds and emeralds, he still refused them as collateral.

Whatever was a man such as he doing on the frontier? He certainly appeared to possess none of the vim and vigor required to survive in this rugged country.

She turned back to the street, reminding herself that she had more to think of at the moment than R. J. Norton's motives, such as how to repay this loan before it came due. Perhaps Mavis could help her find someone to buy the jewels, someone back East. Of course, Mavis would help. Her generosity bordered on being intrusive, but . . . oh, what a friend in time of need!

Approaching the hotel she saw two figures swinging on the porch, and a couple of steps further, she recognized Mavis's buttercup yellow muslin morning dress topped by her fiery auburn tresses. And Quint . . . her eyes caressed him from a distance, sending a warm glow throughout her body. Since the picnic she had not known one moment's peace from the wicked, sweet desire she felt for this man.

Then as the thrill of her success finally managed to break through her barrier of tension, she laughed aloud. She had the money. She could stay in Silver Creek. And Quint had said he wanted her to. Oh, how very lucky she was!

Eager to share her news with the two people who had become such an important part of her life, she broke into a run. They stood up as she reached the steps, but before she could speak, Mavis stopped her.

"Holly, darling, a cowhand is waiting to see you in the parlor. Jed Varner."

Holly looked from Mavis to Quint, who was obviously still engrossed in the conversation he had been carrying on with Mavis, for his eyes twinkled with . . .

While Holly visited the bank, Quint had finished his paperwork and sent a telegram to Sheriff Bales down in Llano County. Then he headed across the street to the hotel to await her return.

He couldn't get enough of her. Instead of quenching his thirst for her sweet, beckoning body, their lovemaking down by the river had only stirred up the coals inside him, until now his need for her was so intense that the only torture worse than being around her and unable to smother her to his aching body was having her out of his sight completely.

She filled his body, his soul, his mind as no woman ever had before. And this at a time when he needed a portion of his senses to lick the rustlers.

Mingled with his sweet reveries of Holly, Quint had worried much of the previous night over the rustlers and had finally come up with what he figured could be a workable plan—if he could gather enough good men to help him carry it off.

So he sent a wire to Bales this morning, requesting an urgent meeting. Llano County ranchers had been as hard hit by these outlaws as his fellow ranchers around Silver Creek had been, and he figured if he and Bales could get together a handpicked posse, they stood a chance of licking this thing.

Waiting for Holly's return in one of the white ladder-back swings on the front porch, Quint felt her presence surround him now like a warm blanket. It was here in this very swing that he had almost kissed her that first night. Swallowing the tightness in his throat, he slapped the side of his knee in chastisement. Lordy, ol' Hoss, you're plumb crazed with calico fever.

Mavis joined him then, her green eyes appraising his Sunday-best attire with a twitter. "It didn't take that pretty little Tennessee belle long to spark a love-light in those flinty bachelor eyes of yours, Sheriff," she teased.

Quint blushed with the truth of Mavis's words. Even the mention of Holly's name increased his heart rate by half.

Finally Holly emerged from the bank and headed toward them. The lightness of her step as she approached the hotel sent a thrill through his taut muscles, and his brain busied itself figuring how to finagle another picnic . . . in a more secluded place, this time.

"It's obvious that *she* feels the same way," Mavis added.

Quint jerked his head toward her. "What do you mean?"

Mavis laughed knowingly and looked from Quint to Holly's approaching figure. "I mean," she looked back at Quint, "that when the parson comes through this way again, we'd best be prepared for a wedding."

Quint's mouth fell open. The idea startled him; he'd

not consciously thought that far ahead. Yet, now that it was mentioned, he knew the idea had been in the back of his mind for a while. He laughed it off weakly, his light-headedness instantly jolted by visions of the photograph of that damned plantation house in Tennessee. "Now hold your horses, Mavis. They're plumb running away with you this time."

At Mavis's mention of Jed Varner, Holly jerked her head away from Quint's obvious rejection and raised her skirts to ascend the steps of the hotel. Jed Varner? Oh, yes, the young rancher whose wife was due to have a baby.

Jed Varner paced back and forth in the hotel's hallway in his dust-covered work clothes. When she entered, he stopped twisting his sweat-stained felt hat in his hands and rushed to meet her.

"Miss Campbell, it's time. Anne said I should fetch you directly."

Holly put a reassuring hand on his arm. "Go on back to the ranch, and I'll get Possum to drive me straightaway."

The door slammed behind them then, and Quint took her arm. "I'll drive you."

Mavis objected. "No telling how long you would have to be away, Quint. Babies take their own sweet time, you know. It's best that Possum drive her."

Quint released Holly's arm reluctantly, damning the rustlers for now another reason. He couldn't go off to a birthing and miss Bales's reply to his message.

Holly stared from Quint to Mavis, while the gold coins clanked inside the black velvet bag, filling her with a hollow, lonely emptiness. How could she have been such a ninny to think she was the only one in Quint's life?

"I've already alerted Possum," Mavis continued, "so get your bag and hurry."

Always the directress, Holly thought furiously, as she reached her room, took up her jacket, a change of clothing, and Papa's medical bag. And upon returning downstairs, she found the waiting buggy hitched and ready to go. Possum stashed her belongings in the carriage.

Mavis handed him a couple of baskets, telling Holly, "Some things for Anne and the baby. Lavender oil—babies need oiling, don't they? And a few other goodies."

"Thank you." Holly offered her hand to Possum for a step up, but Quint took her arm himself, lifting her onto the seat. His hand lingered on hers, and his honey-gold eyes quickened her heart.

"Drive this rig careful, you hear?" he instructed Possum.

Holly smiled down at him, then caught her bonnet in her hand as the buggy jerked forward, and they were off. She looked back at the hotel to wave to Quint and Mavis, but Mavis already had Quint by the arm, steering him toward the back door. Holly caught her last glimpse of them as they simultaneously broke into hearty laughter.

What timing babies had! Before she got back to Silver Creek, Mavis could have Quint all tied up in wedding bows.

She stared at the passing countryside unseeing, until finally the explosion of color around them overcame her wistful mood. Wildflowers in every shade of red, yellow, purple, and blue. She marveled at the blue-bonnets which spread beneath the deep green cedars like a blue mist, their color so intense the sky paled beside them along the horizon.

The contrast between the evergreen cedars and the lighter, brighter new growth of the mesquites and late-budding pecans provided her with a startling symbol of her own contrasting feelings.

A week ago this entire region had seemed threatening: plants with thorns and daggers, animals with horns, and both plants and animals which would poison at a bite or a touch. Today beauty prevailed, and she saw the country Papa must have seen, a country she desperately wanted to be a part of.

What had caused this dramatic change in attitude, she wondered? Papa's property? Quintan Jarvis?

The thought of both warmed her soul, even though she knew she would have to fight for each of them.

But she would win. She would persist, and she would win. Hadn't she done exactly that today with Mr. Norton?

Well, she would win against Tom Farrell, too. She would prove he murdered Papa. She would save that property, and along with it, Papa's dreams and his good name.

She stared up at the few patches of cottony clouds drifting lazily by. Quintan Jarvis. She thought of him more often than either Papa or Tom Farrell these days. But wasn't he the reason she had come to this wild country in the first place? He hadn't had a name back then when she made her decision to come West, or a face. But this was the man she had set out to find.

Not a husband. Not a man. But *this* man. Quintan Jarvis. He took her breath away, and, when she was with him, her fear, as well—her fear of him not being who he seemed, of Papa being right about him. Of finding herself alone without him.

Gradually Possum's words penetrated her consciousness, and she looked in the direction he pointed his quirt. "The Varner cabin'll be showing over the next rise."

Sure enough, from the top of the hill, she saw a tiny log cabin nestled among cottonwood trees, smoke rising from its chimney.

No sooner had they reached the yard than Jed Varner rushed forward, extending his hand to help Holly down. "Thank the Lord you're here, ma'am. She's in right terrible pain."

Inside, Holly tried to conceal her astonishment at the primitiveness of the cabin—rough-hewn log walls and even furniture, earthen floors. A stone fireplace stood along the back wall and completely overshadowed everything else in the room, both in size and in workmanship. The native stones were intricately cut and fitted, obviously by a master craftsman.

She saw Anne Varner then, standing in the passageway between the two rooms of the cabin, disheveled in a wilted homespun wrapper, perspiration streaking her face and matting her hair.

"Jed," Anne's voice was weak. "Fetch Miss Campbell a plate of that stew you have heating." Then looking past Holly, she added, "And some for Possum, too."

Holly took Anne firmly by the shoulders and turned her toward the other room, where a rumpled hand-hewn bed stood waiting. "Stop worrying about us, Anne. We aren't here to be entertained."

With Anne back in bed, Holly removed her jacket and bonnet, while she surveyed the preparations they had made for the impending delivery—a stack of clean linens, a basin, and a pitcher of water.

Rolling up the sleeves of her bodice, she scrubbed her hands and arms with lye soap, rinsed several times, then called to Jed that they would need a clean basin. She asked Anne to describe her other confinements.

"I delivered both times." Anne gasped for breath as a pain racked her abdomen. "They're coming quicker now."

Holly smiled at the frightened girl. "Then we'll get ready. It won't be long." Nor difficult, she hoped, for although she had delivered and helped Papa deliver a number of babies, she had faced no major problems, and a panicky feeling washed over her as she realized that the only thing she recalled Papa saying about birthing was that cleanliness was essential.

But in taking scissors from the medical bag, she came across a bottle of wine of cordui which jogged her memory, so she mixed some in a cup with water and gave it to Anne to drink. "Papa used to say this would clear up the organs, if there was disease."

As Anne drank the bitter elixir, Holly questioned her further about her previous deliveries.

Anne bit her lip a moment and sucked in a deep breath. "One came too early. Such a tiny thing, but it wasn't . . . alive. The other," she broke off and looked at Holly with pleading eyes. "The other came the wrong way. It was blue and . . . and it didn't live either."

Holly sponged the girl's face with a damp cloth. "Mama always told me that hollering helps chase the pain out of your mind, so when it hurts bad, you holler as loud as you want."

And at Anne's first loud scream, Jed rushed into the room.

Holly looked at him sternly. "She's all right, Jed. Go on back and feed Possum. I'll call if we need you."

Jed left, and Anne screamed again. "This is it. I feel it."

"Then put the cloth between your teeth and bite down real hard." She tried to remember Mama or Papa ever mentioning a breech birth. The only way to save the baby would be to turn it around. But could she do that? Maybe . . . maybe it wouldn't come to that. Her thoughts were interrupted by another desperate scream from Anne, and cold perspiration spread over Holly's body as she saw the baby begin to emerge.

Her clothes clung to her limbs, restricting her arms,

her mind. It wasn't right . . . she had to do something . . . turn it around . . . save the baby. Oh, Dear God, help me!

Anne screamed in constant accompaniment, her arms reaching out, pulling at the bedclothes, at last gripping the cornhusk mattress, as Holly pushed the baby, instinctively feeling for its head, turning it, working against Anne's contracting muscles. Then the baby moved into position, and she exhaled her pent-up breath.

First she only felt the wet head, the plastered hair, but suddenly, as she looked into the tiny face, horror beset her, for the entire head of the infant was blue. Pulling it toward her, she saw the birth cord entwined about the little neck.

Frantically she pulled the baby free of Anne's body and disengaged, cut, and tied the cord. She must save this baby.

She must. But how? What would Papa do?

Holding the newborn upside down, she slapped it on the back. Nothing. Again she slapped, and again. Still no sound.

She lay the baby on the bed, cleaned out its mouth and nostrils, and called into the next room for water.

But when Jed arrived with a kettle of steaming water to pour into the basin, she knew that wasn't right. "No, no. Cold water. A pail of cold water," she said. "And whiskey. Do you have whiskey? Hurry!"

Turning the baby onto its stomach, she massaged its back gently with trembling fingers, then held it up and slapped it again.

Possum arrived with a pail of cold water, and she plunged the baby into it, lifted it up, then submerged it again, and this time, upon drawing it from the water, she was rewarded with a small sound.

Jed rushed into the room with a jug of rye, which she

quickly splashed into her cupped palm and forced into the baby's mouth and nostrils. Then she blew her own breath into the infant's throat.

Patting the little face sharply with another handful of rye, she held the baby up and once more slapped its bottom.

A weak cry escaped the tiny creature's throat then, and she felt a faint pulse.

Finally, taking the soft piece of flannel which Jed offered with a limp hand, she wrapped the baby and continued massaging its back, pushing air into and out of its lungs.

"Is my baby all right?" Anne's voice was weak, but anxious, and Holly realized the question had been repeated a number of times.

Jed answered her. "Yes, honey, it's gonna be, thanks to the doc, here."

"Is it a boy, Jed? Or a girl?"

Holly and Jed exchanged startled looks. In the confusion they had had no time to note the sex of the baby.

Holly opened the blanket. "It's a girl, Anne, and she's fine." The baby's breathing had steadied and was closer to normal than her own.

With arms so weak they felt useless, Holly mixed water from the kettle and pitcher into the clean basin, and when the temperature was blood-warm, she bathed the baby, then dried and wrapped her in a clean piece of flannel and placed her in her mother's arms.

Anne's grateful smile reached Holly through a haze of dizziness. Holly finished tending the new mother, and wrapped the afterbirth in a soiled cloth, taking it outside away from the house to bury it. Then she collapsed against the well, finally bathing her own face and arms in water from the drawn bucket, reviving herself in the coolness of the still-young spring evening.

She had saved this baby, and the mother, too—but the cheering would have to wait, for the day had been wholly exhausting from cock's crow to setting sun. First beseeching Mr. Norton for a loan, then Mavis making eyes at Quint, and now a birthing which she hoped would be the most difficult she ever faced.

Through the open cabin door, she saw Possum stirring a pot over the glowing fireplace, and when she returned to the cabin, he handed her a cup of coffee and went about his task.

"Mavis sent this broth," he said. "Told me to heat it up for Miz Varner whilst you was busy deliverin' the youngun."

Anne ate a little of Mavis's broth, and soon both she and the baby were sound asleep. But the doctor, the cook, and the new father were not as easily calmed, and they sat long before the fire, idly discussing first one topic and then another, always returning to the occasion at hand.

"Possum can go back to Silver Creek in the morning," Holly told Jed, "but I'll stay on a few days, since you're so far from town. How long have you lived way out here?"

"Goin' on four years now," he answered. "I was born and raised down around New Braunfels. Anne and me both. I apprenticed to a stonecutter, learned the trade, but cattle got in my blood—cattle and open spaces. So right after Anne and me married, we moved out here."

Holly studied the beautiful work of the stone fireplace. "Did you build that?"

He nodded. "The whole cabin." Then he stared into the fire and dug a circle in the soot with the toe of his boot. "I know this ain't no fittin' place for a family." Taking out the makin's, he asked Holly's permission and rolled a smoke. "I aim to build us a proper stone house," he continued, "soon's I get things together a bit more. Plan on starting it when Farrell brings my money from this last trail drive."

"Humph!" Possum offered with a wiseness surpassing his years. "You'll be an old man 'fore you see money from that drive. Them rustlers up along the Concho have been makin' off with folks' stock all season. This time won't be no different, I wager."

Jed shook his head. "That money is to build a home for my wife and girlchild."

"I thought rustlers were common out here," Holly said, "but everyone talks about those along the Concho River. What's so different about them?"

"We don't have as much trouble with rustlin' as folks back East would like to believe," Jed said. "Oh, we lose stock now and again, but them Concho rustlers—they're different. They hole up in the hills and pick a time when all the hands are needed so's not to make it worth the trail boss's time to send punchers to track 'em straightaway. Then, when he does get after 'em, there's no trail to foller. Organized is what they are."

"Ranching appears to be a risky business," Holly said.

"Same's a bunch of other things," Jed agreed. "Bearin' a child is almighty risky."

Holly nodded. Indeed it was, and who would know better than this man whose wife had lost two babes and almost a third? She sighed, feeling at last the contentment of the successful delivery.

Possum turned the conversation to a topic she had found a favorite whenever people gathered out here. "Treasure-huntin's kinda risky, too. Fact, a feller ain't got much chance of findin' buried treasure, way I figure it, even with a map."

"But folks keep right on trying," Jed said. "Far as I'm concerned, a man working the land in this country owes it to hisself to bone up on those old stories, case he runs acrost one of them pointers. I'd sure enough hate to think that the Lost Bowie Mine was on my land, and my family wasn't makin' the most of its riches."

"Shoot," Possum said. "I'm all the time checkin' out old mesquite trees for silver bars them Spaniards was said to have hidden when that passel of Comanches jumped 'em." He let out a low whistle. "Man! I wouldn't want to pass up a grubstake like that!"

"Do you mean you two really believe those stories?" Holly asked.

Jed and Possum exchanged looks.

"Yes'm, I surely do!" Possum told her.

Jed was more cautious. "Can't say's how I exactly believe 'em," he said, "but it don't stand to reason that there'd be so many different stories floating about without some cause."

Holly sipped her coffee, content to relax with friends. Half her mind was back in Silver Creek with Quint, half on the stories. She didn't believe them, but Jed had a point. All legends were supposed to have some basis in truth.

"I've seen signs," Jed added. "Once I found a turtle carved on a tree trunk with the bark grown over it a ways. Followed the direction its head pointed to, but didn't find nothin'. I've searched the area on an' off for going on a year, but never turned up another marker. Likely most of the old pointers have been destroyed by nature or wild beasts.

"I thought I found a marker for the copper plates once," Possum said.

"What kind of marker?" Jed questioned.

"A spike driven into an old tree trunk."

Jed looked interested. "An oak tree?"

Possum nodded.

"What part of the country'd you find it in?"

"North to west of here," Possum said. "On Farrell's

place, I think it was."

Jed nodded his head in earnest and threw his cigarette butt in the fireplace. Then he pulled out the makin's and rolled another while they rocked and stared into the fire.

Finally Jed cleared his throat. "The copper plates is one of my favorite tales," he told Holly. "Did your pa write you about it?"

"Papa wasn't an adventurer," Holly replied. "After a long day treating patients, he chose the gentler things, like settling down with a good book."

"A tale's a tale, as I see it," Jed said. "Be it wrote down or just spoke. Those stories by that Mr. Shakespeare or about all them knights—why, we had our very own knights right here. Men have found the armor to prove it. And our iron-suited fellers are supposed to have left us a whole fortune hidden in trees and caves and in holes they dug themselves."

"The stories are fascinating," Holly agreed.

"First time I heard of the copper plates was from Old Moses—you recall him, Possum?"

Possum's eyes lighted up. "That crazy old feller—he rode into Silver Creek on a mule one day and stayed on a couple of years, till he up and died just before dinnertime one day in Woody's saloon."

"Old Moses come to town to find them copper plates," Jed told Holly. "Spent his days searching for 'em, talking about 'em, or prying into other folks' business to see what they knowed about 'em. Way he told the story, there was two of the plates, and together, they made a map to the treasure in the banking mission."

"The banking mission?" Holly asked.

"One of them Spanish missions around here where they gathered the money from all the other missions, and gold from mines as far away as Santa Fe."

"And they put the map on copper plates?" Holly asked.

Jed nodded. "Accordin' to Old Moses, them plates was buried at the foot of an oak tree, directly underneath a wrought-iron spike which had been driven into the tree trunk as a marker. Half the map was carved into each plate and painted with red and yellow earthen paints. Old Moses didn't know what part of the country the map was of, only that together them plates would guide the finder to a mess of riches."

Holly listened with increasing interest. "Did Old Moses ever find the plates?"

Jed shook his head. "Not that I ever heard of."

"Some of the paint would have flaked off by now, I suppose," she said.

Jed slapped his leg and winked at Possum. "I do believe we have the good doc interested in buried treasure."

"Don't feel bad, ma'am," Possum said. "Livin' out here, most folks get hit with treasure fever sooner or later."

Holly smiled and rocked, thinking of the two metal plates she had picked up from the floor of Papa's house. They were tarnished nearly black, but she had seen a hint of burnishment that encouraged her to think they could be copper, and somehow she seemed to recall traces of red and yellow.

But copper plates with a map to buried treasure on them in Papa's house? What foolishness! She certainly couldn't let anyone know she entertained such notions. Papa's image must be preserved.

Especially since such an outlandish idea would have to be false. Papa, the conservative country gentleman. Papa, who had never to her knowledge shown an adventurous spirit beyond that required to try a new medical cure.

Or to come West, she thought with a jolt. Pulling up stakes to come West was about the most adventurous thing a person could do. She squirmed in her seat, unable to accept the ideas battling within her mind.

Yet, Papa had been murdered, and now two plates which could well be copper with traces of red and yellow ocher lay in his cupboard undetected.

She thought of his land, his plans to raise horses, of Quint's insistence that the land he had ultimately purchased was not fit for raising horses.

What did it all mean? Papa had never mentioned buried treasure or Old Moses or copper plates, and she found it unlikely he had changed so much as to have fallen victim to these legends, but what if . . .

Suppose someone else put the plates there for safekeeping, knowing Doc Holly's house would be the last place anyone would look for them. And that certainly had been proved true; whoever ransacked the house left them for rubbish.

As soon as she returned to Silver Creek she would find out for herself—set this fantasy to rest. She would polish those two plates and prove to herself that Papa had not been involved in such a common endeavor. She felt guilty even thinking such thoughts of him.

But her mind raced ahead. "Was Old Moses around when Papa came out here?"

"You bet," Possum said. "Doc Holly took to doctorin' the old man's wheezin'."

"He had a right awful wheeze," Jed recalled.

Chapter Seven

Holly sent Possum back to town the next morning with instructions to return for her at the end of the week, a week during which Anne and the baby progressed steadily under the attentions of both Holly and the proud new father.

"The day following the birth Holly rummaged through Mavis's baskets for lavender oil and was amazed to discover an entire wardrobe for the baby—everything from diapers and blankets to dresses and bonnets. And she did not forget the new mother, either, including a lovely blue muslin gown for Anne.

Anne fingered the soft fabric, holding it up to her chin, her bright blue eyes picking up the echoing color of the material. "That Mavis! She's always doing nice things like this."

Holly could not conceal her surprise, and Anne quickly added, "Only she doesn't want anybody knowing. If the ladies started gabbing about the pretties she gives us, Mavis wouldn't like it at all."

"That isn't the Mavis O'Keefe I know," Holly said doubtfully.

Anne smiled and stroked the blue gown. "She's been like a fairy godmother to us ranchwomen."

"I know she's generous," Holly admitted. "She has certainly been overly so with me, but I never noticed her retiring nature."

"Most everybody has two sides," Anne said.

So it seems, Holly thought. But she doubted these women had ever had to challenge Mavis for control of their own lives, an act which she figured she herself might be faced with one day.

The next day Jed followed when Holly took Anne a cup of sassafras tea to help thicken her blood. Sitting on a corner of the bed with his wife and daughter, he watched Anne hold the small bundle up for Holly to take.

"We want to name her Holly—Holly's Miracle—if it's all right with you," Anne said.

"We'll call her Miracle, so's there won't be any confusion," Jed added hastily.

Holly protested. "You surely have mothers or grandmothers you would like her named for."

"No," Jed said. "You saved her life, an' she's your namesake, if you don't object."

"And when the parson comes next," Anne said, "we'd like you to stand up as her godmother."

Holly cradled the still-wrinkled pink baby in her arms. Little did it know the anxiety its birth had caused—or the joy its survival brought these parents. And herself, also, she admitted. "I'll be proud to be godmother to little Miracle."

At Anne's urging, Jed walked Holly up the hill to show her the site for their new home. He and Anne had placed stones to form the perimeter and all the interior walls. "If the good Lord's willin' and that trail money comes back safe, I'll be starting work here directly."

Holly was moved by the simplicity and quiet acceptance of this man and his wife. They were close to her own age, starting a family on an income which was less than meager, yet she heard no complaints. Their dreams were strong, and she had no doubt they would reach their chosen stars. They were the kind of folks it took to build a new land. She hoped she could learn from their example.

Her time was taken up with caring for Anne and little Miracle, but as she worked she thought almost exclusively of Quintan Jarvis, imagining herself taking care of *their* home, *their* babes.

When Jed and Anne stole loving looks at each other, Holly's heart trembled and she recalled the intense magnetism Quint's honey-gold eyes held for her. She could be happy living such a life, she told herself. As long as she shared it with Quint.

Thoughts of Mavis and Quint surfaced from time to time, but she quickly suppressed them, for although Quint had not said he loved her—not in words—his eyes had spoken of such love that goose bumps broke out on her arms and the blood in her veins ran hot all at the same time just remembering.

Rarely did she think back to the conversation of that first night at the Varners'. But when she did, she still questioned Papa's involvement in any kind of treasure-hunting scheme.

If the plates in his cupboard were maps to buried treasure, Papa surely did not know it. And even if he did, the possibility of him being interested in hunting such a treasure was remote, at best.

She sighed. His journal would tell. But what had happened to that journal?

Possum returned for her at the end of the week, and she left amid tears and thanksgivings and promises of a prompt return.

"Take care of my goddaughter," she called to the waving family, as Possum flicked his whip. "And good luck with the house."

Two hours later Possum pulled up in front of the hotel to the sound of Rosie's supper bell. For the last few miles they had raced against heavy black clouds which moved across the horizon behind them.

"You go ahead in, Doc," Possum told her. "I'll take the team over to the wagonyard before the storm hits."

Washing hurriedly, she dusted off her black skirt and basque, pinned her hair back in place, and joined the others at table, where she was besieged with questions about Anne and the baby. Possum had recounted the dramatic birth, and Holly found herself a heroine of sorts.

"And what did they name the youngun, dearie?" Aggie inquired over the rims of her glasses.

Holly answered, discovering to her surprise that names like Holly's Miracle were not uncommon on the frontier. It seemed children were often named after the person who delivered them, or in honor of some momentous occasion.

Herman Crump had returned from his journey to San Antonio during her absence, bringing with him a new wife.

"Luda here drove my extry wagon," he told Holly, his brown eyes livelier than when she last saw him. "I bought so many supplies, what with building materials for the new store and all, that I needed two wagons to carry them. Luda and me figured it was as good a time as any to tie the knot."

Luda's eyes shone from a thick face. Her brown hair was wrapped in heavy braids around her head, and her lined face and stout hands added to her steady, no-nonsense countenance, as did her simple brown homespun dress. The few words she spoke were cloaked in a heavy German accent.

Holly filled her plate with venison steak and gravy. "What kinds of pretties did you bring for us to drivel over, Mr. Crump?" she asked the merchant.

"Lordy, ma'am, you can have your pick. I brung everything a woman could ask for in settin' up hearth an' home." He took a large mouthful of potatoes and washed it down with an ever larger swallow of coffee. "And plenty of necessaries for the menfolk in the bargain."

The diners took up asking Crump for this and that until he said, "Lordy, you'd think I was Father Christmas his ownself, and this being only May."

Talk turned to the brewing storm, then finally Herman Crump asked the question which had burned on Holly's lips since she first entered the dining room and found Quint absent. Disappointment had fallen over her expectations like a pall. She'd spent the last week longing to see the gold in those honey-brown eyes, to feel complete again at his nearness. Now he was gone, and she dared not blatantly ask about him for fear of seeming forward.

"What kind of case is the sheriff off solving?"

Mavis smiled directly at Holly, who blushed and wished she were out in the kitchen eavesdropping with Rosie.

"He's been gone going on a week now," Mavis answered. "A telegram came for him from the sheriff down in Llano County, and he took off faster than a house afire. Didn't, or wouldn't, say what the fire was about."

"Pays to be close-mouthed in his job," Woody said.

The others agreed, while Holly thought what a nit she had been for worrying about Quint and Mavis all week, when Quint was nowhere around.

Supper ended suddenly with a clap of thunder which shook the chimneys of the lamps.

"That's the gullywasher I told you was coming," Possum excitedly informed Holly.

And rain it did. For the next three days. Finally in an effort to stave off complete bordom, Holly borrowed a slicker from the cloakroom behind the kitchen, and during one of the slack periods, went to Mr. Crump's tent to purchase some things for the house, including tins of cream of tartar and saleratus and a measure of salt, which she intended to combine and use to clean the metal plates.

Again, she was reminded of the shortcomings of her upbringing. Before the war she had paid no attention to what one used to polish metals, and after the war the Yankees had carried off everything of value, leaving nothing that required polishing.

But she had learned to cook after the war and knew that water added to cream of tartar and saleratus formed an acid which fizzled and foamed and caused cakes to rise. But adding salt to act as a scouring agent, she hoped to be able to clean the plates. At least well enough to discover whether they were copper.

She could use ashes, but as thick as the tarnish was, she feared ashes would do no good, and she had heard of rotten stone being used to polish metal. Mavis probably even had some, but she wanted to attract as little attention as possible; everyone would think her loony for polishing metal when so much else needed to be done to Papa's house first.

And clean everything else first, she did—even going so far as to hire Possum to haul Papa's demolished furniture and belongings to the dump.

Finally, at the end of the week, when she could find nothing else to hold her back, she bridled the fear of what she would find and gave in to her desperate need to discover if those plates held secrets, hoping to find out also what secrets Papa could have known about them.

Sitting on the back porch with strips of her slashed

petticoats to use as polishing cloths, she spread a thick dose of the cold liquid over one of the plates. It took as much elbow grease as acid to dissolve the heavy tarnish, but she worked steadily, not concentrating wholly on the task at hand.

Where was Llano County? Why hadn't he returned by now? Did he really care for her as much as he appeared to? Or—she cringed inside with shame—was he merely using her to satisfy the physical need she had heard men felt for all members of the opposite sex? No, she prayed. Not Quint. Surely not.

Suddenly she saw a gleam. Lines became visible through the now disappearing tarnish, and, as she depleted her stack of cloths, the sun showed its face low on the horizon.

But the sun she stared at glowed from the plate in her hand, and her body trembled at the thought that these plates actually held a message. Until now she had not entirely believed they would, had actually hoped they wouldn't; but the message was definitely there—etched into the copper, and it at once titillated and repelled her.

The drawing was crude—like a child's design—and depicted two hills with a sun peeking between them. Below one hill a man wearing a tall floppy hat led an animal which resembled a donkey and was laden with bundles. The other hill had a sort of archway drawn inside it.

The second plate was similar, yet different. No man or donkey. No archway. Only the two hills with the rising, or setting, sun. In the middle of this plate, below the hills, three trees were connected by a dotted line, forming a rough triangle.

The second drawing, like the first, told her nothing. She stared at the plates, wondering if Papa could possibly have known what secrets they possessed.

Her spine stiffened suddenly, as the front door creaked, announcing an uninvited visitor. Quickly, she hid the plates and dirty cloths beneath a remaining pile of debris collected for the dump, and just before she stepped into the house, she heard the tinkle of his spurs.

Her breath caught short at the sight of Quint standing inside the front door, hat in hand, not moving an inch. Taking a step forward, she stopped in mid-stride, self-consciously removed the kerchief from her head, and swung her black curls loose.

The liquid gold of his eyes flashed questions to her racing mind and sent shivers down her spine. Why did he stand there so still? Had he changed his mind? Had he never meant it at all? Had . . . ?

"Holly." Quint blurted out her name in an unnatural voice. The sight of her . . . her velvet eyes, her sensuously curling ebony hair . . . lit a fire in his body. He frowned. Why had she stopped so suddenly? "How've you been?" he asked cautiously.

She looked at him anxiously, wanting to rush forward and throw her arms about him, yet some fear she didn't even understand held her back. "Fine," she managed. "You?"

He nodded, twisting his hat in his hands, feeling more awkward than a new colt on a spring morning.

"Would you like to come in?" she asked.

He stepped into the room carefully, as if walking on fresh eggs, and her heart caught in her throat. Picnics do funny things to a person, she thought. And absence can set a man's mind straight. Give him time to regret anything rash he might have done, any statements he might have made on the spur of the moment.

Quint let out a low whistle, thinking how empty the cottage was compared to the last time he saw it. "Looks like you're on bare boards sure enough now," he said.

"Lucky you can stay at the hotel."

At that, all her pent-up emotions exploded in fiery anger—anger which heated her to the roots of her hair. "I certainly cannot live at the hotel for the rest of my life!" How dare him prove untrue! Tears pressed so close behind her eyes that she feared a deluge at any moment, but she could not stop herself from carrying the conversation further toward her own concerns. "Or did you forget that I am making Silver Creek my home?"

He stared at her for a long moment. She looked fragile and beautiful with her smudged nose and tousled hair. And her words . . .

All week long while riding the trails of this vast country alone, while negotiating with Sheriff Bales, half his mind had been occupied with Holly Campbell—and at night she had filled all his dreams. Her sweet love ignited him with desire such as he'd never known. Yet, every time he thought about a future with her, visions of that plantation home and her sheltered way of life haunted him. What kind of life could he offer her? One of hardship and deprivation. And knowledge of the destruction such a life would wreck on his lovely Holly was more than he could stand.

Her cheeks were flushed with anger, and the pain in her eyes pierced his heart. With two short steps, he closed the gap between them, took her in his arms, and held her close to his aching body, all the while damning himself as a weak-kneed cayuse.

"I didn't forget," he said hoarsely. "I didn't forget."

They stood meshed together thus, until finally he bent to claim her lips. Her tender mouth opened to him eagerly, receiving, sharing his probing, intoxicating passion, while her tears bathed their faces. He was all she had ever wanted, and she had been so afraid . . .

Quint felt heat soar through his body at the

sweetness of her kisses—kisses he had longed for these last lonely nights on the trail. As his tongue thrust hungrily into her openness, her small reciprocating tongue flicked spine-tingling shivers up his back and into his brain.

At last he drew back, breathing heavily, and stared into the velvet depths of her teary eyes. Wiping the tears from her soft cheek with the back of his calloused hand, he plucked gently at her bottom lip with his lips.

"Holly! Sweet Holly! What you do to me!" After their one frantic encounter down by the river, he had promised himself that the next time they made love, he would choose the time and place with care. But the fever rising in his body warned him that such a promise would be nigh onto impossible to keep if he didn't take himself in hand right soon.

Clearing his throat, he looked around the room. "Looks like we're going to have to get you some furniture."

Holly, too, was conscious of where their passion would lead them, and she reluctantly stepped out of his embrace, knowing all too well that Possum could burst in at any moment to see if she needed him. "I think I'll get Jed Varner to build me some furniture," she answered. "He could use the money for his new home."

They walked outside, strolling arm in arm along the still swollen river, and she told him about the loan from Mr. Norton and the Varners' baby and Jed's plan to build his family a new home. "Can you believe they even have earthen floors?"

He looked across the muddy water, studied the swirling current, then turned steady eyes on her. "A lot of folks out here have dirt floors."

They talked easily, and a comfortable feeling settled over her at having him with her again, a feeling that this was where they belonged . . . together. She asked about his trip, and he told her little, finishing with, "There's not much about this work that bears repeating . . . especially in delicate company."

She laughed. "Lately I feel anything but delicate."

He stroked her cheek with a work-roughened hand, and, holding her head in his hands, kissed her softly. "You're mighty delicate to me." His eyes took on a resoluteness then, and he clasped her to him in a sheltering embrace. How he had missed her. How he had feared for her safety. And if she left on the next stage, how he would miss her forever.

Suddenly she recalled the copper plates. Pulling away from him, she grabbed his hand and led him toward the house. "I want to show you something. I haven't told anyone, because . . . well, I don't want people getting the wrong idea about Papa, but maybe you can explain them to me."

They sat on the back steps, and Holly leaned against his muscled chest, feeling the quickened beat of his heart against her arm. Quint encircled her with his left arm, while he held the plates in front of them, one in each hand. He looked from one to the other and back again.

"Have you ever heard the legend of the copper plates?" she asked.

He nodded. "Where did you hear it?"

She told him about the conversation with Jed Varner and Possum the night the baby was born. "The signs are almost exactly like Jed said they would be."

"They fit the yarn I heard, too," he agreed.

"What do the markings mean?" she asked, snuggling against him.

Her hair tickled his nose, and he could think of at least one other thing he would rather be doing right this minute than talking about buried treasure, but he complied, knowing buried treasure was the least dangerous of the things he had in mind. "On this plate the sun is coming up between two hills," he began. "The sun always tells of a mine or some sort of treasure, generally gold. This arch is likely a tunnel."

"Of course," she said, awestruck that she hadn't thought of that. "What about the man on the donkey?"

"Burro." He corrected her with a grin. "The man is leading the burro, who's loaded with treasure, into the tunnel."

"The banking mission!" She clasped her hands together in delight. "Tell me about the other plate."

"The way I see it," he said, "this plate with the man and burro tells about the treasure itself, and the other plate with the trees is a map for today, to show whoever finds the plates where it's located." He turned the plates over in his hands. "How did you come by them?"

She drew back and looked up at him. "They were here, among Papa's cooking pans."

He raised his eyebrows.

"He never mentioned them in his letters," she said. "Do you suppose he could have somehow . . . ah, not known what they were?"

"Not likely."

She pursed her lips. "Especially since he knew Old Moses, and Old Moses was hunting this particular treasure."

Quint shook his head, grinning. "I'd plumb forgot about that crazy ol' man."

"Jed Varner told me that Old Moses was one of Papa's patients." She finished the sentence with a gasp. "Do you realize what this means?"

He squinted at her, waiting for an answer.

"Patients pay for a doctor's services in just about everything except cash money."

"And you think . . . ?"

She nodded thoughtfully. "When Old Moses knew

he was dying, he gave Papa the plates in payment for . . ."

"That sure knocks a hole in your idea about Tom Farrell. I'll say it right now, Tom wasn't taken in by buried treasure."

She smiled. "Nor was Papa. The tarnish was awfully heavy. He probably never even touched these plates. It's just that . . ."

"I know what you're getting at, Holly." Quint pulled her head back to his chest. "I lost my folks, too, and I'm mighty curious about anything that comes along that can shed some light on them for me."

She sighed. This was another quiet, serious man. Like Papa. And he understood her so well.

"I need your help," she said as calmly as she could muster.

"Name it."

"I'm sure Sancho knows more about Papa—about his death and everything—than anyone else, maybe even where Papa's journal is."

"Where'd you figure on finding him?"

She shrugged. "Elena Salinas might know."

He didn't respond, and she sat back and looked solemnly into his eyes. "Quint, please take me to the TF to find Elena. Don't say no."

"Now wait a minute . . ."

"Please. Don't say no."

"Holly . . ."

"I've waited all week for you to come back to go with me. But if you won't, I'll go alone."

"You'll play old Billy hell!" he shouted. "I've already explained that we can't go out there stirring up a hornet's nest without anything to go on."

"Please, Quint." Her eyes pleaded with him. "I promise you . . . all I want is to talk to Elena. Besides, with Farrell off on the trail drive, what harm could

I do?"

He cocked his head. "How do you know she's there?"

"I saw her at the graveyard, and she . . . she said she works for Farrell."

He looked at the two plates in his hands and took his time answering.

"Please, Quint."

He studied her a moment, then raised a blond eyebrow. "You're a difficult woman, you know that?"

She smiled.

"All right, I'll take you, but . . ."

In her rush to embrace him, she knocked them off the steps. "When can we leave?"

"Now hold on a cockeyed minute. You have to swear you won't say a thing out of line to anyone Tom might have left in charge."

"On the Good Book."

"I mean it, Holly. This is important. Not a word about your pa."

"I promise."

He looked at her and shook his head. "You're almost too much for a man to handle."

She laughed and kissed him soundly on the mouth. "We can get Farrell later."

He nodded. "But you'll only mess things up if you press him too early. Remember that."

"You didn't say when we can leave."

"First thing in the morning." His hand found the silken curls at the back of her head then, and he pulled her to him, his mouth cupping hers in a surge of desperate longing.

Heat from his body penetrated her blouse and chemise, swelling her breasts and tightening her nipples against their coarse cotton bondage. Blood pounded in her head to the rhythm of Quint's fiercely beating heart.

Wryly, Quint recalled his promise not to take her again in such a hasty, public fashion, and he realized that such a promise was like a fleeting summer cloud that passed quickly out of sight at a gust of warm wind. He had thought, before the picnic by the river, that once he had her, once he consumed her sweetness, he would be satisfied.

But such was not the case, as he had learned these last lonely days. In fact, since that one brief taste of her passion, he had been ravished by the memory of her fiery desire, haunted by the knowledge that he had only begun to sample the limitless pleasure of her body and soul.

The dull clanging of Rosie's supper bell sounded as a knell to their senses. With a last desperate tug at her sweet mouth, Quint drew his lips from hers, and their tongues lingered tip to tip until he spoke.

"Sweet, sweet Holly. We don't have to go to supper."

Unveiled desire flowed from his honey-gold eyes into her heart as a wincing pain. She swallowed with a dry throat. "If we don't, they'll come for us."

They sat without moving, reclined against the steps, their eyes locked in a desperate embrace, as they spoke with no need for words, soul to soul, of their fierce mutual needs.

And love, Holly thought. This must truly be love.

"Damn this town living," Quint breathed in her ear. "It sure puts a crimp in a man's private affairs."

Holly smiled wickedly, her thoughts turning again to Lady Macbeth. But this time they resounded joyously through her mind. Tomorrow and tomorrow and tomorrow . . . Tomorrow they would be alone.

They left directly after breakfast the following morning, with Holly awkwardly attired in Mavis's navy blue wool riding suit. Buckling the dozen or so cordovan leather straps that fastened the tight-fitting jacket over a white silk blouse, she sighed. If loneliness was synonymous with womanhood to Aggie, misery must surely be akin to godliness to Mavis! But, under Mavis's instructing eye, of course, she dutifully tugged on the matching cordovan leather boots which were at least one size too small, then set the navy riding hat atop her black curls and let Aggie arrange the flowing white silk scarf which extended down her back from the hatband to near bustle length.

The right side of the skirt fell beyond her feet for half a yard in order to accommodate the right knee and the saddle prong and still allow the skirt to cover her ankle properly. Tucking her hand through the little navy loop attached to that side of the skirt, she lifted the hem to an appropriate walking length and curtsied to her audience of two. Aggie clucked with delight, and Mavis nodded her approval.

But the time they set out, the early morning fog had burned off, and the remaining dew glistened on the lacelike leaves of the mesquite trees and on the sprigs of new-sprouting buffalo grass beneath the horses' hooves. Though still abundant, the wildflowers were more white now than blue, adding to the ethereal feeling she had of being alone with Quint in some strange and wonderful land.

He had chosen a spirited yet manageable dun for her, and she was glad to be in the saddle again. In the long-gone days at Hedgerow, riding had been one of her passions.

Anticipation of spending this day alone with Quint filled her with a light-headed giddiness and quelled her foreboding about meeting Elena again. She called to him from slightly behind, and he reined up.

"May I ask one more small favor?"

He eyed her suspiciously. "I will not . . ." he began.

"It has nothing to do with Tom Farrell," she added quickly.

He hesitated. "Shoot."

"On the way home, could we ride through Papa's canyon?"

"Sure, why not," he replied, relieved that her request had been so simple.

They rode in easy silence, while Holly rehearsed what she would say to Elena. "This is the best time to see Elena," she told Quint, "with Farrell away on the trail drive."

Quint nodded in agreement, and they both were surprised to find a buckboard and a couple of horses at the hitching rail in front of the TF ranch house.

"Someone must be having a party while the boss is away," Holly said.

Quint remained silent, studying the brands on the horses' rumps.

The house was not what Holly expected. Although she quickly admitted to herself that she hadn't known what to expect—nothing more than a log cabin, probably. But the TF ranch house was a two-story limestone structure, sturdy and attractive.

"Tom built the house for his wife," Quint replied in answer to her question. "If it'd been only himself, he likely wouldn't have built as fancy."

"I never thought of him being married," she said. "I mean, I knew he was, yet I suppose I pictured him as too mean for a woman to live with."

"He isn't married now," Quint said. "She died a few years back."

"Did you know her?"

Quint looked at Holly with an absent stare as he helped her down from the saddle. "Yes."

The second surprise of the morning came when Tom

Farrell himself answered their knock.

"Quint?" he questioned abruptly. "What brings you to the TF?" Then, seeing Holly, he stiffened. "What do you want?"

"Miss Campbell here would like to . . ." Quint began, and Holly slipped smoothly around him, entering the open door.

"Mr. Farrell, what a surprise!" She ignored the tug on her elbow. "However can your trail drive get along without you so often?"

The room was tidier than she had expected, thanks, she was sure, to Elena's care. The oak floors glistened beneath braided rag rugs. The furniture was heavy, rugged, and uncluttered. A large stone fireplace occupied the east end of the room, and beside it . . .

"Mr. Norton! Another surprise!" She made her way across the floor as the pudgy banker fidgeted with his mustache.

The door slammed, and Tom Farrell's voice thundered behind her. "What do you want here?"

Holly turned, but Quint answered the rancher. "Miss Campbell wants a word with the Salinas woman."

Farrell looked suspicious. "She ain't here."

"She does work for you?" Holly questioned.

He nodded curtly. "Time to time, but she ain't around today."

Holly cocked her head at the rancher. "I understand that she . . . well, that you . . . ah, that she lives here at the TF."

Farrell glared at her. "Have you been eating loco weed, lady?" He turned to Quint. "Get her out of here. I have work to do."

"Come on, Holly." Quint pulled her toward the door, but she jerked loose, looking furtively around the room, through the open doorways which led to various parts of the house. He was lying, she thought desperately. Elena must surely be here. Perhaps in the kitchen . . . and she might not have another chance to find this girl who risked so much to warn her.

Taking a deep breath, she raised the back of her hand to her forehead, and in a soft, weak voice, she asked, "I wonder if I might trouble you for a glass of water, Mr. Farrell? I do feel rather faint after that ride. Perhaps I could . . . ah, sit in the kitchen a moment."

Farrell fumbled, then thundered, this time at Quint. "Why'd you bring this harebrained woman out here? Take her back to town." He gave Holly a piercing look. "I warned you to get on that stage and leave Silver Creek."

An uneasy feeling rose along Quint's hairline then, and he reached for Holly again, but the banker moved up beside her.

"Miss, I've discussed our little transaction with Mr. Farrell, and he has no recollection of selling your pa that land."

Holly dropped her hand and turned furiously toward Tom Farrell. "What?"

"You heard him, Miss Campbell." Farrell regained command of both his temper and his voice. "I sold nothing to your pa, especially not Mustang Canyon. I wouldn't be likely to part with that canyon on any terms, would I, Quint?"

"I didn't think so, Tom," Quint replied.

"I'm sure Mr. Norton will be generous enough to let you keep the money he loaned you for passage back to Tennessee," Farrell told Holly.

The banker fluttered. "Whatever you say, T.F. Sure thing. That's fine by me."

Anger and confusion vied within Holly. She started to protest when a figure suddenly strode through a side door, drawing everyone's attention.

"I'll be headin' back to the trail, T.F."

Holly gasped. "Mr. Grant! I thought you were abducted from the stagecoach!"

All of Quint's senses suddenly shifted into order. His aggravation at Holly's persistence turned to fear—not the paralyzing fear that grips men of cowardice, but the careful, calculating fear of the fighting man. His heart rate slowed, his honey-gold eyes pierced Troy Grant, holding him steady, as though with an arrow to a target.

His left hand rose easily, gracefully to palm his hand gun, and he let out a low whistle. "Well, well, Tom. I see you're loaded for bear. What're you doing so far from your stompin' grounds . . . Ah, Grant is it?"

Holly watched wide-eyed as Grant's hands dropped suddenly to his guns, then stopped abruptly, hovering just above them.

"Do you two know each other?" she asked.

Quint jerked her arm forcibly with his right hand, almost ripping the sleeve of her jacket. "Get out of here."

"Wait . . ."

"Now!" He pushed her toward the door with a violence she had not seen in him before.

He followed, walking backward, and as they passed through the doorway, he spoke abruptly to Tom Farrell. "Don't do something you'll regret, Tom."

"You're my only regret, Quint." The voice sounded old, and Holly turned to be sure it was Tom Farrell who had spoken.

A chill swept over her then, and she shivered, but didn't know why. Surely she and Quint were safe anywhere. No one would be foolish enough to harm a woman . . . or a lawman.

Quint spurred his horse to an angry gallop, instructing her to keep up with him. Not until they were out of sight of the house did he let up, and then only slightly.

"Quint," Holly called. "Slow down. Please."

He looked back at her, but she could not read his thoughts.

"You promised to take me to Papa's canyon."

"And you promised . . ."

"I didn't do anything wrong," she shouted.

He pulled back beside her. "You promised not to rile Tom Farrell."

"He brought the subject up, not me," she answered. "And you can see how guilty he is. Come on, Quint, please take me to the property."

"Holly," he argued. "We need to get back to town now."

Holly pulled her horse to a stop. Why did she always have to fight for everything? she wondered. Quint Jarvis was as obstinate a man as she had ever known. "A gentleman never breaks a promise," she said angrily.

"As you can see, I'm not a . . ." His words ground to a halt, and he drew rein and headed west. "A look-see, nothing more."

"I promise."

He glared at her, angry with her for not keeping her part of the bargain; angry with himself for giving in to her whims once again. "Let's you and me put that word away."

Chapter Eight

Quint led the way, chafing with feelings of inadequacy. Not only had he been unable to handle that stubborn woman behind him, but he'd been taken unawares by Troy Grant. Jim Tom had harnessed up with some mighty unsavory characters in the past, but Grant was a whole different breed of animal.

A hired gunman. He wondered if Tom knew what he had gotten himself hitched to. From the conversation it seemed that Grant was part of the trail drive. Could be he needed a place to hide out while his trail cooled, and Jim Tom offered the drive. It had happened before. Many a trail crew included a man or two on the run.

Or was this something different? Could Grant's presence have anything to do with the rustlers? In either case, he presented no threat to them at the moment. What harm could it do to show Holly her pa's place? An uncomfortable ache suddenly filled the hollowness he felt in his gut. But why in tarnation did she have to be so all-fired uppity about it?

Holly followed in silence, the rift between them widening with the miles. A sense of melancholy overtook her when she thought of the lovely way she had envisioned this day alone with Quint. She hadn't intended to make him mad, but . . . well, she must find Sancho, and maybe Papa's land would hold some clue to his whereabouts.

Anyway, she couldn't find it on her own, and he had promised to take her there.

The path they traveled was no more than a deer trail, barely wide enough for the horses to pass single file. Low-growing branches kept her bobbing up and down in the saddle like a bottle in water, and she rode tensed against being dismounted into a bramble patch or clump of cactus.

Everywhere she looked, thorny bushes and trees covered the ground, and where plants would not grow, rocks abounded. Most areas of this country looked as if they had been hit by a hailstorm—of stones instead of ice.

"Isn't there an easier way?" she called ahead.

Quint turned in the saddle and squinted at her.

She shivered at the hardness in his golden eyes. "I am not driveling!"

He stared a moment longer, but his expression did not soften. "It isn't much further now. See those twin peaks?"

Past him in the distance she saw two slightly overlapping hills. "They look miles away."

"We don't have to go."

"Oh yes we do!" she replied.

Soon they left the underbrush and came out onto a prairie which, although still strewn with rocks and cactus, at least allowed them to ride abreast. Holly spurred her horse next to Quint's.

"You knew Troy Grant," she said, voicing a concern which had nagged at her the last few miles.

Quint tensed, but shook his head.

"You spoke to him as if you did," she insisted. "And he knew you."

"We crossed trails a couple of times," he answered. "That's all."

She wondered what he meant, for the scene back at the TF definitely portrayed the two men as more than passing acquaintances. She shrugged. If he didn't want to talk about it . . . but what was Troy Grant doing at the TF? And why had he left the stagecoach during the holdup to ride there?

"Farrell didn't answer my question about why he wasn't with his trail drive," she said.

"Nothing unusual about that," Quint replied. "Hugh Perkins oftentimes takes charge of Tom's drives. That frees Tom to ride ahead and tend to business in Kansas City before the cattle arrive."

Holly accepted that. She knew little of trail drives, and what he said made sense enough to her, with one reservation. "He certainly isn't in Kansas City now," she said. "And why did he lie to me?"

Quint cocked a blond eyebrow.

"I told you what he said," she argued. "He told me he was on his way back to the trail drive."

"A man's plans are his own business, Holly."

"I didn't ask him where he was going," she insisted. "He offered the information, and it was a lie."

He gave her a stern look. "Don't let anybody but me hear you call a man a liar."

"Truth is truth," she said. "And a lie is . . . Besides, no one would harm me. You said yourself it's considered unhealthy to accost a lady."

"Don't count on everybody playing by the rules."

She flinched at the sharp edge to his voice, and he continued. "Your escort would be obliged to back up your statements—likely with a gun. Where you come from they call it chivalry."

She drew a quick breath.

"Don't go acting so shocked. You've likely caused

your share of duels. It's all the same, except out here we don't stand on form—no setting up or fancy seconds. More often, it's simply draw or die."

She clenched her teeth against an outburst at him.

"I've seen men killed over some half-baked notion a female comes up with," he finished.

His accusations stung, but the comparison rang true. Perhaps civilization was the same the world over, beneath the surface, anyway. "I have never caused a duel," she told him quietly. "And I never will."

Coming to a cleft in the hillside that she would have called a gully, but he termed a draw, they turned up it, and the horses picked their way along the steepening sides, which eventually forced them to travel in the rocky-bottomed stream.

"I was afraid of this." He spoke aloud, surveying the country before them.

"What?"

"The creek hasn't run down from last week's rain. We're liable to get wet before we get out of here."

"Is this the only way?" she asked, alarmed that they might not be able to get to Papa's canyon after all.

"It's the best," he said. "We're lucky to get in at all. Whenever it comes a hard rain up the country, this draw will run high for days." He motioned to the sides of the bank, where she saw driftwood halfway to the top.

"Does it happen often?"

"No, but don't get caught out here in bad weather. The wall of water rushing out of that canyon will wash you away before you can say jack rabbit."

She shuddered. Not exactly the rolling, green pastures they raised thoroughbred bays on back in Tennessee. But they weren't to the canyon, yet.

The next thing she knew, however, the sides opened up, and they entered an area of several hundred acres surrounded by staggered, jagged cliffs of limestone.

The creek wound around one side and appeared to run the length of the canyon. In here the ground was covered with more grass than the country they had passed through outside, but it was strewn with the usual number of rocks, and dotted with prickly pear, mesquite trees, and a scattering of scrub oak. In fact, the thicket to their right appeared impenetrable.

A feeling of isolation overwhelmed her. "Are you sure this is the place?"

He nodded, spurring his horse forward.

She followed, and the horses raced to the opposite end of the canyon with no problem, but she reminded herself dismally that they were sure-footed cowponies who were used to dodging rocks, not spindle-legged thoroughbreds.

When they reached the head of the spring, Quint helped her down and showed her how to drink from the bubbling water by lying flat on her stomach, stretching over the water, and blowing to scatter the tiny water bugs away, then quickly sucking in the cold water.

The drink invigorated her, and the water was cool as it splashed on her face. She coughed and spat out a water bug, stood up, adjusted her jacket and riding skirt, and caught Quint's eye as he prepared to drink. He didn't speak, but she read approval, and a little surprise, in his glance.

"Is swallowing water bugs one of the tests you put a tenderfoot through?" she asked.

When he smiled, she thought she saw a touch more warmth than before. "As a pilgrim, you're plumb full of surprises."

While he drank, she leaned against a huge cottonwood tree, removed her gloves, and, loosening the string, pushed her hat back off her head.

Beyond the spring she saw a number of centuries-old

oaks, and an appreciation of the timelessness of this place penetrated her disappointment that it was not the rolling pastures she had hoped to find. A chill passed along her spine as she imagined that few civilized people had ever stood where she stood now.

As if reading her thoughts, Quint motioned to a circle of blackened rocks. "An ancient campfire," he said, "used for nobody knows how long by tribes of wandering Indians. You'll find all manner of arrowheads and other sign around here. Not just from the Indians we know about, but weapons and pottery like modern folks have never set eyes on before."

She looked at the circle of rocks, at the sides of the jagged cliffs, at the overlapping peaks of the hills. "It's beautiful," she admitted, "and humbling." She thought about the war, about Papa's death, and her present situation. "No matter what conflicts we conjure up for ourselves, life goes on here the same as ever. Man is the instigator, the violence-maker."

He grinned. "You haven't been around when the heavens go at it. They put on a show that'll top Old Scratch hisself."

Her attention kept returning to the overlapping peaks. "What direction is that?" she asked.

"North."

"Oh, then it can't be . . . ?"

He shook his head. "No. Not the hills on your copper plates."

She turned about slowly, studying Papa's land, searching for some clue to why he bought this canyon. "Are those caves up in the cliffs?"

Quint nodded. "This country's lousy with caves."

"And rocks," she added. "You're right. Papa couldn't raise thoroughbreds here. But why did he buy it?"

Quint studied her thoughtfully, seeing her confusion,

her vulnerability, tempted to take her in his arms. "Tom says he didn't."

She stared at the late-afternoon sun which shone through the mouth of the canyon. "I must find Sancho—or Papa's journal—or both." Scanning the cliffs again, she asked, "Could he be here, in one of the caves?"

"Won't hurt nothing to scout around a bit and see what we come up with." So they spent the next couple of hours searching the floor of the canyon for any sign of the boy, although, as Quint warned her, "Unless he's been about since the rain, we aren't liable to find any tracks."

They rode around the far end of the canyon, where the two hills converged. "This isn't a true box canyon," he said, showing Holly how to ride carefully in and out through the muddy maze of a trail which zigzagged to an exit on the east end. "Most folks don't know about this way out."

She noticed the debris along the side of the hill and realized he was right. Had they come a few days earlier, this very spot would have been under water.

At several points he stopped to study the ground and surrounding rocks.

"Do you see sign of him?" After a while she repeated the question, this time breaking through his concentration.

"Not unless he drives a wagon," he answered.

He didn't elaborate, and she was beginning to learn that even upon questioning, he wouldn't answer if he didn't want to, so she turned her attention to other matters.

"Is there some way we can get up to those caves?"

He looked at her in astonishment. "Whatever . . . ?"

"If Sancho were here," she reasoned, "he might have taken shelter in a cave."

Quint scanned the steep cliff doubtfully. "I don't cotton much to climbing. Besides, even a goat couldn't get to most of them."

"What about the ones within reach?" she insisted. "Couldn't we at least check them out?"

He inspected the walls behind them, then suddenly fell from the saddle, pulling her with him toward the ground.

She landed cushioned on his left side, his arm squeezing her to him. At the same instant, flying rock stung her face, and she heard a zing and thump, and the report of a rifle.

"How did you know . . . ?" She heard the trembling in her own voice as he pushed her behind him and fired at the hill to their right.

"Let's get out of here." He helped her to her feet. "And hurry. We'll lead the horses—you go first and keep to this side of your mount."

He gave her horse a swat on the rump, and at the same time jerked his Henry rifle free of its boot.

"What's happening?" Her legs wobbled as she stepped forward at his urging. "How did you know?"

"The sun glanced off his rifle barrel."

They rounded the last jag into the canyon, and he fired a succession of rapid shots at the hill, scattering rock and dust with each.

Leaning their backs against the limestone wall, they used their horses for a shield. She felt her body tremble against the hardness of the rocks. "I can shoot a gun, if you have a spare."

He hesitated.

"I can," she insisted, feeling some sort of need to have a hand in their defense. "Every year I outshot all the boys at the county fair."

Smiling, he reloaded and handed her his pistol. "I don't have much of anything to spare," he said, "including ammunition."

She inhaled tremulously, taking a lungful of caliche dust. "What does he want?"

Quint shrugged. "To shoot us . . . or scare us. But as to his reason, I'm stumped. He let us get into the canyon, but . . ."

"How did he know we would be here?" Her eyes flared wide in horror. "Tom Farrell!"

Quint took a deep breath, but ignored her question. "We'll keep to the shadows till dark, then make our move."

"Won't he be waiting for us at the other end?" She imagined the racket the horses' shod hooves would create striking the rocky ground.

"We'll make it."

His voice was very sure, as if he had faced adversity before and won. The tension which had formed a polite but distant barrier between them since their strained visit to the TF, melted in the strength of his words.

They stood together, scarcely breathing, and she jumped every time the horses snorted or stamped.

Without taking his eyes off the opposite hill, he reached over and squeezed the back of her neck. "It don't pay to get spooked. We'll make it."

Sweat trickled from beneath her hat, then streamed down her back and neck, in contrast to her dry, parched throat. If they were killed here, no one would ever know why . . . like Papa. She said this to Quint.

For an instant his eyes left their vigil and gazed reassuringly into hers. He lifted her trembling fingers to his lips. "We're not going to die here."

And somehow she knew he believed it.

Gradually the setting sun, which shone as a beacon of light through the canyon entrance ahead of them, settled behind the mesquite trees in the pasture outside, and they were immersed in a darkness illuminated only by the whiter, more opaque light of the rising moon.

Finally he gave the signal to move, but not across the canyon floor, as she had expected. Instead, they went back the way they had just come, through the labyrinth of mud and rocks. Although the trail was a mere wagon breadth wide, in most places they could lead their horses side by side. He let her go slightly ahead, while he continually checked above and behind them.

When they neared the pasture outside the canyon, he motioned for her to halt, and he moved forward alone, studying the area. Then, at his sign, they mounted, and he led her horse behind him.

Once out of the canyon, they hugged the side of the cliff to the north. Her heart pounded in her head louder than the sound of the horses' hooves on the rocks beneath them.

He drew up and spoke in hushed tones. "We'll ride to my place, if you don't mind."

She nodded in agreement, and he continued, looking at the crescent moon. "The night's too bright to be on the trail with a gunman after us. My cabin is close by. It isn't too fancy, but we'll have protection, and I can pick up some ammunition."

She nodded again, and without further discussion, they rode through the night, Quint keeping a constant vigil, alert to every sound.

When at last they stopped, it was behind a live oak thicket. "I'll ride in and see if we have company," he said. "You stay here and shoot at anything that moves."

"But . . ."

He reached over and squeezed the back of her neck again. "If I don't have sense enough to halloo the camp when I return, I deserve to get shot." He flicked the reins and rode off, leaving her alone.

And a more oppressive loneliness she had never

before felt. Totally lost in this vast land with an unknown gunman . . . or gunmen . . .

Fretting would get her nowhere, she chided, and she attuned her ears to the sounds about her, trying to distinguish one from another. Inexplicably she recalled someone saying that Indians imitate coyotes or other wild animals in their communications when they are out on nocturnal raids.

But Indians prowled about only to steal horses nowadays. Papa had said so, and everyone in Silver Creek told her the same. The settlers credited soldiers at nearby Fort San Saba with protecting them from the hostiles, but, evidently, gunmen were not as easily discouraged.

Suddenly she heard a low whistle, followed by a hushed voice, and her heart flip-flopped in the second it took her to recognize Quint's resonant voice.

"Things look safe enough," he told her. "Follow me, and we'll take it slow and easy."

They rode over the rise and straight to the barn, where they silently stripped saddles, blankets, and bridles from the horses and gave them feed and water. "Once we get to the house," Quint whispered, "we'd best stay put."

The ground was bathed in moonlight as they crossed the twenty-five yards or so to the house. At the back door, Quint stopped, cocking the handgun that she had returned to him in the barn. "Stay close behind me."

They stepped inside, and he told her to stand by the door until he found a light. Then he lighted a kerosene lamp, and the glow immediately cast shadows about the tiny cabin—two rooms as best she could judge from where she stood, shaking with both relief and left-over fear. She shifted her stiff legs from foot to foot, and as her heels struck the stone floor, her mind reeled back to the prior conversation. No dirt floors here.

Quint turned at the sound. His eyes met hers in amusement. "I'm not entirely heathen."

Quickly he surveyed the room and checked the locks on the shuttered windows, then instructed her to step away from the door, which he bolted from the inside with triple levers.

She stared around the sparsely furnished room. A couple of chairs and a rickety table, a cot in the corner with a blanket pulled tightly over it. And the dust—at least an inch covered everything. It hung heavy in the air. She tasted the grit in her mouth.

With the last bolt in place, Quint returned to Holly and placed his hands on her trembling shoulders. "I'm real sorry about this, Holly. We'd be like sitting ducks out on the road in the moonlight." He cleared his throat, and his voice became husky. "There's likely to be talk in town—what with us being away all night and all."

She laughed into his golden eyes. "I'd rather endure a little loose talk than end up dead on the road."

He relaxed and kissed the top of her head. "This isn't exactly what I had in mind when I dreamed of getting you alone to myself."

She bit her lip, recalling the fear she had felt in the canyon. Taking a deep breath, she tried another laugh. "Quint Jarvis, I'll bet you paid that sniper yourself—just to get me alone in your cabin."

He looked down into her twinkling velvet eyes, then he kissed her roundly on the lips. "Like hell I did. You and me, sweet Holly, we don't need help from nobody."

Then, without warning, he swatted her on her bustle and busied himself building a fire in the fireplace. He told her to fill a pot with water from the hand pump.

"Running water? Not many homes have such a luxury. Why here?"

He grinned. "I can tell you don't think much of my

batching set-up." Taking a packet of ground coffee from his pocket, he emptied it into the pot of water she handed him and set it in the coals. Then he turned serious. "The water pump is a precaution. With enough water, a man can hold out in here for quite a spell."

She looked at him curiously. "You told me Indians rarely come about anymore." Yet, security was the tightest of anyplace she had been. The two doors were barred in three places each, as were all the shutters . . .

"And the fireplace," he spoke up, following her gaze around the room. "I have a contraption on the chimney that allows smoke out, but prevents anything from being thrown inside, like torches or shotgun shells."

She shivered as a chill gripped her. "Whatever in the world for? Who are you keeping out? I mean, besides the person who shot at us today."

"Tom Farrell—or, rather, his men."

Her eyes blinked and her mouth dropped open. "This from the man who wouldn't believe Farrell capable of murdering my father?"

"I never said he wasn't capable," Quint responded. "I told you he would have to have a darned good reason."

She stared at him a long time, not sure she wanted to ask the question that sprung instantly to her mind, not sure she wanted to hear his answer. "What's his reason for wanting you . . . ah, out of the way?"

Quint's eyes never left the dancing flames. "I didn't quit him on the best of terms. He doesn't exactly want me out of the way, but no sense letting him make life miserable for me." Then his mood changed, and he stood up. "We'd best see about scaring up some grub."

While he searched the cupboard, she washed her hands in the cool water from the pump, and finding nothing which was not permeated with dust, she dried them on the edge of her bloomers.

"Looks like we've had a visitor," he said, turning

from the cupboard with a can of tomatoes and a hunk of jerked meat.

"Someone broke in?" she asked through a suddenly constricted throat.

Hearing the panic in her soft voice, he set the food down and put his arms around her. "We're safe in this house, Holly. I leave it open when I'm away so folks passing by can make use of what they need. Now that we're here, I've locked up tight. No one could get to us, even if they wanted to."

Turning back to their supper, he reached for a spider-legged skillet. "I had a knife around here somewhere," he said, searching the small cabinet.

They looked in vain, and finally he took a wicked-looking knife from the scabbard on his belt. "Be careful with this," he instructed. "It's been known to cut the hair off a buffalo's tongue."

She turned the knife over in her hand. It didn't resemble any hunting knife she'd ever seen. "What kind of instrument is this?"

"Bowie knife," he answered. "Named after the famous Indian fighter, Jim Bowie, who invented it. He was mighty handy with that knife, or so the stories go, before he died at the Alamo."

"Bowie?" she asked. "I've heard that name recently.

He grinned. "Like as not in talk about the Lost Bowie Mine."

"Another of those treasure stories."

"The granddaddy of the lot." Taking the knife away from her, he recounted the legend while he opened the can himself. "Can't have you cutting your hand off on your first visit to my fireside."

She looked around the primitive room and laughed wistfully. "Your home could use a little attention."

"This cabin's way past help," he admitted. "It was here when I bought the place, and after I left the TF, it was the only place I had to go. I fortified it some, as I said, but I've been intending to make a trade with Jed Varner to build me something respectable."

"If his cattle are rustled on the way to market, he's going to need some extra income." She tilted her head, thinking about the trail drive. "Do you have stock on that drive?"

"Not this time." He sliced the jerked meat, and checked on the coffee. "Bring the skillet, and I'll show you how to cook on this thing."

"What thing?" She looked around for something that resembled a cook stove.

"The fireplace," he said. "It's the best place around to get smoke in your eyes."

She put her hands on her hips. "You don't think I've ever cooked over an open hearth?"

"Well, have you?" he challenged.

She smiled. "Actually, we did have one of the first cook stoves in Tennessee, and I even learned to cook on it after the war." She knitted her brow. "As for an open hearth . . . well, I can't see that it would be very demanding."

He raised his eyebrows, his eyes glittering with reflections from the fire. "Maybe not to your pioneering instincts, but . . ."

She shoved his shoulder, toppling him off his perched feet. "I think I'm taking to this country pretty well," she said. "In fact, if I recall correctly, you told me so yourself."

He studied her seriously, his body warming with both the memory and the anticipation of her many pleasures, while his mind argued the deprivations a life in this wilderness would rain upon the body and soul of his sweet Holly. "That you are," he answered finally. But he retained his hold on the skillet and stirred the jerked meat and water until its thickness suited him.

"You'll find plates and cups on the shelf, or did our visitor . . . ?"

She nodded. "There's only one plate left, but I did find these two tin cups."

"The list is adding up." He carried the skillet to the table, and she poured their coffee. "Plate's for the lady. Many's the supper I've eaten out of a skillet over a campfire."

They ate in silence, Holly trying to settle her nerves from the earth-jarring events of the day. She stared at him unconsciously, thinking how little she knew about this man—this man who fulfilled her needs and longings and fantasies as she had never dared to dream a man could do. Finally he looked up.

"What's on your mind?" he asked.

"I'm curious about something, but I doubt you'll answer my questions."

"Fire away."

She sighed. "I can't decide how you feel about Tom Farrell. What's the big secret between you two?"

He cocked his head, surprised. "I sort of figured Mavis or someone in town would have told you by now."

She shook her head.

Shrugging, he said, "Seeing's how you're mixed up with both of us, I guess you have a right to know—my part of it leastways."

So, as they cleared the table, he told her the story in his full, rich voice, beginning simply with, "Tom Farrell is my uncle."

She stared at him dumbfounded for a moment, then finally managed to swallow the lump in her throat. "Your uncle?"

"Ma's brother. But actually, he's more like a pa to me himself."

She frowned, her mind furiously attempting to deny

the words he spoke. She had sensed some bond between them, but this close a connection . . . the man she knew she was coming to love and a hated enemy, like father and son.

"My pa was . . . well, not exactly a loafer, but he wasn't a real go-getter, either. All he cared for was riding wild horses, and that didn't make much of a life for Ma and me. When I was just a tyke, Aunt Jen talked Tom into taking Pa on, so we moved to the ranch. It was the first real home I'd ever had."

She shook her head absently, and he paused. "Not your blue-blooded plantation family, I reckon."

"Quint," she reprimanded. "Go ahead."

"Not long after we settled in, Pa was thrown for the last time. He lingered a spell, but died after about a month. Ma passed on a year later of the ague. So Uncle Tom and Aunt Jen raised me up."

"Alongside Jim Tom," she said, recalling the antagonism between the two men at the dance.

"Jim Tom didn't come along till later. I'm ten years older than he is. I was only five when Pa died."

"So Tom Farrell really is like your father," she said simply, settling into the rocking chair before the fire.

He nodded and seated himself on the hearth facing her.

"Leaving him must have been difficult."

"Worse'n when my folks died," he admitted. "But it had to be."

"Will you tell me why?" There's a logical explanation for all this, she thought. After all, one has no choice in relatives. Many a good man must certainly have found himself with intolerable ruffians for parents.

"I'm getting to that part," he continued. "While Aunt Jen was alive, I guess you'd say she kept Tom in line, but when she died three years back, he went plumb loco."

"What do you mean?"

"Just say things got out of hand. Jim Tom took up with the wrong crowd, and Tom expected . . . well, he expected things of me I didn't cotton to."

"You and Jim Tom must be close, like brothers."

He grunted. "Brothers oftentimes don't get along together. Tom thought Jim Tom ought to grow up to be like me, and he wasn't cut out thataway. Jim Tom turned bad just to prove himself to Tom."

"What did Farrell do, exactly?" she asked. "I mean why are you afraid of him?" She swept her arms about the fortified room.

"He hasn't done anything, yet. And he won't cause me any physical harm. I figure he might try to burn me out—so I won't have anything left and will have to go running back to the TF. Tom sort of feels like he owns me and everything else around him, including Jim Tom. And he doesn't turn loose of his belongings without putting up a fight." He paused, seeing the fear in her eyes. "We're safe here, Holly," he assured her. "Tom had nothing to do with our visitor. That was some passerby needing a grubstake. Meant us no harm."

Her heart flipped into a tight knot. And the rifle shot? she wondered. What did that mean? Who was it meant for?

She said nothing, but he sensed her uneasiness. "You're safe here," he repeated quietly. "I don't want you to be afraid."

She looked around the fortified cabin, realizing with a start that she wasn't really afraid—not here in this cabin with Quint beside her. She smiled, and with a sigh stretched her weary muscles. "I'm fine."

He fidgeted uneasily. "I'm afraid the accommodations aren't up to the Hotel O'Keefe's."

Eyeing the rickety cot in the main room, she crossed

to the doorway of the bedroom, but the bed she saw there didn't look much more promising. She laughed. "A little roughing it never hurt a body."

Behind her water splashed from the hand pump, and when she turned, Quint had set a bucket of water over the coals to heat.

A mischievous light twinkled in his eyes, sending spine-tingling flickers down her back. "Thought you might like to freshen up a bit before bedtime." He turned away from her to busily rummage through a trunk in the corner, finally pulling out a number of quilts.

Damn it! he thought. Why did such great good fortune come cloaked in beggar's garments? Ever since that day by the river, he'd dreamed of, longed for, ached to have Holly alone to himself. But now that he'd gotten his wish, he was conscious only of the crudeness of this hovel he lived in.

He sighed, spreading the quilts in a thick pallet before the fire. They said a man had to make hay while the sun shone, he thought. Tonight had been given to him, and by damn! he'd take it . . . and make it a night they would both remember.

Holly watched Quint with increasing curiosity as he laid the pallet, then extinguished all the lamps in the cabin except the one on the mantel. After he tested the water with the inside of his wrist and set the bucket on the hearth, he turned to her with outstretched arms, and, towering like a god in the small room, he beckoned her to him wordlessly . . . with his disarming, glittering eyes.

Her pulse quickened with the growing understanding of what he was about. The delicate aroma of musky woodsmoke filled her nostrils, titillating her senses even further as she inhaled a tremulous breath and walked to him slowly, savoring the delicious glow of anticipation that made her skin ache for his touch.

The fire in the fireplace, which had taken the chill off the late spring evening, had now died down to a few live coals and embers. She stared at Quint, transfixed by the halo of light from the single lamp that danced brightly in the golden highlights of his tousled hair, while the golden circle spread across the pallet, leaving the rest of the room in deep black shadows.

She stopped before him. He cupped his hands gently on her shoulders, and her entire body thrilled with the erotic promise flowing into her soul from the golden depths of his eyes.

Eagerly they slid into each other's arms, and every concern outside this one dim circle of light vanished—dissolved in the heat of their shared passion.

His lips found hers, demandingly devouring her sweetness. When her tender mouth opened to receive him, such a tremendous shaft of heat swept through his body that he knew he could throw her down on the pallet and take her this very instant.

His mouth closed over hers, leaving her dizzy with the expectation of remembered pleasures, yet a little frightened, too. This time they were alone—truly alone. This time he would have his way with her, and she was not at all sure what that meant. Shuddering as a flurry of expectancy coursed her body, she answered his probing kiss with a bold quest of her own.

His heart thumping wildly, Quint endeavored to quiet his trembling arms, while he stood her back from him and caught her face in his hands. Soft shadows flickered across her features. Gently, he kissed her eyelids, her pouty lips. Then, slowly, he took the pins from her inky black hair and pulled her long curls through his fingers.

Overcome by an urgency to feel his body next to hers, Holly tried to pull him to her, but he held her back, resting her hands easily on his hips. "Wait, sweet Holly. Wait. Remember what I promised you?"

His husky voice sent tremors down her spine. His eyes held hers, and she could barely restrain herself from grasping his hair in her hands, drawing his lips to hers, and pressing her hungering body to his firm, masculine form.

But she submitted to his wishes, standing stock-still except for her runaway heart which beat fiercely against the boning in her corset, while Quint painstakingly unbuckled all twelve buckles on her jacket without ever taking his eyes from hers.

The jacket discarded, he kneaded his hands briefly in the silky softness of her blouse before his arms encircled her, holding her tantalizingly close, yet apart from him, while he unbuttoned her blouse from behind and threw it aside, as well. Deftly then, he dropped her skirt and petticoats, and she stepped out of them with shaky knees, standing before him shyly now in her chemise, corset, and bloomers.

His heart caught in his throat at the thought of what was to come, and his large, impatient fingers fumbled with the tiny hooks on her corset, tormented, as they worked, by her heaving breasts, until he was want to tear the garment off her and ravish her trembling body then and there.

Holly stood on weakening limbs while his hands removed her corset, her lacy white chemise, stimulating her already sensitized body to unbearable heights. A sigh, as a sob, escaped her parched throat at the explicitly carnal passion with which Quint stared at her ripe, swollen breasts, and she instinctively arched her throbbing nipples toward his parted lips.

Her sigh sent a tremor through his aching loins. Urgently, he grasped her silken body at each side, then gradually brought his hands around until he had squeezed her breasts together. Her tiny, hardened nipples beckoned him closer.

Blood clamored through his veins as his lips closed hungrily on her offered gifts, suckling first one, then the other, while Holly wrapped her arms about his hips and moved her still-clothed abdomen against his fevered body.

Loosening his hold with one hand, Quint fumbled to find the tie of her bloomers, but she pushed his hand away, her head swimming mindlessly.

"Wait," she breathed, and before he realized what had happened, she had stripped his shirt from his body and rubbed her breasts against the heated flesh of his midsection.

Reaching for her lips once more, he bathed her face, her ear lobes, her neck with smothering kisses, finding at last the intoxicating sweetness of her breasts. His great hands roamed the silky smoothness of her back, holding her close while he teased the already taut peaks with his lips and tongue.

Driven by unbridled desire, Holly arched herself into the heated cavern of his mouth, her hands kneading the rippling muscles of his back in rhythm with his urgent tugging at her inflamed breast. Then he stopped to roll an aching nipple teasingly between his teeth, and she cried out, moaning at the unbearable sweet fire which sprung in the pit of her stomach and spread like wildfire to her thighs. Her aching flesh tightened with a sudden jerk, and she thrust her hips against Quint's, seeking solace from this torturous suffering.

When he felt her passion-racked body jerk against him, Quint knew the end was near for both of them. But this was not the way he planned it: he had intended to languidly explore every luscious nook and cranny of her exquisite body; he wanted to bring her pleasure so great, so intense, that she would never forget this night, not if she lived to be a hundred and forty years old.

With one last, determined nip at her sweet breast, Quint held her back. "We're getting way ahead of ourselves, my sweet Holly." And with that he untied her bloomers and let them fall from her slender hips. While she removed her boots, he, likewise, stripped the rest of his clothing from his heated body.

She gasped at the undeniable proof of his desire for her. Her arms weakened by raging desire, she reached for his body and ran her hands wondrously down his sides from his muscled shoulders and powerful chest to his small waist and . . . Shivers of delight ran up her spine as she thought of what lay ahead. The undulating lamplight played across his body, and a painful sweetness swept over her. Never had she dreamed of anything as blatantly erotic as this moment.

Quint removed her hands from his hips slowly and began to bathe her with a cloth he had wrung out in the warm water from the bucket. She stood straight, outwardly calm, fascinated by the pleasure in his eyes as he bathed and caressed her body, stroking the fire within her to greater and greater intensity.

He began with her face—her fevered brow and love-parched lips; progressing past the pulse points on her creamy throat, he paused to fondle and tantalize her sensitive nipples with the coarse cloth; past her tiny waist and flat stomach to the aching triangle of curly black hair, where she put her hand on his to stop him.

His breathing coming in ragged gasps, Quint let out a low moan as she took the cloth from him, wrung it out in the fresh warm water, and bathed him in turn.

With slow, measured movements she washed his chiseled brow, closing first one eye, then the other, to tenderly stroke his lids. His lips nibbled hungrily at her fingers as she passed; the throbbing veins in his muscular throat echoed her own clamoring heartbeat, and she hurried to his matted chest, where soft golden hair glistened in the lamplight. Caressing him with both hands, one covered in the cloth, the other bare, she reveled in the fine hair which covered his tightened muscles. With a surprise she found his rigid little male nipples, and his groan at her touch built pressure to a frenzied peak behind every pore in her body.

Their lips met fiercely then, and she continued her bathing of him by feel, while he dropped a hand to her thighs and slipped inside her satiny core. When she urgently moved against his probing fingers, he knew she was ready to receive him, so with one arm around her back and another under her buttocks, he lifted her small frame and eased himself slowly, sensuously inside her.

The shock of their joining was so intense that they gasped in unison, fused together not only by their fiery molten flesh, but by their eyes, their hearts, their very souls.

They stood as a statue, Holly thought. She heard no sound except that of their own ragged breathing, their beating hearts; felt no movement but the sweet burning that pulsated within her.

Holding her firmly in place, Quint knelt slowly, lowering them to the pallet without taking his eyes from her shimmering face. They lay on their sides, still linked as one, and he lifted a hand to fondle her small, taut nipple.

"Holly! My wild Tennessee lover!"

"Texas lover," she murmured, exhaling heavily through dry lips.

He shook his head. "I've never known anything like this in Texas . . . or anywhere else."

His erotically husky voice and his intolerable ministrations to her aching nipple inflamed her with a frenzied delirium, and she rotated her hips provocatively, urging him on with sensual undulations. Her fingers pulled his head toward her, her lips sought his, and with a half-sob, half-plea, she arched her back, her breasts reaching to feel the soft curls on his chest.

Responding to her urgency, Quint rolled her over and began to thrust wildly within her tightened core, driven deeper and deeper by her turbulent movements below him and her warm moist breath on his ear, whispering, "Oh . . . oh . . . oh . . ." in rhythm with their heated bodies.

Holly moved her hips with a wanton abandon brought on by the fiercest sweetest hungering she had ever known. The very feel of his body filling hers, answering her clamoring quest to reach some distant summit of pleasure, brought wondrous joy to her heart and tears to her eyes.

The sunburst she expected came on gradually this time and lasted longer. Instead of the one great explosion she had experienced that day by the river, this time she recognized the beginning of the end, which came to her as a falling star, trailing fiery magic across a blackened sky. Her hips moved faster and faster against this increasingly brilliant sensation, wishing it would never end, wanting to prolong the glorious agony forever.

Then at the moment when her body felt it could not stand another second of such unbearable torment, it came. Like a giant meteor smashing to earth, her passion exploded in startlingly fiery blasts from every sensitized pore in her body, leaving wave after wave of undulating repercussions flashing light and heat through her brain.

It didn't take long for either of them this time. Quint held back until he felt her shudder in his arms, then he released himself in great heated waves. They clung to each other limply, their perspiration-streaked bodies sticking where they touched, their hearts and minds slowly winding down to normal.

Finally Holly moved her head back and gazed into the golden depths of his sleepy eyes. "My God!" she whispered in awe. "That was wonderful."

Quint pulled her wet, naked body tightly to his own. "It just gets better and better, sweet Holly. Better and better."

They slept then, awakening later in the night to love again. This time less urgently, more slowly, but even better. As Quint had promised, she thought.

Satisfied by Quint's loving, she slept deeply at first, then, as morning approached, her dreams became anxious, and turned a glorious experience dark and ominous. A face floated in her dreams. A face she recognized. Papa.

His voice came to her, harsh with condemnation. "Why, Daughter? Why?"

"You didn't know him, Papa. He's wonderful. You would love him, too. I know you would."

But the voice came again. "Why?"

Quint roused at her restlessness, and, hearing her whimper, he tightened his arms around her, pushing her head into the protective hollow of his shoulder.

Chapter Nine

Light filtered through slits in the shutters, arousing Holly from an uneasy sleep. Drowsily, she stretched her arm across the empty bed, then flushed with remembrance of the night before . . . the joy . . . the wonder. Waking now in this rather lumpy bed, their bathing and lovemaking in the shadowy flickering light seemed almost a dream.

But it wasn't a dream, she thought, as her still-nude body thrilled with delight at that glorious coupling. They had drifted off to sleep on the pallet before the fire, only to awaken later in the chill of a room where the fire had died out.

She blushed, thinking that the flames of desire inside the two of them burned hot enough to stave off the severest of winters. So they had made love again, and sometime after that, Quint had carried her to bed.

Now with the morning come, he was gone, and her body ached with disappointment . . . and longing.

His absence did not alarm her, though. He had left coffee on the coals, and after she dressed and started breakfast—which, owing to their limited rations, would be a repeat of supper without the tomatoes—she smiled, realizing their first night together had been spent in this rustic stone cabin.

By the time Quint returned, the jerky was ready, and she'd had a chance to fantasize about fixing up the place; a woman's touch was definitely in order, beginning with a thorough housecleaning.

She turned expectantly at his entrance, but he avoided her eyes and crossed the room to the fireplace. She went to him, put her arms around his neck, and kissed his lips lightly. "Good morning."

Still he wouldn't look at her. "This won't work, Holly . . ."

She stared at him, confused by his strange behavior. "What won't work?"

She stood before him, the embodiment of everything lovely he had ever imagined, and her sweetness filled him with bittersweet longing. Never, not in his most far-fetched dreams, had he ever pictured himself with a woman like Holly Campbell.

Yet, here she stood, his for the taking. And she belonged in a palace with a king—his heart thudded like lead in his chest—not here in this . . . this sorry excuse for a home.

Clearing his throat, he spoke in a deep tone, purposefully harsh. "I can't do this to you."

Still she did not understand. "Quint! You didn't do anything to me. I . . ."

He turned away, and his apparent indifference struck a discordant note within her. She loved him; she knew she loved him. And his tender caring manner convinced her that he felt the same way, but . . .

Storming to the table, she slammed down the one plate, demanding, "What do you think I am? I don't do that every night. In fact, you're the first man I've ever even wanted to . . . to be with."

He stared at her, unspeaking, and the thought of losing him brought tears to her eyes. She crossed to him, put her hands on his arms. "Quint, look at me. I love you. Don't you know that?" she asked softly.

He diverted his eyes again. "You don't know what you're saying, Holly. You didn't come out here to live . . ." He flung his arms out suddenly, and she tottered backward. ". . . like this," he finished.

Regaining her footing, she stood up to her full height. So that's was it was, she thought. Hedgerow again. His pigheadedness infuriated her, and she spat out her words. "I certainly did not."

Quint blinked at her vehement admission.

"And you don't plan to live like this any longer than you have to, either. You told me yourself that you intend to get Jed Varner to build you a house."

"That won't be for some time," he argued. "And besides, even then it wouldn't . . ."

She frowned at him, tilting her chin to look into his distressed eyes. "Like Hedgerow?" she asked viciously. "Why can't you understand, Quint? Hedgerow isn't like that photograph, either. Not anymore."

Slowly, with a reverence born in grief, he lifted one of her small hands to his lips. With his other hand he stroked her rosy firm cheek and gently patted the tender unlined skin around her eyes, seeing her youthful beauty aged to leather by the unrelenting sun and wind, by tragedy and hardship.

"This land's too harsh, Holly." He trembled at the moisture brimming in her eyes, and as he looked into their velvet depths, the fire and fight he saw there reminded him of the despair he'd seen in his own ma's eyes, and, at the end, even in Aunt Jen's. "The grief and loneliness around here are too great. They'd soon put out that flame in your eyes."

Looking deeper into the dull glitter of his golden eyes, she flinched at the pain they reflected. But she saw no rejection, and with a mouth parched by fear, she answered him softly. "You're the flame in my eyes, Quint. As long as I have you, nothing else matters." She squeezed her arms around him, laying her head against his chest. "I want to spend the rest of my life with you. Wherever you live. However you live."

He returned her embrace desperately, his heart pumping wildly in his chest. God, how she wrenched at his heart and soul. "Holly, oh Holly," he crooned in his rich voice, which never failed to turn her spine to jelly. "You don't know what you're saying."

She ached inside, praying for some way to convince him. "Quint, will you at least promise me one thing?"

He drew back and looked at her silently, waiting.

"Promise me that you won't ever regret last night. It was the most important night in my whole life, the most wonderful. I couldn't stand to think it wasn't important to you, too."

His heart leaped to his throat, and he studied her intently, finally kissing her deeply. How did he think he could live one single day without this woman by his side? "You're something else, you know that? You're really something." He hugged her to him, their hearts pounding as one. "I couldn't ever regret last night, Holly. Not ever."

They stood holding each other a moment longer, and her head whirled. He was a confusion to her, indeed he was. One minute he loved her so fiercely, the next moment he withdrew from her in some mistaken effort to shield her from a life she passionately wanted to share with him.

When he pushed her back, she smiled up at him, expecting a kiss. Instead, he gave her a swat on the bottom. "We'd best get moving."

Disappointment swept over her. "So soon?"

"Yes, ma'am, so soon." While they ate, he told her about the small footprints he'd found this morning around the cabin and barn.

She was instantly alert. "Sancho?"

He shrugged. "If it was, he's in a peck of trouble."

"How do you mean?"

He shook his head, thinking about the situation. "He shouldn't have to go sneaking about, stealing. Anybody in Silver Creek would help him out, even give him a job and a place to live."

"Then why . . . ?"

"I figure somebody must be after him."

Quint saddled the horses, while Holly cleaned the dishes and straightened things inside the cabin, smoothing blankets over the cornhusk mattress. At the door she turned for one last look. "Can we come back soon?"

He kissed her soundly, in a manner which said he'd returned from his previous pensive state. Guiding her out the door, he said, "You bet we'll come back. But right now I need to read our sharpshooter's trail before it gets any colder."

The countryside was less threatening in daylight, but they rode with vigilance. Quint studied the ground, the trees, anything that might indicate that someone other than they themselves had passed this way.

"Why the trees?" she asked. "What do you expect to find there?"

"A broken twig," he responded, not taking his attention from the thicket he studied. "Or a scrap of cloth, a thread. You'd be surprised how big a trail a man leaves unless he rides wary."

"But wouldn't the gunman have been extra cautious?"

He nodded. "Nighttime poses its own problems, though. Even on a moonlit night, a man can't see every twig and branch. It's mighty unlikely a fellow could travel through a piece of country at night and cover his trail completely."

They rode on in silence, and she began watching for signs herself. But she enjoyed watching Quint more. He was so proficient, so sure of himself—not the same man who quaked at the vision of Hedgerow Plantation. This was his land, and he was as much a part of it as the prickly pear and cactus, the mesquite and oaks, the antelope and wild mustangs . . .

"What're you staring at?" he asked suddenly.

She blushed, realizing she had indeed been giving him a thorough inspection.

"Am I that funny looking?" He moved his horse closer to hers and studied her face as intently as he had the landscape. He was so open, so free, so at home here.

"I wasn't laughing at you," she protested. "I just like to watch you. Is there anything wrong with that?"

Stretching in the saddle, he leaned over and kissed her lips. "It's damned distracting, that's what's wrong with it."

"What's wrong with being distracted?" she asked coyly, reaching for his lips with her own.

While he stroked her cheek, quivers ran along her spine. He inhaled deeply. "Holly, sweet Holly. You'll be the ruin of me."

They continued their ride, Quint inspecting their surroundings carefully. But he found no indication that they had been followed from the canyon, and before she knew it, they drew up in a thicket. Quint pointed to the opening in the hills where they had exited the canyon the night before.

"I don't expect to find anybody around today. He likely gave up on us last night, but we'd best play it safe."

He staked the horses and studied the ground, finally pointing to a scuff in the side of the hill. "Here's where he climbed up."

She looked at the place he indicated, but it was

merely another scuffed place to her.

Quint sized up her boots with a grin. "I guess they'll do for climbing."

She returned his stare to his own boots. "I can't see that mine are much different from yours. Except for your slanted heel."

He nodded. "Mine weren't made for climbing, either. For the most part, work that can't be done ahorseback doesn't need to be done."

She tilted her head back to look up the hillside. "But this time?"

"This time we'd be wise to see what trail that feller left up on the hill. And the only way up is to climb."

It was steeper than she had thought. Not over a hundred feet high, yet the dirt was loose, and they had to hang onto branches of low-growing bushes to pull themselves along.

At the top she slipped her hat back, wiped her brow with a dusty handkerchief, and stood with hands on hips, rotating until she had admired the country from a full circle.

Isolating. Intimidating. Exhilarating.

"Why can't I see the cabin from here?"

"What?" he asked absently, concentrating on tracks he had located in the crusty soil.

"Your cabin? Why can't I see it from here?"

He rose to stand behind her, resting his arms on her shoulders, and his blood stirred, heated by even this simple contact with her. "See those trees?" He pointed to a group of pea green leaves with some bare branches still showing. "The cabin is down there by the creek, hidden under the trees."

Her shoulders tensed beneath his arms. "You mean the rifleman could have seen the smoke from our chimney last night?"

"Not likely," he assured her. "The pecans are already

leafed out enough for some protection. And I used mesquite wood. That's the closest thing this country has to smokeless firewood."

She cocked her head, and he questioned her. "What's going on in that noggin of yours?"

She smiled, staring at him. "You amaze me . . . all the things you know."

He grinned. "Not everybody out here is so ignorant he can't teach a setting hen to cluck."

She laughed at his expression. "I didn't mean it that way."

"I even got some schooling. Aunt Jen saw to it that I had a tutor, so I can actually read and write," he joked.

"You didn't learn all this in school," she protested.

He took her by the arm. "Let me show you what I found, then you'll know something, too."

"All right, but I'm proud of you."

He squeezed her around the waist as he knelt, pulling her with him. What a woman! What an incredible woman, he thought.

"Our man must have smoked a dozen cigarettes." He took on the tones of an instructor. "Now, what do you suppose he was doing setting up on this hill smoking?"

She considered this information seriously, then stood up and looked down into the canyon. She swallowed hard. Fear crept along her spine, choking in her throat, as she stared at the place directly below them. "That's where we were when the shot . . ."

He nodded.

Wrapping her arms about her body, she tried to stave off chills which suddenly rose in whelps. "He waited up here; then he shot at us. I don't understand." She turned to Quint, and he gathered her in his arms, soothing her fears.

"I don't either, yet," he said. "But you can bet I'll find out."

Guiding her back to the hillside where they had climbed up, he motioned for her to go first. "Going down will be easier on your feet, but harder . . ." He grinned, rubbing his behind.

And sure enough she slid partway down and reached the bottom thankful for not having collided with any of the outcroppings of sandstone or prickly pear, and for not having tangled herself hopelessly in Mavis's by-now-not-so-elegant riding suit.

"Keep a sharp lookout," he warned as they entered the canyon. "I figure we're safe enough, but since we don't know who or what . . ."

She smiled mischievously. "In other words, I'm not to distract you."

He winked at her. "You got it."

As they rode out of the tunnellike trail and into the canyon itself, he pulled up.

She stopped alongside him. "What are we looking for?"

"Tracks to match our smoker on the hill," he answered. "Or the intruder from the cabin. At least, now we know for sure they were two different people. And you wanted to see these caves."

Her eyes opened wide in surprise. "Really?"

He nodded. "First, let's mosey over to the spring. Our trigger-happy friend might have left a calling card."

They rode to the cottonwood, where they dismounted, and Quint preceded her to the spring, holding her back so he could study the tracks beside it before she drank.

While he was busy with the tracks, which she saw at an instant were a jumbled mess, she scanned the area. Looking tentatively behind her, prickles arose along the back of her neck when she saw that even here they had been under the watchful eye of the gunman.

"He could have killed us easily." She felt weak with

recollection, with foreboding.

"If he'd been of a mind to."

"What do you mean?"

"I figure he only meant to scare us off."

"They knew we were coming here, because this is Papa's place? Is that what you mean?"

He shrugged. "I don't figure your pa had much to do with it." He looked around the canyon, then back at her. "But he must've stumbled onto something."

"What?"

"I don't have the answer to that," he admitted. "Yet."

"And they think we have, too?"

He nodded.

Alarm rose in her voice. "So they're going to kill us, too?"

He stood up and held her tightly to him. "Not likely," he said. "That gunman had half a dozen good chances to fire on us yesterday, but he didn't. Not until we got . . ."

"Into the maze going out of here," she recalled.

He nodded, tightening his hold on her.

"What's so special about that place?"

He shrugged, but didn't answer.

"You're the tracker," she reminded him. "What did you find?"

"Not enough."

And that was all she could get out of him. "Don't you want a drink?" he asked when she repeated her question.

When she finished, she stood up and tightened her hat on her head against the suddenly warm sun. The water did not taste as sweet today.

They continued around the canyon, Quint watching the ground for tracks, occasionally looking up the cliffs, then back at the ground.

Finally he halted. "We'll climb up here."

She eyed the steep narrow animal trail.

"What's the matter?" He challenged her with a grin. "Lost your curiosity?"

She dismounted and followed his lead up the incline which started gradually enough, but rose steadily to a steep grade. "Why did you choose this place?"

"Part of a footprint . . ."

"Part?"

"Like those outside the cabin."

She frowned. "Shouldn't we look for more than part of a track?"

"We take what we can get. Whoever this feller is, he's mighty good at covering his trail."

She climbed after him, hand over hand, grabbing at jutting rocks, crawling as much as climbing, expending as much energy pulling her cumbersome skirts out of the way as she did actually motivating up the hill. How she longed to remove her jacket, which soon became wet and restricted her movements even more.

"Be careful where you put your hands," he called back. "This sunshine'll draw out every rattler in the country."

She recoiled in horror. "Rattlesnakes?"

"Don't get spooked. If there's one on the trail, I'll likely scare him away before you come along. Pays to be on the lookout, though."

The next move was the hardest she could recall ever making. Stiffened muscles froze her joints, and she spent more time searching for snakes than she did climbing.

Pausing to rest a moment, she glanced back, but the spring was hidden now by trees growing on this side of it. The opposite hillside was not, though, and as she looked across the canyon, she wondered if the gunman had been a good enough marksman to pick them off the side of this bluff.

Finally Quint heaved himself onto a flat ledge of limestone above her. He reached his hand down and pulled her up beside him.

After she caught her breath, she removed her jacket, and let the slight breeze cool her through her—or Mavis's—silk blouse. She had almost forgotten what they came for when she heard a low whistle behind her.

"Looks like we hit the jackpot."

Sure enough, the cave was well stocked. In the center she saw a ring of blackened rocks with charred wood inside.

"That's an Indian midden," he told her.

She smiled. "Yes, I know. We had Indians back in Tennessee, too."

He grinned. "Never thought of it thataway."

While she searched for anything belonging to her father, Quint searched, also.

"It's all here," he said at last. "Everything missing from the cabin."

"Do you see anything that belongs to Sancho?" she asked.

He shook his head. "I'm not the one to ask. I didn't know the boy that well. But I'd lay you a dollar to a hunk of bear sign that . . ."

"To what?" Most of the time she could figure out what he meant. Then there were times, as now, when he might as well have been speaking a foreign language.

"Bear sign," he repeated, grinning. "Don't tell me you never heard of bear sign."

"No, but it doesn't sound like anything I would want, even if I won it."

"It's some of the finest eating you've ever sunk your teeth into, that's what it is," he replied. "Why, any cook worth his salt knows how to make bear sign."

She walked over to him and put her arms around his

waist. "Even you?"

Sighing with his intense delight in her, he replied, "Even me. I'll stir you up a batch one of these days."

She raised her lips to him provocatively. "In the cabin?"

He squeezed her tight against him and nipped at her lips. "What I started to say, when I was interrupted, was that I'd lay you . . ."

"A dollar to a hunk of bear sign that what?"

"That our thief and friend Sancho are one and the same critter."

She stepped out of his embrace, instantly intrigued by this information. "Where do you suppose he is now?"

"No telling."

She looked around the cave. "Then we'll wait."

"Now hold on a minute. What're you figuring on doing?"

"We'll wait for Sancho."

He shook his head. "That's not such a good idea, Holly."

"Why not?" she asked.

"For one thing, we aren't certain it's Sancho."

She shrugged. "We'll wait and find out."

"It might turn out to be somebody you'd rather not meet up with," he said. "Besides, you've already been gone from town one night. If I don't bring you in there before sundown today, Mavis will have my hide."

She thought about it. Of course he was right. She shouldn't worry them more, but she had to find Sancho.

"They'll know I'm safe with you."

He raised a blond eyebrow. "After two nights, Mavis will think what everyone else in town will think," he said. "And you don't want her thinking that."

A smile lit her face at his mention of the previous night, but when she looked up at him, her smiled faded. Something was wrong . . . the tone of his voice, the . . . Suddenly she heard Aggie instead, suggesting that Quint and Mavis were . . .

"I don't want her to think?" she demanded. "Or *you* don't want her to think? Which is it, Quint?"

"But your reputation . . ." he began, confused.

She clenched her jaws against the tears that sprang to her eyes. A great sense of despair engulfed her as she recalled his eagerness to get away from the cabin this morning, his determination that she didn't belong in this country—as if Mavis were better suited for this country than she herself! she thought bitterly. And now his concern that Mavis not discover that they were lovers. How dare he? How dare he! "My reputation." She spat the words at him in fury. "How convenient."

She walked around the darkened cave, searching for something to write on. She would leave Sancho a message.

Quint grapped her arm, but she pulled away.

"Holly, what . . . ?"

"Don't worry," she said. "I'll be ready as soon as I find something to leave a message on."

He helped her, and they ended up writing on a flat rock with a piece of charcoal from the dead fire.

"Do you think he'll be able to read this?"

"Of course he can read," she snapped. "Papa taught him."

She stared out the mouth of the cave into the morning sun, its warmth fueling the hurt within her. Papa had tried to teach her, too, she thought, but she hadn't listened.

Quint offered to help her on the way down, but she refused. The trip was not easy, though, and before she reached the bottom, she carried, not only the jacket, but the boots, as well.

He led the horses to where she stood, but held her reins in his hands, and did not move to lift her into the saddle. When she started to mount on her own, he gripped her arm with a force that caused her to stare angrily at him.

"Hold your horses," he said. "Before we ride out of here, you're telling me what's got you so riled up."

"Nothing." She jerked to free her arm.

He shook his head. "Something I said set you on the warpath. Something about Mavis or your reputation or . . ."

"It really doesn't matter," she muttered between clenched teeth.

He spoke in deep, barely controlled tones. "It damned sure does matter. Now what is it?"

Her heart raced, and she felt claustrophobic. "I . . . ah, I had forgotten a few things the past couple of days, that's all." She tried to sound offhand, as if it really didn't matter, as if she . . . She swallowed back a sob.

"Forgotten what?" he demanded.

She eased away from him, determined to put her foot in the stirrup, but he grasped her about the waist, turning her around and holding her in a savage embrace.

She struggled furiously.

"Damn it, Holly! Be still. What's gotten into you?"

She stopped struggling, blinking desperately to hold back tears. Why had she forgotten about Mavis? Why hadn't she remembered what Aggie said?

"Holly, last night was special for me. I thought you said it was for you, too."

"It was," she whispered before she could stop herself.

And what about your nights with Mavis? she thought. Were they special, too? One thing she knew, she could not, would not, share him with anyone—not with Mavis, not with anyone.

He forced her chin up and kissed her lips brutally in an effort to force her to relent to him . . . to love him, and in spite of herself, she returned his kiss with growing ardor.

A sense of relief and fear mingled to flood her with confusion. Where was the fight in her anyway? Couldn't she fight for the man she loved? She didn't have to fold like a wilted bluebonnet at the mention of a rival, not even one as beautiful as Mavis O'Keefe.

Molding herself to his powerful body, she sighed with unabashed passion. There last two days had been so wonderful, just the two of them alone . . . so peaceful . . .

Peaceful? She giggled, and he looked at her with a mixture of curiosity and relief. "What is it?"

She stared to the depths of his glistening, questioning eyes, throwing him a challenge with her own. Whoever the enemy, she'd defeat her; whatever the fight, she'd win. And the victory would be theirs to share—hers and Quint's. She gave him a quick peck on the lips. "Let's go now."

After helping her into the saddle, he handed her the jacket she had dropped. "Here's your jacket."

"Mavis's jacket," she corrected, stuffing it behind her saddle. Everything around here seemed to belong to Mavis.

Well, she'd fix that. Tomorrow she would move out of Mavis's hotel and into Papa's house. That would be a start, anyhow.

* * *

It took a little more time than that. A week to be exact, during which time Holly worked on the house daily, determined to make good her promise to herself to move from the hotel as soon as possible.

The week, however, did not hold what she had envisioned, for upon their return to Silver Creek, Quint found a telegram waiting for him from the Llano County sheriff, requesting a meeting at Fort Mason. So Quint set out immediately, stopping only long enough for a clean shirt and a bite to eat.

She stood on the steps watching him ride away, the feel of his touch lingering on her arm where he had squeezed it and said, "This won't take long."

Not even a brief kiss. She knew he was thinking again of her reputation, what with all of Silver Creek on the porch beside them, but it wouldn't have embarrassed her, not one whit.

Mavis linked arms with her drawing her toward the hotel, and half-whispered in her ear, "Holly, darling, you have a lot to tell."

"It will have to wait, Mavis. Right now all I want is a hot bath and a long rest. I'm exhausted."

Mavis smiled. "I can imagine. Two days and a night in the wilds, alone with Quintan Jarvis!"

"Mavis! How could you?" Holly swished past the proprietress and up the stairs, indignant, but with a burning on her cheeks she knew was obvious to all.

In her room she took off the soiled riding habit and threw on Mavis's robe. Mavis's this. Mavis's that. Her entire life seemed to belong to Mavis O'Keefe. Would she ever again have anything truly her own?

A knock came at the door, and she opened it to admit Possum and the welcome sitz tub. She sighed. Mavis's thoughtfulness.

"Glad you're home safe, Doc," Possum greeted her.

"I'll bring your hot water directly."

She thanked him and fell upon the bed as he closed the door. How long would Quint be gone? Already her heart ached with loneliness, and her limbs were weak with longing for his touch.

Was he on a dangerous mission? What business did he have with the Llano County sheriff this time? And why did some other sheriff need Quint? Especially right now. *She* needed him now.

But she worked things out on her own, and when Quint rode back into town a week later, he was amazed at the progress she had made with the house.

"You've been busy while I was gone!" He walked in on her arranging furniture which Mavis insisted she bring from the attic of the hotel.

This time there was no hesitation on either part. They rushed into each other's arms, eager to fill the yearning emptiness brought on by their separation.

Reeling with the impact of his lips, his mouth, his probing tongue—back where they belonged, consuming, devouring, ravishing her senses, Holly was conscious from the beginning of a very different feeling this time.

This time she had known he would come back to her. She had known he would rush to her side, smother her with his dizzying love. And in that knowledge security and contentment had grown within her. Now, pressing her body to his, she opened her lips wider, anxious to follow wherever this newfound freedom led.

Drinking in the familiar sweetness of her kisses, Quint's arms roamed her small back, caressing, massaging, kneading her to his love-starved body. Her passionate response set his blood to boiling, and he kissed her deeply.

Suddenly his wandering hands stopped; his fingers

examined her scantily clad back through the flowing calico dress. No corset?

With a grin, he pulled their lips apart and stared mischievously into her questioning brown eyes. "Were you expecting me, sweet Holly? Or do you have some other feller hidden in the woodpile?"

She blushed, recalling her immodest attire. Since she intended to spend the morning working around her house, she'd decided to wear one of Mavis's black calico wrappers. Its high neckline and long sleeves covered her properly, but underneath she wore only bloomers and one petticoat, and although the wrapper's lining buttoned snugly over her bosom, outwardly it was a totally unrestrained garment, requiring no corset.

Encouraged by her newborn confidence, she grinned back at him, teasing, "And you, sir? What am *I* to assume with you coming in from a week's hard ride, smelling of bay rum instead of horse sweat? Did you think you were calling on a loose woman?"

He swallowed against his rising Adam's apple and gazed longingly into the velvet depths of her challenging eyes, pleased she had noticed his efforts to spruce up for her. "I'm calling on *my* woman," he said, his rich voice veiled with rising passion. "And she'd better be loose . . . for me."

Her whole body quivered with warm desire, and her smiling lips reached for him, but his eyes glanced about the clean, barren room—no sofa, no bed . . .

Reading his thoughts, she took his hand and quietly led him into the bedroom, where she closed the door behind them.

Still no bed, he thought, recalling how the mattress had been shredded. But the pile of quilts in the middle of the floor would do . . . this time.

He reached toward her, and with sure hands, grasped her wrapper and attempted to lift it over her head. When it caught up somehow, he looked at her quizzically. "How do you women come up with such damned troublesome contraptions?"

Laughing delightedly at his confusion, she showed him the lining, which he unbuttoned. Then, quickly discarding the dress, they cast aside the remainder of their clothing and came together on the tumbled heap of quilts, holding each other close with all the longing their separation had brewed within them.

Finally they drew apart, and he bathed her with his eyes, seeing for the first time in broad-open daylight the sheer beauty of her fragile loveliness. His sun-bronzed hand stroked her alabaster breasts, the contrast filling him with both tenderness and raw desire.

Trailing his fingers down her skin, he played leisurely around the small indentation of her navel, then slowly progressed to the breathtaking sight of the tight little curls, black as soot, which guarded her womanhood. Trembling with anticipation, he pulled his fingers lightly through the soft curls and watched them spring languidly back into place.

His hands cooled her fevered breasts, and Holly lay her head back lazily, relishing his light touch on her midriff, her navel. When he reached the matted curls at the junction of her thighs, she arched herself against him, swooning with swelling desire for what she knew would come.

At her sensuous movements, Quint swept her to him with his other arm. His lips met hers, demandingly warm and wet, while his fingers slowly, enticingly, inched through the silken curls to stroke her tender, heated flesh.

The infuriating slowness with which Quint caressed

her sent Holly's mind spinning. Desperately she pushed against him, willing him to find entrance to her secret core. And when finally she felt his fingers slip inside her tightened flesh, she was overcome with such fierce passion that she pulled her lips from his and wantonly offered him her aching, throbbing breasts.

Once he had gotten past his terror of making love to a lady, and his bugaboo about Holly not being happy in this country, Quint had feared their relationship would change.

And it had, he now recognized. But subtly, and in a way he would never have dreamed. At last he felt free with her. He knew he loved her; and he knew she loved him. And despite what he had always believed about married love, he was now inclined to feel he had been right when he told her their love would keep on getting better and better.

As he stroked, caressed, and fondled the most intimate parts of her, he knew she was all the woman he would ever need or want, and this knowledge brought him joy as great as the bursting desire she called forth from every nerve ending in his body.

Their desire, intensified as it was by a week's separation, brought their lovemaking to its peak long before either of them wanted. But after their joining, lying together comfortably, they felt satisfied with the act completed, and with the mutual understanding that there was more, much more love ahead for them to share.

Lazily she moved her head around and looked into his honey-gold eyes, her voice soft and quiet. "I can't wait to move into this house, even if most of the furnishings will belong to Mavis. Someday . . ."

"Someday we'll have a place of our own with our own things." He leaned down and kissed the top of her head. "I'll try hard to make you happy, sweet Holly, to make up for all that's happened to you."

She snuggled against him. "You've already done that, Quint. I'm happier than I ever dreamed possible."

Later, they dressed, and he watched her loop and pin her hair. "I'm only sorry Papa can't be here to see how happy I am," she told him.

He grunted. "After reading his letters, I've an idea he wouldn't approve of me at all. Fact is, he'd likely send you as far away from me as he could get you."

"Not even Papa could separate me from you, Quint Jarvis. You're stuck with me, whether you like it or not."

But she sighed as the mention of Papa's letters turned her thoughts to Tom Farrell and Papa's property and Farrell's claim that he never sold Papa any land.

She said nothing then, not wanting to bring a sour note to Quint's homecoming. A few days later, however, when she walked back to the hotel for supper, she saw Quint talking with Wilt and Luther in back of the livery stable. They sat on the corral fence, boots hooked over the rail, engaged in what looked to be an intense conversation.

A frown creased her brow, and a tightening came in her stomach. What did this mean? She recalled seeing them in the same kind of conversation outside the saloon the day she returned from visiting Papa's grave for the first time.

After supper, when she and Quint sat alone in a swing on the porch, she broached the subject. "What are Wilt and Luther doing back from the trail drive?"

He looked surprised, then replied, "Perkins sent them in for supplies."

"Is that what you were discussing at the corral?" She

didn't want to sound nosy, yet a sense of foreboding pushed her along.

"They're old friends, Holly." He studied her a moment, seriously. "They had nothing to do with the trouble between Tom and me."

She wanted to believe that that was the extent of their relationship. Common sense told her to accept it as that and forget about it. But something nagged at her, telling her things were not as he said. What could he be keeping from her? And why? Hadn't he practically said they would wed? Practically.

And had Tom Farrell not raised Quint as his own son? Blood ties often proved stronger than any others. Didn't much of her uneasiness come from her own father labeling Quint a renegade? Struggling against Papa's opinion had been hard enough, even when Papa wasn't here to reinforce or deny it. But what about Quint?

Surely he had bonds with Tom Farrell which went deeper than the tender new ones he professed to be forming with her.

And if Tom Farrell were indeed responsible for Papa's murder, as she was sure he was, how could she and Quint ever have a life together?

The days that followed were filled with mixed pleasures. When she was with Quint, she was sure he loved her and was incapable of condoning wrong-doing, no matter who was responsible. But when they were apart, she doubted.

And her doubts plagued her. Why had she fallen in love so freely? Why had she not remained the level-headed daughter who came here fired with resolve to find her father's killers, then return home to Tennessee where she belonged?

She realized nothing would ever be the same for her

again. And her fear of loneliness was stronger, now that she had known Quint. He had filled her to overflowing, body and soul, with his passion and his love. She recoiled in a terror more real and decimating than any physical fear she had ever known at the thought of life without him. But if he proved untrue? What would life be then?

He was around almost constantly, however, and she had little time to worry over the future. One afternoon he arrived with an armload of supplies from Mr. Crump's store and busied himself in the kitchen while she arranged the bedroom with a day bed which Mavis had sent over.

She would tend patients on it by day, and use it to sleep on at night. Combined with Papa's desk, a shabby old armoire, and a screen to shield her personal toiletries, it turned the bedroom into a respectable office.

When she finished, she followed the aroma of Quint's cooking to the kitchen, filled with curiosity as to what he was about.

"Doughnuts!" She clapped her hands in delight at his culinary ability.

He grinned like a schoolboy. "Bear sign!"

As final preparation for moving into the house, she stopped by the mercantile—still a tent, but the building was quickly taking shape—to add to the provisions she had already purchased. She asked Mr. Crump about calico, thinking how lovely curtains would look on her windows. And they would be one thing in the house of her own doing.

"Lordy, ma'am," Herman Crump responded. "Calico was fetchin' a right handsome price when I was down to San Antone. Fifty dollars a yard or better. Luda said folks could weave their own cloth, 'fore spendin' hard-earned dollars thataway."

After carrying her packages back to the house, she returned to the hotel shortly before noon. She hadn't heard a word from Elena. And Sancho hadn't replied to her message.

Had he found it? Was the thief in the cave really Sancho? Perhaps the boy was far away from here by now, and the thief merely that, a thief.

Being early for dinner, she decided to check on Davy Westfield and found him sitting in his window, as usual. But she knew he was better since cutting out the calomel, because he had been eating more at mealtime. He looked up when she entered and responded to her conversation.

"I visited Mr. Crump's store today," she told him. "Have you seen the building going on over there?"

He shook his head, interest creeping into his eyes.

She held out her hand. "Come on, then. Let's go take a look before dinner."

He stood, and although he didn't take her hand, he followed her into the hallway.

Stopping at the tall windows on the landing, she looked down at the vulnerable child. "We can get a good view from this window," she suggested, fearing to push him to go outdoors.

They watched Herman Crump measure and saw boards on a sawhorse in the rear, while Possum nailed the boards onto a side wall. It was a lively scene, and Davy rested his chin in his hands, enthralled with the activity.

"Possum looks like he's having a good time," Holly said.

Davy nodded.

"I'm sure Mr. Crump could use your help, too," she suggested.

His eyes widened.

"Would you like me to talk to him?"

He paused, then gave a minute nod of his head without taking his eyes away from the building across the street.

Holly inhaled deeply, prayed she was doing the right thing, and asked Davy the question she had wanted to put to him ever since she first learned that he and Sancho were friends.

"Have you . . . ah, have you seen your friend, Sancho, around lately?" She tried to sound casual and was startled when he abruptly turned his head and stared at her with hostility.

"Why do you want to know?" he demanded.

She shrugged. "I just wondered. You were friends, weren't you?"

He cocked his head slightly.

"Sancho was a friend of Papa's, too. I would like to find him, to see if he's all right. I'm sure Papa would want me to watch out for him."

He continued to stare at her, but she could see his features relax a bit.

"I don't want him to be alone and hungry," she said.

"He isn't hungry." Davy stood up and walked toward his room without another word.

Holly's heart sank. Had she undone everything she had accomplished with the boy? Perhaps she should have kept quiet about Sancho. Perhaps . . .

She stood up, deep in thought, her eyes traveling absently over the scene across the street, down the street.

Suddenly she saw two men ride out of the brush behind the saloon. Wilt and Luther.

They sat their horses at the edge of the clearing, looking about, searching . . .

She stood transfixed, watching them with an eerie

sense of foreboding.

Then another rider emerged from behind the livery stable, and hot panic swirled in the pit of her stomach.

The three riders disappeared behind the thicket.

Wilt and Luther.

And Quintan Jarvis.

Chapter Ten

Of course he denied that they had been hiding—that he was engaged in anything sinister or secretive with the TF ranchhands.

"You'll have to trust me, Holly," he said. "Please."

She looked into his honey-colored eyes, seeing not the golden passion which had lighted her life with so much love, but a cold, metallic-hard reflection of her own wrath. Trust him? She sighed, holding back welling tears. How she wanted to trust him.

But someone had murdered Papa. Someone connected with the TF, she was sure. And the things Papa had written about Quintan Jarvis . . . If she were ever forced to choose between the trustworthiness of the two of them . . .

Please don't let me have to make that choice, she prayed, and she clung to him fiercely, trying to drive the rendezvous with Wilt and Luther from her mind, while his kisses rekindled her need for him and pushed Papa's letters into the past.

A few afternoons later as she returned to the hotel, she was of a lighter frame of mind. Tomorrow morning she would move into Papa's house for good. And surely Sancho would come soon. If not, she would get

Quint to ride to the canyon with her again. Perhaps he could use his friendship with the TF ranchhands to get in touch with Elena. Why hadn't she thought of that before?

Stepping onto the boardwalk which ran along past the saloon, Mr. Crump's Mercantile, and the sheriff's office, she was so immersed in her thoughts that she jumped at a yell which jolted her back to the present.

"Waahoo! Lookee who I see!" Jim Tom Farrell stumbled onto the boardwalk, leaving Wilt to tie his horse and Luther to step after him cautiously.

"If it ain't Little Miss Nightingale herself sashaying down the walk."

At his first step he appeared lame, but the next step revealed the obvious, Jim Tom Farrell, drunk as usual.

Her pulse quickened and her one thought was to escape. She wasn't afraid of him here in broad-open daylight with Quint in his office a couple of doors down, but neither did she intend to pass him and risk a pawing. So she stepped off the walk—a second too late.

Jim Tom lunged with a quickness that surprised her. He grabbed her arm and pulled her around.

"Wait up a minute, cutie pie. Ain't you even gonna say howdy to ol' Jim Tom?"

His grasp was firm, and she knew she couldn't get loose by force, so she gently maneuvered her arm about and smiled weakly. "Good day."

"Good day?" His mouse-colored beard was unkempt, and his coarse breeches and shirt showed signs of being worn several days too long. He gave another wild whoop and turned to Wilt and Luther. "Good day, she says. Now, ain't it a fine day for sure to be arunnin' into a fetchin' skirt like this?"

Wilt and Luther exchanged glances, and Wilt spoke first. "Let's get that drink, boss. I'm plumb dried out."

"Yeah," Luther added. "Come on in and let 'er be."

Jim Tom turned dancing eyes on his two sidekicks. His whiny voice was casual enough, but his words struck fear in Holly's heart. "Go ahead, boys. I don't need you for what I'm after."

She felt her knees quake, but she stiffened her back and jerked to free her arm. "Unhand me, Mr. Farrell."

He laughed. A menacing, rotten, drunken laugh. "Ah, you don't mean that, sugar." His fingers bit into her arm. "Come on, cutie pie. One little kiss for ol' Jim Tom."

She dodged as he leaned into her, smelling with drink and uncleaniness. He planted a slobbery kiss on her cheek and moved toward her mouth. She turned her head, at the same time, jerking to free herself.

His grasp was dislodged, but, as she flung herself away from him, he tightened his grip, tearing the sleeve from the left shoulder of her white shirtwaist, propelling her backward.

A shudder of repulsion overcame her as she landed with a splash in the water trough, where horses drank and Woody, in spite of her admonishments, insisted on washing out the spittoons.

"What's going on here?" Quint's voice rose in alarm when he saw her struggling to escape both the water trough and Jim Tom's threatening approach.

"Keep away from her," he shouted, rushing to Holly's aid. He helped her up, while fending off Jim Tom with his other hand, and nodding to Wilt and Luther. "Quieten him down, boys."

Jim Tom didn't give Wilt and Luther time to reach him before he dived at Quint, sneering, "Let's see what you're made of now that Pa ain't around to stop us."

Quint caught Jim Tom's arm in full swing and held it, but the younger man jerked away and landed a blow to the sheriff's jaw.

Quint wrestled with him, struggling to pin Jim Tom's

arms behind him. Finally he succeeded in throwing an undercut to the young man's knees. Jim Tom stumbled to the ground, where Quint twisted his arms behind him and called to Wilt and Luther.

"Come get him and take him home."

Holly's mouth dropped open. "Take him home?" Quint had obviously been interested only in restraining Jim Tom, not fighting him, and now he was merely sending him home? No reprimand? No jail? She stared, silenced by an apprehension that crept up her spine, freezing her in her tracks.

Quint didn't look at her, addressing instead Jim Tom. "What are you doing back from the drive?"

Jim Tom spat into the dirt in front of Quint, splattering the latter's boots. "That damned ol' Perkins," he said. "He's so straitlaced you could shave with him. Don't allow a feller even a smidgen of a drink."

Quint shook his head. "So you got kicked off the drive for drinking? I'm sure Tom's real proud of that."

Holly regained partial use of her senses then, and stepped closer to the fracas. "I want to press charges, Sheriff," she demanded, loathing her soft, trembling voice.

Wilt and Luther stopped in their motion to pick up Jim Tom, then proceeded when Quint nodded to them to carry out his orders.

"You ain't got no right to treat me thisaway, Quint." Jim Tom sounded a trifle less drunk, but still threatening. "Pa ain't gonna like it. You owe him, Quint."

"Take him home, boys." Quint stepped aside as Wilt and Luther took hold of their young boss in a manner which said they were accustomed to such occasions.

"Quint," Holly protested. "I demand that you put this . . . this scoundrel in jail. He accosted me, and I am pressing charges." A strange sense of unreality swept over her. She stared incredulously at Quint, blinking back tears. What in the world was the matter with him? Didn't he even care how she was treated?

He refused to meet her eyes, and his words could as well have come from a total stranger. "Stay out of this, Holly. I'll handle it."

Wilt and Luther dragged a hollering Jim Tom to his horse.

"Are you going to ride out on your own?" Quint asked. "Or do we tie you across the saddle?"

Jim Tom looked from one to the other, as if deciding whether they would really do it, then apparently realized he was outnumbered. "You'll regret this, Quint. I swear it. Pa'll have your hide."

Wilt led Jim Tom's horse behind his own, while Luther pulled around behind and slapped the boy's mount on the rump.

Jim Tom swayed in the saddle, still hollering at Quint over his shoulder. "You owe Pa. You owe him, and you know what he expects in return."

Holly watched them go, dazed, empty, disgusted. She glared at Quint, who picked up his hat and slapped the dust off it against his leg.

Turning quickly toward the hotel, she heard him call her name, but she squared her shoulders and went inside, holding the sleeve of her torn dress in place.

She brushed aside Mavis and Aggie, who emerged from their window view with questions, and went straight up the stairs, not even stopping on the landing to reassure a startled Davy.

She walked straight and ridged and dry-eyed all the way to her room, carefully closed the door behind her, and stood with her back to it, her hands holding tightly to the cold doorknob, and tears began to flow silently down her cheeks.

They rolled gently at first, then faster in rivers, until

great sobs racked her shoulders and heaved in her chest. She threw herself on the bed and cried and cried and cried, stopping now and again to draw a handkerchief from her sleeve and blow her nose, only to have the sobs start up once more. She shook from head to foot, her eyes closed tightly, her muscles tensed.

All the way from the street, up the stairs, and to her room one question had echoed through her brain. Why? Why? Why?

Finally the sobs subsided, and she rolled over on her back and stared up at the gaily flowered ceiling paper. But that only reminded her of the flowers along the river where she and Quint had walked this week, talking of their future, and her sobs returned in full force, this time to the accompaniment of her inner voice: you should have known; you should have listened to Papa.

Papa had always been right. He had always known what was best for her. And he always would.

Except he wasn't here anymore.

Sobs again engulfed her, smothering, choking. Oh, Papa, Papa, Papa. They took you away from me. They killed you. And I almost . . .

The pain was physical, like someone actually squeezed her heart in his fist. Why? her heart cried. Why? And her soul echoed her desperate cry.

The answer to her supplications came as a powerful surge of fury, welling from deep within her—from the doubts and uncertainties she had felt about Quintan Jarvis, even before she met him. Quint had betrayed her. No, she had betrayed Papa. No . . .

The door opened, and Mavis entered and seated herself on the bed. Mavis, so beautiful in her delicate yellow dress . . . so beautiful. But here's nothing delicate about her, Holly thought, as visions of Quint and Mavis sent her into another fit of sobbing.

Mavis put her hand gently on Holly's back, and Holly flinched. "Now, now, darling. Things can't be as bad as all that."

Still sobbing, Holly turned her anger on Mavis. How could she know? How could she, the frivolous and insensitive . . . ? Mavis, the widow, who should know. Mavis, who would never be alone.

"Darling, Quint is waiting for you downstairs. I'm sure there's a simple answer to all these tears."

Holly bit her knuckles so hard she tasted blood, but she didn't answer. She couldn't be rude to Mavis, but . . .

"Get up now, Holly. Let's find you something fresh to put on."

Holly gritted her teeth, her head swirling with more despair than she had ever imagined. She had to get away from this place. Far away. Quickly.

Mavis spread a fresh waist on the bed. "This one doesn't look too mussed. And here's some water to wash away all those tears." She wrung out a cloth in the basin and brought it to Holly.

The cloth felt cool on her feverish eyes, but her body remained numb and leaden.

"Up we go." Mavis eased gently at Holly's arm.

Holly jerked away. "Will you leave me alone, Mavis? Please. I'm not going downstairs."

"But he wants to explain, Holly."

Holly's fury rose. She pressed the cloth to her pounding temples and spat the words at Mavis. "There's nothing to explain."

"He looks so miserable, Holly. And he has a bad cut under his eye. You really should see to it."

Quint cut? A flicker of worry dampened her hurt, but only a flicker. It served him right. "He can take care of himself." Then an additional thought filled her with more anguish, and she said, "Why don't *you* tend his wound?"

"Holly, he asked me to fetch *you* . . ."

"I am not a dog, nor a horse, to be fetched at will." She sat up and took the fresh cloth Mavis extended to her, patting it on her swollen eyelids, hoping the coolness would relieve her aching head.

"But, Holly . . ." the proprietress began.

Holly raised her voice. "You entertain him, Mavis. It's evident from the way you flirt and carry on that you're the one who's after him. Well, you can have him. I want no part of this dastardly place or anyone in it."

"Me?" Mavis's Irish blood flamed in her face. "I am not after Quintan Jarvis. He isn't my type, and I certainly am not his. That's why we can flirt and carry on." Her voice lowered. "We're merely good friends, Holly, comfortable together."

Tears suddenly overflowed as Holly recalled that she and Quint had been comfortable together, too. But that was all over now.

"Besides, Holly, you won't get by with condemning me for flirting. You know as well as I that a girl doesn't set her cap for every man she flirts with." Mavis smiled indulgently. "You, darling, are just as guilty of flirting with Quint Jarvis as I."

"I have not flirted with him . . . I mean, that is . . . ah, that was different."

Mavis nodded her head. "Precisely. You and Quint do have something different—something very special."

"No! No, we don't!" Holly denied vehemently. "We never did."

Mavis glared at her. "What has he done that's so ghastly you deny ever caring for him?"

Holly buried her face in her hands. "Leave me alone, Mavis. Tell him I can't see him. Tell him I'm returning to Tennessee."

Mavis stood over her with hands on hips. "Oh, no. You're not getting by with that. That man down there loves you, and from the look of him, you've led him to believe you feel the same. If you've changed your mind, then you will tell him yourself."

Holly clenched her hands together. A sick feeling rose to her throat at the thought of facing Quint ever again. She couldn't. She couldn't.

But of course Mavis was right. Hadn't Mama told her the same thing a hundred times? And hadn't she seen girls brush off their beaux without so much as a word, to the horror of everyone who knew the poor young men?

This was different, though, she argued desperately with herself. She wasn't brushing Quint off in order to flit from beau to beau. And she couldn't face him. Tears squeezed through her closed eyelids and slid down her cheeks. Oh, dear God, how she loved him!

Mavis pulled her to her feet. "Come on."

Holly sagged limply back to the bed. "I can't, Mavis."

"That's a good man down there, Holly. You're not going to find one better, no matter how far you look."

Holly wiped furiously at the new, silent onslaught of tears.

"Give him a chance to explain." She handed Holly a glass of water, which Holly sipped, then crossed to the looking glass and vacantly patted her hair into some semblance of order. If only he would explain. If only he would. But she knew already that he wouldn't.

Hadn't she given him any number of chances? Hadn't she begged him to tell her about Wilt and Luther? About Troy Grant and whatever was going on at the TF? And hadn't he refused every time?

Mavis helped her change the torn blouse. "You're doing the right thing, Holly. I know you are. Everything will work out fine. You'll see."

Holly blinked her stinging eyes and looked around the dressing table, disoriented. "Tell him I'll be down in a minute." She would see him briefly, she told herself. Then she would feel better for having it over.

Mavis patted her shoulder, her voice indicating that she figured things had returned to normal. "Hurry up, now, darling. Don't keep him waiting."

The trip from her room to the parlor downstairs made her journey from Tennessee to Texas comparable to skipping a mud puddle. Her heart beat furiously in her chest, and her knees felt like the joints were frozen in place. One step she rebuked herself for going down in the first place, the next she prayed this whole mess was only a bad dream from which she would suddenly awaken, and the next step she knew there was no hope at all—until at the bottom she found herself in such a tumbled-up state that she feared she might swoon at his feet. She reproved herself sharply. She would not cry. She would not.

He met her at the foot of the stairs, and for an instant his hand on hers recalled that first night when he had handed her down from the stagecoach. She drew a sharp breath at his touch and gulped back a sob.

"Holly?" His voice betrayed his anxiety.

Avoiding his eyes, she lifted her chin and walked ahead of him into the parlor, taking a seat on a damask chair. She dared not risk the closeness of sitting beside him on the sofa.

"I'm glad you saw fit to come down." His voice was steady, she noticed, but apprehensive. Perhaps he knew what he had done and was sorry. Perhaps he . . . When he pulled his chair closer to hers, she scooted away as from an unclean person.

Sitting straight-backed on the edge of her seat, scarcely breathing, she clasped her hands tightly in her lap to keep their shaking from showing to him. "Mavis said I should give you a chance to explain, " she began, "but I told her that explanations don't appear to fit your character." She clamped her jaws together. Why did her voice have to tremble so?

"Do you always throw brickbats before you hear one word?" he demanded. Her puffy red eyes and pale cheeks sent pains of remorse through him, but her highfalutin tone infuriated him. They had a good thing between them, and he was sure if he could take her in his arms, he could soothe her ruffled feathers. He also knew any attempt to do that would be rebuffed.

"I would say I'm entitled to throw brickbats," she retorted. "I was just accosted on the streets of this town, and the sheriff did nothing but send the offender home to the protection of his father. The sheriff who . . . who professed to . . ." She broke off, too near tears to continue.

Helplessly he reached toward her, but she drew away. "I stopped him, Holly. I didn't let him hurt you. I got him out of your sight . . . and out of mine." He finished with such vehemence in his usually mellow voice that she looked up, startled.

But still she persisted. "Any other drunk would have been arrested and thrown in jail for such behavior. But not Jim Tom Farrell."

"Holly . . ."

"Your alliance with the Farrells is obvious," she broke in. "I've been addlebrained to believe you're any different then they are."

Her accusations rankled him, but he held onto his anger. "It isn't what you think," he said carefully. "I swear it."

She looked directly at him for the first time, then, and her fiery ardor met his with the power of a thunderbolt. She turned away quickly to avoid surrendering herself on the spot to those glistening eyes she had loved so . . . Desperately pushing past pleasures from her mind, she continued. "Then tell me, who are Wilt and Luther?"

"Old friends," he answered stubbornly.

"Why do you hide behind bushes and buildings to talk with friends?"

"Listen to me, Holly. Wilt and Luther . . ." He stopped, suddenly filled with exasperation for this stubborn woman. He couldn't tell her about the posse; that would endanger her life and everyone else's. But why did she need to know, anyhow? Why in hell couldn't she take his word for it? Why couldn't she trust him?

Looking at her once-passionate body sitting there so prim and proper, his exasperation rose as heated anger from the pit of his stomach. His jaws clenched, and he felt like walking out right this minute. But he continued. "As sheriff, I make the best judgments I know how—for *all* the people in this community."

Lowering his voice automatically, he found himself trying, for some reason unknown to himself, to explain to her. "I have a job to do, Holly, and a lot of folks are depending on me. If I'd put Jim Tom in jail today, it would have ruined everything."

She stared unseeing at the patterned rug on the parlor floor. His words made no sense to her; they were just alibis, excuses. And she needed no more of either. "I thought *I* could depend on you, too." She flung the words in hostility, trying to cover the hurt she really felt. "But obviously we have different views of the job of a sheriff." She inhaled deeply. "And of a gentleman."

He knotted his fist and fought down the urge to knock some sense into her. He'd never hit a woman, and pray God he never would, but damn it all! This woman put a burr in his saddle blanket! "Give me time, Holly. You'll understand if you'll give me time."

She lifted her head and stared at the opposite window for a long time before speaking again. "I've thought about it a great deal this week, Quint," she said finally, "and I do understand. Truly, I do."

Not trusting her suddenly agreeable tone, he raised his brow curiously. When she spoke again, his eyes dimmed as if a coal-oil lamp had suddenly been extinguished in a dark room.

"Tom Farrell is your father in much the same way that Papa is mine," she explained. Holding up her hand to gesture, she saw it quiver and quickly returned it to the protection of her lap. "And Jim Tom, your brother . . . and Wilt and Luther . . ."

Her image blurred before the red-hot anger which seeped into his spinning brain from his gut. "Stop it, Holly." Why was she so confounded hardheaded? he wondered. She always did have trouble listening, but he hadn't known until now that she didn't reason worth a damn, either!

"It's true," she continued. "I love my father; you love yours. I know how dedicated I am to Papa—to his ideals, to his opinions." She looked at her lap and had no heart to speak, yet she knew she must finish. "I can expect no less from you. I understand your ties with Tom Farrell."

Suddenly she found herself looking at him, pleading with him. "Don't you see? I know Tom Farrell murdered my father, so . . . so you can't have us both, Quint. I won't have Jim Tom sitting at my table and Wilt and Luther at my fire. You have to choose between the Farrells and me." She looked away quickly, hoping he hadn't seen the tears brimming in her eyes. Swallowing back a sob, she forced her way back to anger, continuing with her voice low and slow and final. "And today you chose."

Quint glared at her, dumbfounded by her reasoning.

She loved him. He'd seen it in her face, felt it in her passionate response to his loving. She couldn't just turn it all off. "I chose you, Holly," he said simply, in that deep, rich voice that caused her to melt inside. "The first day I saw you, I chose you."

It took a moment for her shaking to subside enough that she could answer. "Not today, Quint," she whispered. "Today you chose your brother."

Jumping to his feet, Quint pulled her to face him, and she quaked at the fury she saw in his face. His fingers bit into the flesh of her arms; his voice, when he spoke, was hard and cold as steel. "I have a right to expect something, too," he shouted. "Your trust and patience for a change."

She pulled away, the memory of his touch still burning her arm. This was nonsense, she thought. Why couldn't they stop it? They loved each other. Nothing else mattered. Tears rose in her eyes, and she quickly doused them with rage, recalling Jim Tom's menacing attack on her. Yes, it did matter. Quint's alliance with the Farrells would affect their future.

"How patient must I be?" she demanded. "I've asked you three times this week about Wilt and Luther. And today . . . today you . . ." She pressed her lips together, thinking of his rejection in the street today. "Don't you think I want to trust you? But after . . ."

"When the time comes, Holly, you'll understand everything. When the time comes . . ."

"When the time comes for what, Quint? What are you waiting for? For Jim Tom to drag some woman down and rape her on Main Street?"

His fury incensed, he shouted at her again. "You know me better than that. I would never let anything like that happen." He clamped his jaws tight, then continued in a lowered tone. "I promise you, Holly. I will take care of the Farrells . . . when the time comes."

She shook her head in disgust. "The time will never come for you to cross Tom Farrell. I've seen that from the beginning." She left, then turned in the doorway and met his gaze head-on. The pain in his golden eyes was almost her undoing, but she took a deep breath to steel herself against a future she knew would be unbearable. "And the time will never come for us, either," she whispered across the room.

They didn't say good-bye, but it was in their eyes, the bitterest of all the good-byes she'd ever had to face.

And her idea that she would feel better when it was behind her was wrong. She felt worse, she soon discovered, much worse. Worse, even, then when she had received the telegram announcing Papa's death. Or when she found Mama lying dead from yellow fever that misty morning at Hedgerow.

Quintan Jarvis had been the one good thing that had happened to her in all these dastardly years. And now that dream, too, had become a nightmare.

Why hadn't she listened to Papa? He had warned her, but she had ignored him. Why?

She sat on her bed until dusk. Not crying. She had cried all her tears. Now she sat dry and hollow and empty.

Empty.

Rosie's supper bell sounded a painful reminder of the meals they had shared at Mavis's elegant table. A few moments later the door opened a space, and Davy Westfield's towhead peered around, his eyes as big as saucers in his pale face.

"You want to go to supper with me?" he asked.

She shook her head.

He tiptoed across the room and sat beside her. After a while he spoke in a voice which had been matured by tragedy. "I used to cry a lot, too."

She looked at him, startled, then reached for his

hand, and he did not resist. "I haven't been acting very grown-up, have I?" she asked.

"That's all right. Everyone gets sad sometimes. When Ma and Pa were killed by those Injuns, I was really sad. Granny was there, but it wasn't the same."

She swallowed the lump in her throat. "I know."

"Granny's awful nice, but . . . well, when Sancho and me got to be friends, everything was better."

"I'm sure it was." Her heart warmed at this dear, troubled boy trying so hard to comfort her. Then he quietly made his greatest effort to offer her solace.

"I saw him 'bout a week ago."

She was too numb for his statement to sink in at first, then she realized what he had said. "Sancho?"

He nodded.

She looked closely at his pale, still face. "Where?"

"It was dark, and he acted like he didn't want anybody to see him, so I stayed real quiet and watched him from my window. He crawled from one bush to another. Then he went 'round behind the smokehouse."

So it was true. Sancho had been here. "What was he doing back there?"

Davy shrugged. "I saw him sneak back, and he had a bundle in his arms. Like a big ham or something. I guess he was hungry."

Last week, even this morning, this information would have elated her. Now, it fell as on deaf ears, but for Davy's sake, she tried not to show it.

"Why do you think he was hiding?"

"He couldn't come out in the open, 'cause someone's after him with no good in mind."

She frowned. "How do you know that?"

"Two men stopped me down behind the springhouse one day," he said after a brief pause. "Not long after Doc Holly died. They wanted to know if I knew where Sancho was."

"What did you tell them?"

"Nothing. I didn't know where he was. But they were real mean-like. Said if I found out and didn't tell 'em, they'd have my ears for supper."

Holly gasped, and Davy snickered.

"Doesn't sound like a very good supper, does it?" he asked.

"Who were they?"

Davy shrugged.

Her heart quickened. "Do you know Wilt and Luther?"

"Sure."

"Were they the ones?" she asked, sure she had found another ghastly piece to the puzzle which tied Quint to these terrible men.

"Nope," he said. Then after a moment of silence, he added, "But they were dressed like 'em."

She sighed. Ninety percent of the men out here dressed like Wilt and Luther.

Davy pulled at her arm. "Come on. We'll be late for supper."

Much to her surprise, she was hungry, but when she thought of sitting at table with Quint, her heart beat a fevered staccato. "I'm not coming down tonight, Davy." He looked so disappointed, however, that she added, "You can have Rosie send me a tray."

He smiled and ran for the door. "Sure, Doc."

"And Davy," she called after him. "Thanks for coming to see me . . . and for sharing your secret. Maybe together we can find Sancho.

Woody picked up the near-empty rye bottle and wiped the counter underneath. Replacing the bottle, he studied his lone customer. "There goes Rosie's supper bell, Sheriff. If you think you can hobble acrost the street with a bottle of rye in your belly, we'd best get movin'."

Quint poured the last of the rye into his glass. "Go ahead without me."

Woody eyed his customer. "There ain't enough rye in the state of Texas to cure calico fever."

Quint cocked his head. "Hell, Woody, I ain't got woman troubles. I just swore off 'em . . . for good." He belted down his drink and slapped the glass on the bar. "What I can't figure out, though, is how come the good Lord'd make something so sweet to look at, and then pour her brains in with a teaspoon."

Chapter Eleven

Holly's misery took the form of no appetite for breakfast, or rather, no appetite for sharing a meal with Quintan Jarvis; nor for the inquisition she knew Mavis and Aggie had in store for her.

So she dressed hurriedly and, while the others were at table, sneaked out the back way to Papa's house, leaving behind a note on the hall table instructing Possum to bring along all her remaining belongings, including the trunk.

Last night, determined to start life anew, she had gone through the trunk and removed the shredded garments. These she left, along with a message, asking Aggie to reconstruct them into simple wearable costumes.

Her transformation might as well begin with shedding Mavis's widow's weeds. Then she would find Elena. Perhaps Elena would return to Tennessee with her. That was a thought. Although, once she escaped this miserable place, she wanted nothing in her life to ever remind her of these last dastardly weeks.

Her well of tears had been restored during the night and now continually threatened to overflow. But she was tough. She had come through troublesome times before, and, as Papa told her before he left for the war, they needn't expect life to be anything but difficult—not ever again.

One more instance when she had not heeded his warning, she thought dismally. How she regretted not listening to him. To the truth he wrote about Tom Farrell and his men, especially Quint. Why had she given her heart so freely, so quickly, like a schoolgirl?

And her body? She cringed inside, sick with the recollection of their wanton lovemaking. What a fool she had been. Would she ever shake these memories?

But the most painful part of all—and the hardest for her to understand—was that she loved him still. Even though he had lied to her and tried to cover up who knows what; even though the bond between them was broken forever, her thoughts of him were not bitter. All the bitterness she reserved for herself, for her own foolishness.

Her thoughts of him were . . . his hand squeezing her neck, touching her face . . . She slapped herself hard on the cheek. Stop it. Stop it. Stop it. She could handle this . . . this unpleasantry. She *would* handle it.

Tears rolled silently down her face. But could she live without Quintan Jarvis? Did she even want to try?

The sound of running feet alerted her, and she rushed to the door in time to see Davy Westfield dash full speed into the yard and up the steps.

"What is it?" she asked, alarmed.

He drew in his breath excitedly. "I just felt like running."

Kneeling down, she hugged him to her. He had emerged from his cocoon, and she prayed he would not be crushed by life again. But, like Papa said, the going wouldn't be easy, and soon Davy would have to learn to pick up the pieces of his life himself and go on.

Not long before noon she became alarmed that

Mavis, in her ever-helpful way, would send Quint with a basket for dinner, so to stave off such an unthinkable occurrence, she turned to Davy. "How would you like to have a picnic?"

"Oh, boy!"

"Then run up to the hotel and ask Rosie to fix us a lunch. Just for the two of us. No one else. We have a lot to talk over."

He was off in a flash, and she felt guilty for using him in this manner. But wasn't this exactly what they had hoped for—Davy out and running about again? A picnic couldn't hurt him, and it might save her own sanity.

The picnic, as it turned out, was not such a good idea. For even though she chose a different spot from where she and Quint had sat, it was still the same grass, the same river, the same flowers and trees.

Stop it, Holly! she admonished herself. She could learn to live in the same world with him and still forget. It would take time, that's all. A little time.

They had finished the fried chicken and started on the mincemeat pie, when Possum burst onto the scene.

"It's Soly, Doc! He's in his wagonyard, and he's broke his leg. Bad. You gotta hurry!"

Taking up her shawl and the medical bag, she rushed after him with Davy close behind.

"Tell me as much as you can before we get there."

"Didn't you hear it?" Possum asked.

"What?"

"The break?" he said. "It sounded like the report of a rifle. You didn't hear it?"

She shook her head. "What happened?"

"A wagon he was fixin' fell smack-dab on top of him. Broke his leg, the left one, I think, a ways above the knee."

She sucked in her breath, which was already coming

in gasps. The large femur. That was the most dangerous break she had seen during the war. Few men with such a break made it from the battlefield to the hospital alive.

"They aren't moving him, I hope."

He shrugged. "They was talking 'bout carrying him over to his house. It ain't but a few paces behind the pens."

The yard was empty when they entered, and sure enough, all the commotion came from a small cabin to their right.

Quint met them on the walk, his eyes wide, questioning.

She brushed past him, pulling her arm away from his offered hand. "That was a foolish thing to do," she snapped. "He should not have been moved."

He turned sharply to hold the door open.

Inside the one-room cabin, she was relieved to see windows on all walls. At least she would be able to see what she was about. Activity surrounded her, coming from all directions. Mavis restrained a distraught woman in her arms. Mrs. Wiseman, Holly thought.

Soly lay on a rickety bed in one corner, and he was extremely large—larger than she recalled. She had seen him only a few times since coming to Silver Creek, for he rarely came to the hotel, staying with his wife in this tiny cabin back of the wagonyard.

She had assumed he would be unconscious, but as she drew near, he started flinging his arms about, trying to rise.

"Get her outta here," he hollered.

"Hold on now, Sol." Quint held the man's shoulders. "The doc here's gonna look at your leg."

"Oh no she ain't! No lady doc's gonna touch me."

Holly looked at Davy, whose eyes were wide with a touch each of fear and wonderment. "Davy, fetch me some water and a cloth, please."

She turned her attention to Soly Wiseman, steering herself unsteadily to the opposite side of the bed from Quint.

"You're going to be all right, Mr. Wiseman," she assured him. "I've seen a number of injuries such as this, and I'm perfectly capable of handling it."

"You ain't touchin' me," the man bellowed in a voice that she knew was at least a pitch below normal. "Get her outta here, boys."

Mrs. Wiseman appeared suddenly at his shoulder beside Quint. "Sol, dear, you must calm down. It ain't good for you, gettin' riled and all. This lady's yer only chance of savin' that leg, and there ain't nothing that's not proper and fittin' about it." She patted his heaving shoulders. "Of course, if you want, Herman'll fetch one of them saws from his new store and take the leg right off."

Soly turned pain-filled eyes on his wife. "Mama! You know better'n to talk thataway." But he calmed down a bit, and Holly gently examined the leg through his coarse trousers.

She had seen an open fracture of this magnitude only once or twice before—a clean cut with the bone protruding through the torn homespun material of his overalls. She pursed her lips, trying to keep a lid on the panic she felt rising in the pit of her stomach. Or did this one seem more severe since she alone was responsible for treating it?

Thoughtfully, she turned the accepted method of treatment over in her mind. Most doctors would amputate without further dalliance, yet fully half of all amputees died, and a goodly number of those who survived the operation died later of infections.

She pulled back a bit of the material, and Soly jumped at her touch. When he did, the leg jerked in spasms.

"There, there Mr. Wiseman. Quit making such a fuss. Every time you move, it only starts the pain all over again."

"Little you know," he retorted, as angry as his weakened condition would allow. "It hurts like old Billy h—like Hades all the time."

"That's because you move," she said. "The muscles are trying to return to their normal positions, but with the bone out of place, they can't. You lie as still as you can, and we'll get on with . . ."

"You ain't takin' my leg off," he insisted.

"No, Mr. Wiseman. We'll try to set it first."

He settled down at that, resigned, but obviously not liking it one bit.

Holly turned toward the door. "Mr. Crump, I'll need some boards for splints. They must be stout."

The kindly German stepped to the bed, studied Soly's leg, then rushed quietly out the door.

She then looked at Slim Samples who stood beside her. "May I use your knife, Mr. Samples?" But she had no sooner spoken than Quint handed her the Bowie knife he carried. Looking at it, memories of their night in the cabin lashed out at her. Blood rushed to her head, and she made no move to take the knife. He held it steady, just in front of her.

"That one looks mighty sharp, Doc," Slim said. "You'd best use it."

Hesitantly, she reached toward the handle, and Quint almost dropped the knife on top of Soly before she had a good hold on it.

Straighten yourself up, she admonished. This man is in grave danger. Personal feelings cannot interfere with your work.

Davy returned with the cloth as she finished cutting away Soly's pant leg. Soly still tossed about, and she recalled how patients with this type of break often went into shock. No one knew what caused it, but some doctors felt it had something to do with the force of a blow hard enough to break such a large bone. She wiped a sleeve across her damp forehead. Soly's was the largest leg she had ever seen.

"He needs a shot of whiskey or something, Holly." Quint's voice was tentative, almost as weak as Soly's, and she looked at him in alarm. Their eyes met briefly, painfully.

"In the medicine bag." Her voice came out a mere whisper. "Get the chloroform and cotton wool."

He brought it to her, and again they had a juggling match to keep from touching hands.

She instructed Mrs. Wiseman to loosen Soly's collar, then she waved a small bit of chloroform in front of his nose. "I can't give him much of this, so you'll still have to hold on to him tightly. Can't risk sending him into shock."

Mrs. Wiseman became visibly anxious. "Will he be all right?"

Holly smiled into the woman's harried eyes. "He'll be fine, ma'am. Why don't you let Mavis take you over to the hotel until we're finished here?"

"He's my man," Mrs. Wiseman insisted, her eyes expressing her horror at being sent away. "He needs me." She clung to Soly's hand, stroking it, wiping his pain-dampened face with the cloth.

Holly watched her loving ministrations with a lump in her throat. "It's going to be rough before we're through."

"I know," the woman answered.

At that moment, Herman Crump returned with the splints, and Holly looked down at the protruding bone. She took a deep breath. "We'd best get on with it, then." She glanced up at Quint, and his eyes quietly reassured her.

Calmed, somehow, she began. "Mr. Samples, take his good leg, here. And Mr. Woodson, you and Mr. Crump hold his shoulders." She glanced again at the broken leg. "Quint, you help me."

They positioned themselves according to her instructions. "When I give the signal, you men hold him firm and still. The sheriff will pull his leg straight out, and I will guide it into place. Don't let go until I finish."

It wasn't as difficult as she had expected, although, for a person her size, the procedure would have been impossible alone. As the bone slid into the exact place, she bound it quickly with flannel, then added the splints, and finally strips of sheeting which Aggie had silently placed by her side.

Once she saw Mrs. Wise sway.

"Mavis, quick, the salts from my bag." And Mavis took care of the wife.

They all congratulated her, and she weakly accepted Soly's grudging thanks before he passed out. He supposed she'd done well enough, considering the pain had eased up.

She turned to Mrs. Wiseman, who was recuperating with a cup of tea Mavis had provided from only Mavis knew where. "He must stay completely off that leg. A break like this will take a long time to heal, and we can't be sure what to expect. I hate to alarm you further, but we may still have to resort to amputation."

"I'll take good care of 'em, miss. That I will." And when Holly finally walked outside, the woman followed.

"We got nothin' to pay you with right now."

Holly held the woman's roughened hands tenderly in her own. "Please don't worry about that. See that he stays down and check the wound every day. If you see sign of putrification, call me immediately."

"Bless you, miss, bless you. We'll repay you somehow one of these days . . . when Soly's better. I promise you that."

Holly smiled and turned and walked away. The late afternoon breeze felt cool on her damp body. She hadn't realized she was so exhausted.

When she rounded the corner, Quint stood with hat in hand. "That was a mighty fine job, Holly."

"Thank you," she mumbled, tensing at his unexpected appearance.

They stared at each other, and she had the sudden feeling that her heart had been shattered, much the same as Soly's leg. Finally she succeeded in tearing her devastated eyes from his, but the electricity of the encounter sent shock waves resounding through her body.

Gritting his teeth in a fierce effort to hold his emotions in rein, he stretched his hand toward her. "Come with me."

Her heart pounded up in her ears as she stared at his proffered hand, wanting nothing but to rush into his arms, to feel that hand caress her back, her neck, her face. A sob rose quickly in her throat, bringing tears to the spilling point before she could stop them. But she shook her head almost imperceptibly.

Narrowing his eyes, he spoke through still-clenched teeth. "Why not?"

"Nothing has changed," she whispered.

His hand formed a fist as he dropped it to his side, listlessly. "You're right about that. Nothing has changed between us. It's still there, Holly, if you'd give it a chance to work out."

With a deep sigh, almost a groan, she shook her head again. "It won't work out, Quint. Can't you understand? Life isn't just you and me alone, clutched in each other's arms. It's all we are—all we've ever been, all we've become, the people we've known and loved." She pressed her lips together and swallowed the bitter lump in her throat. "We're too different."

"You're wrong," he argued. "I thought that way, too, once. Before I knew you. Now I know that idea's nothing but hogwash."

She thought of him meeting Wilt and Luther in the bushes. Of his gentle treatment of Jim Tom even after the man accosted her. "No, Quint. *You're* wrong."

She looked at him, then, and was stunned by the hard, metallic glint in his eyes. Her heart froze from the coldness of his words when he spoke.

"If that's the way you want it, that's how it'll be. I won't be bothering you further." He turned a bit, then added, "You're a damned stubborn woman, Holly Campbell."

The hollow clinking of his spurs echoed in her muddled brain as he walked away from her. Finally she moved toward her house—toward Papa's house.

Was she stubborn, as so many people claimed? She thought about that a lot during the next couple of weeks while she straightened her house and tried to order her thoughts and her life.

Perhaps she was stubborn. But the occasions when she had been called that were the times when she stood up for what she thought was right.

Right? Hadn't the war taught her that what people considered right was usually their own way of looking at things? What was right for one person might be dead-wrong for someone else.

And what could be right about the hopeless ache in her body and soul? Would that ever be healed? Would . . . ?

But right or wrong, she had made her decision, and she had only to think of a future filled with Wilts and Luthers and Jim Tom Farrells to know that life with

Quint would not be right for her—or for him. She would only grow to hate him.

But she didn't hate him now, far from it. So she didn't go out. In fact, she scarcely went to her front door, for fear of seeing him ride by or seeing his horse hitched in front of the sheriff's office, which was distantly visible from her yard.

And, of course, Mavis objected.

"You can't lock yourself away from society, Holly."

"Society?" Holly questioned. "Thanks, anyway, but I have no desire to be part of your society. I'm returning to Tennessee as soon as Papa's death is settled."

Aggie came with one of the dresses completed, and Holly hurriedly changed from the depressing black to the lighter yellow frock, which she hoped would raise her spirits.

It was a lovely dress of voile with a heavier banding of white around the bottom and sleeves. The skirt, inset with gores of print, swayed gaily as she traipsed about the parlor to Aggie's clucking.

"Oh, Aggie, it's beautiful. It reminds me of a pieced quilt, one that's been made from all the worn-out dresses. This voile was a ball gown Caroline wore at our last May Day party. And the white is from a dress Molly fussed over every time she laundered. Said she couldn't take one stroke with the flatiron without scorching it, and she didn't see why I persisted in wearing it." She giggled. "Of course, it was my favorite dress. And the print—Mama had a dress from this same material. She was so handsome in it, sitting on the veranda in the afternoons with the honeysuckle and jasmine in bloom."

Aggie picked up her basket. "I'll get on back and finish up the others, now that I know this one fits." She turned at the door and gave Holly a stern look. "Them's mighty pretty memories, dearie, but it appears to me that you'd best be makin' some new ones. Right here."

"I'm going back," Holly replied in clipped tones.

Aggie shook her head. "To what, dearie? There ain't nothin' back there for you. I've seen it in your face. Your life's here now, and you'd best stop running away and start makin' the best of things."

Aggie was right about one thing, Holly thought after she left. The only thing she had to go back to was the same thing which faced her here—loneliness.

At night she worked on Papa's papers by the light of a coal-oil lamp. The letters from Mama during the war were personal and poignant, reminding her of the love the family had shared, and making her anxious to return to the fold. However shabby and dead end it might be, it was still home.

Davy became a constant companion, arriving early every morning with news of his scouting expeditions around the smokehouse looking for signs of his friend Sancho. He had yet to find anything, but he never gave up hope that one day soon Sancho would return, and he was going to be the first to see him.

And more important to Holly's way of thinking was the health returning to the boy's cheeks and limbs. He became stronger each day and before long was as brown as a pecan shell. And he always brought a lunch to share with her.

One day Mavis arrived in a flit. "The coast is clear now, darling. You can return to the hotel for supper."

"What do you mean?"

"He's gone. Off on a mission of some kind. Anyway, you can stop neglecting your friends and come out of hiding now."

Holly retorted in a huff, but she knew Mavis was right. She had been hiding from Quint, and she had neglected her friends and patients.

The first thing she did after Mavis left was visit Soly Wiseman with Davy by her side.

Mrs. Wiseman met her at the door. "Oh, miss, ain't it a marvel? Look at him."

Soly was sitting up in bed, and although she looked him over good, the only difference she saw was that he wasn't writhing in pain, nor in anger at her for attending him.

She stepped tentatively toward the bed. "Hello, Mr. Wiseman."

The voice that boomed out at her was indeed different. Not only was it stronger, but it lacked the belligerence of a week ago. "Come on in and sit a spell, Doc."

She blinked and tried to conceal her astonishment at his turnaround. "How's the leg?"

"Could be better," he admitted. "But if it weren't for you, it was be a h—, ah, a heck of a lot worse, Doc." He shook his head in amazement. "And you such a mite of a thing."

She laughed. "Papa always told me I would have to work hard to make up for my size, but I didn't realize at the time this was what he meant."

"That pa of yourn, he was quite a doc. We surely was at a loss without him," Mrs. Wiseman said.

Her husband nodded in agreement. "But now we got ourselves another'n. Another Doc Holly." He beamed as if he were the first to think of this strange turn of events.

A lump came to her throat. These were such kindly people, and she felt right at home. How wonderful it was to be needed and able to respond to their needs. "I didn't do this alone," she said. "I had a lot of help from your neighbors."

"'Specially from that sheriff of our'n. He's a fine one . . ." Mrs. Wiseman began.

Holly nodded stiffly. "If you're getting along all right, I'll be going. I'll stop around again in a day or so. Now, you remember not to get out of bed."

"You can bet on that, Doc," he said. "I might bellyache a bit, but I sure enough don't hanker to be ahobbling about on one leg."

As she started to leave, Soly turned to his wife. "Mama, where's that mess o' pokesalad you picked for the doc here?"

Mrs. Wiseman fetched a bunch of smooth green leaves and thrust them into Holly's protesting arms. "It ain't much, after all you've done for us. But there's more where this come from."

Outside the June sun shone brightly, and Holly basked in the bigness of this land and the hearts of its people. Her people. At least, they could be. Yet . . .

She put the greens on the cabinet, recalling that first picnic when Quint told her that pokesalad was poisonous if not properly prepared.

Even that memory brought tears to her eyes. Would she ever get over the pain? Every reminder, every time someone called his name, she flinched inside as if stabbed with his razor-sharp Bowie knife.

"Come on, Doc." Davy pulled at her skirt. "That's Rosie's dinner bell, and you promised to eat at the hotel today."

She smiled down at him. "Indeed, I did." But before leaving the house she went to the trunk and took out the piece of lace left from Caroline's wedding veil. It should be put to some use.

After dinner she gave it to Aggie. "Can you make a christening dress out of this?"

"Christening dress?" Aggie held up the length of lace.

Holly nodded. "For little Miracle. I'll take it out to the Varners' in a day or two." She noticed Aggie's reticence. "You told me a traveling preacher comes through every now and again."

"That he does, dearie, but not often enough that a youngun won't outgrow a christenin' gown in betwixt."

"Then make it big. After all, she is my namesake, and she's to be my godchild, too. I should see that taken care of before I leave."

"Humph!" Aggie snorted. "Sometimes I think you're so blind you can't see the hand in front of your face."

Holly looked puzzled, but gave it little thought. There was a lot to do before she returned to Hedgerow.

Most important of which was to see that Tom Farrell was charged with Papa's death. She had been putting off going to find Elena, but now it must be done. Tomorrow.

To be certain she didn't back out, she stopped by the livery stable and arranged to use a horse the next morning.

"And Mr. Samples, I'll need it early. I must get away from town before Davy is up, else he'll insist on going with me."

"Where'll you be headed, Doc?"

"Just for a ride," she hedged. "But I would like to go alone . . . to look over Papa's property for the last time before I return to Tennessee."

"You can count on me," he said. "I get up with the crows."

"Not the chickens," she teased.

"No'm." He spit carefully to one side. "Them crows'll beat chickens ever time."

She laughed. Such easygoing folks. She would miss them, for sure.

At the door, she turned suddenly at the sight of a dappled gray horse. "Is that . . . ?"

"Yes'm, the sheriff rode into town not over an hour ago."

Fear—or was it anticipation? she wondered—swept

through her veins like a prairie fire. So he was home.

She felt as if she had been free and was suddenly caged once more. Hurrying to her house, her shoulders tightened against any noise behind her. Wanting to hear the jingle of his spurs, his voice calling her name—not wanting to.

You silly nit, she admonished. He said he was through, and he meant it. She winced, recalling the hardness in his eyes, the determination.

Yes, he meant it all right. And that was exactly how it should be. But she knew she wouldn't venture out again as long as she stood the slightest chance of running into him; the pain would be unbearable.

For supper she opened a can of tomatoes and did not light a fire. Eyeing the pokesalad suspiciously, she finally took it out back, hoping varmints would devour it before the Wisemans saw it. She wouldn't have a chance to get it to Rosie, now, and she dared not try cooking it herself.

After changing into a blue muslin gown and robe, she hung the new dress on a hook and wondered what kind of memories would cling to any future garment made from this dress—painful ones that she hoped to put behind her someday, she thought.

Sitting at the desk she went through the letters again and tried to rekindle her desire to return to Tennessee. How could she stand to be that far from him? Yet she knew she couldn't bear to live so close.

She put off going to bed as long as possible. It would be no different, unless worse, than all the other sleepless nights she had had lately. During the day she could keep her thoughts from straying too much, but at night, when she lay in bed alone, her memories gave her no peace.

First she would recall his softness, his gentleness—then she reminded herself how he had hedged and lied.

Then again she thought of his golden eyes, his loving touch, his passionate embrace . . .

No, she would put off going to bed all night, if need be. So, taking down *Twelfth Night,* she tried to lose her thoughts in comedy.

Finally when she couldn't keep herself from gazing out the window at the gathering clouds and wondering where Quint was at that very moment, she gave up.

As she bent to blow out the lamp, a scratching sound at the back door stiffened her spine. Silly, she admonished. She had jumped at every creaking board the last two weeks, thinking Quint had returned.

But at this hour? Only the rising wind, she assured herself, but she went to the porch to be sure the door was pulled to against night-crawling creatures.

She stood a moment watching the pecan limbs sway. The moon was shrouded in clouds, and she saw a faint flash of lightning to the south. A storm was building somewhere.

Suddenly a shuffling sound outside the door alerted her, and she jumped back, then cautiously peered around the doorway. Only a varmint, but she surely didn't want it inside the house, no matter how friendly Davy thought them all to be.

The shuffle came again, and this time fear spread rapidly throughout her body. "Who's there?"

More shuffling, and a form appeared at the side of the steps. "Ma'am, it's me . . . Sancho."

Relief whistled through her teeth, as she expelled the breath she didn't know she was holding.

Opening the door wider, she called to him. "Sancho."

"Shhh!"

She bent low then, beckoning him inside silently.

"You got my message?" Holly whispered inside the porch.

"No'm." He spoke in barely audible tones. "Elena told me to find you. She's in real bad trouble."

Holly gasped. "What can I do?"

"I brought a horse to hitch to Doc Holly's wagon." He stopped suddenly. "The wagon's still around, ain't it?"

She nodded. "In the carriage hou—ah, the shed."

"She's too bad off to ride a horse, but I figure if we can get her in the wagon and bring her here, you can fix her up. Your pa told me . . ."

". . . that I'm as good as a doctor," she finished for him.

"I sure hope you are, ma'am. She's awful bad off."

Sancho hitched the horse while Holly slipped back into her yellow dress and a pair of shoes, got the medical bag, and then ran back into the house at the last minute for a blanket for Elena, all the while worrying frantically—what could have happened to Papa's friend?

Chapter Twelve

Distant rumbling thunder added to Holly's distress as they set out in the wagon with Sancho driving. On the way he recounted how he had stumbled across Elena.

"I was on my way to Silver Creek when I run acrost her tryin' to make her way to get help from you."

Holly raised her voice above the wagon clatter. "What on earth happened to her?"

"She was beat up real bad," Sancho said. "Ol' man Farrell's men done it."

Holly gasped. "I should have known something like this would happen." She caught the ends of her shawl as a gust of wind whipped it about, then held it tightly under her chin while the edges flapped around her shoulders. "If only she had stayed with me."

"She was plumb scared to death of 'em, ma'am. Ol' man Farrell, he told her he'd kill her if she ever let the cat out of the bag."

"The cat . . . ?"

"You know, if she told, but that ain't it. I figure the ol' man don't know 'bout this."

"What happened?" She asked the question, fearing the answer, yet knowing she must find out.

"It was that drunkard son of Farrell's, Jim Tom. He tried to . . . well, he . . . he wanted to . . ."

Holly stared at the tongue-tied boy, the memory of Jim Tom's attack on her filling in the gaps of his broken phrases with horrendous details. "Oh, dear God! Is she . . . ?"

"She hid out, an' when she got the chanct, she run out on 'em. But they come after her, and well, it ain't no pretty sight you're 'bout to see, ma'am. I can say that for sure. She might'n even be alive."

Fear swept over Holly in a wave of cold sweat—fear mixed with anger and guilt. If only she had persuaded Elena to remain in town. If only Quint had put Jim Tom in jail. Curiously, she felt vindicated in her condemnation of Quint's cronies, but it was a sour, very bitter victory.

The miles seemed endless, and finally she turned her attention to Sancho, the boy she had tried so hard to find, whom she felt sure held answers to the puzzling questions about Papa and his death.

Studying him in the dim light, she saw only a boy-man of about her own size, somewhere around ten years of age, but closer to thirty by the way he had taken charge tonight.

"You did get my message?" she asked.

"No'm, I never got no message. Where'd you leave it?"

She told him about the visit to the canyon and being fired upon, and the next day leaving the message in a cave where they discovered the provisions from Quint's cabin.

Sancho hung his head. "Yes'm, it was me broke into the sheriff's cabin. But I was getting mighty desperate for something to eat and some ammunition for your pa's rifle, and I figured with him living in town and all, the sheriff wouldn't be needin' everything. I didn't take all he had."

"He appreciated that, Sancho, and he didn't mind sharing with you, but we did worry about your safety. That's why we left the message in the cave."

"I never seen it," he said. "Somebody messed up the cave real good. I ain't got nothin' left."

Momentarily stunned by this news, she then thought of Papa's house. "It was probably the same people who ransacked Papa's house," she said. "What are they looking for?"

"Me, I reckon," he replied. "An' maybe your pa's book. They knew he kept records, 'cause I heard him tell ol' man Farrell that he had all their dealings down in writin'. Farrell couldn't stand by and let someone get hold of that book."

She inhaled deeply, then spoke as calmly as her racing heart would permit. "Tell me about the book." At last, at long last, she was going to hear the truth.

"I'll be glad to, ma'am, but it's a mighty long yarn, an' this here's where I left Elena."

Sancho pulled into a clearing surrounded on three sides by a dense thicket.

"Does the road end here?" she asked.

"No'm, I left the road a piece back. I was cuttin' acrost country when I run into her." He peered into the black night. "But she ain't here now."

Occasional flashes of lightning illuminated the darkness, and Holly saw no sign of Elena, either. "Are you sure this is the right place?"

"Yes'm. She must've crawled back under cover."

Holly climbed down from the wagon seat, and they looked around. Her chest tightened and the back of her neck prickled. She kept wanting to look behind her. Jim Tom and his beastly friends could be anywhere.

Suddenly a whimpering in the brush alerted them, and a flash of lightning revealed a bare leg at the edge of the thicket where Elena had tried to hide.

Sancho called to her softly, reassuring her they were indeed friends. "I brung her, Elena. She was there, like you said she'd be, an' I brung her."

Holly knelt beside him. "Can you get out by yourself, Elena?"

"You are sure they have gone?" The voice was weak, barely more than a whimper.

"We're alone," Holly assured her, then wondered if she had lost her senses. She had brought no weapon of any kind. A quick look at Sancho revealed only an old Navy pistol she recognized as Papa's. That would do for one shot, but would be little help against a group of determined men.

Elena dragged herself from the thicket, as a sudden flash illuminated the area, and they stood revealed in a stark, ethereal daylight. Holly gasped at the sight of Elena's face—beaten, bloody, swollen, and her almost nude body clothed only in shreds of a garment.

Quickly, she wrapped the blanket around the girl, and they lifted her gently and carried her to the wagon. Elena tried to speak, but Holly shushed her. "Don't talk now. We'll get you home and put a nice poultice on your wounds."

Elena's eyes darted from side to side, and her body shook, while Holly's fear of being set upon turned to anger at the men responsible.

"Jim Tom Farrell is an animal!" She spat out the words. "And his murdering friends, as well. They will pay this time, Elena. Jim Tom, Wilt, and Luther. They'll all pay this time. I promise you."

Elena rolled her head back and forth, her body trembling.

"Don't be afraid," Holly soothed. "We'll protect you." But she knew they must hurry to reach the safety of town before they were discovered.

She couldn't push the images of Jim Tom, Wilt, and Luther from her mind. Whelps of goose flesh arose along her arms when she recalled the terror these men had instilled in her from that first meeting at the dance in the hotel, and later when Jim Tom accosted her in the street.

She clenched her teeth against her rising anger at Quint. Some sheriff he was! His collaboration with these ruffians was apparent; they were all conniving animals, all of them. Even the man she had . . .

Tears sprung to her eyes. Even the man she still loved. She could not be rid of this hostile world soon enough.

Holly tried riding in the bed of the wagon alongside Elena, but the girl soon passed into a sleep-like state, so Holly climbed onto the more comfortable seat beside Sancho.

They rode silently, Holly clutching at her shawl, which whipped in the still rising wind, and at her courage and sanity, which she felt being swept away, also.

Suddenly Sancho tensed beside her, and a moment later she heard a horse approaching. A rider at this time of night?

Sancho pulled the wagon off the road, headed for a clump of trees, but the lone rider rounded a curve in the road and caught sight of them.

"The pistol!" Holly instructed Sancho. "Draw it."

He lay the weapon across his leg. "It ain't always wise to show yourself a threat, ma'am."

"A threat? Who would be riding this way, except those hunting Elena?"

He remained silent, and, as the horse approached, he relaxed. "It's only the sheriff, ma'am."

The sheriff? Quint? Then she, too, recognized the familiar form approaching through the flashing lightning and her heart pounded furiously inside her. What a time he chose to be on this road.

He reined beside the wagon. "What's the trouble?" he demanded, knowing his anxiety sounded more like anger.

Sancho started to reply, but Holly spoke over his words. "As if you didn't know."

He returned her stare with a level gaze, relieved that her voice sounded all right, but wondering why in tarnation she had gone off with no more than a boy in the middle of the night. "Matter of fact, I don't."

"It's Elena Salinas," Sancho told him, indicating the rear of the wagon, and Quint nudged his mount closer.

"What happened to her?" he asked, unable to make out the problem inside the darkened bed of the wagon.

"Farrell's no-account son and some of his hands had a go at her," Sancho said. "I found her alongside the trail leadin' from the TF."

"Your kith and kin," Holly fumed, each word heavy-laden with bitterness.

Quint gave her a hard look, then glanced briefly at the stirring sky. "Take my horse, Sancho, and I'll drive the ladies. Looks like we'll have to make a run for it to beat the storm back to town."

He dismounted as he spoke, and Sancho readily obeyed over Holly's ardent objections.

With thunder crashing all around them, Quint settled himself easily on the wagon seat beside her. Noticing Sancho's trouble mounting his mustang, he spoke lightly. "Go easy on him, son. He's a bit feisty, like Miss Holly here."

Holly gasped indignantly. How dare he? The very idea of poking fun at a time like this! "You weren't merely happening by." Her voice seethed with unstated accusations, and his puzzled eyes met hers briefly. The flashing sky gave him the eerie countenance of an undeveloped photograph.

Flicking the reins, he concentrated on sounding casual as if he hadn't heard the reproaching tone in her voice, as if he weren't aching to take her in his arms and crush her body to his. "I just rode back into town today, Holly. Thought I'd look in on you and see how things were going."

"Now you see." She crossed her arms tightly across her heaving chest.

Determined to get through to her in some rational way, he continued steadily. "When I found the shed open and the wagon gone, and then you yourself having gone off and left a lamp burning, I figured trouble must have come up. So I took out after you."

Chilled more by the knowledge that she had been right about his connection with the Farrells than by the coming storm, she pulled her shawl closer about her shoulders. "And you knew exactly where to look," she said with a sigh of resignation.

"A horse and wagon track easy, Holly," he answered.

"On a night black as sin?" she retorted.

"With the sky lighting up like the Fourth of July, it's a regular picnic."

The weight on her shoulders settled heavily over her heart. "Especially when you know where that wagon is going."

Quint bit his tongue to keep from shouting at her. "How do you figure that?"

She stared hard at him, and he finally turned and spoke, this time with exasperation. "Like I said, Holly, a lamp was burning, and a woman don't . . . a woman and a boy don't set out on a night like this unless there's something mighty wrong."

"How'd you know Sancho was along?"

He exhaled loudly, wondering why he didn't just give up on her. Wondering why she mattered so much to him. Knowing the answer with every throbbing beat of his heart. "Tracks, Holly, tracks."

They rode in silence, Holly recalling his proficiency at tracking—reading sign, he had called it. She doubted not that he could find her on the blackest night. But why did he have to prove those skills tonight? Tonight, when she wished him to have been miles away.

Quint cleared his throat. "Riding through the countryside like I've been doing the last few days gives a man a chance to clear the cobwebs out of his brain. And I've done a lot of that." He turned to face her, but she was unable to see his expression until a bright flash lit the sky and his glistening golden eyes as well, bringing an unbidden whimper to her throat.

"And I've about got you figured out," he finished.

"Me?" she shouted, becoming as angry at the betrayal of her own emotions as she was with him.

He nodded, turning back to the road. "At first I figured you to be strong, with courage enough to face life in this wilderness. But I was wrong."

Holly bristled, and raising her chin defiantly, she looked across at him. "How dare you! You have no idea what I've been through these last years—during the war . . . and after." Her thoughts raced back to the hospitals, the plantation, the family plot. "All the dead and dying—hordes, droves of dead and dying—unending, it seemed, and when the war was over, we were left with . . . with nothing but destruction. And the death and destruction didn't end with the war; they followed me here." She thundered her wrath upon him. "Not strong and courageous? You have no idea . . . no right."

His voice rose strong and steady above the rattling wagon wheels and rumbling thunder, but it held no sympathy. "You've been through mighty trying times, no question about it. But you survived, Holly. And you should be able to face life now without all that fear you have inside you."

"What fear?" she demanded. "Wasn't it I who faced Tom Farrell? Who insisted on going to the TF? To the canyon? Wasn't it I who . . ."

"I'm not talking about that kind of courage," he said. "I mean the courage to trust . . ."

"To trust?" she interrupted, aghast at how little he understood the situation. "To trust you? Give me one good reason why I should. I have a dozen not to, the latest being tonight."

His hands froze on the reins. So that's what she thought! How could she? She who had lain with him, loved him? Glancing back at Elena, he shook his head sadly. "You know me better than that, Holly. I wouldn't be a party to such . . ."

"But you and Jim Tom, and Wilt and Luther . . ."

"Now hold on a cock-eyed minute. Wilt and Luther had no part in this either. They were . . ." He paused. The situation had somehow gotten completely out of control, like a runaway horse, and he knew he had no choice left but to tell her the truth. "They've been with me all week."

She smiled, satisfied at his admission, considering her point made. "And where were you?"

He sighed. "Holly, I can't tell you all of it. But I'm doing an important job, and they're helping me."

"Wilt and Luther?" She looked toward him, wondering what story he would concoct this time.

"Don't you go spilling the beans for a while now."

She frowned. "How could I tell anything? You've told me nothing."

"It's a job on the side of the law, Holly. And Wilt and Luther are helping out. No one can know until we've wrapped it up."

He spoke so calmly that she listened, and listening, she began to doubt. Not Quint this time, but herself. Could she have been wrong about him? Dared she hope? Looking back at Elena, who appeared to be merely sleeping in the jostling wagon bed, she dreaded to discover how badly the girl was injured. Her mind whirled in circles. Not Wilt and Luther? Who then?

The wind had picked up greatly, and she felt it pushing them forward. Quint urged the horse ever faster and faster with his whip and exclamations.

Laboring with her whipping shawl, she at last tied the ends in a knot so her hands would be free to grip the wagon seat as they bounced across the land and over rocks and bushes. The side of her hand brushed the coarse fabric of Quint's trousers, and she flinched as if struck by one of the sparking streaks of lightning.

"This way's quicker than the road," he said. "It's rougher, but it'll give us a better chance of beating that storm to town."

She held on for dear life, while they raced through the stormy night as through a mystical wonderland out of some fairy story. The lightning streaked in brilliant bolts and zigzags, then the entire sky appeared to be full of falling stars which were not falling at all, but rather exploding in place, all to the accompaniment of an orchestra provided by nature—crashing, clopping, rumbling thunder; whistling, gusting, blustering winds, accompanied by the creaking of harness leather and the clatter and squawk of the wagon wheels.

"Is this what you meant by the heavens going at it?" she asked.

He nodded, looking around at the blazing sky. "It's sure enough a sight to behold." Even though she knew he must have witnessed such storms many times before, his voice was filled with wonder.

The storm didn't frighten her, and she started to say

as much. To point this out as another example of her courage. But she wondered how much was personal courage, and how much simply feeling safe with Quint. She had no doubt that he would get them home safely. And, of course, he had kept Jim Tom from molesting her. She squeezed back tears. But that hadn't helped Elena.

Trust him, he asked of her. In some ways she did. Yet, he seemed to have his own standard for determining how and when to help; and of what was right, what wrong. Sometimes his views coincided with her own beliefs, but often a chasm divided them. And there lay the problem of trusting him: she would have to change her entire system of judging right and wrong.

She fidgeted on the wagon seat beside him. What was right and what wrong? Oh, dear God, she wailed inside, once she had known. Once things had been simple: the war was wrong, and so were Yankees and carpetbaggers and what had happened to Elena.

And Quint was . . . She took a deep, quivering breath. Sitting beside him now seemed right. Yet, how could it be, when he was in many ways the exact opposite of all she had been taught to respect?

For twenty-four years her family had been the standard by which she judged right and wrong. With them she knew when to trust, whom to trust, and when to be suspicious of someone. Papa had taught her to trust her own instincts, but now she knew her instincts had been his. She had learned to measure life by his standards.

Again she shifted in her seat. If only Papa were here now. He would tell her what to do, whom to trust. And it probably wouldn't be Quintan Jarvis.

"It isn't supposed to be easy." He spoke quietly.

"What?"

"Life," he said. "It isn't supposed to be easy."

"That's what Papa said, but . . ."

"Some folks want too much control over life. That's Mavis's trouble. And Tom's." He switched hands with the reins and rested a hand on his knee, the hairs on his hand brushing hers slightly. He swallowed. "And yours," he added softly, barely above the din surrounding them.

"Mine?" The accusation jolted her. "How can you say such a thing?"

He shrugged, his shoulder very close to hers. "Likely comes from always having someone fetch and carry."

The wind blew as a barrier between them. "You certainly have a low opinion of me and my upbringing."

"No," he said. "I've been studying on it, that's all. Trying to decide why you're so confused in your ways."

"I am not confused."

"Afraid to take a chance, then."

"That again! How can anyone who left home to come alone to this wilderness be afraid to take a chance?"

He shook his head. "Not that kind of courage, Holly. You're afraid to take a chance on me, on the feelings we have for each other. I'll admit I'm not your pa. I think you're looking for your pa, and you're scared to take a chance on me, because I'm different from him."

"That isn't true!" She pressed her lips together against anger, against tears. How could he say such a mean thing? No one would ever be like Papa. And Quint Jarvis didn't even come close. "That isn't true," she repeated.

"Something's holding you back," he continued. "You want me as bad as I do you, but there's something inside keeping you back."

Yes, yes, she thought, as tears stung her eyes. How desperately she wanted him. Sitting next to him like this, it was almost impossible not to forget all that separated them.

But a great gulf of things came between them, and she could not—would not—give in to purely physical attraction.

"That's why you sound so angry with things I do and say. It's to hide your real feelings."

"You're quite the philosopher!" she retorted.

He shrugged, hiding the despondency that filled his heart and soul. He'd failed with her again. "I had to tell you one more time how I felt," he said. "That's all there'll be. I promised not to bother you, and I won't."

Terrified suddenly that he would desert her—that he would give up—that she would lose him after all, she rushed on. "What about Jim Tom? I'll bet you don't arrest him, even now."

"He'll pay for this. And for what he's done to you, too." He cleared his throat. "There's a lot more involved here than you know about. In time . . ."

"If there is more involved, then I'm entitled to know what it is," she stormed, furious at his insistent pigheadedness. Unsuccessfully, she tried to tuck the strands of hair lashing about her face back beneath her shawl.

"See? That's what I mean. You want control over every situation."

"That isn't true, Quint. I want to know what's going on so I *can* trust you. Can't you see? Your silence is what keeps us apart. Silence can be as much a lie as spoken words."

He took a long time answering, then said, "This one's too dangerous for you to be involved in, Holly. I can't put your life in that much danger."

"You mean you *won't,*" she said. Just when she thought he had finally come around to explaining this whole dastardly affair, he only refused once again. And this, she thought, more than anything else would be what kept them from having a life together. She could not live with someone who wouldn't include her in his life. Papa had shared all his troubles with Mama, and she with him. They drew their strength from each other. If this thing were dangerous for her, it would be for him, too. And in a sharing relationship, they would support each other.

"Holly, listen to me. You came to town in the middle of a . . ." Quint stopped short, then yelled "Fire!" He flicked his whip across the horse's rump.

At first she didn't understand, but then she suddenly realized that the light on the horizon was not lightning after all, but a steady yellow glow straight ahead of them. "Where is it?"

"Looks like it's on the edge of town."

She held her breath. Papa's house was the nearest building to them as they approached Silver Creek.

They rode hard, eyes fastened on the lighted sky ahead of them. The nearer they got, the brighter it grew, and soon the air became heavy with smoke and cinders.

It was Papa's house. As they raced up, flames bellowed skyward in bursts of heat and fire and cinders. Several townspeople rushed about, hollering, trying to start a water line from the river.

"The lamp!" Holly cried, grasping for reasons, causes. She had just moved into the house. All her belongings were there. Her head whirled, and she clutched the edge of the wagon seat, her eyes staring, yet not seeing.

For a time after arriving in Silver Creek she had believed that someone was trying to drive her from this town, and now it appeared she had done so herself by carelessly leaving the lamp burning in her haste to reach Elena.

Quint dashed her guilty feelings to the ground. "I put

the lamp out when I found you gone."

She stared at him, a note of disbelief striking a brief blow in the midst of her dismay and hopelessness. Her entire world of material belongings disintegrated before her very eyes. There had to be a reason.

As Quint drew the wagon to a halt, Sancho reined beside them, panting. "It burst into flames the second I rode up," he said. "I seen a couple of fellers ride off toward the river, but by the time I got there they were nowheres about, and their tracks got lost in the underbrush on the other bank."

"Good work, son." Quint jumped from the wagon, handing the reins to Holly. "We'll be able to follow them come daylight."

"Daylight?" She glared at him through the grotesque light images fashioned by the blowing smoke and fire. "If you could track me by night, why not them?"

"Holly, there's work to be done here."

Holly started down behind him, forgetting in her anxiety, her patient in the wagonbed behind her.

Quint put a restraining hand on her shoulder. "You stay put. There's nothing you can do, except see to Elena."

She froze for a moment, angry that he, of all people, should tell her what to do. It was her house, and he could very well be the one who set the fire, or . . . ?"

Two men? Wilt and Luther?

A step away he turned back. "Pull the wagon around so the horse won't be looking into the flames. He'll be easier to handle thataway. I'll come back directly and take you to the hotel."

She stared into the blinding flames, seeing only her own helplessness, her own insignificance. Shuddering, she buried her face in her hands, shielding it against the heat and sudden terror which clamped around her chest like an iron band. She could have been inside that house. He wouldn't have gone that far, surely.

Flicking the reins, she turned the jittery horse, then set the brake and moved to the back, where a whimpering sound told her that Elena had roused and was anxious at the commotion.

Holly sat facing the blistering heat, cradling the injured girl's head in her lap, while the townsmen worked furiously against reality. Their only success could be in keeping the flames from spreading, as not even a valve opening from heaven could save the house now. With the wind blowing, it was fortunate that no other dwellings were located to the south.

She wiped a hand across her face, then held it out, palm heavenward. Raindrops.

But she was so stunned by her loss that her head whirled in a rush of static, and she could neither feel the rain nor consciously protect herself and Elena against it. Her thoughts turned to incongruous mush, which soon devoured her fears, leaving her with nothing.

Nothing.

After a while she became aware of a voice calling her name. "Stay where you are, darling. I am driving you and Elena to the hotel."

Holly bolted up, dropping Elena's head on the wagonbed in her haste to climb out. "No! No!"

"You can do nothing here." Mavis's voice was calm, but insistent.

Holly could not answer. She struggled to the side of the wagon, unable to tear her eyes away from the mesmerizing flames.

"There's nothing to stay for, Holly. Everything is gone." Someone pushed her back to the bed of the wagon as Mavis clucked to the horse, and they moved away.

Gone. Her mind seemed to trudge along, dulled by the fire. Gone up in flames. She had heard that expression all her life. Now its reality danced before her.

Gone up in flames. Everything she owned. The letters she had so painstakingly pieced together after the break-in. Mama's jewelry. The money she borrowed from the bank. The copper plates.

She stared as the flames cremated her memories, her belongings, and flung their ashes to the heavens. Eventually they would drift back to earth, unheralded, unrecognizable.

She looked down at her dirty yellow dress, stained with Elena's blood, torn in her haste to bring aid to this friend of Papa's who had obviously suffered greatly because of her involvement with him. Warm tears trickled from her eyes, leaving wet trails along her fire-dried face.

They halted behind the hotel, and Mavis took Holly's arm. "Come, darling. We must get you and Elena out of the rain."

Holly moved as in a trance, realizing vaguely that others were in the wagon.

They helped her in, and she let Aggie bathe her off and dress her in fresh nightclothes and tuck her into bed. The thought of Elena lay somewhere in the back of her mind, intermingled with memories of tonight and long ago.

For a while she slept, suddenly awakening in the darkness with orange flames licking a building—the dream she had lived with these last years, yet different somehow.

Groping for her slippers, she stumbled to the landing, where she stared in the direction of Papa's house and knew the dying embers were those of a new nightmare.

Long she stood staring at the smoldering fire through the falling rain, until finally the firelight dimmed under the growing light of day. Sinking to the floor, she rested her head on the windowsill, and slowly the thread of her memories rewound itself as yarn on a spinning wheel, and she began to think more clearly.

The house had caught fire while she was away fetching Elena. Chills shook her through the thin cotton nightgown when she realized how narrowly she had missed being in that house.

Would she have been able to get out in time? Had she been there, could she have prevented the fire?

Quint? Suspicions rose instantly at the thought of him. Why?

He found them in the pasture in the middle of the night, but . . . Her brain, although recharging, remained too dull to recall the past night with any clarity. What difference did it make now? she wondered.

Today she was faced with a whole new set of problems. She must return to Tennessee, but with the jewelry gone, along with the money from the bank, she was, for the first time in her life, truly destitute.

She looked down at Mavis's nightgown, once more finding herself dependent upon this woman's charity. And it appeared she would have to borrow money from Mavis to even be able to return home.

She sat staring through the rain at the pile of rubble and smoke and ashes until the rooster crowed, jolting her brain more firmly into the present.

Elena, so badly injured. What had happened to her? How could she have forgotten Elena? Quickly, she fetched Mavis's buff wrapper from her bed and looked through the empty rooms until she found the girl in a room next to Davy's. A lamp burned on a table beside the bed, and Aggie dozed in a rocking chair alongside it.

Holly stood quietly in the doorway, watching Elena's breathing, which was a bit raspy although not irregular enough to cause alarm.

But her face was a fright, swollen with knots over her eyes and forehead, cuts everywhere, and all of it turning a sickly mottled color, which Holly knew would soon be black and purple. Only savages could perform such brutal acts.

A faintness washed over her at this latest development. A foreboding. This was no country for a woman. The moment Elena was well enough to travel, she would take her home with her to Tennessee. Convicting Papa's murderers was not that important anymore. Now she must get Elena and herself to the safety of civilization and leave these heathens to kill off each other.

Chapter Thirteen

Holly would forever after remember the following day as among the most devastating of her life.

After assuring herself that Elena was resting well, she returned to her room and dozed fitfully until Rosie's breakfast bell sounded.

Not that she felt the least bit hungry, but Sancho might be there, and, although she was still light-headed and thoughts fluttered through her mind as dizzily as butterflies, she seemed to recall Sancho saying that he knew where Papa's journal was.

So she dressed quickly, glad not to have to worry about clothing. With Mavis around, who would? Not stopping to choose, she picked the top dress of the remaining garments Aggie had remade and which she found hanging in the wardrobe in her bedroom. And it was a lovely dress, she thought, examining her reflection briefly in the looking glass—a gay combination of blue-flowered muslin and a blue, magenta, and purple plaid. Its princess lines were accented with strips of purple velvet she recognized as a former Christmas gown. Ruffles of buff lace trimmed the cuffs and added extra height to the fine lawn collar.

Holly shook her head at such orderliness. In the

midst of a threatening fire, burdened by one badly injured woman and another who was addlepated, Mavis had seen that she would be properly attired! Everyone should have a Mavis in times of trouble.

Sancho was not at breakfast. In fact, no one at table recalled seeing him the night before, and since Quint wasn't to be found, either, Holly didn't know where to turn. As events of the previous evening took clearer shape in her mind, she decided that the two of them must be off together, investigating the tracks of the men Sancho saw ride away from Papa's house.

The other diners offered their condolences on the loss of her house, and her spirits rose as they discussed ways to help rebuild her home and restore her life here in Silver Creek.

Herman Crump, who now ate at his own fire with his wife Luda, sent word that he would travel to San Antone himself to bring back supplies to rebuild the house. Such generosity, she thought, recalling his relief only a few weeks before that he wouldn't have to make that miserable trip again for a long time.

"Since there's nothing you'll likely be needin' from the saloon," Woody said, "you can count me in on the building."

"I'll help, too," Slim Samples added. "And in the meantime, bring your wagon over to the stable. I've more than enough room."

Possum, Mavis, and Aggie put in their contributions, while Davy sat very still beside her and squeezed her hand beneath the table. "I can build, too," he said.

She smiled at each of them. They had become a family to her, and she would surely miss them. But there were neighbors back in Tennessee, she reminded herself, and a great deal of rebuilding to do there, too.

Her light-headedness had abated somewhat, and in its place she felt a growing need to escape Silver Creek, and to take Elena with her. As soon as talk at table would allow, she dismissed herself and hurried to Elena's room, where she found the young woman awake, but in great pain. Her battered face had begun to turn a darker blue-black and the swelling, if anything, was greater this morning.

She bathed Elena's face in cool water from the basin on the washstand, and soothed it with a poultice of Chamberlain's Pain Balm which she found alongside the tinctures of opium and morphine in Papa's medical bag. Then, with foreboding, she pulled back the covers and discovered Elena to be clad in a fresh white nightgown much the same as the one she had worn. Bless their hearts, Mavis and Aggie had been busy last night.

Holly lifted the gown gently and winced at the extensiveness of Elena's bruises and abrasions, some of which she probably got by crawling and stumbling through the underbrush in her escape.

But not all. Holly looked gently at her new friend. "I'll try not to hurt you, Elena."

Elena's swollen eyes fluttered perceptibly, then she closed them as if against the memory of unspeakable horrors.

"I won't be long, but I must discover whether you have any broken bones or other injuries we should deal with." She pushed the covers further back and turned Elena onto her side, an action which elicited a muffled groan as the girl stuffed a fist in her mouth.

Holly poked here and there, drawing a wince, but no comment. "I can't see anything threatening, except this bruise on your right side. What happened there?"

"Cob kicked me, I think. Very hard."

"Who is Cob?"

Elena shuddered. "One of them."

Holly stared past the injured girl into space, Quint's

words from last night filtering into her memory, and she asked Elena, "Wilt and Luther had nothing to do with this?"

Elena shook her head slightly. "No. They would have stopped it, I think, if they had been there."

"And Jim Tom?"

The name caused a violent quaking throughout Elena's body, and Holly soothed her as best she could. But Elena trembled still, while tears rolled down her battered face.

"He finally . . ." Elena groaned with a fierceness that brought tears to Holly's eyes.

She held one of the girl's hands, and smoothed her matted hair away from her forehead with the other. She didn't ask Elena to finish the sentence; she didn't need to. Hadn't Jim Tom Farrell made his intentions clear to everyone around? If only Quint had put him in jail and kept him there.

Elena suddenly stopped crying and forced herself to sit up, against Holly's objections. All the pain she felt released itself in the intensity of her voice.

"I will never return to that place. I will die first."

Holly tried to comfort her. "You don't have to, Elena. Believe me, I won't let anyone make you go back to the TF."

Tears brimmed in Elena's eyes, but she squeezed them back. "I must tell you about it."

Holly plumped the pillow and tried to keep from crying herself. Gently, she eased Elena back to the bed. "Shhh. You're safe from those beasts now, and you need to rest. Try to put it out of your mind."

Elena shook her head. "I must tell you."

So Holly listened, her despair growing from disbelief to shock to horror. Drawing a chair to the bedside, she listened to Elena's halting yet carefuly phrased English, realizing that Papa was responsible for the girl's ability to express herself so well in a second language.

"Jim Tom Farrell is an evil man," she began slowly. "It is common for men to make eyes at young ladies they pass on the street, even at married ladies such as myself. Especially if the ladies are Mexican, no one seems to mind. But Jim Tom is different. He thinks that since his father is so powerful, he can take as well as look."

"I know." Holly's words echoed the hatred she had learned to feel for this demon. "He tried to attack me right here on the streets of Silver Creek."

Elena's concern immediately transferred to Holly. "I did not know."

"It was nothing. I mean, nothing like this. He only tore my dress . . . and my self-respect. But go ahead."

"Jim Tom has been trying to . . . well, you know what I mean . . . for a long time."

"Oh, Elena! How dreadful for you, having to live out there with those ruffians."

"I was safe most of the time. Tom Farrell would let nothing like this happen." She looked at Holly. "And Wilt and Luther, they protected me, too, when they could."

Holly's mind recoiled at the idea of Wilt and Luther in the roll of rescuers. "I can hardly believe that. They stand behind Jim Tom as if they'll back up anything he chooses to do. And they certainly didn't come to my rescue that day."

"Who did?" Elena asked.

Holly looked away, torn by the memory of that fateful day. "Sheriff Jarvis," she answered in clipped tones. "But he only broke it up. He did nothing to let Jim Tom know that such behavior would not be tolerated." Anger at Quint mounted within her. If he had acted like a real sheriff, he might have prevented this atrocity. "And now look what has happened," she hissed.

"This was not the fault of Sheriff Jarvis," Elena said. "No one could have prevented it. Jim Tom is like a wild beast. I knew one day he would finally succeed." Tears rolled down her cheeks, and she gingerly covered her battered face with scratched and bruised hands. Finally she raised her head and continued, determinedly. "But I must tell you. You must know."

Holly wondered at the girl's stamina, thinking that somehow the shock of actually being raped must have triggered a need to talk about it. Surely it would be best to try to forget such a dastardly act, but perhaps talking about it would drive some of the fear from her mind.

"What happened yesterday has been building up for many years," Elena said. "Every time Jim Tom came to town, I tried to hide, because if he saw me, he would grab hold of me and kiss me. Raphael, that was my husband. Raphael did not understand that Jim Tom acted the same to all women. Skirts, he called us."

Elena paused a moment, her mind somewhere in the past. Holly poured a glass of water and held it to her lips. After sipping, Elena continued with what Holly began to think of as a self-purging.

"Raphael was a good husband."

"Papa wrote about him," Holly told her. "Papa thought highly of your husband."

"Your papá did not tell you about Raphael and Jim Tom?"

"He mentioned the tension," Holly said.

"Raphael worked for Tom Farrell, and because of the way Jim Tom treated me, Raphael and Jim Tom fought often. Someone always broke it up, until . . ." She pressed her lips together for a moment before she continued. "I told Raphael that he was a fool to make such a dangerous enemy, even though we were in the right."

"You certainly were. Why didn't you go to the sheriff?"

Elena sneered. "The sheriff? We are Mexicans. We cannot go to a gringo sheriff and say the boss's son is making trouble."

Holly thought of her own lack of cooperation from Quint and realized that what Elena said had merit.

Looking vacantly out the window, Elena shrugged. "What could he do, anyway? Jim Tom had broken no laws. At least, not then. But one day Jim Tom was in town, drunk as always, and he caught me beside the stables and tore my blouse, bad. And he left scratches on my . . ." She blushed through the bruises, but continued, "on my chest."

Holly sucked in her breath. "Surely you could have gone to the sheriff then."

"Jim Tom is not just any gringo," Elena said, her voice perplexed. "He is the son of a powerful man. They would have said I caused it. But you will see."

"I understand what you mean, Elena. It could have happened the same way in Tennessee. The carpet-baggers have no concern for my people, either."

Elena continued. "I hid the blouse and tried to conceal the scratches, but . . ." She tensed, recalling something painful. "But Raphael saw them anyway, and the blouse." She clasped her arms about herself then, holding her shaking body. Holly dreaded what was to come.

"The next day at the ranch," Elena said, "Raphael confronted Jim Tom, called him names and threatened to kill him if he ever looked at me again. Tom Farrell was there. When Raphael came in that night he told me that Mr. Farrell was so mad at Jim Tom when he saw my blouse—Raphael had taken it with him—that he struck his son across the face in front of all the hands.

"I was afraid for Raphael to return to the ranch, but

nothing happened the next day, until . . ." Her voice faltered and a sob shook her chest. "When Raphael left the ranch the following evening, he was . . . he was shot in the back of the head."

Holly gasped. "But I thought . . ."

Elena stared at her. "Jim Tom got off because your papá testified before the court that Raphael was *not* shot in the back, that it was a fair fight. But I dressed the body."

"That cannot be. Papa would never . . ." Then the truth dawned on her. "Why didn't Papa see the body?"

"He did." Elena's voice was soft, barely audible, and, contrary to the words she spoke, not accusing. Holly's mind whirled.

"I don't understand."

"I do not understand, either. Your papá was very good to me and to Raphael, to everyone. He spoke many times of Jim Tom's wickedness."

Holly stared through Elena, trying to grasp the meaning behind the words, but she saw only Papa, his contagious smile, the bear hug he gave his most prim patients. Papa wouldn't . . . he couldn't . . . A phrase from one of his letters buzzed around in her head like a disoriented honey bee. "He wrote . . ." she began. "But he couldn't have . . . he didn't mean . . ."

"What did your papá write?"

"I don't understand it," Holly said. "Maybe you will. He wrote that he had done something he wasn't proud of, but that he hoped it would improve the life of two young women who were very important to him."

Elena shook her head. "How could setting free the murderer of my husband improve the life of anyone? I was not only widowed, but afterward Tom Farrell took me to his ranch and would not let me leave. He did not want me to tell anyone what I knew."

"And he killed Papa to keep the secret in the family?

But what about the ranchhands? They knew . . ."

"No one knew except Tom Farrell, Jim Tom, your papá, and me. The story Tom Farrell told your papá was that Jim Tom hid out and shot Raphael, then he got scared and told his papá. Mr. Farrell, himself alone, brought Raphael's body to the house of your papá. I was there when he came." She sobbed, then controlled herself.

A strong woman, Holly thought. Or a woman in shock. "The story doesn't make sense, Elena," she said. "If Tom Farrell wanted to keep the murder a secret, why did he bring the body to Papa? Raphael was already dead."

Elena nodded. "Yes, he was dead when they arrived at the house. But you see, everyone knew about the fight the day before, about the blouse and Raphael's threats. If it could be proved that Jim Tom was shot in a fair fight, he would be cleared. It would be self-defense."

Still Holly could not understand . . . could not believe these absurd accusations. "Why not hide the body and forget about it?"

Elena shook her head. "Mr. Farrell could not take that chance," she said. "If Raphael's body turned up murdered . . . shot in the back, everyone would know to blame Jim Tom. Jim Tom has enemies around here. It was safer to see him acquitted in the first place."

Holly nodded slowly. That made sense, she supposed, but nothing else did. "Papa wouldn't do that," she insisted. "Did you hear him agree with Farrell?"

Elena shook her head. "They did not talk of such things in my presence. I dressed the body of my husband, there in the house of your papá, and I stayed there beside him all night. Your papá went off with Mr. Farrell, and when he returned, he had the box . . . the coffin. The funeral had been arranged for the next morning."

"The next morning?"

Elena nodded. "I was too much shocked to think. It was kind of your papá to do such things for me. Then as soon as I returned to my house from the funeral, Mr. Farrell was there. He took me to the ranch, and I never saw your papá again."

"Not even at the trial?"

"I did not go to the trial."

Oh, Dear God! Holly thought. Her light-headedness from this morning turned into a strong, persistent throb. This could not be true. It wasn't. The story had far too many discrepancies.

She looked hard at Elena. Surely she wouldn't lie, yet . . . Delirious? The shock of being raped? Hadn't she herself almost fallen to pieces last night? And over something as simple as losing a house. A house could always be replaced, but Elena had lost much more. Delirious. Of course.

"Where is Sancho?" Elena asked suddenly.

"I don't know. He wasn't at breakfast."

"They will kill him."

"Farrell?"

Elena nodded.

"When Farrell took you to the ranch, why didn't he take Sancho, too? He must have feared Sancho telling this awful secret as well as yourself."

"Sancho was not at the house of your papá when Mr. Farrell brought Raphael to town. I do not think he thought of Sancho until much later."

"What do you mean, much later?"

Elena shrugged as though not sure herself. "I did not hear them mention Sancho until after they talked about the death of your papá. Then they questioned me many times about Sancho and where he could be."

Holly's brain was twisted in knots. She must have

answers, so many answers she hardly knew the questions. She was sure Elena was delirious. Yet, her need to know something, anything, was so great that she pressed on.

"What do you know about Papa's death?"

"Nothing, except that I am sure Mr. Farrell had something to do with it," Elena answered.

Thinking aloud, Holly asked. "He could not keep Papa prisoner, so to protect the secret, he had to kill him?"

Elena nodded, indicating that she agreed with this reasoning.

"But . . ." Holly could not even form the question. "My father was such an honorable man, so just, so . . . He would have risked being killed himself rather than see a murderer set free." She walked to the window and stared out across the pecan trees and the river to the wilderness beyond. "I know him, Elena. He would never lie. Especially not about murder."

Elena looked at her with large, sad eyes. "He did."

"No!" Holly's belief in her father was unshakable. He had been her foundation. Not only because he was Papa, but because he had such high principles. He was a man who would risk danger, ridicule, estrangement. It was in his blood, in his breeding. He wouldn't have . . . If Holbart Campbell said the man was killed in a fair fight, he knew it to be a fact.

"The other wounds? What about the other wounds on Raphael's body?"

"The body of my husband had only one wound," Elena answered simply.

Holly glared at the injured woman. "You are wrong, Elena. There must have been other wounds. You missed them."

Elena shook her head. "No. There was only the one. It entered from the back of the head." She shuddered at the horror of this recollection.

Holly stared at her with unseeing eyes, unable to comprehend . . . to believe . . .

"I am sorry . . ." Elena began.

Sorry? Holly grasped at the tight lawn collar, suddenly frantic to relieve the swirling pressures which enclosed her head, her body. She jumped up and raced from the room, ran down the hall, onto the landing, and straight into Quint's arms.

"Whoa! What's your hurry?"

Unconscious even of who he was, she tore herself loose and ran out the back door and down to the river, where she flung herself onto the ground, gasping for breath.

Her fingers tore at her collar, unfastening the garment around her neck. She felt the cold, wet grass cool her flushed skin. It must have rained last night, but she could not recall. Would she ever be aware of the normal things in life again?

She felt isolated, stranded, heartbroken. Not that she believed for a moment that Papa had committed the crime Elena blamed on him. He wouldn't. He couldn't. It simply was not in his nature. Criminal instincts didn't suddenly appear in a man; they were detected early in life. No Campbell had ever been a criminal.

And no Campbell ever would.

But what had happened to Elena that she would turn against Papa in such a dastardly fashion? Holly thought of the girl's life as a Mexican woman on the frontier—a fiery, beautiful Mexican woman. She could relate to her feeling of not trusting gringos; Holly knew she would have been hard-pressed to make a charge of rape stick against a carpetbagger while Sheriff Willard ruled their home county back in Tennessee. He held strong grudges against the plantation families.

Before the war the Willards had been hard-scrabble people, then afterward, the Yankees had played on their sympathies, further antagonizing them against the plantation families, and putting them in positions of power so they wielded control with a firm and uneven hand. Revenge was an unjust master.

But Elena could have had none of those feelings toward Papa. Papa treated her like a daughter; he taught her to read English; he was preparing her to be Silver Creek's school marm. How could she have turned against him like this?

Holly sobbed into the wet earth. How could Elena turn against Papa? How could she?

She cried herself into exhaustion and lay on the ground, feeling as though she would never have the strength to rise again. And why should she? What had she gotten herself into by coming out here? Caroline had certainly been vindicated in calling her headstrong.

As she lay breathing in the wet grass, her heart gradually slowed its beat, and her mind settled on a new idea. Elena said she wasn't permitted to attend the trial. So, in fact, she didn't really know what had taken place.

The new thought greatly relieved her. Of course, Papa had not done as Elena suggested. Someone, obviously the Farrells, had tried to malign him, to discredit him for their own purposes. Of course, he hadn't perpetrated such an unspeakable offense, and now Holly knew she must correct this idea before it became common knowledge.

She was unaware of time, the elements, her surroundings, until finally sensing someone beside her, she looked over her crossed arms into Quint's troubled eyes.

He squatted before her on his heels and reached to smooth her hair back from her eyes. "I talked to

Elena," he said. "I'm awful sorry, Holly. If I'd listened to you, this would never have happened."

"You couldn't have stopped it, Quint," Holly said bitterly. "Jim Tom would have attacked her eventually. He had been trying to for years, or so she said. Actually, she might not be telling the truth."

Quint cocked his head, confused by her lack of sympathy. "What do you mean?"

Holly still did not move, and she spoke in a monotone. "I don't think she knows what she's saying. She's delirious."

"She isn't making up all those cuts and bruises," he argued.

Holly glared at him. "Go ahead and take her side. But Papa didn't do it."

"We're talking about what Jim Tom did to Elena," he said, frowning. "Your pa had nothing to do with that. Nobody's saying he did."

A weak listlessness seemed to permeate her muscles, and she struggled to find enough energy to convince him. "What she told you about Papa is all lies."

His concern deepened. "She didn't say a word about your pa, Holly."

"Oh." She sat up then, and stared vacantly at the river. She must find out the truth so she could prove Papa's innocence before Elena told anyone. But she was suddenly so very tired.

Quint reached to brush the mud from her face, but she pushed his hand away. "Come on, Holly. This ground's too wet to be sitting on. It came a gully-washer last night, remember?"

She looked at him with an uncomprehending stare, then fell against his body when she tried to stand. He held her steady.

"Are you sure you're all right?" he asked.

Her legs wobbled, and she could see nothing but

shadows through her daze. With some effort she managed to hold back a rising feeling of panic. "Yes, I'm fine."

Quint guided her toward the house, supporting her with his arms. "I'll see Jim Tom locked up for this, Holly. I'm sorry I didn't do it sooner."

She smiled, unhearing.

"I'll bet you didn't sleep a wink last night after the fire and all the commo—"

"Fire?" She looked at him with glazed eyes, and he scooped her up in his arms and carried her the rest of the way to the house.

Recalling the fire, the haze in her brain cleared a bit, and she remembered seeing Sancho. Sancho would know the truth. And he had been here last night.

"Where's Sancho?" she asked.

"Last I saw of him was when he rode over to the wagon when we arrived at your pa's house. He took off sometime during the fire."

She sagged against him. Sancho gone? Sancho was her last hope.

"I'm worried about that youngun," he told her. "He's almighty scared of something. And he isn't one to scare easy."

Inside he sat her down at the kitchen table. "Give her something to eat, Rosie. Then see to it that she gets to bed and stays there."

Holly looked at him blankly, seeing only Sancho and Papa. Sancho would never turn against Papa. She must find him.

Kneeling beside her chair, Quint hugged her to him quickly. "I have a job to do, Holly. It'll only take a day or so, then I'll be back to help you out." He kissed her lips softly, then stood. "Promise me you won't leave town until I return."

She looked at him curiously.

"Promise?"

She sighed. "Where do I have to go?"

The door slammed behind him when he left, and the next thing Holly was aware of was Rosie's dinner bell three hours later. She awoke with a clear head, but the fuzziness returned gradually along with the realization of what had happened during the morning.

And with the fuzziness came panic. What was she to do? Her first instinct was to run away from this place before she lost her mind completely, but now she had to stay to clear Papa's name. Suicide was bad enough. Now they were accusing him of a crime. Papa!

She didn't go in to dinner, but left by the back way and went straight to the burned-out shell of Papa's house.

Last night's rain had been hard enough to put out even the smoldering embers, leaving a mound of soggy soot, incompletely charred timbers, and fire-blackened rock. Nothing had been left unburned.

She walked through the mess, oblivious to the soot which clung to her already muddy blue skirts. In the kitchen area, she found the copper plates, and where the bedroom had once been, a metal box in which she had put the last of her jewelry. Although somewhat melted and badly in need of cleaning, the jewels themselves appeared unharmed.

The money she borrowed from the bank was nowhere to be found. The velvet bag would have burned, of course, and the coins would be blackened and lost among the rubble. Only a thorough sifting would be likely to turn them up, and she certainly didn't feel up to that. The jewelry would be enough to get her home.

Back of the house she found the river flowing well out of its banks, indicating that the rain had indeed been a hard one—the gully-washer Quint had proclaimed it.

She leaned against one of the pecan trees, staring at the muddy, swirling water, feeling it echo her mind. Not even one clear thought would surface, and that frightened her. She tried to reason that Elena was in bad shape, not responsible for her ramblings. In a few days when she was better, they could talk about her accusations and perhaps get to the bottom of it—at least, Holly could find out who had told her such a tale.

Of course, the story was all lies perpetrated by Tom Farrell. But for what reason, she could not even guess. Papa wouldn't have been a party to such an act, and she couldn't imagine why Farrell would slander him in such a manner. What could Farrell hope to gain from such talk?

Her swirling mind cleared somewhat, and Quint's voice came to her as plainly as if he were standing beside her, telling her the same thing he had said on their first picnic beneath this very tree—something she had dismissed at the time.

She had asked him what he found in Papa's letters, and he answered, after acknowledging the unsavory reputation Papa had saddled him with, "The only puzzle in the letters is why he didn't mention the trial. That trial was the talk of the country, and your pa's testimony saved Jim Tom's bacon. It's curious he didn't see fit to mention it, since he laid out everything else that happened around here."

She grasped her throbbing head in her hands and screamed. It could not be true! It was not true! No! Turning, she ran wildly, blinded by her disbelief.

"Whoa there, miss."

The shout brought her to an abrupt stop before the carriage of R. J. Norton.

Banker Norton looked down at her muddy, soot-stained attire with a disdainful eye, shying back in his seat as though he feared she might somehow contaminate him.

"I have come with regretful news, miss."

She stared at him, trying to bring her mind into focus. At first she thought he had been merely passing by and stopped to prevent her running into his carriage. But at his words, she realized he must have ridden here specifically to find her.

Wary of his intentions, she backed off a bit, stumbling, catching her balance, absorbing his dislike for her, which for some strange reason caused her to straighten her shoulders, tilt her head up, and pat her straggling hair into place. Her gestures reminded her quite incongruously of old Mrs. Hobbstadt back home, whom Mama always accused of putting on airs, and she almost giggled.

"I'm afraid you have caught me slightly unprepared for callers, Mr. Norton." She turned and gestured with a sweeping motion toward the mound of burned timbers and rubble. "My parlor is quite indisposed at the moment."

His eyes clenched in a frown, as if he wasn't sure whether he addressed a sane woman or one completely off her rocker.

Off her rocker she felt, but she also knew the enemy when she saw him, and Banker Norton was the enemy in her book—right along with the Farrells.

Mr. Norton cleared his throat. "I have come to call in your loan, miss. Mr. Farrell found the deed to the property you claim as your pa's. So there goes your collateral—up in smoke, you might say." He smiled, obviously pleased with his attempt at a joke, and she wondered if he joked with sane women, or only those he considered a trifle demented.

But she did not smile. His placating, condescending tone, his ostentatious manner as he sat holding the reins in his limp, namby-pamby hands, suddenly clotted all her disillusion and disbelief into a mass of outrage and anger.

"I am sure you have nothing left of the money I loaned you," he continued, "so I shall confiscate this property in return."

Holly's back arched, and she raised her chin a notch higher. "You are welcome to what is left of it, Mr. Norton. And you'll find the remainder of the paltry sum you advanced me somewhere in that mess."

He stiffened. "I suggest you be on the next stage, miss. I recall telling you myself that Silver Creek was no place for a lady of your ilk."

Holding her chin steady at its haughty angle, she spoke in precise tones. "How right you were, Mr. Norton. And I certainly intend to heed your advice this time. It will take me no longer than that to wind up my business here."

He looked at her suspiciously.

"You see, Mr. Norton. I have known for some time who murdered my father." She paused, shifting her gaze to where she could watch his expression. "Now I can prove it."

Chapter Fourteen

Within an hour after leaving Holly in Rosie's care, Quint rode out of Silver Creek headed along the stage road to his rendezvous with Sheriff Bales and their hand-picked posse.

His mind, however, was not on the business at hand, but back in Rosie's kitchen with Holly. Every time she got her feet on the ground, it seemed like something else came along to knock her down. The next few days should take care of some of her problems, but now he feared she might never recover from the blows she had already taken.

Some folks didn't. He swore to himself. And he hadn't been any help last night, jumping on her like that about not having any courage. He'd thought at the time that he might jolt her to her senses.

But now, after what Jim Tom did to Elena Salinas, he figured his own chances with Holly were slim to none. She'd likely never forgive him for not putting Jim Tom in jail that day in Silver Creek.

Not that he blamed her. He'd have a hard time living with himself, too. But with so many other folks' lives and property at stake, he knew if he had it to do over again, he'd have to saddle the bronc the same way.

He spurred his mount to a trot. If he could've told her the whole tale, she might have understood . . . But that was water under the bridge now. It went with the job, he supposed. If he'd spilled the beans, he couldn't have expected the others not to. Then before a feller knew what was happening, word would leak out, and the whole supper would be lost.

No, he couldn't have done things any different. In another day or so, if they played their cards right, the ranchers in these parts would be free from worry over rustlers.

Only he stood to lose in this game. Way he saw it, he had dealt himself a bust hand this round—as far as Holly Campbell was concerned, anyhow.

He nooned at Little Sandy, riding up on it unawares, which spooked him, and he warned himself to stop pining over the past and start watching his backtrail, else he'd not be long for this world. More than that, this little chore was risky, and other men's lives depended on him staying on the lookout for trouble.

After that he minded his business and whiled away the hours giving any cayuse who might have come across his trail time to make himself known.

Then, as the evening star showed itself in the late afternoon sky, Quint approached the camp where his companions waited.

All appeared quiet. He circled the area around the camp, trying to discover how close a man could get before being hailed by a guard.

Satisfied at last that they had chosen well, he relaxed. These men were risking not only their lives, but also their property and the lives of their families.

Vigilantes, some would likely call them. But they weren't, not in the sense of the fellers in that Sutton-Taylor feud down in De Witt County. Quint knew, though, that the bitter taste in his mouth came as much from the idea that they were in any way related to a vigilance committee, as it did from the fact that the rustlers they were after happened to be his own family.

He had left the TF with his eyes open, or so he thought back then. After failing to persuade Tom to get rid of the riffraff Jim Tom brought around, Quint knew it was only a matter of time before Jim Tom hit the outlaw trail. He had never suspected Tom could be dragged along with him.

Even as his principles had prevented Quint from becoming a part of the outlaw crowd Jim Tom took up with, so the thought of taking the law into his own hands rode uneasy on his mind. He was, however, the acting sheriff of Silver Creek, and as such he'd found himself unable to take on a whole gang of rustlers single-handed. Same with Clyde Bales, down in Llano County.

Sure, they caught up with a few now and again, but this was a big country, and these rustlers were so well organized that a couple of lawmen would be hard put to stop their maraudering on their own.

So the time had come for banding together to catch the leaders in one sweep. If men were to live in this country, were to be able to bring their families here, to build homes and businesses, they must be able to control lawlessness and violence. And at this time, Quint was satisfied that what they were about to do was the only way for the law to get the upper hand.

After Tom and his men were behind bars, he hoped regular lawmen would be able to keep the peace.

Reconstruction couldn't last much longer. As soon as the state could rid itself of that carpetbagger governor and his murdering State Police, they could set about bringing real law and order to Texas.

But for now—tonight—their chosen trail was the only one he could see for them to travel. He prayed it would be bloodless.

Jed Varner sat on his haunches in the early evening dusk at the base of the gnarled mesquite tree fifty yards in front of the camp. Quint saw Jed before Jed saw him but only because Quint knew where to look.

Jed waved him forward, signaling that he recognized the sheriff as being part of their group. Quint pulled rein beside him.

"Benford's back with the horses," Jed offered. "An Sperry's off to the right in that thicket on the hill." He pointed until Quint nodded, then continued. "Mac's down left fifty yards or so, hid behind that outcroppin'."

Quint nodded again. "Has Bales showed up yet?"

"Nope, but Jefferies is at camp stirring together something his missus sent over. You'd've thought we was going off to a barn-raisin', the way them womenfolk loaded us down with eats."

Quint smiled. "Where did you tell your wives you were headed?"

Jed twisted a boot toe in the ground. "I told Anne that Mac needed some help bringing in a herd of mustangs he run acrost whilst on the trail drive. The other boys told their missus the same. Said we'd be gone one night, but I swear, they sent food for a month."

Quint pulled a silver star from his shirt pocket. "Raise your right hand, Varner."

Jed complied, and Quint pinned the star on his homespun shirt. "Do you swear to uphold the laws of the State of Texas?"

"Sure do," Jed answered. "Hanging's too good for 'em."

Quint flinched. "Don't even whisper that word until this shindig's over. I don't hanker to have a lynch mob on my hands."

"Some of the boys are thinking thataways, though

Sheriff. You might as well know it now."

Quint removed his hat, dried his forehead with his bandana, then wiped the inside of his hatband, all the while trying to figure how best to settle this problem before it arose. He would not be party to a lynching, yet if he were outnumbered . . . He wished to hell Bales would get here. That'd even out the odds a bit. He looked deep into Jed Varner's face in the growing darkness. "Can I count on you, Jed?"

Jed nodded.

"Can I count on you?" Quint repeated. "No matter what your neighbors do?"

"I come from down south, Sheriff, and I seen first hand what vigilance committees do to a man's life. That Sutton an' Taylor feud, why it spilt blood onto ever one about. I've got me a family to raise now, and I don't aim to do it looking over my shoulder. You bet you can count on me. If need be, I'll speak my piece for you."

"Thanks, Jed, I may need it."

Jed resumed his vigil while Quint rode around the camp, leaving his horse with the other saddle stock. Jeremiah Benford stood guard there, and Quint took another star from his pocket. "How're things going, Benford?"

Jeremiah spat tobacco juice to one side. "Fair to middlin'," he answered. "Can't say I ain't looking forward to what lays ahead of us. It's about time we took a rope after them fellers. You're to be thanked for getting this little party together, Sheriff."

"Jeremiah." Quint spoke in as firm a voice as he could command. "There will be no lynching. This is a posse, and it'll remain law-abiding. Sheriff Bales and I figured we weren't doing much good alone in bringing those rustlers to justice." He paused and looked Jeremiah Benford hard in the eyes. "Reason we chose you boys is for your honesty. We could've turned everything over to the State Police, but you know as well as I do that they don't stand for justice on any man's terms."

"I've lost a fearful number of livestock to them fellers," Jeremiah said. "An' it's cost my family a lot of worry, not to speak of all the things we've gone without because of them thieving rascals. They don't deserve any man's justice."

"I agree with you." Quint wondered how riled Jeremiah would be when he learned that Jim Tom and two of his sidekicks had molested Elena Salinas. He prayed no one would come up with that news until he got through the next few hours. "But justice is what they're gonna get—from me and from you boys. I chose you because I know you to be fair-minded men, and I'll hold you accountable." Quint held out the star. "I'm going to trust you, Benford. Hold up your right hand."

Jeremiah complied, and Quint pinned the star on his vest with a goodly portion of misgivings. "Do you promise to uphold the laws of the State of Texas?"

Jeremiah stared at him. "I guess so."

"You're a peace officer now, Benford, sworn to uphold the law. I know I can count on you. In my book there's nothing worse than an officer of the law gone bad, and I know you feel the same."

Jeremiah took his own time answering, saying finally, "I'll go along with you, Sheriff, long as I see them outlaws are headed for a real trial."

Quint slapped him on the shoulder. "You'll be called to testify. You can tell your whole story to the court. Those rustlers aren't going to get off. They'll end up in Huntsville Prison, and to my mind that's worse than hanging. Locked away from family and these wide-open spaces."

"You've got yourself a point there, Sheriff."

Quint made the rounds, deputizing Mac McPherson and Bill Sperry before he approached the camp. He could have waited until the men came in from guard, but he had anticipated their anger and wanted to talk to each man separately. If he stood a chance of winning them over, he knew he must do so privately, and he felt jittery as a june bug, not knowing for sure whether he had convinced them beyond rebellion.

By the time he got to camp and deputized Hank Jefferies, Sheriff Bales arrived with four additional ranchers, these from Llano County. They, too, had been victimized by the rustlers and were fed up with the poor results law enforcement had been able to accomplish against the perpetrators in the past. Quint studied them, feeling their raw edges, realizing that he and Bales had their work cut out keeping this motley crew in line.

Bales's men replaced the Silver Creek men at guard, and the camp bedded down. Quint remained up, sitting well back from the fire, waiting.

Finally, as the dipper began to fade, he heard riders approach the camp.

Wilt and Luther ground-hitched their mounts, and Quint met them at the fire. The three men sat with coffee discussing final plans.

"They're moving the cattle at first light," Wilt said.

"How many boys do you figure they'll have with 'em?"

"All told I'd say ten," Wilt answered. "There's Jake on the wagon with his buffalo gun, and six boys on the herd, not counting Farrell himself and Jim Tom."

Luther grinned. "You might ought not count Cob or E. A., either. They come into camp early this morning looking like they'd been in a cat fight."

"Don't forget Jim Tom," Wilt added. "He was the

worst off of the lot. Can't figure what them sinners got themselves into, but it surely wasn't healthy."

Quint held his tongue. They would find out soon enough. No use fueling the fire at this stage. "What about Tom?"

Wilt and Luther sobered up. "He's to meet us in the canyon," Luther said.

"Plans are to get all the cattle in the canyon and change the brands before heading on west to Mexico. Tom's to be waiting for us in the canyon," Wilt finished.

"You boys've done a fine job," Quint said. "We'll all set a mite easier when this one's over."

They refilled their cups, one after the other. Wilt moved from the log he sat on to the fire and back again. Luther stared into the coals, leaving his coffee untouched.

Quint studied them carefully. He had ridden with these men most of his grown life. He knew them, and they knew him, like family. And something was troubling them. Something more than the difficulties at hand. Finally he asked, "What's on your mind?"

Wilt and Luther exchanged looks.

"We'd be in a mess of trouble going into this shebang blind," Quint said. "What's on your mind?"

"Troy Grant." The men blurted out the name at the same time, as if spitting hot coffee onto the ground.

"What about him? Quint asked.

"He's after you, Quint," Wilt told him.

"He left camp an hour before us with a thousand dollars gold jingling in his pockets," Luther said.

"There's another thousand when he brings you back to Tom—dead," Wilt finished.

Quint sucked in his breath. He took another swallow of coffee, and it went down like a hard rock boulder.

"Farrell's getting edgy," Luther told him. "Says you're riding too close to the truth. He wants you out of the picture before you stumble onto something . . ."

"Something you've no business knowing," Wilt said. "Them's his words, exact as I recall."

Quint crossed to the fire. He'd never figured on this. Oh, sure, he'd fortified the cabin, but his precautions had been against harassment—against being burned out, or the like. He'd never figured Tom would have him killed.

Or try to.

He slapped Wilt on the back. "What's the matter with you two, anyhow? You look like you swallowed a handful of pillbugs. Ain't you got no confidence in my shooting?"

They looked up at him, worry showing in their faces.

Wilt spoke first. "Damn it, Quint, he won't give you a chance at a fair fight."

"That's right," Luther said. "He'll lay up for you somewheres, and . . ."

"I've traveled a rocky road before, boys. He won't get me."

"You'd better ride wary," Wilt warned.

"And leave here with a plan," Luther said.

"Sounds fine to me." Quint filled his cup and took another swallow of coffee. He couldn't recall when his mouth had been so dry, but he would not give in to fear. He could not. "What kind of plan do you have in mind?"

"We talked about it on the way over," Wilt told him.

He should have guessed, Quint thought. His two best friends. They'd ride herd on him, for sure, if he wasn't real wily.

"We figure on riding with you when you leave here in the morning," Luther said. "Let Bales and the others go after the rustlers. We'll ride along with you and take care of Grant for oncet and for all."

Quint tried to sound jovial. "Hell, fellers, this ain't

your fight. You don't think I'm going to lower my head value by letting him get three of us for the price of one, do you? Why, never in all my born days did I figure I'd come so downright expensive."

"You can't ride into this alone," Wilt said. "We're coming with you."

Quint turned serious. "We've spent a lot of time setting up this scheme to catch Tom and his rustlers." He motioned around the camp. "These men are counting on us—our own ranchers back in the trees asleep, and the Llano County fellers out there risking their necks standing guard. We can't let them down, boys. Not over some foolhardy notion Tom Farrell takes of wanting to see me dead. You get on back to that herd, like we planned, and I'll ride out in the morning with Bales. If Grant catches up with me . . . well, I'll wrastle that bobcat when I get to it. Right now, my job is to make this country a law-abiding place to live in."

Luther squinted at him through the smoke of the campfire. "You promise you won't go riding off on some harebrained scheme of your own?"

Quint nodded. "Now, you fellers get on back to camp before our rustlers miss you. We can't slip and spill the beans this close to suppertime."

Wilt and Luther stood, signaling their compliance, but their sagging shoulders told him that they didn't completely trust him.

"You gave us your word that you won't ride out of here alone," Luther said.

"And we'll have your hide, if you don't keep it," Wilt threatened.

Quint shook his head in amusement. "Looks like you'll have to stand in line for that, boys."

* * *

When R. J. Norton drove away from her house, Holly wasted no time. Whatever else the banker had done, he had brought her to her senses, and she was grateful for that.

At the livery stable, she inquired about the horse she had arranged for earlier.

"I saddled the dun you rode before, Doc, but," Slim eyed her disheveled blue dress, "I'll hold onto him for you, whilst you mosey back to the hotel and change to your ridin' get-up."

Holly shook her head. "No, thanks, Mr. Samples. I'm . . . I'm in a hurry."

As she mounted, tucking her skirts behind the saddle horn and exposing not only her ankles, but an inch or so of leg, as well, she wondered at her lack of propriety. Even during the war she had never been in a position to reveal a bare ankle, but now she found she didn't even care. Such frivolities belonged to a lifetime with totally different priorities.

But riding toward the canyon, she wondered what her priorities actually were these days. At the moment her thoughts centered on getting to the canyon, Papa's canyon. For, whatever Mr. Norton or Tom Farrell or anyone else said, that property had belonged to Papa. She may not understand his method of obtaining it, and Elena may even be proved right, but no matter what he had done, Papa had not deserved to be murdered.

She spurred her mount, vowing to keep her promise to find his murderers and see them punished before she returned to Hedgerow.

She wished she could believe that Elena was either misguided or lying. In fact, she had believed exactly that for a time this morning. But now, recalling Quint's statement about Papa's testimony saving Jim Tom's life, her belief faltered beneath mounting questions.

And the questions resulted in a heartache such as she had never known before. The physical pain was so severe that for a time she feared she was about to expire, but she continued to the canyon, determined to complete her task before anything fatal should befall her.

Quint should be returning from the TF at any moment with Jim Tom and his cohorts in tow. Earlier she would have relished seeing Jim Tom locked behind bars. But everything had changed now. She must tend to her business and get away from this wretched place.

So deep in thought was she, so anguished and alone, that she paid little attention to where she rode, until finally drawing rein, she surveyed the country. At least the rain hadn't been heavy here. Perhaps the creek wouldn't be up after all.

She had been to the canyon only one time—during the spring when the countryside was vibrant with wildflowers. Now the landscape was beginning to fade beneath the summer sun, and the only colors besides varying shades of brown were occasional red and yellow blossoms of prickly pear clumps, waxy white clusters of blooming yuccas, and a smattering of muted greens here and there.

On that earlier trip with Quint, they had not ridden straight to the canyon, but had approached it in a roundabout way on their return from the TF. She didn't doubt her ability to find her way there now, however, since from the time she was a little girl going on calls with Papa, she had had a good sense of direction. He always said so. In fact, many was the time that she drove them home after a late call while he slept in the buggy beside her, exhausted from a difficult case.

Often she had had to find her way by the stars or in daylight by landmarks. He had taught her well.

She drew a sharp breath, recalling the innumerable

things she had learned from this man. How fortunate she was to have had a father like him.

She wiped tears from her face. And how lonely and confusing life was without him.

Using the powers of observation she had sharpened through the years, she located the twin peaks and headed for them. Sancho had mentioned a second cave, but she had no idea where it might be. She wanted only to get to the cave she knew, to set her thoughts in order, and to somehow find a way to understand the man she had thought she knew so well.

If only she had his journal . . . If only Sancho would be in the canyon.

Finding the canyon was easier than she anticipated, and quicker, and it was only when she pulled up at the rocky wash and saw the dun eagerly put his muzzle into the muddy stream that she realized she had been riding hard.

A large sign posted on a gnarled cedar tree at the canyon entrance struck her with the force of a bolt of lightning: Trespassers Will Be Shot on Sight.

For a moment her mind traveled back in time: had the notice been here on her first visit?

It hadn't. She was sure of that. Fear swept keenly up her neck at the memory of the sharpshooter on the hill, and her first instinct was to turn and run for town. Sancho had even said someone ransacked the cave.

She sighed. They had posted the notice after finding Sancho's hideout. It wasn't meant for her alone.

Besides, when Quint rode into town with Jim Tom, all the TF hands would be sure to follow. She was probably safer, and more alone, out here than she would be in Silver Creek!

Practical thinking, as always, did little to relieve her physical symptoms of fear, but she was at least able to prod herself into the canyon.

Wading her mount through the muddy stream, she was glad the rain hadn't been upcountry, for when she left town, she had given no thought to Quint's warning not to come out here in bad weather.

Inside, the canyon looked still and uninhabited. She kept to the left, hugging the wall whenever possible, and when brush grew heavy against the sides, she rode around it, then quickly back to the bluff.

Finally she made her way to the place where she and Quint had climbed to the cave. A large outcropping of boulders which had fallen from the face of the cliff long ago protruded in an arch, and she found ample space behind them to tether the dun.

The climb was not as steep as she recalled, but the journey to the top seemed more perilous with her thoughts divided between the sign at the entrance and the one-time sharpshooter on the opposite hill.

In the end, however, she pulled herself safely onto the ledge and sat for a moment catching her breath.

Inside the cave she was disappointed to find no sign of Sancho, even though truthfully she hadn't expected him to be here. A thorough search revealed no journal, either, nor anything else for that matter, including food.

That last thought reminded her of the many hours that had passed since her hastily consumed breakfast, and she patted her growling stomach, assuring herself she wouldn't starve before supper. If she arrived too late for the meal, Rosie would have something left in the kitchen.

Sitting on the ledge in the shadow of the overhang, she scanned the opposite cliff intently, studying each detail of the stratified rocks. The many caves dotting the cliffs all looked like black, scooped-out indentations in the walls, and she could tell the depths of none of them.

A desperate feeling overtook her as she studied the cliffs. Suppose Sancho never came.

Hours passed and Holly chided herself for coming here. What had she hoped to learn? Nowhere did she see anything to tell her why Papa had bought this land. She had only deluded herself into thinking that every question had an answer, that every problem could be solved.

When she had almost given herself up to despair, a noise at the bottom of the cliff startled her. And here, as on the prairie last night with Sancho and Elena, she belatedly realized she had come away with no weapon.

Quickly searching the cave for a substitute, she found a chunk of firewood.

Footsteps scraped the side of the hill, growing louder as the climber approached the cave. Her mind raced in a torrent of speculation. It must be Sancho, yet . . .

It must be. Only two people were aware that she knew about this cave—Sancho and Quint. And Quint would be busy in town with his arrests. It must be Sancho, but why did he not call to alert her?

Anxiety rose within her as she struggled to keep from thinking about the other possibilities. It could be anyone else. Anyone who had spotted the dun hidden behind the boulders, or . . .

Or—her mind rushed forward—anyone who had seen her leave the livery stable on the dun, followed her here, and . . .

The noise grew louder, and she positioned herself close to the ledge where she hoped to remain unseen until she had a good look at the visitor. Drawing back her arms and holding the stick of firewood high above her head, she waited.

Her hands sweated against the rough cedar bark, her breath caught, and she held it in with pursed lips. Her eyes stared transfixed at the edge of the rock surface.

Suddenly she saw fingers—brown fingers—and she stifled a scream at the sight of a head of black hair. Two forces struggled within her, one demanding that she wait to see a face before striking with her club, the other urging her to swing now before it was too late.

At last a face showed itself, and she exhaled her pent-up breath. "Sancho!"

"Lordy, ma'am, you could've swiped me clean off the hill."

Holly's throat contracted in a spasm. She dropped the chunk of firewood and wondered at her fraying nerves. She would surely be fit for a madhouse before she got home to Tennessee.

"What are you doing up here, ma'am?" Sancho asked. "I told you ol' man Farrell knows 'bout this hideout."

"I didn't know where else to go." Her voice shook, and she was frightfully near tears. "How did you find me?"

"Followed you from outside town," he said. "I hid out at the edge of town, hopeful to see what Farrell and his men was up to, burning your pa's house an' all." He settled himself back of the ledge, and she sat also, clasping her still-shaking arms about herself.

"How's Elena getting on?" he asked.

"She's all right. She was badly beaten, but I think she'll recover." Holly still cringed at the thought of Elena's molested body. "What do you know about her, Sancho?"

He shrugged. "What'd you want to know?"

"Everything."

"Well, your pa sure set store by her. Said she was smart as a whip."

"Smart enough to make up a lie about him?"

"About your pa?"

Holly nodded.

"What for? What'd she say?"

Holly wanted to tell him, but she couldn't bring herself to voice the dreadful accusations Elena had made against Papa.

Finally she tried. "Elena said Papa's testimony at Jim Tom's trial was false. That Jim Tom really murdered her husband."

Sancho looked at her. "I've heard such."

"I know my father," Holly said. "He would never swear to a falsehood, especially one involving murder. Never. It would be against everything he stands . . . or stood for."

"Times of trouble, I reckon a man has a right to change what he stands for."

Holly's anger grew. "Papa was the most honest man I have ever known," she insisted. "He would not do something so . . . so wrong."

"It ain't easy, ma'am, judgin' right and wrong."

She stared at him. Quint had said almost exactly the same thing. Did they all think she was crazy? She knew Papa better than any of them. He wouldn't . . .

"There's a whole long story to it, ma'am. You'll see. But right now, I think we'd best get on back to town. Who all knows you're gone?"

She thought a minute. "I didn't tell anyone where I was going. Except Mr. Samples, and he wouldn't tell anyone. Besides, when Quint comes back . . ." She paused, realizing that Sancho probably passed Quint and his prisoners on his way from Silver Creek. When she asked him, however, he hadn't.

"Why'd you think the sheriff went to the TF?"

She told him about the events of the morning. "And the sheriff left, saying he had a job to do. I'm sure he intended to ride to the TF and arrest Jim Tom and the two men Elena called Cob and E. A. Do you know them?"

"Yes'm," Sancho answered. "They're a hazard, all right. But I never seen the sheriff ride out that way. I was up on a rise, watching the road he would have taken, and he didn't travel it."

"He may have cut across country."

"Not till he was up the road a piece," Sancho said. "The brush is too thick back of the livery stable. He'd have taken the road, then maybe switched off after he crossed the river."

She thought about it and decided Sancho could have been napping. They had all had a late night.

"Anyway," she said, "I'm sure Quint has arrested Jim Tom and the others by this time, and all of Farrell's men are probably in town right now. So we don't have to worry about them finding us here in the canyon for a while." She looked toward him anxiously. "Do you have Papa's journal?"

He nodded. "Yes'm. It's in the other cave. 'Long with some food we stashed there." He looked out across the canyon floor. "Folks in town will likely be worrying about you. Seems best for us to head on back."

Holly bristled. She had considered other people all her life, and look where it got her. She was tired of it. She was sick of it. Tears stung her eyes as she thought that this was to be her lot in life from now on. When she got back to Hedgerow, it would be Caroline and her nieces and nephews. There would always be someone to put before herself, before what she wanted out of life.

However, at this moment, she was hard-pressed to define exactly what she did want from life. She had wanted the war not to happen, but it did; she had wanted to be with Papa, and he was dead; she had wanted to start a new life, and here she was in the midst of a worse nightmare than she could have ever dreamed up; she had wanted, desperately wanted, Quintan

Jarvis, and she finally realized that even if she had gotten him, their life would have been a great disappointment. It seemed that she couldn't even leave with Papa's honor and good name intact—even that had been tainted.

She swallowed hard and held her head high. All she had left was her own spirit and gumption, and she was not going to relinquish that, at least not for this one day.

Tomorrow, of course, she might take to her bed and never get up, as Mama used to say, but for today . . .

"Let them worry," she told Sancho. "As I told Mr. Norton this morning, I am through with Silver Creek. My business here is finished. Now that I know who murdered Papa and can prove it, I . . ."

"You told Norton that?" Sancho stared wide-eyed at her.

She nodded. "As soon as . . ."

"Oh, ma'am. We'd best get a move on. Quick. If you told him that, we're in a heap of trouble."

"How do you mean?"

He looked at her, alarm bringing out the white in his eyes. "He went straight and told ol' man Farrell, that's what he done. I saw him ride out of town this morning headed in the direction of the TF like he was chasing a fire, and that's what it was all about." He jumped up and pulled Holly to her feet. "We'd best get moving."

"Won't they find us on the way to town?"

"We ain't goin' to town, ma'am. It'd be plumb loco to ride out of here now. We'll go to the other cave, an' come morning, we'll figure what to do."

Chapter Fifteen

Quint sat back from the fire chewing on a stick and mulling over the events of this day and the day ahead like a squirrel worrying a pile of leaves.

After Wilt and Luther left, he had discussed things with Bales, and they agreed that the success of the raid depended on them tending strictly to the business at hand.

At first Quint had thought to go along with the original plans—to leave camp in the morning with the boys, as he promised Wilt and Luther he would, then take care of Grant after the rustlers were safely under arrest. But if Grant should ambush them on the way to the canyon, one or more of the posse might be killed in the fracas.

He couldn't risk that; nor could he endanger the success of this raid. So, reluctantly, he had sought out Bales.

Not one to confide personal matters, Quint found it hard to tell Bales that Tom Farrell himself had set a hired killer on him, yet he saw no other course.

"What'd you propose?" Bales had asked.

"I figure you boys ought to carry on as planned," Quint replied. "Loose-herd the rustlers out of sight until they get into the canyon. Wilt or Luther will slip away and signal us when the branding starts . . . and when Tom arrives." He paused, then continued, trying to suppress his own welling emotions. "We have to sit tight and catch Tom at the scene, else he'll likely wriggle out of any blame."

"What about you?" Bales asked.

"I'll head out by myself and take care of business. With luck I'll meet you boys outside the canyon in time for the shindig."

Quint and Bales sat silent, their stares crossing paths into the darkness beyond the campfire. Finally Quint spoke again. "You shouldn't have any trouble with the Silver Creek boys. They're itching for a hanging, same as yours, but I'll be back in time to help you hold them in line."

Bales inhaled deeply. "You as confident as you make out?"

Quint laughed. "Ain't much use being otherwise."

"Where'd you figure to catch up with Grant?"

Quint shrugged. "That's a fair question. I'll likely study on it a bit between now and sunup."

So here he sat with a faint glow tinting the eastern horizon. And still he wasn't sure how to approach the coming day. He and Bales had agreed that he should hang around camp until they all left at first light. Thataway the boys wouldn't wonder where he'd gone off to.

And Bales wouldn't be stuck with nine deputies who knew they had only one sheriff to control their lynching instincts. It would be simple to ride out with the others, then lose himself behind a hill or growth of brush.

So the beginning would be simple, he thought. Nothing else figured that way. Where would Grant look for him? How much time had Tom given him to do the job? Quint threw the stick into the fire. And more important to his mind, how much did Tom know about the posse?

Likely not much, Quint decided, since Tom evidently saw him as the only threat to their rustling operation. He clenched his jaws against a nagging feeling of commitment to the man. Tom hadn't hesitated to hire a gunman to kill him.

Quint wondered why that surprised him. Through the years Tom had become more and more cocksure, evolving now, it seemed, into a cold-blooded killer . . . if one without the guts to commit the deed personally, a man who nevertheless considered himself well outside the reach of the law.

But Tom Farrell had not always been that way. Time was, Quint recalled, when he had hung on every word and action of this uncle-turned-parent. Perhaps it began with Ma. She had looked on Tom as a great man, one who saved them from a life of roaming the country following Pa.

Of course, the only man Ma had to compare Tom with was Pa. But Pa, for all his shiftless ways, wasn't a killer. He might have been single-minded and selfish, but he was not lawless.

Quint stared into the campfire, mesmerized by memories of his life at the TF. Tom had put him right to work, and a firm taskmaster he was. But he worked right alongside Quint, and Quint took to the work and attentions of the older man like a thirsty steer to a gyp-water stream.

When the war came along, Quint found himself completely under his uncle's spell. Boys his age stopped by the ranch at mealtime on their way to sign up, and Quint was eager to go fight, too. But Tom said no, and Quint obeyed.

Tom was a rancher, pure and simple. The only thing that mattered to him then, as now, was land.

And the only land he was interested in was his own—that being defined by himself as not only the property to which he held deed, but any land bordering his titled property to which he happened to develop an interest.

Land divided into states, controlled by governments did not interest him. Quint had often heard him say that he didn't care which side won the war, as long as they stayed clear of his land. If they came too close and tried to harness him with laws and provisions, whether North or South, or even the State of Texas, he considered them the enemy and treated them as such.

And Quint, after his initial disappointment at not being allowed to go to war abated, was content to stay home and tend stock.

He wasn't even sure he would have made a good soldier. He was a good shot, yes. He would match his shooting with the best, but killing had never been a thing he cared for. So staying home from war, once he realized he would be required to kill men he didn't know, men with whom he had no personal disagreement, became a blessing in his book.

He had learned to shoot, because shooting was a necessary skill—both for protection and for putting meat on the table. First, he had shot at bottles Tom lined up on a fence, then at bottles thrown in the air. Tom considered him a natural, and his pride spurred Quint to greater and greater heights of marksmanship. Whenever Aunt Jen wanted something special for supper—wild turkey, antelope, quail, or such—she sent Quint, and he never disappointed her. But neither did he slaughter game needlessly.

Like Jim Tom. When Jim Tom became old enough for them to ride together, Quint continually scolded his young cousin for recklessly killing animals, then leaving them to the buzzards.

Recalling Jim Tom's bloodthirsty nature, Quint felt

a chill rise along the roots of his hair. As a boy, Jim Tom had delighted in filling a fawn as full of buckshot as he could, or in seeing how many antelope in a herd he could shoot before they darted out of range.

And the years had not matured him. In fact, it seemed to Quint that age had only deepened his cousin's mean streak—a streak which had been directed at Quint more than once. Since leaving the TF, Quint had often thanked the Man Upstairs that he had escaped without being pumped full of buckshot himself.

Now it appeared his time had come. A story Ma used to read him from the Good Book danced in the flames before his eyes—a troublesome story of two brothers called Cain and Abel.

But however repellent the idea might be to him, Quint knew he would have a better chance in this showdown if Tom had sent Jim Tom after him instead of Troy Grant. Grant's reputation as a hired gun was well in place across Texas. If tales were to be taken from Gospel, Grant had figured in half the prominent killings in this state in the last three years. His reputation was beginning to rival that of John Wesley Hardin.

Although Quint was the first to caution that a man's true colors could only be seen by those with a personal stake in the game, he was not about to discount these tales as fancy, not just yet, anyhow. On the other hand, it was too late to start running scared.

The dice had been thrown. So he figured he'd best count up his tally and decide where he stood.

First off, he had the advantage of knowing that Grant was after him. If Grant was to be careless in any way, it might be in thinking he rode unsuspected. But that would be an advantage for Quint only if the two came face to face. Try as he might, Quint could come up with no more points in his favor.

He shrugged in the darkness. What had to be, had to be. He would ride out in the morning, hunt Grant down, and take him in a fair fight. Anything otherwise would not sit well for any longer than it took a sunfishing bronc to wrinkle his spine.

He would ride wary and try not to give Grant a shot at his backside. And he had to be finished with Grant in time to help Bales. These law-abiding ranchers in their bedrolls behind him could not be allowed to turn themselves into heathens no better than Tom Farrell himself.

Holly and Sancho waited for darkness to envelop the canyon before climbing down from the cave. She slipped a number of times on the trail, and by the time they reached the bottom, a light rain began to fall.

She expected to take the dun. She had never left a horse uncurried and unfed at the end of the day. However, Sancho had other ideas.

"He'll be fine here, ma'am. There's grazing enough, and he's out of sight behind them boulders."

She wiped the mist from her face. "Where's the other cave?"

"Yonder, past the entrance," he answered, pointing toward the mouth of the canyon. But in the darkness she was unable to see much beyond the extension of his arm.

"We'll have a good view of this spot from over there," he told her, "so if we see 'em nosing around, we'll have time enough to get down and out of the canyon before they see us."

Perhaps, she thought, guessing that he had silently added that word himself. So far nothing had worked in her favor, and she permitted herself no illusions about being able to escape Tom Farrell's men unseen and on foot.

She said nothing, however, and followed him back the way she had ridden this afternoon, trying to quell her misgivings at leaving her only form of transportation out of reach.

After a few yards, he motioned her to stop, while he worked patiently to remove any sign that they had passed this way.

Her stomach felt queasy as she recalled Quint saying that even a skilled man would leave some kind of trail at night. Then she chastised herself with his counterstatement that Sancho was an expert at concealing a trail.

Moving on they crossed the still muddy stream, and she became more alarmed. "Quint said this stream becomes a torrent after a rain," she called ahead to him.

"Yes'm, it surely does."

"It's raining now. On top of what we had last night, we could be trapped in here." Her voice quivered in her ears, but whether from fright or mere exhaustion, she wasn't sure.

"This is a shower, ma'am. It ain't no thunderstorm."

She looked up at the sky and found it less threatening than she had feared. In fact, she felt strengthened by holding her shoulders up and her head high. She hadn't realized she was hobbling along the ground. A second later, however, she discovered a reason for hobbling when she stumbled over a rock and tripped on her frayed skirts.

Suddenly Sancho stopped at the opposite edge of the cliff, where he pulled a matted tangle of brush away from the wall of limestone.

"There's a trail here, ma'am," he said. "Runs right along the hillside."

The narrow trail was bounded on one side by the cliff

and on the other by a wall of brush which protruded in unexpected places, scratching and stabbing at her in the darkness. Sancho led, and she followed once more, stumbling and crawling, praying that she would not tumble over the edge, nor fall through the brush onto the canyon floor below.

Although not as steep as the path to the other cave, this trail was booby-trapped with boulders and brush, all unseen until she smashed into them. Her hands and knees were raw, her feet ached through her thin-soled shoes, and she felt utterly lost and alone.

Only the image of Elena's beaten and abused body pushed her forward. She had no doubts that Quint had by this time arrested Jim Tom and Cob and E. A., but Sancho was frightened, and she had no choice but to trust his judgment.

Finally she felt Sancho pull her onto the ledge of the second cave, where she sat with her muddled brain quivering in rhythm with her shaking arms and legs and the frantic pounding of her heart.

The darkness which had settled over the canyon hung in and around the thickets and trees more densely in some areas than in others. She decided that a circle of ebony in the center of the canyon must be the spring. And thoughts of the spring reminded her again of her thirst and hunger. She said as much to Sancho.

"We brung some vittles up for such times as these." He handed her a canteen, which she turned over in her hands in the dim light.

"It was your pa's," he told her.

She drank and the water was brackish, but wet and satisfying.

Sancho disappeared into the dark cave, and suddenly she saw a light flare, then flicker to a dim glow.

"Is it safe to have a light?" she asked.

"Yes'm. Back this far, it is. Come on back, an' I'll find you a place to set."

Hesitating briefly at the thought of granddaddy longlegs and other creepy-crawly things, she felt her way toward the faint light.

The ceiling of the cave was a good foot too low for her to be able to stand erect, and touching the stones, she found them now smooth, now porous with hairy protruding roots which tickled her sensitive hands and sent icy shivers down her spine.

Following the cave around a slight el, she found Sancho at the rear, rummaging through a stack of supplies. A lantern stood on the floor in the far corner.

"Do you truly think they will come after us?" she asked.

"Yes'm," he answered without taking his attention away from his search. "Maybe not tonight, but they'll show up tomorrow—or soon. They gotta."

"Why? What harm can we do them?"

"Ma'am, you gotta know ol' man Farrell. When he sets his mind to something, he's like one of them snapping turtles that bites you an' won't let go till it thunders. He wants this canyon back, an' you're standing in his way. And me . . . well, ma'am, I saw him kill your pa, an' he can't let me get away with word like that to spread around."

Holly's exhaustion vanished at the mention of Papa's murder, and in its place a new terror gripped her. Now, at last, she would hear the truth. "Tell me about it."

Sancho looked at her. "We was here at the canyon, your pa an' me, when ol' man Farrell, he rode up all by hisself and just . . ."

Holly stopped him. "Tell me the whole story, Sancho. Start at the beginning. Why did Papa buy this canyon? What did he want with it? Why did Tom Farrell sell it to him?"

Sancho glanced down at their stores, then took two pieces of jerked meat from his pocket and handed one to Holly. "I don't reckon we oughtta risk a fire, ma'am. Chew on this, and you'll get some of your strength back."

Holly bit into the meat, and the piquant flavor of the brine the meat had been soaked in stung her taste buds. Then, as Sancho began the tale she had traveled so far to hear, the story she had tried to learn from so many different people, all of her other senses sharpened, as well, and images suddenly appeared to her, painfully vivid in the shimmering darkness.

"It was the treasure, ma'am. That's what he wanted the canyon for."

Holly bit her lip and shook her head slowly back and forth. The treasure?

Surely not. "It had to be more than treasure, Sancho," she argued. "He wanted to raise horses—blooded horses."

"Yes'm, that too. But not here. He wanted this canyon for the treasure, then he would be able to buy land for horses somewheres else."

She was still not convinced. "You don't need buried treasure to be able to buy land out here. That's nonsense."

"Well, it wasn't only to buy land for his horses that he wanted the treasure. He thought to give some of it to Elena. He felt real bad about Raphael's killing. Real bad. And he wanted to help Elena get a new start."

Holly chewed on the salty meat. "I know he was fond of Elena, but that doesn't explain . . ." She stopped short. What was she saying? Did she believe Elena's story herself? But driven by some incomprehensible need to understand her father's actions, she was unable to change the questions. "Did he ever talk about Raphael's death?"

"No'm. Only that it was a . . . a tragedy, and that Jim Tom'd get his due someday."

Holly thought about it. Surely Sancho would know if the trial had transpired as Elena described. "How did Papa get this property?" she asked. "Did he buy it? Or did Tom Farrell give it to him?"

Sancho was quiet for a moment. "He must've bought it," he answered finally. "Ol' man Farrell don't give nothing to nobody."

Holly felt a moment of triumph. That was exactly the way she had Farrell pegged. "Did you ever hear that Raphael was shot in the back?"

"I've heard tales, but that ain't what Doc said."

"Were you at Papa's house when they brought Raphael's body to town?" she asked.

"No'm. Davy an' me, we'd gone fishing up to a yellow cat hole. Caught a passel, too. Rosie cooked 'em up mighty fine."

Holly washed the salty taste from her mouth with another swig from the canteen. "Who was there?"

Sancho shrugged. "I dunno. Doc an' Elena, I reckon."

So, it was Papa's word against Elena's, she thought. And Papa couldn't even defend himself.

Sancho took some blankets from the corner. "I'll shake the dust and granddaddies out of these on the ledge, then you can lay yourself down. I'll stand watch."

Holly helped him with the blankets, coughing as weeks of settled dust boiled in her face. Her skin crawled with the thought of a granddaddy on her leg or in her hair.

"Did Papa and Tom Farrell haggle over this property?" she asked.

Sancho shrugged. "Doc told me he was trying to buy the canyon, but that Farrell wouldn't sell."

"You weren't around when they discussed it?"

"No'm. Your pa rode out to the TF a time or two, but I never went along."

"Wouldn't he let you go with him?" she asked, then bit her tongue, feeling the traitor to her own father.

Sancho thought a while, obviously not having given it any thought before. "He never told me I couldn't go along," he said. "It just happened that something always came up for me to do 'round town those times."

"For Papa?"

"Sure for Doc, who else?"

Sancho spread the blankets into a pallet at the rear of the cave and motioned Holly toward them. "This here's not the best kind of bed, ma'am, but it'll likely give your tired bones rest enough."

She smiled at his consideration for her welfare. Seating herself on the pallet, she returned to the story. "Tell me about the treasure."

"Well, ma'am, to hear Doc tell it, it's some treasure." Sancho's voice expanded, and Holly primed herself for a story which she was not sure she could let herself believe.

"Ever'body who comes to these parts gets the treasure fever," he began. "There's hundreds of them legends, an' your pa and me, we talked about 'em a lot . . ."

His voice trailed off, and Holly realized then that she wasn't the only one who had lost a friend and companion with Papa's death. Sancho, too, was left lonely.

"What about the copper plates?" she asked.

"How'd you know about them?"

"I found them in Papa's house, but since they hadn't been cleaned, I thought . . . I don't suppose he knew what was on them, did he?"

"Old Moses give 'em to him," Sancho said. "Doc never cleaned them, 'cause Old Moses told him what the pictures was, and Doc drew it down in his book. Said if he cleaned them plates, folks was likely to see 'em, an' he didn't want nobody to find that treasure but hisself an' me."

"And Papa thought the treasure was in the canyon?"

"Yes'm."

"Did he look for it?"

"He dabbled around, but it took Doc a while to convince ol' man Farrell to sell, and he couldn't locate a treasure on another feller's property. Don't you see, ma'am?"

She nodded.

"Then it was quite a spell after that 'fore Farrell would let us come into the canyon. Doc was fighting mad 'bout that, for sure. Ever'time we'd come out here, one or two of the TF hands was around outside the canyon to run us off."

"What did Papa do about that?" she asked.

Sancho sat silently studying the flickering light of the lantern. "I ain't sure how he done it," he answered finally, "but one day he rode out to the TF, and when he come back, he said we'd have no more trouble with 'em. That we'd start digging for that treasure come morning."

"Did you?"

"First we looked around for a camping spot," he said. "You see, we brung the wagon an' a load of supplies. Doc said we ought to find a place to hide 'em, case trouble broke out."

"What kind of trouble did he expect?"

Sancho shrugged. "With ol' man Farrell, you never could tell."

"Go ahead," she encouraged. "Where did you put the camp?"

"We found the first cave over yonder," he said. "An' after we'd packed our food and belongings up that cliff, Doc figured how we should have a second hiding place, to be on the safe side. So we located this cave here an' packed part of our things down that cliff and up this 'un."

Holly rubbed her aching back. How had Papa ever climbed up and down these cliffs so readily? He must have been driven by a very real fear to have placed his camp up in these cliffs instead of on the ground close to water as folks usually did.

"He didn't tell you what he was afraid of?" she asked.

"Said he didn't want us to be taken unawares. Seeing's how he'd finally convinced ol' man Farrell to let us in here, he wasn't going to take a chance at bein' run off."

That made sense, she supposed, as far as it went. But the story must be larger than what Papa had confided in this boy.

Sancho continued. "When we finally got things stowed, it was nigh onto sundown, so we fixed us a meal an' decided to start looking for that treasure at first light. But that's when . . ."

Sancho again appeared lost in his thoughts, and Holly kept quiet, tensed against the events she knew would follow.

Sancho spoke again. "The next morning ol' man Farrell rode up. We'd just finished with breakfast, an' Doc climbed down—we stayed in the cave over yonder. Doc'd already sat a good hour out on this ledge here the day before studying the layout, an' he'd determined where to commence to digging. Then he told me to put away the vittles, an' he climbed down the trail. But he'd no sooner got to the spring, than ol' man Farrell rode up on that big stallion of his."

"What did he want?"

Sancho shrugged. "I didn't hear the first part. Soon's I saw the ruckus, I skeedaddled on down the hill. I went real quiet-like, an' they couldn't see me, 'cause the trail is hidden from folks down at the spring by them trees."

Holly nodded, recalling her first climb to the cave. Tears pressed against her eyelids as she thought of standing beside the spring that day. The only thing on her mind at the time was Quint Jarvis. How could she have been so wrapped up in herself when she stood on the very spot where Papa had stood, where . . . "Go on," she whispered.

"Ol' Farrell had started in on Doc before I got there. I could tell something unhealthy was going on, so I hid myself and kept edging closer, figuring to find some way to help Doc out, if need be."

"Did you get close enough to hear what they said?"

He nodded. "I heard 'em say Elena's name a couple of times, and mine. That was 'bout all I could understand till the ol' man raised his voice and hollered out how he wasn't figurin' on giving this canyon to nobody, and he wanted Doc to hand over the deed. Then Doc told him that he had sent the deed by mail to his daughter—that would be you, I reckon—back in Tennessee."

She gasped. "What did Farrell do when Papa told him that?"

"He didn't let on like he believed Doc at first. But finally I guess he started to believe him. Anyhow, the two of 'em had a right smart shoutin' match, if ever I heard one, with Doc sayin' that this land was his now, that a deal was a deal, an' a man don't go back on his word. But ol' man Farrell, he didn't hear one word, I reckon, for his own huffin' and puffin'. His face got real red, and then he pulled out that gun, and I figured he was goin' to blow Doc away right before my eyes, and me with no weapon at all."

"Wasn't Papa armed?" she asked. "After all the preparations against attack, why would he go about the canyon unarmed? And you, Sancho? You didn't take a gun with you?"

Sancho hung his head. "Guess he didn't expect anything to happen right away like that." He took a deep breath, then continued. "Besides, we'd gone off an' left our guns over here. What with all the hauling things up and down, we got back over yonder without 'em and was too tuckered out to go back an' fetch 'em. I was to fetch 'em soon as I finished up that morning."

He nodded toward a Sharps rifle in the corner of the cave. "This an' that ol' Navy Colt is all he had, and they was both over here. Believe me, ma'am, if I could've, I'd of got one of them an' shot ol' man Farrell dead. Believe me, I would've done it if I could."

"I know, Sancho. And Papa knows, too." She stared out into the darkness. How she had hidden from reality. All this time, while searching for the answers to Papa's death, proclaiming to all who would listen her determination to hear the truth, she had not known what hearing that truth would mean. She had not envisioned the pain and agony each word would bring . . . bombarding her in an avalanche of horror.

"But Tom Farrell did shoot Papa?" she asked finally.

"Yes'm," he replied. "After a while, he did, not right then. First, he drug a paper from his pocket an' showed it to Doc, and they talked quiet-like for a while, and then he took out this piece of lead and Doc began to write, and I figured how they was writing a new deed or something . . ."

Sancho's voice faltered, and Holly wrapped her arms about herself tightly. She listened intently as he continued his simple emotion-filled recitation of this tragedy which bound them together.

"Anyhow, 'fore I knew what was happening, ol' man Farrell, he took the paper and looked at it, and stuffed it in his pocket. Then he hauled off an' shot Doc right through the head. Quick as that. Right there by the spring."

Holly closed her eyes, and tears rolled quietly, softly down her cheeks, warming and stinging at the same time. Suddenly she realized what he had said. "I didn't know they found him by the spring," she said softly.

"They didn't," Sancho answered. "That's where ol' man Farrell shot him, out there underneath that big ol' cottonwood tree. Then Farrell stepped in the saddle an' rode off, asettin' tall an' whistling like he killed a man ever'day after breakfast."

Holly pursed her lips, but the tears wouldn't stop. Sancho continued.

"I hurried on over to the body, but he was . . . he was gone. So I went to fetch the wagon, but 'fore I got to it, I heard the thundering of horses. I hid out again, an' here comes ol' man Farrell aridin' back with two of his men, Cob and E. A."

Sancho's voice picked up, and Holly felt him relive the terror of that day. No wonder he was frightened now.

"Ma'am, they come up so fast, I figure they must've been waiting not far from the canyon. Waiting for the ol' man to . . . Anyhow, they rode up with him, and he told 'em exactly what to do, and 'fore I knew what was happening, they hauled Doc's body up the cliff to the cave. Well, I figured I was hid out for sure, but one of 'em come to the ledge there—ol' man Farrell had stayed behind on the ground—and he called below that there must be someone else in the canyon, 'cause they found sign of another person."

"In that cave?" she asked, thinking of when she and Quint had looked there for Sancho. Why hadn't Quint told her then? She spoke her question aloud.

"I don't reckon he knew which cave it was, ma'am," Sancho replied. "I hid out an' watched Woody and Slim search through the caves till they come upon him, an' then they hauled Doc's body to town. The sheriff wasn't with 'em."

"Oh," she said, then nodded for him to continue his story.

He looked at her, and she could see the soft glow of the lantern reflected in his stricken eyes. "Well, ma'am, ol' man Farrell started huffin' an' puffin' again, an' he hollered back that it had to be the boy—meaning me, I figured—an' to get back down here and find him quick-like." He drew in his breath, then rushed forward.

"Fortunate for me, I was to the other side of the canyon this time, so's I could get to this trail here without bein' noticed. An' I hid up here till they was done with their looking."

"How did they keep from finding you?" she asked. "It was daylight, and they must have been good at tracking."

"Not them," Sancho said. "That's where I got off lucky, you might say. If Farrell'd brung some of his other men, they'd have found me for sure, but Cob an' E. A., them are good-for-nothing's, same as Jim Tom. I figure the ol' man keeps 'em on for work like this that he don't hanker for folks to know about. They tired out lookin' for me after a spell an' convinced him that I'd high-tailed it out of the canyon."

They sat silent for a while, their thoughts on a man needlessly killed, loved and mourned by both of them. And of the terror which still surrounded their every move.

Finally Holly broke the silence. "When did you . . . ah, go back to the cave?"

When he answered, his voice was soft and low, reverence replacing the fear she had heard earlier. "I waited till dark, and then I went, intendin' to carry him to town in the wagon. But then I started worryin' over the ol' man finding me on the trail, so I left him there, and made my way to town an' told the sheriff how I'd run acrost him in one of them caves. Then I hightailed it."

He hung his head low. "I know I should've owned up to being there and told the sheriff how it happened, but . . ."

"That's all right, Sancho," Holly said. "No one can blame you with Tom Farrell's murderers after you. Where did you go?"

"Back in the hills. I'd thought to get clean out of the country, but then I recalled how your pa set store by Elena, an' how ol' man Farrell had spoke her name, so I figured it was the only thing left I could do for Doc—to stay around and see if I could take care of her."

They fell silent again, Holly thinking about Elena now. Then Sancho spoke. "I reckon I didn't do so good by her, seein's how things turned out."

"You did fine, Sancho. With Farrell holding her at the ranch, you could have done nothing more than keep track of her."

"You reckon she'll be all right?"

Holly nodded, and Sancho stood up suddenly,

startling her.

"We'd best get some shut-eye. I'll take first watch, an' you can roll up back here," he said.

As she settled down in the blankets, a few stars shone through the mouth of the cave, and she thought that the rain must have stopped and the clouds receded. But inside her heart, clouds and stormy weather brewed, and as often happened at night, despair overtook her.

"Sancho," she called softly. "Why do you suppose Mr. Norton rode to the TF?"

"Like I said, ma'am, you're a threat to 'em now. It ain't just the canyon anymore. If you can prove who killed your pa, you can have the ol' man convicted of murder. He won't stand by an' let that happen, no, ma'am."

"And you're certain you didn't see Quint leave town?"

"No'm, I didn't."

"Where do you suppose he went?"

Sancho turned to the back of the cave. "We maybe should be finding out. We could be needin' him ourselves come morning."

"How's that?"

"Well, ma'am, even if the sheriff arrested Jim Tom and two of the TF hands, his pa ain't likely to hang around tryin' to get Jim Tom out of jail, when you're hidin' out with enough proof to convict the ol' man hisself."

"What can we do?"

"I've been studyin' on it, ma'am, an' I reckon I'd best get myself on back to town an' locate the sheriff."

Holly drew a sharp breath which echoed through the cave.

Sancho turned to her. "You'll be all right here, ma'am. They ain't never set foot in this cave; they won't never find you here. That's how your pa planned it—we'd keep this place for a special kind of hideout. They'll likely search the first cave, but . . . I can even lead your horse out behind mine. Thataway the tracks'll show that you come an' went, an' when they see that, they'll leave, too. They'd never think you'd stay inside the canyon without a horse."

Her heart beat up in her ears. She knew Sancho was probably right, but . . . "No, I couldn't stay here alone without a way to escape," she pleaded. "If they came, and I needed a way out . . . No, you must leave my horse."

He nodded. "I'll leave him then, ma'am. An' don't you worry none. There ain't a chanct in the world they'll find you. Our tracks are covered real good. And when I leave, I'll go up over the top."

"Where's your horse?" she asked.

"Outside," he answered. "In a safe place Doc an' me found."

He sounded willing to take a chance, and since he had survived alone these last months with Tom Farrell hunting him, and even before that, before coming to live with Papa, she was sure he knew his way around.

Sad, she thought, how differently things turned out from what she had expected back in Tennessee. She had looked forward to meeting Sancho, getting to know him, and here they spent the entire evening running from death or talking about it. She had learned nothing about him, except that his love for Papa had been great, as was his feeling of loss. It occurred to her then that this loss she and Sancho shared erased all past experiences. Their relationship began with Papa's death.

Sancho rummaged around in a corner, while Holly walked to the mouth of the cave and looked down into the canyon. Now that the clouds had lifted, she could make out some of the trees and an outline of the spring itself. In her mind's eye the clear water bubbled before her, and suddenly Quint's face appeared, full of life, smiling broadly as he had done so often during their happier times.

Then, unexpectedly, Papa's face appeared, superimposed over Quint's. But Papa wasn't smiling. His expression was . . . admonishment? No, a supplication? Could it be she had never known him?

Sancho interrupted her thoughts by pulling her back from the ledge. "You shouldn't stand so far out, ma'am. Ain't likely no one's down there tonight, but we don't need to take no chances."

She moved back, and he put the rifle in her hand. "I'll be goin' now, an' don't you go wandering about till I get back with the sheriff. Keep this ol' Sharps by your side—an' these here shells . . . an' this." He held a book toward her. "This here's what your pa wrote things down in. I tried to read it, but I never got far enough in my learnin' to know all them loops an' squiggles. When it gets daylight, you can commence to readin', an' the time'll pass right quick."

He handed her some more jerked beef, also. "This'll tide you over, along with the stores in back, but don't go lightin' no fire."

She watched him go, her mind in a slow whirl. She wasn't afraid, but with all his warnings, thought perhaps she should be. Then she wondered why. Quint would come, and everything would be all right.

But what if he weren't in town? How silly, she chided, of course, he would be in town.

Her mind spun to a sudden stop, and in that instant she realized that she had transferred her trust, and yes, her dependence, from Papa to Quintan Jarvis.

She would have to work on that, she decided. If

things turned out the way Sancho and Elena said, Quint probably didn't have a hand in the affairs against Papa. Perhaps there was a chance for them after all. But trusting him, even loving him, was one thing. She would never, never again find herself dependent upon another human being.

Never.

Chapter Sixteen

The sun shone high overhead when Quint drew rein outside the entrance to Mustang Canyon. He removed his hat and ran a sleeve across his forehead, studying the tracks he had followed since soon after breaking away from the posse this morning.

The tracks led into the canyon, sure enough, but if he barreled headlong after them, he was likely charging into the very trap he had been shying clear of.

He'd lain awake most of the night puzzling over the difficulty, finally setting his mind in order. His first aim was to put as much country behind him as he could before he ran into Troy Grant. Gunfire at this point would do more than booger the men; if the rustlers were to hear it, it would play havoc with the posse's raid, as well.

Once he'd cut himself away from the others, Quint turned to more personal concerns: since he didn't hanker to find himself shaking hands with Saint Peter before nightfall, he must find Grant before Grant found him.

But where would a bushwhacker be looking to ambush a sheriff? None of the places he frequented were the out-of-the-way sort preferred by a dry-gulcher.

Of one thing he was sure, he intended to ride shy of Silver Creek. The idea of Holly witnessing a shoot-out between himself and Grant brought chills to his spine. She might step in the way of a stray bullet, or Grant could decide to use her as a shield. To say nothing of the danger such a showdown would pose to the townsfolk.

Then he thought of the only place outside Silver Creek where he could be expected to show up—his own ranch. If Grant stayed patient, sooner or later his prey would go home.

So, deciding that he couldn't wrestle this steer unless he took it by the horns, he had turned his pony's nose toward the cabin. Riding easy, yet alert, he began to look for sign, all the time keeping an eye open for a likely spot for an ambush.

And finally his diligence had paid off. Northbound tracks crossed his trail. He dismounted to study them: one rider, medium build, riding easy. He had crossed these tracks twice before, and he'd lay odds that this was the horse Troy Grant rode.

The first time was following the stagecoach holdup when Holly's trunk was stolen. The tracks then led to the TF, where Grant later turned up. The second time was in the canyon when he and Holly were fired on by that sharpshooter. Yes, he'd bet his pony these tracks belonged to Grant.

He rode on cautiously, attuned to every detail of the country around him. If the stories he'd heard about Grant's bloodthirsty ways had any truth in them, he figured Grant would shoot to wing him or in some way to put him out of commission, then move in for the kill face to face. Not that Grant was known to give his victims a last-minute chance to defend themselves, but word was Grant didn't want the poor fellers to die without giving credit where it was due.

Trees sparkled as the morning sun touched their still wet leaves, and the whole countryside took on the fresh look it always had after a rain washed the dust off plants and rocks. The musky earth-smell which exuded from the ground following a rain filled him with more than the usual sense of pleasure today, and he was suddenly seized by his love for this land and a keen hungering to stay alive.

His contentment soured with the thought that Tom Farrell had other plans for him. The shock of Wilt and Luther's news had worn off somewhat since last night, and no matter what Holly thought, Tom had ceased being a father to him long ago.

Yet, Tom had raised him, and when he was a boy, Quint looked on Tom as his hero. Tom was strong and took pride in a boy who could shoot and ride as good as any full-blood Indian. And Tom provided a solid example that hard work paid rewards—while Quint's own pa was weak and shiftless and died letting another man care for his family. It was only later—after Aunt Jen died and Jim Tom grew up mean—that Tom turned wicked.

Quint had never thought these things through before, and he knew Holly had led him to see Tom in a different light.

At that moment the tracks he followed showed signs of turning toward the canyon.

He sat now at the mouth of the canyon, figuring how best to ride this bronc. Finally drawing a determined breath, he hitched his mount to a thicket, took out his field glasses, and climbed the cliff. At least he could take a look-see without showing his hand.

Steadying his elbows on the ground, he swept the canyon with his glasses, focusing at last on one area, studying it until he was sure of what he saw: a horse hitched behind an outcropping of boulders. As he watched its tail swish to swat a fly and its rump twitch again, he swore aloud, recognizing the dun horse from Slim's livery—the same pony he had hired for Holly when they rode out here that day. What the hell . . . ?

Could his memory be playing tricks on him? He was sure the tracks he had followed all morning were the same as those he'd found in the canyon. Could he be mistaken?

Was he confusing these tracks with tracks he'd seen that same day—tracks of Holly's mount?

Reason told him that anybody could hire a horse from Slim, but Troy Grant would have no cause to. If his mount went lame, Tom would have him one saddled from the TF remuda.

Then he considered Holly, but dismissed that thought, too. The rider he followed to this canyon was a mid-sized male. He was sure of that. And those were the only tracks in the fresh mud at the mouth of the canyon.

In fact, the more thought he gave it, the more likely it seemed that the rider was someone who intended to hamstring the arrests.

And that could include a number of folks on both sides of this trouble—those wanting to hang the rustlers, as well as those hankering to set them free.

Quint put away his field glasses. Whoever was in that canyon must be headed off. These rustlers needed punishing, but he intended to see it done lawfully, not the other way around.

So he climbed down and remounted his pony, disgusted with folks who take the law into their own hands. Unless notions like that were put to rest, this country would become a badlands for every two-bit outlaw looking for a place to swap lead.

* * *

Holly slept intermittently after Sancho left, waking often to relive the events of the past day.

Once she awoke to hear rain falling again, and her fears of being trapped inside the canyon returned.

Now she clutched the journal to her chest, waiting for enough light to read Papa's words.

She rubbed her fingers back and forth across the pebbled leather cover—pigskin, she supposed—and thought that her mission to this canyon was finished. She was anxious to return to Silver Creek.

Sancho had warned her to wait for him, and she would for a time, but if he didn't return by midmorning, she would ride into town on her own. Sancho and Quint would likely go straight to the TF to apprehend Tom Farrell and Mr. Norton.

With daylight the rain stopped, and she relaxed. Eating the last bit of jerky and drinking a measure of water from the canteen, she settled herself in the mouth of the cave, where the new light was strongest. Laboriously she repinned wayward strands of black hair away from her face.

Her fingers were sore and swollen from scrambling up these cliffs yesterday. The delicate buff lace on her cuffs hung torn and loose, and with little effort she impassively ripped a portion of unattached lace from her sleeve and discarded it. All this she viewed with no emotion—as an observer, rather than a participant—all her emotion being reserved for the journal clutched in her batterd hands.

How long she had waited to reach this book! Surely it held answers to the questions she had traveled so long and tried so hard to discover. But hope was not fresh inside her anymore. Sancho's lack of knowledge had been one more blow to her determination to discover the truth.

He had seen Tom Farrell murder Papa, of course,

and that was what she had professed to be searching for—the identity of the person who killed him, proof that he had not taken his own life.

With the accusations that had surfaced now, though, she knew finding his killer was only part of the answer.

Why had Papa purchased this canyon? And how? Would the journal clear him of Elena's hateful accusations?

She opened it hesitantly, dreading the disappointment that the truth might hold for her, or, if he had not written of these things, the frustration of never learning the truth. She wanted to know, yet she was afraid.

Soon the sun rose to the top of the jagged maze of cliffs opposite her, and after that she lost herself in the intimacy of Papa's writing.

She had never read another person's private writings before, and she did so now with the misgivings of an eavesdropper. Would she regret opening this inner door into the very soul of another human being? Especially that of her own father?

The journal began with the war years, and much of the first part contained sentiments Papa expressed upon returning home, or later in letters after he left Hedgerow: an aversion to war and to man killing man; disillusionment with crowded places and the pretenses of society.

To her dismay she discovered the reason he had come to Silver Creek. Up to now she had accepted the fact that he, like thousands of others, fled the multitude of horrendous memories facing him at the end of the difficulties. Beyond that, she had not even wondered why he chose Silver Creek, a village hardly large enough to be widely known, one certainly not on any map.

Now she found that he met a young man from Texas during the war. This man, David Westfield, talked of

Silver Creek and the treasure to be found in the region.

Westfield was wounded in the leg and helped Papa around the hospital until he recovered enough to be discharged and sent home.

David Westfield. Holly recalled the four graves of Aggie's family. Some fortune Westfield found in Silver Creek, losing his scalp to Indians. Now he and Papa lay in the same graveyard.

This news stunned her. Not that Papa had failed to reveal his true intentions, but . . . Papa a fortune hunter? She had doubted, disputed, insisted it wasn't true. Now here it was, plain as day, in his own handwriting. But he did not explain his deception to his family.

And he wrote as though he had entertained such dreams for a long time. Not specifically dreams of finding buried treasure in Texas, but dreams of shedding the cloak of responsibility which everyone from time to time dreamed of discarding.

She recalled the endless hours and days, weeks and months she spent in the hospital. Often she had dreamed of escaping for a while, hiding from this responsibility. But she couldn't then.

After the war Papa could. And if he proved to be a more complex person than the staid country doctor she knew him as, why not? Weren't we all more intricate than we appeared to the world? She thought of Jacob and his coat of many colors—each color representing not a different tribe, but a different attitude, a separate and quite opposite approach to life.

Perhaps this wanderlust was what had driven her to Silver Creek—a questing not merely for a new life, but for a different one.

Quint accused her of wanting to rebuild Hedgerow here in Silver Creek, but she didn't. She had told him so then, and she knew now how deeply she meant those words. She didn't want the same kind of life here. She came for something new and different—something to wash her soul clean from the festers of that old world.

Her insight had stopped with herself, however. She knew Papa came to Texas to start over, yet she had thought of it as revitalizing the emotional aspect of his life, not restructuring life to fit a different set of attitudes and goals.

Through his writing, Holly became acquainted with a side of him she had not seen before, and she realized how rigid a set of rules she had applied to him—and to herself, as well.

That he was excited by the prospects of finding buried treasure was inescapable. He thrilled at following in Coronado's footsteps, traipsing across the very land on which the conquistadors had searched for the fabled seven cities of Cibolo. The very same land where, within the lifetime of men living today, Indians mined silver, and where Spanish missionaries and soldiers searched for gold and buried some of their own for safekeeping from mauraudìng Indians.

Reading his words, she recalled the animated conversation between Jed Varner and Possum the night little Miracle was born. And the recollections of the men on the stagecoach. Perhaps they had been trying to ease her mind, but they had also enjoyed the tales they told.

Through Papa's experiences she no longer saw treasure hunting as an idle endeavor. She began to understand that sane and otherwise sober men searched for gold. Not that she envisioned herself discovering buried treasure. To the contrary, she probably wouldn't even search for it. But then again, if . . .

Her thoughts drifted to Quintan Jarvis. If she were to remain in Silver Creek . . .

She pulled her eyes back to the journal and was soon

rewarded for her persistence. The first mention of Tom Farrell concerned a piece of his property on which Papa thought treasure was buried. He detailed his approach to Farrell with an offer to buy the land, using the same reason for wanting it he had written her, that he was looking for a place where he could raise horses.

Farrell turned him down flat-handed, but Papa wrote of his determination not to let the matter stand. "I am sure of the location," he wrote, "and I cannot give up. I must discover a way to convince Farrell to sell."

Later he recounted Elena Salinas's confrontations with Jim Tom, and Raphael's impatience at having to accept these indiscretions. Papa had advised Raphael to look for work at another ranch, but Farrell had the only operation around large enough to hire dayhands.

Then Raphael was killed, and Papa saw a chance to acquire the land he had dreamed of having. At first, when Farrell delivered the body demanding that Papa help convince a jury that the shooting was self-defense, Papa had refused to do it.

Later that evening, though, as Papa described it, he discussed the exchange with Farrell—Farrell's land for Papa's perjury. And Tom Farrell, distraught father, accepted the offer.

Most of this she had already heard from Elena; the rest she had pieced together from Sancho's and Quint's recollections. But still the shock unsettled her.

Looking up from the book into the bright summer morning, she was appalled at what she had read, at being here in the disputed canyon at this very moment, hiding in a cave, discovering the truth. The truth that her beloved Papa had been . . . human. No . . . less than human . . . involved in a disgraceful scheme to set a hated murderer free for no more than a treasure of gold and silver.

She stared without seeing, her sight dimmed by the

words Papa had written—words which spun a poisonous web within her brain.

How long she sat thus, she did not know, but suddenly a horse and rider moved before her on the canyon floor, restoring her to the world of the present.

She watched in stunned silence as the man stopped at the spring, dismounted, drank, then remounted and rode slowly toward the maze end of the canyon. He paused twice to look behind him, and her heart flip-flopped in her throat when she recognized the rider.

Troy Grant.

Grant entered the maze, and without altering his pace, disappeared behind jutting boulders. Suddenly she felt herself once more in the maze with Quint the day the sniper fired upon them, and she scootched back into the cave to find the rifle.

What had Sancho said? Was it loaded? Checking, she found it to be, and took up the extra shells in her hand.

Scarcely breathing, she watched the hill until at last she chided herself. Grant had paid no attention to her part of the hillside and had not looked toward the boulders where her horse was tethered. He could very well have been cutting through the canyon to another part of the ranch.

Finally satisfied that Grant had gone on his way leaving her undetected in her hideout above the canyon floor, she returned to the journal. Only a few pages remained, and she prayed that Papa would explain his despicable actions.

He did. And his reason resembled somewhat the garbled message he had written her about doing something he regretted, but which he hoped would benefit two young ladies. In the journal he spelled it out, and she tried valiantly to understand his thinking.

As a widow of Mexican descent with no landholdings, Elena was left to a life of hardship and poverty by Raphael's murder. Papa couldn't restore life to Raphael, but the treasure would give Elena a chance at a better life.

Then there was Holly. She was coming to live with him in Silver Creek, but the life-style here was less than luxurious. He wanted her to have a life as near to the old days as possible, especially after all the travail she had suffered during the conflict.

Holly closed the book with a sigh, tears flowing in silent rivers down her cheeks. Oh, Papa. Papa. She didn't need buried treasure to be happy any more than he did, than Elena did. There was always honorable work to be had, and they could find it.

She was struck by the senselessness of his reasoning—of his quest, and of his death. The answers she had searched for were supposed to make sense, to justify his death, but they didn't.

Perhaps tragedies never made sense. If everything added up, if right was clear and wrong definitely distinguishable from it, tragedies need never occur. Only muddled, confused, and senseless thinking resulted in catastrophes from which people did not recover.

Papa was bitten by the treasure bug, she thought angrily. And to make matters worse, the whole tone of his writing indicated that he actually believed he had located the treasure, when, according to Sancho, they had yet to begin digging. Had he lost all semblance of sanity?

The remaining pages of the journal contained the directions he intended to follow the morning of his death. In fact, the last entry must have been made the evening before he died, and she studied it, still doubtful, yet desperate to discover something about him with which she could identify, something which would indicate that he was indeed the man she had always believed him to be.

Looking from the journal into the canyon and back several times, she pursed her lips in deep concentration, finally recalling that Sancho said he had sat on this very ledge when he determined where they would dig the following morning.

The sun had risen high above the jagged maze now, but earlier it sat right on top. And the trees fit . . . the oaks to her right and the cottonwood there by the spring. The very cottonwood where . . .

Suddenly the book dropped to her lap, forgotten, as a second rider crossed her line of vision, headed toward the first cave.

Quintan Jarvis!

Holly gasped and bit her lip to keep from calling to him. She had no idea how far her voice would carry, nor for sure that Troy Grant had left the area.

Quickly scanning the hilltop opposite, she saw no one. Across the canyon Quint dismounted, studied the dun, and looked for tracks. He climbed to the cave, then came down again, remounted, and cautiously, it seemed to her, rode in and out among the trees to the spring.

Anxiety built within her, and she struggled with whether to call to him or not. He had obviously come at Sancho's bidding, but why didn't he knew where to find her? Hadn't Sancho told him about this cave?

Suddenly, as she watched with mounting terror, Quint jerked in the saddle. At the same instant, the report of a rifle rang through the hollow, piercing her senses. Quickly raising the rifle, she scanned the hills again.

Nothing.

Quint sagged, then dropped to the ground, and she knew she must do something.

At that moment Troy Grant emerged from the maze, walking. He headed straight for Quint, and Holly stared, frozen with fear, not knowing what to do, how to save Quint if indeed he were still alive, while a nightmare took shape before her eyes.

Quint moved slightly then, and when Grant stopped and braced his legs, she reacted.

Steadying the Sharps rifle, she sighted and fired . . . and prayed. She could shoot, as she had told Quint, but never had she fired when her speed and accuracy counted for so much. She breathed deeply, feeling dazed.

She watched Grant fall, her mind moving at an annoyingly slow rate of speed. He jerked backward, hit the ground solidly. Then she switched into action. Taking time only to reload, she rushed down the trail, her mind abuzz with fears for Quint.

Was he dead? Had she killed Grant? Or would he fire on Quint again before she could get another shot?

The trail, she saw in daylight, was protected from view of those on the canyon floor by brush which she had only felt the night before. It grew thicker in some places than in others and threatened to obscure not only her view, but also her passage. She marveled that she had made it up in the darkness.

Three paces from the bottom another shot pierced the air, and her heart froze in her breast. Throwing herself around the remaining brush, she watched Grant fall a second time. Quint knelt, as if rising, his handgun dropping to the ground.

Stumbling over the purple velvet trim on the bottom of her skirt, she rushed toward him, crying. He turned to stare in disbelief.

Dazed by the shot, it took his befuddled brain an instant to recognize the wild woman who ran toward him, her black hair flying, her clothes rumpled and tattered. "Holly!" Her eyes were large as silver dollars, and a new terror gripped him at the alarm emitting from the near black depths . . . at the rifle in her hand. "What the hell are you doing here?"

Ignoring his question, she fell to her knees in front of his rising form, her only thought to protect Quint from Troy Grant. Scanning Grant's body for any sign of movement, she finally found her voice. "Is he . . . ?"

By this time Quint had risen and reached the body. He picked up the gunman's pistol, kicked his rifle away, then looked back at Holly. "I reckon he's dead," he said, and, turning, they fell into each other's arms. "What're you doing here?"

Clinging to him desperately, she pressed her face into his muscled chest. Tears burned like hot coals behind her clenched eyelids. She'd been so afraid for him. So afraid.

Finally she answered, but her voice was small, constricted by the fear which gripped her throat. "I came out yesterday, and Sancho . . . Didn't Sancho find you? Isn't that why you came?"

"I haven't seen Sancho." Then he held her back and looked at her anxiously, as the realization hit him that she had been in this canyon all along and would soon be caught in the fracas. "You're waiting here in the canyon for Sancho?"

She tried to smile into his golden eyes, but her chin trembled instead. "He said it wasn't safe to leave . . . that Tom Farrell would be after me since I told Mr. Norton that . . ."

Quint broke in. They couldn't stand here talking any longer. "Where were you hiding?"

She pointed to the cave.

The thought of her being in this melee filled him with near-panic. He gripped both her shoulders. "Then get back up there. All hell's fixing to break loose around here, and I want you out of the way."

Her eyes wide, she looked from him to the body of Troy Grant, then suddenly recalled that she hadn't even looked at Quint's wound. "Where did he hit you?"

Quint felt his shoulder. "Up here, I reckon," he answered, drawing a bloody hand from inside his shirt.

Immediately she took charge of the situation. "Let me look at it . . ."

"Holly." He spoke with enough authority to cause her to draw back. "Time's short. Do exactly as I tell you, and no questions."

At her objections, he added, "I'm all right." He stuffed a bandana inside his shirt and pressed it to the wound, which he figured had only grazed his shoulder, causing a lot of blood to flow, but likely no serious damage. "You can tend to this later. Right now I have to figure out where Grant came from and get him out of the way."

She transferred her stare to the body of the man she had shot, and revulsion shook her with a resounding wave.

Quint looked around the canyon. "Did you see where he came from?" he asked. And when she told him how Grant rode through the canyon before him, he nodded toward the gunman's lifeless body. "Give me a hand." He grasped Grant's body by the shoulders and dragged him toward a thicket to the left. "Grab his rifle and kick dirt over any blood you see on the ground."

Sick with a churning in her stomach, she did as he asked, following him with Grant's rifle and hat. "I don't understand. Why are you . . . ?" Questions raced through her brain, but none of them made any sense.

She had killed a man. Helped kill him, anyway. A man who had been nice to her once, but a man she'd had many questions about these last days.

Quint stepped back through the brush, blood from

his wound forming a dark circle on his vest. He looked into her frantic eyes. "You know those rustlers you've been worrying over?" he asked. "They're headed this way, and our posse's right behind them. If the rustlers were to find Grant's body before the posse gets here . . . Well, our boys would likely find themselves walking into an ambush."

Her shaking subsided somewhat with this explanation, spoken quietly, matter-of-factly. She drew a deep breath and swallowed the lump in her throat. "What now?"

Tension drained from him at the sound of her soft Southern voice offering her help in such simple tones. He clasped her to him in a tight embrace. "You'll do to ride the river with, Holly Campbell. You surely will."

She returned his embrace fiercely, and he pressed her to him, feeling complete, at peace, for one instant in her arms. But then his thoughts turned quickly to the situation at hand, to the danger she faced here in the canyon.

Looking at the boulders behind which her dun was hitched, he thought of sending her back to Silver Creek right now, but no . . . "If you ride out of here now, you're likely to run smack dab into trouble." He spoke as much to himself as to her. "You'd best skeedaddle on back to that cave and stay put till this shindig's over. You'll be safe there, and you'll have a front row seat when the Farrells get their due."

She tightened her arms around him and tried to steady her trembling voice. "Where will you be?"

"I have to locate Grant's horse and get him out of sight. Can't have an empty saddle spooking our rustlers." He took her arms from around him and kissed her soundly on the lips. "Get going, sweet Holly. We're about to run out of time."

Quint mounted then, and she watched him through a

veil of tears, wanting to protest that he wasn't fit to ride, that he needed to have the blood staunched now, that she wanted to ride with him—but she did none of these things. Sensing his urgency, she knew she must obey him without question.

When he saw her start toward the cave, he headed for the maze, wishing she had stayed in Silver Creek as he had instructed her to; grateful that she hadn't. Without her shot, Troy Grant would have got him for sure.

Walking back toward the cave, Holly breathed deep draughts of fresh air into her constricted lungs. She was thankful that she'd stayed in the canyon. If she hadn't been sitting in the mouth of that cave, Quint . . .

She turned to longingly watch him disappear into the maze, and a strange marking on the tree trunk beside her caught her attention. Suddenly she recalled the directions to the treasure that Papa had recorded in his book.

Down here in the midst of the trees, the directions didn't appear as logical as from the eagle's eye view of the cave, and she thought how one event connects to another, like the links of a chain, until they are all meshed together into a situation that could not exist if any one of the links were missing. If Papa hadn't been afraid of Tom Farrell, he might never have discovered the second cave. And if he hadn't sat in that cave and viewed the terrain from that perspective, he might never have been as certain where to dig for the treasure.

She ran her hands over the rough bark that had curled into a circle around the patch of smooth tree trunk. A now-faint turtle was carved inside this circle.

Not that the discovery had done Papa any good, she thought bitterly. If he hadn't been infected with treasure fever, none of this might have happened. None of it. She touched her lips where Quint's kiss still calmed her racing heart.

Suddenly the stillness around her was shattered by a thundering of horses' hooves, and three riders burst through the mouth of the canyon.

Without thinking, she dove behind the nearest boulder, almost dropping the rifle in her haste. When the riders raced past her toward the spring, she recognized only one of them.

Jim Tom Farrell.

Chapter Seventeen

Quint followed Grant's tracks through the maze and out of the canyon, driven by an urgency to find Grant's horse and stake it out of sight before the rustlers came upon them.

Grant had not tried to conceal his tracks, and Quint found the bay horse staked in the same thicket where he had staked his own and Holly's horses that day they returned to the canyon to search for tracks of the sniper. This time, though, Grant had fired from the opposite hill.

Knowing the horse would likely raise cain when he sensed the approach of the other riders, Quint secured him with an extra stake rope of his own. Then, giving a backward glance at the canyon and wishing that Holly were in Silver Creek instead of in a cave in the middle of this difficulty, he rode out to meet the posse.

Not that he worried about her. The rustlers would be too busy with their own doings to search the caves, and once the posse took charge, he didn't look for more than a couple of shots to be fired, if any at all. As soon as the arrests were made, he would take her back to

Silver Creek himself.

He fussed at himself for fretting so, and put it down to the throbbing in his shoulder. The bandanna he'd stuffed inside his shirt was soaked with blood, and the numb shock of impact was wearing off. He'd been shot before and didn't look forward to what lay ahead: the pain and stiffness he could handle, but his strength must hold out until the rustlers were well in hand.

Riding east, he kept well south of the path he figured the trail herd to take, and a few miles further he got a whiff of their dust. The ground shook, and, as always, he thought about the buffalo herds Pa told him tales of—how the great rumble set a man's blood to pounding as it spoke of power and freedom. Civilization had run most of the buffalo off from around here, but one of these days he figured to ride up to the Llano Estacado and marvel at that sight for himself.

He spurred his mount toward his meeting with Bales. Once he thought he heard the report of a rifle, but the sound was muffled by distance, and he knew it could as well have been a branch snapping over a creek or a couple of old bucks knocking horns.

Reflecting on his job—a job which he never imagined himself holding down, and one he had not sought—he knew it was in his blood.

He hadn't planned on being a peace officer, but now that he was one, he was proud of it. Lawbreakers would always be around, and so would the need for folks like himself to corral them.

Finally he pulled up behind a thicket that grew along a draw. The cattle were not visible yet, but a couple of outriders appeared in the distance. As they approached, the herd came into sight beyond them to the north, and he drew a satisfied breath that this day had arrived clear and warm. So many things could have gone wrong that didn't. Now, except for keeping the posse in rein, the job was mostly done.

His sudden liking for this sheriff's job surprised him. Until now he had thought of himself as acting sheriff only—a rancher helping out in time of trouble.

Now, however, he felt a pleasure he had never known before. The work of building a safe, law-abiding place for folks to live in was work a man could take pride in doing.

He wondered what Holly would think about marrying a peace officer, then, removing his hat, he wiped sweat from his forehead and grinned to himself. Was he getting plumb loco in his old age? After what she'd been through since coming to Silver Creek, it was going to take all hands and the cook to convince her to stay.

The outriders came closer, and he identified them as Wilt and Luther. They met behind the thicket, sitting their mounts in the late June heat, their clothes and rigging blending in with the dusty, nondescript scenery as well as any creature of the Lord's own design.

Luther eyed Quint carefully. "Where're you ridin' from?"

"The canyon," Quint answered. Then they both noticed his shoulder.

"Looks like he got a little lead into you," Wilt said, taking out the makin's.

"Grant's worse off than me," Quint assured them.

"Want us to tie it up for you?" Luther offered.

"It'll keep for now. Let's get this shindig over with."

"Where'd you leave Grant?" Wilt asked.

"Back in the canyon. Holly helped me hide his body behind some brush. It won't be found in time to hurt us."

Luther raised an eyebrow. "Doc's daughter?"

"Where's she at now?" Wilt asked at Quint's nod.

"In the canyon. There wasn't time to get her out, so she's hiding in one of the caves."

The two men exchanged glances.

"She'll be safe enough if she stays put," Wilt said.

"You didn't run acrost Jim Tom with Cob and E. A.?"Luther asked.

Quint shook his head. "Should I have?"

"They were already liquored-up by sunrise and headed for the canyon. Said they'd get the branding fire going for us," Wilt said.

"It didn't look to be no problem, 'cept . . ." Luther started.

"Long's they don't run into Miz Campbell," Wilt finished.

A sick feeling gripped Quint's gut as he suddenly recalled the sound he heard earlier, a sound he had vaguely associated with a rifle shot. What if . . . ? How could he have been such a damned fool to leave her alone? If anything happened to Holly . . .

Drawing rein sharply, he spurred his horse and called to Wilt and Luther to follow. "Get a move on. We can't let Jim Tom . . ." Visions of Elena Salinas choked the words in his throat.

Holly squeezed herself further behind the boulder, tucking her bright blue and purple skirts out of sight beneath her. Cautiously, she peered around the corner.

When the three men reined up at the spring, her eyes froze on a wriggling bundle across one of the saddles. They had captured Sancho!

The men dismounted, wobbling with drunkenness, and the heartrending thought occurred to her that these must be the same two men who helped Jim Tom rape Elena. Then, as they turned her way, she bit her lip to keep from crying out at the sight of the red scratches and wounds on their faces. The burly one removed Sancho from the horse, carelessly chunking him beneath the cottonwood tree.

She sat as still as possible, fearing even to breathe. Her mouth felt like it had been swabbed with cotton wool, and perspiration trickled down her cheeks along her hairline, causing tickling sensations as it dripped to her ears. Perhaps, she thought, trying to quieten her nerves, they would remain around the spring and not venture out into the canyon.

Sure enough, after drinking at the spring, an act which caused her to lick her own cracking lips, they set about building a fire. At first she thought they intended to make coffee, but then they took out branding irons and placed them on the ground beside the tree.

From time to time she scanned the rest of the canyon, anxious for Quint's return. He couldn't have gone far.

She gripped the rifle in a wet hand. One shot would not go far in defending herself against three vicious, drunken men who could hardly be counted on to give her time to reload. She must remain perfectly still and undetected until Quint returned. She must.

The sun was well overhead now and warm. From her position, the canyon was still and quiet, except for an occasional grasshopper jumping from here to there in the summer-dried grasses . . . and the querulous voices of the men by the spring. She could not make out what they were saying, hearing only a string of swear words now and then. They seemed to be having trouble with the fire, and she decided that last night's rain must have left the wood too wet to catch hold.

As she watched them argue, suddenly one of the two

men threw down the sticks of wood he was using and started toward the thicket where she and Quint had hidden Troy Grant's body.

She stared in horror, scarcely breathing. They must not discover the body until the posse's raid was complete. It could mean death to the posse . . . to Quint. He had said so himself.

She expelled her breath slowly, her mind whirling like a dervish in midsummer. Staring at the man's back, she willed him to stop . . . willed him to turn around. But he didn't, and when he was within a few steps of the thicket, she threw the rifle to her shoulder and fired.

The man's body jerked, and as he fell to the ground, screaming, she watched in terror. Jim Tom and the other man started toward their wounded companion, but he rose to one knee and dragged himself back toward the spring.

They ran about wildly, then, shouting and grabbing rifles from their saddle boots, trying to calm the horses and the wounded man. Holly reloaded, sure they could hear her heart beat above their own ruckus. With great trepidation she moved from the slight shelter of the boulder toward the cave.

Sliding behind a thicket, she scraped her arms against the sharp branches, tearing one sleeve partway from her dress. Ripping the torn fabric completely off the garment, she risked another look at the spring.

This time she was alarmed to see a more organized look about them. They had evidently decided the shot came from her side of the canyon, and, leaving their wounded friend with a rifle of his own, they mounted their horses and headed toward her.

She scooted farther into the thicket, hoping they were still too far away to hear her movement. If she could make it to the path, she would have some protection, and, with luck, she could get to the cave.

By that time Quint would surely have returned. Stay calm, she told herself, frantically pushing her flying hair behind her ears. Stay calm and out of sight.

But the memory of Elena's battered body did nothing to bolster her courage. She must get to the safety of the cave soon.

On trembling legs she moved again in the direction of the path. Again without being seen. Then the thought of being cornered in the cave by these vicious men brought cold beads of perspiration to her arms and neck. She would have no chance there. No chance at all.

She must get away . . . outside the canyon . . . quickly. Quint would return any moment; he surely heard her shot.

Loud whoops from not too far away alerted her, and she peeked from behind her hiding place to see them hunkered around the boulder where she fired the shot.

Jim Tom picked up her spent cartridge, and the two men held it up, shouting to their wounded friend by the spring.

"Watch the hillside, Cob," Jim Tom called. "If you see him, shoot to kill." They took off up the hill afoot.

Panic threatened to overwhelm her, and she desperately tried to slow her shallow breathing. Scanning the cliff above her, she tried to recall what Sancho said last night about going over the top. There was a way; she would have to find it. If she could get higher up, perhaps Quint would see her from outside, or she could find somewhere to hide. She could run. She could escape. She must get out of this canyon.

Her fear was so great now that her limbs were almost paralyzed, but she knew she had no time to waste bemoaning her state. They would find her soon enough if she stayed where she was. She must move now while they weren't looking her way.

Quickly she stepped around the thicket, then cut up and ran for the top of the hill.

Before she had taken more than a few steps, though, the men shouted, and she heard them crash through the brush behind her. When she turned to look, she stumbled over her mud-caked skirts and fell facedown onto the ground.

Their whoops and shouts upon recognizing her sent new shivers up her spine.

"Don't shoot," Jim Tom called, and Holly turned to see him knock his companion's rifle away. "Shooting'll come later. This here filly's been aching to be rode, an' I'm the wrangler who's gonna break her."

The other man laughed. "I'm after you, boss. Reckon we have time for a couple of go-rounds a piece, 'fore yore pa gets here?"

"Hell, yeah, if we hurry." Jim Tom's voice stung in her ears, and the vision of Elena again tore through her brain. She sprang to her feet, running for the nearest boulder.

She could hear the men below her, gaining on her, egged on by Jim Tom's drunken verbiage.

Reaching the boulder, she swung herself behind it and looked back down the hill. Her heart beat wildly, and her brain struggled to produce a coherent thought. All she wanted was to lie down and catch her breath, but that was not possible now. Later, she told herself. Later, after she escaped these madmen.

Below she saw the men stop and exchange words. They looked back up the hill, momentarily disoriented in their drunken state, and she took this chance to look to the top of the cliff.

Tears sprang to her eyes when she looked directly

overhead. So far away. And no possibility of going straight up. She would have to wind around and hope she didn't slip into their arms.

Flashes of anger hit her then, like jagged streaks of lightning. Anger at Papa for getting her involved with such barbarians; anger at Quint for leaving her here alone; anger at herself for coming to the canyon, for firing that gun. She gripped the rifle tighter. She had one shot left now. Only one. Against two savage men.

Rocks flew from beneath her thin, leather-soled shoes, and she spent as much time on her knees as she did actually running. She had the panicky feeling of merely slipping around in the same place, but finally she made it to another boulder.

They whooped and followed her, and she knew they were closing the gap between them. Tears of anguish blurred her vision: they were even dressed for such an occasion with their heavy boots and pants and thick leather chaps, which protected them against falls and prickly pear and thorny branches.

About the only advantage she had was that they were drunk and she wasn't. Although thinking about it, perhaps she wouldn't be as frightened with some of her senses dulled. As it was, her spine was afire with sharp prickles of fear, and her breath caught in jabs of pain with each gasp.

How did she ever find herself in such a dilemma? Why hadn't she stayed in Tennessee? Or at least in Silver Creek like Quint had told her to?

But if she had, Quint might be dead right now—as she might be herself at any moment.

She looked around for her next avenue of escape repeating over and over in her brain: He'll come in time, he'll come in time, he'll come in time.

Suddenly, when she had decided she must leave the

shelter of her boulder and run further, Jim Tom stumbled, then pitched forward onto the ground swearing loudly.

"Help! Get my foot out of this goddamned varmint hole, E. A.," he called.

E. A. stopped to work on Jim Tom, and Holly took this chance to run to another shelter.

E. A., she thought. And he had called the other man Cob. These were the same men, all right. The same men who had molested Elena; the same men who chased Sancho and gave up. If only she were so lucky. Yet, she knew their reward this time was much more enticing than when they chased Sancho; they wouldn't give up on her.

She wove back to the right, then around to her left, progressing only six feet or so along the hillside before she heard them running after her again. She took shelter behind another boulder.

This one was not as large as the others, and they soon spotted her and were on their way anew. Jim Tom's injury did not affect his running any more than it was already hampered by his intoxication, and as they drew near, she suddenly had an idea.

Waiting until they came close enough for her to see the creases in their faces, the individual hairs in the beards, the red veins along the sides of their noses and around their cheeks—close enough that she shuddered with the thought that they might finally get their wicked hands on her . . . When they were close enough that she did not think they could jump clear of its path, she shoved the boulder into them.

Then she turned and ran, not waiting to see the results of her desperate attempt to slow them down.

Where was Quint? What had happened to him? Someone must have shot him, killed him. Tom Farrell, perhaps. He must come, she thought, frantically searching both entrances of the canyon. He must.

Diving behind an outgrowing cedar, she turned to inspect her handiwork and was surprised to see that she had actually knocked Jim Tom back ten yards or so.

Her mind buzzed. With Jim Tom down, if she could stop E. A. with her one shot . . . Aiming carefully, but quickly, she fired and saw his hat fly off his head. He fell to the ground and grabbed his hair.

Jim Tom was up in a flash. He jerked E. A.'s hands away from his face. "You ain't killed. She just singed you. Come on."

With that they charged after her afresh, not in much worse shape than when they set out. Now, however, in addition to being drunk and anxious to get to her, she sensed a new determination in their movements, their voices. Embarrassment, she thought, at being taken advantage of by a woman. Their angry, threatening shouts pierced her ears.

Threats . . . and promises. Promises of what they would do to her. Fear surrounded her with a suffocating closeness as she racked her brain for a way to escape these demons.

Quint will come, she thought. He will. But she knew now it would not be in time.

Stay calm, she told herself. It's your only chance. Stay calm. You can circle up, and when you get them on this side of the thicket, circle back again. Keep them running until help comes.

It was a good plan. The best one she could come up with. It would work. It had to work.

But it didn't.

Jim Tom reached her first, and she should have given up right then, she thought later. It would have been easier on her. But she didn't.

Giving up was not a part of her makeup. And what did it matter if fighting made things worse on her? How could things get worse than they already were? Worse than they had been for Elena?

It took both men to carry her down the hill, and they paid for it. She kicked and screamed and bit at any part of them she could get to.

When they reached the bottom of the hill, they began arguing on where to take her. E. A. wanted to carry her to the spring, but Jim Tom said no, they must get what they were after right here, quickly, before his pa came.

"Then we'll take her down to Cob and see what he's up to, 'fore Grant gets here to put her outta her misery."

She had stopped resisting while they spoke, but when they put her down at the chosen site, she jumped to her feet and ran. By this time the bottom of her dress hung in blue and purple ribbons about her calves, so it did not hamper her escape.

Jim Tom did. Grabbing her arm, he jerked her back to the ground.

"Wowee!" E. A. whooped. "You sure you're up to goin' first, boss? I told you she was a fighter. Just the way I like 'em."

"Let me at 'er." Jim Tom stumbled forward, and Holly jerked to free her arm.

"Let me go," she demanded in a quivering voice. "The sheriff will be here any minute."

Jim Tom laughed—the same menacing, rotten laugh that had filled her with revulsion that day in Silver Creek. Her stomach churned violently, and she doubled over.

"Your ol' sugar daddy won't be ridin' up to save you this time, cutie pie. He's busy with a gunfighter on his tail." His pupils were tiny dots of black floating in a mass of red jelly, and they taunted her with their insolence.

"Grant won't get him," she said. "He'll come."

Jim Tom grinned at her, grabbed the front of her dress, and she gritted her teeth, willing herself not to cry. It's only a body, she thought furiously. Only a body.

"Grant's the best gunfighter in this whole goddamned state outside ol' Hardin hisself. He'll take Quint in the bat of an eye."

"No," Holly protested. She had to keep them talking, to buy some more time. Quint would come if she gave him time. "Quint will shoot Troy Grant," she said. "He probably already has."

Jim Tom swayed before her, still holding the front of her dress, but seeming to have been distracted from his mission. "Ain't nobody gonna save you this time, sugar. Nobody." He swayed again, and she flinched as his hand slipped and gripped hold of her breast. This refocused his attention, and he leaned his foul-smelling mouth toward hers.

E. A. stopped him. "I told you I heard a shot 'fore we got to the canyon, boss. Two or three of 'em."

Jim Tom turned his head toward his companion. "Then it was Grant shooting Jarvis. Pa don't hire nothing but the best."

"Get on with it, then," E. A. said. "We'll have hell to pay if yore pa catches us."

Holly wriggled backward, her mind searching for some way to hold them off. A little longer, she pleaded with herself. Just a little longer.

"Why did your father hire Troy Grant to kill Quint?" she asked. "Quint's a part of your family."

"Humph!" Jim Tom snorted. "Quint ain't never been family to me. And he turned on Pa, too. Pa figured it'd be best to put him out of the way, 'fore he took it into his head to bring the law down on us."

"But . . ." Holly began.

"No more talking," Jim Tom demanded. "Me an' you got business. Right now." When he tightened his grip, she heard her fine lawn collar rip and her bodice tear apart. He wrenched at her breasts, sending searing pain through her body, and she bent her head forward and sunk her teeth into his arm.

He reared back, freeing his arm, and slapped her hard across the face. Then, thinking her subdued, he dived for her lips with his open mouth, and she drew her head back and spit in his face.

Wrestling her roughly to the ground, he tore and tugged at her dress, while she struggled mightily beneath him.

Her thoughts were on survival now, fierce and sharp; all else was muddled beyond recognition. During the war she had friends who had been raped. Always she had felt compassion for them, believing she knew the depths of their feelings.

She was wrong. The horror and fear and very real terror were beyond her imaginings. As was her digust at herself. Why had she dawdled at the spring? Why hadn't she gone directly to the cave as Quint told her to?

Why, oh, why, had she come to Silver Creek in the first place? And why had Papa come here? The treasure be damned. It had brought them nothing but suffering and pain and death.

Writhing on the ground, kicking, struggling, screaming, she resisted, determined that he should not consummate this final outrage.

The turmoil addled her senses: Jim Tom's putrid odor—whiskey and stale sweat; his curses and those of his cohort; his heaving breath and the movements of their bodies against the earth and each other; his boots scraping against rock, clothing ripping and skin breaking beneath her fingernails.

Suddenly the din ceased, abruptly silenced by the report of a single rifle shot. A deafening, threatening command filled the ensuing silence.

"Get up off that woman and get down here, you good-for-nothing drunken excuse for a son!"

Chapter Eighteen

The uproar reverberated through Holly's hysteria, bringing hope to her addled brain.

For a moment she thought Quint had come. She had fought Jim Tom off long enough, and now Quint had come to save her. She knew he would.

Jim Tom's actions bore out her thinking. He lifted himself from her struggling body, cursing loudly. Hatred gushed from his eyes to hers in an almost physical stream.

Hatred for her, she thought, and hatred for the man who pulled the strings of his life with such force.

Tom Farrell.

The shouted words took form in her mind then, and anguish and disappointment fell upon her like a heavy cloak. Quint hadn't come. She chided herself for playing the ostrich game; she had such a knack for hoping, and now . . .

Jim Tom trudged down the hill, followed by E. A., while she grappled with her own hatred for these men.

She had won, though. She had fought them off, and she had won. As her senses cleared, she became conscious of a loud racket which filled the canyon.

Standing up to better observe the commotion, she

brushed her tousled hair away from her eyes. Tom Farrell paraded below her, strutting like a bantam rooster before his son, and she was suddenly overcome by a nauseating combination of aches and pains. A great throb at the back of her head turned out to be a rather large knot. Her hands, as well as both legs, were scratched and bleeding, and she sagged like a limp rag at her first step.

Sinking to a boulder on the side of the hill, she looked toward the activity. A stream of milling, bellowing cattle flowed into the canyon through the maze-end, followed by a wagon and a number of men on horseback.

She stared at them dumbly. With the cattle and riders at one end and Tom Farrell himself at the other, she was shut in. She closed her stinging eyes and drew a shaky breath. Escape would be impossible.

Determination stirred within her, however, and ugly as the outlook was, she vowed to be the last to give up heart and hope, especially now, after she had survived Jim Tom's attack.

Terrified, grasping for the strength and wisdom to escape, she put her hand to her heart, and as her fingers chilled her bare bosom, an overwhelming sickness took her breath away.

In a fury she looked from her naked body to the gaping eyes of the men standing down the hill. Quickly she turned the back of her skirt over her shoulders, as humiliation brought fresh tears to her eyes.

But a crazy terror warned her that she could never escape the danger which faced her without the use of both hands, so working as fast as her quivering fingers would allow, she tore a strip from her already frayed skirt, and hastily pulled the skirt underneath her arms. She then laced it together across her bosom by weaving the strip in and out between the holes in the tattered garment.

With one eye on her work and one on the scene below, she worked feverishly, repeating over and over the words of Marie Antoinette, "I count upon my courage; I count upon my courage," while E. A., apparently at Tom Farrell's orders, started up the hill toward her.

With one last tug she tied the strip into a knot, and gasped, finally recognizing E. A. All during their frantic chase around the hillside, she had the nagging feeling she had seen him before. His voice was even somehow familiar. Now she placed him. He was the highwayman who had treated her so indecently during the holdup. Although she hadn't seen his face at the time, his movements now assured her she was right. Well, he wouldn't get another chance at her.

Looking around quickly for something that she could use to fight him off, something that would hit hard and come readily to hand—she thought of her rifle.

But where had she left it? Then she remembered. Feeling no need for the encumbrance of an empty rifle after her last shot, she had discarded it. Now, as E. A. approached, all she could do was run.

But that was not enough. Even though he came slowly, still breathing hard from their chase, he caught her handily and dragged her fighting back to the canyon floor where Tom Farrell still upbraided Jim Tom in his usual caustic fashion. When he turned his attention to her, she flew at him in a rage and tried to box his ears.

He shoved her away from him, frowning her down severely. "You've only yourself to blame, Miss Campbell. I warned you to leave Silver Creek, but you refused to listen to me. Now your troubles have thickened."

"I hate you all. . . ." Her voice shook, and every fiber in her body quivered.

Jim Tom sneered. "A lot of good it'll do you now, Miss High-Toned-Uppity-Uppity." He pulled back her pieced-together skirt to peek at her bosom.

She recoiled from his touch, as if from a dreaded rattlesnake, and Tom Farrell suddenly backhanded his son across the face with such force that Jim Tom fell to the ground, where he lay huddled in a heap.

"You goddamned whorin' sonofabitch," Farrell hollered at his son. "It's a good thing your ma's dead an' can't see what a drunken mess you've turned into. I spit on the day she bore you."

Jim Tom cowered on the ground, and Tom Farrell turned his wrath upon Holly. "And you've got me into a fine fix, yourself—you and that lyin' pa of yours."

Holly glared at him, her heart in her throat. "You murdered my father. I can prove it."

"You can prove nothing," he retorted. "Your pa killed himself by his own hand."

"That isn't true," Holly screamed. "You bribed him and then murdered him."

Tom Farrell shook his head, undaunted by her accusations. "Your pa was exactly like all them other treasure hunters. He was caught up in his own greed. That's what killed him."

"Liar!" As her mind focused on the diary and her reason for coming to Silver Creek, she momentarily lost all fear for herself. "You never intended to let him keep this property. All you wanted was to save the life of this . . . this demon. Then you killed the best man who ever lived." Tears brimmed in her eyes, ready to spill at no notice. She tried desperately to control them.

"Your pa was misled," Farrell said. "Misled by a foolish notion which I reckon I understand well enough."

She stared at him, knowing he could say nothing to set the matter straight. He had killed Papa; that was all that mattered. He killed Papa, and he must pay.

The thought of convicting Tom Farrell brought her own precarious state to mind, and a violent quaking took hold of her once more. Who would be left to bring the Farrells to justice? Oh, they might be tried for rustling, but they deserved more. They must pay for Papa's death, and for Raphael's. If they killed her and Sancho, no one would be left who knew the truth.

Except Elena and Quint. And they didn't know enough. Quint knew about the cave, though, and when he found her gone, he would look there. The journal would convince him of Farrell's guilt, but without Sancho's eyewitness account, the journal itself might not be enough to convict Farrell of murder.

At least Quint would look for her. He wouldn't let up until he found her body, but . . .

"Your pa and me was guilty of the same thing, I reckon," Farrell said, and she glared at him, daring him to compare himself with Papa.

"He wanted the treasure for you. And the things I've done—they've mostly been for . . ." He looked down at Jim Tom with complete disgust and continued. "What I've done was for a son, but I was a fool, thinking I could raise him up like his ma wanted. He was bad from the start." He shook his head regretfully. "She wouldn't claim him now, any more'n me. He doesn't care one fig about this land . . . this land his ma and me sweated our own blood over . . . land that would've been his someday, all of it, as much land as I could put together. More land than most folks lay eyes on in a whole lifetime. It would have all been his . . ."

Holly stared, startled at this unraveling of a man she had grown to hate more than she ever hated Yankees or carpetbaggers.

And her skin crawled at the sight of Jim Tom. How dare Tom Farrell speak of his relationship with Jim Tom in the same light as her relationship with Papa.

"Papa wasn't like you say. He knew I cared nothing for treasure." Her voice was steadier now, and as she spoke she saw the lines in the journal, lines which repudiated all she knew and believed.

"He wanted you to have a better life than he could give you without it," Farrell said. "Your pa an' me understood each other in that respect. He wanted a better life for you, wanted it for your ma's sake, likely. And for his own. It's the way we have—a way of keeping ourselves going after we've left this life."

"You're wrong . . ." Holly began, but Jim Tom interrupted her.

"You never asked me what I wanted," he hollered at his father. "You always told me. Well, I ain't the kind of feller you want, an' you can't make me out to be. I never will be another Quintan Jarvis. I'm me, an' you're stuck with me."

"No." Tom Farrell's eyes hardened. "After today I have no son."

"If that's the way you want it," Jim Tom stormed. "I'm lightin' a shuck."

"Not quite yet," Farrell answered. "I have one last job for you. And I intend for you to get this one right." Farrell looked directly at Holly. "Take her out of sight and kill her. I don't want the cattle scared by the shot, or the drovers to hear it."

Jim Tom sneered at his father. "Why don't you do it, Pa? I ain't never seen you kill a man." He winked at Holly. "Much less a high-toned lady. You always send someone else to do your dirty work."

Holly swayed with faintness. It was one thing to know what they intended, but quite another to hear the order given. She turned to Jim Tom. "You're wrong," he said. "He murdered my father himself. He shot him nder that cottonwood tree by the spring, and he had is men drag the body up that cliff." She pointed to the rst cave. "He left the body up there along with the essage he forced Papa to write. Sancho saw it all."

Tom Farrell glared at her, and she knew if by some are chance he had planned to let Sancho live, he would ertainly kill him now.

"Sancho wrote it all down," she claimed, "and his ritings, along with Papa's journal which describes ow he lied about Raphael Salinas's murder are in a afe place where Sheriff Jarvis will find them and rosecute you both."

"Quint will prosecute no one," Farrell said, and Iolly tensed against the fear that he had killed Quint imself.

"After today," Farrell continued, "we'll be looking or a new sheriff. Matter of fact, we already have one in nind. And he won't settle for the word of a dead man."

"If you mean Troy Grant, whom you hired to kill the heriff, forget it," Holly said.

Farrell stared at her. "What's this all about?"

She hesitated, recalling Quint's warning. But the erd was in the canyon now, and the rustlers, too. If she ould persuade them to look for Grant's body, the osse might arrive in time to save her.

"Troy Grant's body is in the brush over by the spring here the sheriff and I hid it."

Tom Farrell cocked his head, obviously uncon-inced. "You're wasting my time," he answered finally.

"It's true," she repeated, pushing a strand of hair way from her face. "Are you afraid to look?"

Farrell's back stiffened. He called to Cob, "Get on ver there and take a look-see."

Cob strained to hear, and Jim Tom answered. Cob's shot up, Pa. She done it."

Farrell glared from Cob to Holly, then to Jim Tom. "Jingle your spurs . . . pronto," he told his son.

Jim Tom headed for the spring, but at his own defiant pace, while Tom Farrell shifted from foot to foot impatiently. When Jim Tom was almost there, he turned to E. A. "Give him a hand. On the double."

E. A. sprinted across the canyon floor, and he and Jim Tom arrived at the thicket at the same time. They stared only a moment before looking back at Tom Farrell.

"Yep," E. A. called. "He's in here, sure enough. An' dead as a doornail."

"Then take care of this woman. Now."

At that Holly broke loose and ran for the canyon entrance, but Farrell caught her arm. He held her until E. A. and Jim Tom returned, then he shoved her toward E. A. "Take her up there where you put her pa," he said. "That way if Quint comes back, he won't see you." He thought a moment. "And don't use a gun. The shot would carry too far."

"I'll do it, Pa." Jim Tom tried to pull Holly's arm from his father's grasp.

"Get your hands off her," Farrell demanded. "You've done enough harm as it is. I wouldn't be in this mess if it wasn't for your horseplay. I should've listened to Quint when he warned me to get rid of your outlaw friends . . . should've sent them packing, and you along with them. You ain't fit to live with civilized man."

Holly's mouth dropped open. "And you are, Mr. Farrell? Even though you murdered my father, and you now intend to murder me."

"You got yourself into it," he fumed. "This is my land. I fought Injuns for it, outlasted the war and droughts and blizzards, and I won't let some two-bit doctor or his harebrained daughter cheat me out of what's mine." He shoved Holly toward E. A.

"Get on with it," he ordered.

E. A. reached for Holly's arm, and Jim Tom spoke again, his voice a whine. "But, Pa, give me one more chance. I won't mess up this time."

Tom Farrell exploded. He slapped his son hard across the face once more. "Never speak to me again," he shouted. "I have no son." Turning to E. A., his eyes were livid with rage. "Get that woman out of my sight. Now. And if she gives you any trouble, shoot her on the spot."

E. A. dragged Holly after him, and she followed in a daze, not knowing what to do . . . frantic to think of some way to save herself.

When they crossed the center of the canyon, she became aware of the cattle filling the once empty spaces, of horses and riders. Vainly she looked for Quint, but recognized no one. She considered yelling to attract the drovers Farrell didn't want to know of her murder. They might help her. But by this time the noise engulfing them was so great that she knew her cries would go unheard.

He dragged her past the spring where Sancho still struggled with his bonds, his eyes frightened. Cob reached toward them, jabbed his rifle butt at her leg, and she stumbled.

E. A. let up a bit. She realized that he must still be tired from the chase around the canyon and from his race to the spring and back. Quint said men out here didn't do much of anything that couldn't be done on horseback. Strange, she thought vaguely, how a person remembered trifling things at such a desperate time. She recalled the babbling of dying men during the war. Now she understood the mind's inability to control itself. She supposed in self-defense, to keep the mind from disintegrating before . . . She wondered what difference it made.

When they reached the bluff, she looked up, and her heart leaped to her throat. Was this it, then? Was this where she would die?

Fury and rage stirred inside her, but she could think of no way to save herself. Even if she could get loose from E. A., he or someone else would shoot her.

E. A. dragged her behind him up the hillside. Thinking perhaps she could somehow escape into the herd, she looked back at the cattle, but their sheer size—they were the largest animals she had ever seen—and the length and sharpness of their horns appalled her.

As did dying. But regardless of the method, a growing certainty weighed on her thoughts—her time was here and now. She followed E. A., unwilling to give in to these dastardly men. Surely she could find a way—some way.

Things were never hopeless until they were done, or so she had always believed, so she stopped climbing and forced E. A. to pull her up the hill behind him, a feat that he soon found impossible.

After a few steps, he made way for her to go ahead of him. She started not to obey, but decided she had no choice.

Suddenly, as she climbed ahead, she numbly recalled how Quint warned her of rattlesnakes on their first climb to this cave, and an idea struck her . . . a chance, probably not a chance to escape, but a chance for a little more time. Now that she knew Farrell hadn't killed Quint, she must give him more time to come.

If she pretended to see a snake, she might frighten E. A., and if she could cause him to fall, she could get to the cave. Once there, surely she could find something in the cave to fend them off with until Quint returned.

Desperately she fought for the courage to continue,

to believe, to hope. She turned her head over her shoulder to look back at Tom Farrell, and at that instant what she saw almost caused her to fall off the bluff instead of E. A.

Quint entered the canyon, then stopped short, apparently seeing the Farrells, who had their backs to him.

She looked down at E. A. who saw Quint at that same moment. Quickly, before E. A. could call a warning, she steadied herself with one foot, took a firm hold on the rock above her, and kicked him in the head with all her might, sending him teetering down the cliff.

Tom Farrell saw the commotion in the split second Quint opened fire.

Holly looked hopefully for the rest of the posse, but Quint sat his horse alone, facing Jim Tom and his father.

Then she thought of Cob, down by the spring. And of Farrell's drovers. She must do something, anything, before Cob fired on Quint. Quint wouldn't know how many men he faced, and he hadn't shot at the Farrells with the intent to either kill or injure. He had merely fired a warning shot to draw their attention.

Quint wouldn't know about Cob. And he wouldn't know about E. A. Holly wriggled down the bluff. At the bottom she found E. A. unconscious from his fall, so she pulled his guns from the holsters and picked up his rifle where it had fallen.

Since they had been out of sight from the spring at the time she kicked him, there was a chance Cob didn't know what had happened yet.

She took a step away from E. A., then realized that he could come to at any moment. So she swallowed hard, raised the rifle, and struck him in the head with the stock.

A quick glance at Quint told her that he had the

Farrells under control. Then she turned her attention to the spring, where she quietly approached from behind the thicket. She apprehended Cob as he raised his rifle to fire.

"I wouldn't do that, if I were you," she whispered. "I've already shot you once today, and I killed Troy Grant."

"Don't shoot, lady." He fumbled with the words. "You got me dead to rights, but don't shoot."

"Then pull yourself up slowly and see if you can hobble on over to where the sheriff is. We wouldn't want him not to recognize you here under the tree and shoot you by mistake."

Cob grumbled, but he followed her instructions, and the two of them crept slowly toward Quint and the Farrells.

When Quint saw Holly, his face went ashen. Quickly he noted that she was walking, alive, had captured one of Farrell's men. But his blood turned cold when he saw how her dress hung in tatters from her bare shoulders, how her hair tumbled in matted masses every which way. Scratches marked her face and shoulders with streaks of blood. Furious and terrified at the same time, he spoke through a cottony mouth. "Are you all right?"

She nodded, and he turned to Jim Tom in a blind rage. Only the discipline of always putting first things first kept him from leaping on the younger man and strangling him with his own hands. Deliberately he moved his finger away from the trigger. "If you've laid a hand on her, I'll kill you."

Jim Tom grinned. "You? I've known you all my life, Quint Jarvis. You'd never murder a man in cold blood. Neither you nor Pa . . . although, if what she says is true, the ol' man here may have changed his ways." He sneered from Quint to his father and back again. "If he id kill her pa, he won't never own up to it."

Quint felt himself relax at the familiar whine in Jim 'om's voice. Why should he risk everything he held ear for revenge when, this time, a court would put iem all away for good?

"Drop your guns and belts," he instructed them. The posse will have your men under guard by now." 'alling for the men in the thicket at the edge of the anyon to come forward and take the Farrells' guns, uint reholstered his rifle in its saddle boot and turned ack to his prisoners.

Holly watched the scene, mesmerized as much by the elief she felt that she and Quint were both alive, as by ie tense physical drama before her. Although resent-ient and scorn showed on his face, Tom Farrell beyed Quint's order.

Jim Tom did not. He fiddled with his gun belt, his yes twitching as he looked at Quint, obviously still not onvinced that he had lost the game—that his father ad lost any game. From the contempt in his expres-on Holly wondered whether he and Quint hadn't ought like hyenas all their lives.

She saw more in Jim Tom than anger and hatred, owever. He didn't seem sane. His jerky actions, dart-g eyes, curling lips—all were symptoms she had wit-essed during the war in men who had gone crazy from ie horrors of battle, from seeing friends or family die efore their eyes.

But Jim Tom's insanity was different. To her nowledge he had suffered no unusual trauma other ian the too-high expectations of a father he could ever please.

As she watched, Jim Tom slowly untied the holster rings from around his legs. First the left, then the ght. His eyes never left Quint . . .

Until Wilt and Luther showed themselves, obeying

Quint's command to take up the weapons.

Then at the sight of Wilt and Luther, Jim Tom's madness exploded in a frenzy. His eyes danced to a stop, frozen in disbelief. "You lily-livered, double-crossing sons-of-bitches."

If she hadn't witnessed it, Holly would never have believed anyone capable of the perfect precision with which Jim Tom drew his gun and fired. One single, fluid motion, taking but an instant from a moment fixed in time.

One single instant, following which the world exploded, paused, then collapsed.

Everything occurred in slow, measured time—beginning with Jim Tom's simple liquid movement as his gun rose majestically, then fell by degrees, followed by his body jerking backward, crumbling to a heap on the ground.

Outside the perimeter of that one scene, everything else was fuzzy. Tom Farrell shrieked, a piercing cry which seemed to come from a long ways off, from an old, gray woman; Cob fell to his knees in front of her, meeting Tom Farrell over Jim Tom's fallen body.

Slowly lifting her head by degrees, she saw Quint, shoulders slumping, gun sagging, smoke rising from the barrel. She stared at him in horror, then rushed to his side, her hands searching, caressing, searching . . .

"Where are you hit?" she cried, but the words sounded in her ears as a whisper.

Quint tried to wet his lips with a too-dry tongue. He couldn't tear his eyes away from Jim Tom's body.

Tears streamed down Holly's cheeks. "Quint, answer me. Where are you hit?"

He heard her voice, felt her arms around him, tried to speak. But all he could manage was to stare dumbly at Jim Tom. No life. None. Damn it! He should have taken their guns himself, sooner. He should have . . .

"Quint," Holly sobbed. "Where are you hit?"

"He ain't hit, ma'am," Wilt said, and she stiffened at his somber tone, the tone used in the House of God . . . at a funeral. "Jim Tom never even got a shot off."

Relief swept over her at the words, and she tightened her hold on Quint, her eyes pouring tears.

Then Jim Tom moved. Only a foot, but Quint saw the movement, and removing Holly's arms, he squatted on his heels to get a better look.

At that moment life and time resumed their normal pace for Holly, as if someone had lighted a lantern and thrown life back into the world. She stood silently watching Quint study the man he had shot.

Jim Tom moved a bit more, tried to sit up, but then fell back onto the ground, twisting with pain.

Tom Farrell caught his son's head before it hit the ground, and the gesture drew Holly's eyes away from Quint to Farrell, himself, his eyes brimming with tears.

Suddenly he looked up at her. "Don't just stand there. Get down here and save my son."

Her mouth fell open. "What?" she asked, staring at the writhing, groaning form of the creature she had so recently struggled against.

Farrell shoved Cob away from the body, making space for her. "Get on down here before he bleeds to death." His voice trembled, she thought, as one on the far side of reason.

With Cob out of the way, Holly had a good view of the wound, the entry of which she judged to be slightly below the heart, but whose trajectory could be anywhere.

Her mind whirled with contradictory thoughts, opposing emotions struggling within her. Here was a human being who needed help, yet a man who had ruthlessly tried to rape her not an hour earlier, then begged to be allowed to kill her; a man who murdered Raphael Salinas in cold blood and had only now been shot trying to murder Quint.

A cold wave washed over her body, drying her tears and leaving her mind in a stupor. Save him? How could she? "I've no instruments," she said.

"We'll take him to town," Farrell replied urgently.

"He can't ride a horse," she objected.

Farrell looked sharply to the other end of the canyon, then back to her, his eyes betrayed his loose hold on hope. "The wagon," he said. "We'll unload the supplies and make him a bed."

"He wouldn't make it." Holly stared at the father and son, the father now appearing to have shrunk from the pompous figure of earlier today to the shriveled size of the son. She turned and walked silently toward the spring, stopping beside the ancient oak with the turtle carved on it. The curse of treasure fever, she thought bitterly.

Pressing her lips together until she felt the blood flow stop, she ran her trembling fingers up and down the bark of the tree. Its roughness stung her numb hands.

Save Jim Tom Farrell? Why should she? All her life she had watched Papa save lives, and those he could not save, she had seen him grieve over. She had never known him to refuse to treat anyone, yet . . .

She still quaked with the fright of thinking Jim Tom had shot Quint. And the hatred she knew Jim Tom felt for Quint, could, if he lived, give him cause to kill him later.

Save Jim Tom? Visions of his deeds swept madly before her eyes—Elena's beaten, raped body and her distress over the murder of her husband; the fiendish way Jim Tom had pursued Holly herself since she arrived in Silver Creek, and his very near rape of her today; and Quint . . . She would forever see Quint's trembling body and feel the pain of thinking him killed.

"Miss Campbell, you must . . ."

The words reached her, and although she did not turn around, she saw his eyes as she had seen them last; the pleading eyes of a father about to lose a son—a father unaccustomed to losing anything. No longer filled with rage, they now begged.

Suddenly she clasped her head angrily, hearing again Tom Farrell's words against her father. So Papa wasn't perfect. So he made mistakes. Papa's greed was nothing compared with Tom Farrell's own greed—a greed so great that he couldn't let a man have a small piece of his property in exchange for what he now begged for a second time—the life of his son.

No, she thought, why should she try to save Jim Tom's life? One Campbell had already done so and had been repaid by being murdered. It was time to stop this dastardly cycle. Time to end it all with Tom Farrell paying at last for his own greed.

Why should she . . . ?

Quint's hands sent chills up her arms as he grasped her shoulders from behind. "Holly . . . ?"

She quaked at his trembling. Turning toward him, the pain in his golden eyes bore into her heart, answering her question.

"Get the wagon," she whispered.

Chapter Nineteen

Her decision was made, Holly knew, for Quint's sake, and her apprehension abated somewhat at the flicker of hope which brightened his eyes at her reply.

He held her body close to his and was eased by her nearness, by the hope that she could save Jim Tom. "Holly . . . Holly . . ."

She squeezed back tears. "It may be too late, Quint, but I'll try."

While Wilt fetched the wagon, Quint conferred with Sheriff Bales on the transporation of prisoners.

"Can you keep the posse in line, Bales?"

Bales nodded. "The way they figure it, you've got the ringleaders. What's left ain't worth hanging."

Holly glanced toward Jim Tom and shuddered, then she continued to the spring where she found Sancho struggling to loosen his bonds.

Jed Varner approached at the same time. He looked Holly up and down. Curiosity and apprehension showed in his eyes, but politeness sealed his lips.

She touched her hair and for the first time thought what a frightful appearance she must present. He said nothing about it, though, and set about untying Sancho.

As soon as the gag was off his mouth, Sancho started talking. "I'm right sorry, ma'am. They snatched me 'fore I could get to town. Are you all right?"

She nodded and lowered herself to the spring, where she let the cool water bubble over her cracked lips and into her mouth.

"You plumb saved the sheriff's bacon," Sancho continued. "No doubt about it. He'd've been a goner for sure if you hadn't got hold of ol' Cob's rifle when you did."

Splashing cold water on her face, she drank long, then sat up and spit out a water bug. "I guess we saved each other this time, Sancho," she told him. "Are you injured?"

"No'm." The boy stood, flexing his legs. "But it surely does feel good to be moving about."

Quint came up then, urging Holly to see to the loading of Jim Tom, but she thought of his own wound and made him let her bathe it with spring water.

"It's only a flesh wound," he protested.

She ignored him and looked down at what was left of her petticoats. "We need some clean bandages." Nothing on her body even resembled cleanliness, she thought.

Quint pulled his shirt back over his shoulder. "Come on, Holly, we're wasting time." He took her by the arm, but she hesitated.

"Troy Grant," she said. "What about his body?"

Quint looked at her for a moment, then focused on her meaning. "Varner, Grant's horse is in a thicket behind the canyon."

Jed followed Quint's glance to where Grant's body lay, now only partially covered by brush. His eyes opened a smidgen wider. "This here's one shindig I'm sure proud to've missed."

"Yeah," Quint answered in a near whisper. "Wish I

could say the same." He took Holly's arm and pulled her toward the wagon.

She faltered, knowing she was purposely tarrying. And when she returned to examine Jim Tom, her skin crawled with her affinity for the man.

For Quint's sake, she coaxed herself. Do this for Quint and be done with it.

Tom Farrell hovered above her while she had Quint help turn the body to look for an exit wound. There was none.

"How bad off is he?" Farrell asked.

She stared up at him without disguising her hatred. "If you hadn't murdered the only doctor in this whole country, your son might have a chance. As it is, he will probably get what he deserves."

Quint helped Wilt and Luther arrange a bed in the wagon, then they gently lifted Jim Tom into it.

Holly watched Cob and E. A. hobble in beside him, but when Quint tried to lift her into the wagon alongside the wounded men, she stifled a scream. "I will not ride with them."

Quint felt her body flinch beneath his hands, and turning her toward him, he saw the terror in her eyes. He looked back at Jim Tom, seeing still the tattered vision of Holly's ripped clothing, her injured body. At this, his shock of the shooting turned to anger, and he held her tightly in his arms and murmured into her hair. "You don't have to, sweet Holly. You don't have to."

Motioning for Wilt to move the wagon out, he sat Holly on a fallen log while he retrieved their mounts, and the two of them followed the wagon from the canyon.

As they passed the trail that led up the side of the bluff to the second cave, Holly jumped from her horse, handing Quint the reins.

"I'll only be a minute," she called, and was off up the trail before he could respond.

Returning with the journal, she remounted, and they rode silently toward town until Quint found words to speak.

"Damn, Holly, I'm sorry. If I hadn't been so taken up with catching the rustlers, I would have put him away before he hurt you."

"You had to catch the rustlers, Quint. Too many people have suffered from their deeds." She sighed. "Too many."

He shrugged. "Pigheaded me, I refused to believe that the Farrells were connected with the rustling until not long back when Wilt and Luther finally convinced me. After they got wind of it, they worked their way into Jim Tom's confidence, and he let them into the gang." He rode silently awhile, then continued. "That wasn't long before you came to Silver Creek. But I still couldn't believe Tom had anything to do with your pa's death. He was never a murderer, and I couldn't figure why he'd start killing folks without any reason. Then that telegram came about the canyon, and after I saw those tracks the day we rode out here . . . Well, things began to fall into place after that."

Holly showed him the diary. "This is Papa's journal. He writes about Raphael's murder. He also says Tom Farrell deeded him the canyon in exchange for the testimony that cleared Jim Tom."

He looked at her sad brown eyes, thinking of the deep hurt she must feel, knowing that this man she had set such store by had pulled the rug out from under her.

"Sancho saw Tom Farrell himself shoot Papa," she told him quietly. "The journal ends with the morning of Papa's death, so it provides a good record to Sancho's eyewitness account . . . and Elena's claims."

He gazed long at her tattered face and clothing, and

anger grew inside him—anger at the men who had hurt her—Jim Tom, her pa, himself. "I'll never let you down again, Holly. I promise you that."

She looked across at him, aching inside for him and for herself. For Elena and for Papa.

She recalled Aggie Westfield's words her first morning in Silver Creek . . . something about loneliness being a woman's lot in life. Pain and suffering were, too, she supposed.

But seeing Quint now, she knew that not only women suffered out here on the far side of civilization. "We each do what we have to, Quint," she told him. "To have arrested Jim Tom back then would have been the same as doctoring a scratch on a dying man. It's the whole picture that's important. The only person who could have stopped Jim Tom before now was Papa. Papa could have prevented all of this—perhaps even stopped the rustling by helping convict Jim Tom of Raphael's murder. But he didn't. He wanted the treasure."

They rode quietly, neither of them hearing or seeing the sounds and commotion around them, as the entourage made its way to Silver Creek—the wagon leading the rustlers with their hands tied to their saddle horns, followed by the posse and cattle.

Quint thought of the photograph of Holly's family at that grand home, of her way of standing by her pa and what she thought were his beliefs, and of her hurt on learning the truth. "He loved you, Holly."

"I know," she said. "That's why he wanted the treasure—for Elena and me. But I can't understand why he thought it was necessary."

Quint looked at her. "Give yourself time," he said. "You will."

She nodded, thinking of her children yet to come. Who knew what drove a parent to such ends?

"I did learn something, though," she said.

"What's that?"

She sighed. "That security can't come from your family—from their name or who they are or who you think they are." She thought of her terror earlier today when on three different occasions she had thought Quint had been killed. If such a thing happened, it would be dreadful—but she could live with it. She knew that now.

Her heart caught in her throat when she looked at him. Dear God, how she loved him. "In the end the only security you can really count on must come from within yourself."

He studied her, knowing that his feelings for her were stronger than anything he had ever run up against before in his life, that somehow he was going to protect and love her for the rest of his life. Knowing, too, that that might not be long enough. He nodded solemnly at her wisdom, thankful for her strength.

"It's strange," she said, "I thought I learned that leasson during the war, but . . ."

"Some lessons come a mite harder than others," he told her. "Some need repeating time to time."

As they neared town, Holly became more troubled. If she was going to tell him, it must be now. She had to tell someone, and she wanted Quint to know. So she gulped at the lump in her throat and blurted out the words.

"I fought them off."

He turned to her, startled, and from the depths of his golden eyes, she found the strength to go on. "It was the most . . . the most terrifying experience . . . but they didn't . . . they didn't do to me what they did to Elena." She held her head high and stiff, and although their eyes locked together, he could not read her feelings.

She continued. "They might have finally . . . succeeded, if . . . They might have killed me this time, too, but now I know I can fight them off. Next time . . ."

"My God, Holly! Stop!" Hsi heart pounded in his temples like a thousand horses' hooves. He took a breath and in a gentle voice said, "Stop, Holly. There won't be a next time."

She pursed her lips in a straight, rigid line. "But if there is, I know I can beat them."

Only a couple more hours of daylight remained when they pulled up before the Hotel O'Keefe. Every inch of her body ached with fatigue, and she thought longingly of a hot bath with her own rose-scented oils. But that would have to wait a while yet.

Quint handed her down from the saddle, and she gave him the journal. "Put this in a safe place. We might not be able to find it if it disappeared again."

She stumbled on the steps, and when he took her arm, she felt his hands tremble. She glanced at him reassuringly. "I'll do the best I can for him, Quint."

He gripped her arms, and his eyes fierce. "You don't have to touch him, Holly."

"Yes, I do," she answered simply.

Mavis met them on the porch, taking charge with her usual aplomb. "Sancho rode ahead," she said, "and we're ready for you. Bring him into the dining room. The table will serve nicely as an operating table." She held the door open for the men who carried Jim Tom, while talking to Holly. "Your medical bag is already there, and . . ." She stopped in midsentence to give Holly a thorough inspection. "Good God, Holly! Whatever happened to you?"

Holly ignored the question, but somehow felt the tension drain from her at having Mavis take charge. She was too exhausted to direct the situation herself. Performing the operation would be difficult enough.

"I need to wash up, and . . ." she began.

Mavis interrupted her. "Rosie has plenty of hot water, and Aggie can bring you fresh clothing."

"There's no time to change, Mavis," Holly said. "We're running out of time, as it is."

Washing her hands and splashing water on her face brought a measure of feeling back to her senses, and as she pinned her matted, wet hair out of her way, she heard the men in the next room following Mavis's directions about where to place Jim Tom on the table.

The dining room was full of people when Holly entered, and she immediately noticed the inadequate lighting. Even though all the lamps were burning and the drapes drawn back, the almost total lack of sunlight cast a subdued pall over the room.

"We'll have to move outside, Mavis. I can't see in here."

"Holly . . ." Quint began.

Holly stopped him. "I'm not stalling this time, Quint. I must be able to see what I'm about."

Without further discussion Mavis organized the men, and they carried Jim Tom, the table, and Holly's instruments out the back door and set up beneath the towering pecan trees. Rosie followed with a kettle of steaming water which she poured into a basin on a sidetable.

Approaching her patient, Holly shook her head in amazement. Davy and Sancho stood at either end of the table waving large fans to shoo the flies away. Mavis still thought of everything.

Tom Farrell positioned himself staunchly beside his son. "Now get to work," he demanded.

Holly looked at his frazzled countenance, surprised by the bit of sympathy she felt for him. "There's nothing you can do here, Mr. Farrell. Why don't . . . ?"

"You're not sending me away," he insisted. "I intend

to stay and see you do your job."

"This time things will be done my way, or not at all," she told him. "Now, you leave me alone to perform this operation."

Mavis took Farrell by the shoulders. "Come, Tom. There's coffee in the kitchen, and I think I can scare up a spot of brandy."

He didn't budge, however, and Mavis stood with her hand on his arm. Holly turned to Quint and their eyes held expectantly. "You have prisoners to tend to," she said.

"Bales will handle them till this is finished." His brain reeled at the final ring of that word. "I'm not leaving you, so you'd best get started. Tell me what to do to help out."

She looked down at the patient, fighting to put everything else out of her mind, everything that had happened this day—and before.

Mavis handed her a cloth which she had wrung out in the basin, and Holly bathed Jim Tom's face, then pulled back his shirt. His smooth chest lay exposed, and visions of hundreds of previous patients swarmed before her, while she desperately tried to convince herself that she now worked to save someone else—someone other than the hated, the feared . . .

"Mavis has your instruments," Quint said, breaking her reverie. "Which one do you want?"

Holly looked up at him, knowing she must pull herself together. Now. She saw the instruments along with Papa's medical bag . . . Papa, whom Jim Tom . . .

Stop it! she demanded of herself. She breathed deeply to quiet her own heart, while listening to Jim Tom's ragged breathing. It wasn't shallow or irregular, not like men she had seen with a bullet in the lung, yet, where else could the bullet have gone?

Finally placing her bare hand over his heart, she

found to her surprise that she wasn't as squeamish at touching him flesh to flesh as she had feared, but when she gently placed her ear on his chest to listen for his heartbeat, the hairs of her face bristled.

"What are you doing?" Tom Farrell demanded. "Get on with this, I tell you."

She listened a bit longer, concentrating intently, trying to close out every sound except the rhythm of the heartbeat.

"What the hell are you doing?" Farrell raged.

"It's called auscultation," she answered, without stopping her examination. The bullet had entered a couple of inches below the heart, but it could have traveled anywhere.

Slowly, gently she felt his body with her fingertips, willing her fingers to distinguish something irregular, something . . .

"Now what're you doing?" Farrell bellowed in an increasingly distraught manner.

"Palpation," she answered.

"You don't need to do that," Farrell said. "His heart's working fine."

"Not palpitate," she answered quietly.

"What's that supposed to do? When're you gonna get the bullet out, woman?"

Quint took Farrell by the arm. "For God's sake, Tom. Let her do her work."

Holly continued the examination, and when she touched the bottom rib, Jim Tom flinched and hollered out.

So the bullet deflected off his rib, she thought. But where was it now?

Quint helped her turn Jim Tom to his back, where she continued feeling for the bullet. Finally when she had almost lost hope, she touched another sensitive area. This one near the right hip bone. When she ressed, Jim Tom cried out again.

Up to this point he had drifted in and out of onsciousness, but now he began to flail his arms about ınd yell and curse. Although at less than full strength, he whine in his voice still sent shivers up Holly's back.

"Take your goddamned hands off me and let me up," e muttered.

Quint helped Tom restrain his son. "Hold still now, im Tom," Quint told him. "The doc's gonna fix you up ;ood as new."

Other men stepped forward to help hold Jim Tom on he table, but Holly knew for what lay ahead, that vould not be enough. She had located the area where he bullet was lodged, but she still must probe to find it, nd a conscious man would have a hard time standing uch pain.

She stepped back from the table and searched the ıedical bag for medicines that she vaguely recalled eeing there: tinctures of morphine, hysocine, and actine—the doctors had used such injections during he war whenever they had the supplies on hand, so she ıow filled a hypodermic with the proper measure of ach and injected it into Jim Tom's arm while Tom 'arrell stood aghast, and Mavis comforted him with ooing sounds.

As the medicine began to take effect, Holly made an ncision, then probed for the bullet. She had seen this one more often than she had actually done it herself, nd she knew she would never get used to it. The very ct gave her gooseflesh, and when she finally reached he slug, the contact of metal on metal caused her to rimace and grit her teeth.

Sensing Quint staring at her, she looked into his eyes hich were filled with enough worry to contradict his ttempt at lightheartedness.

"Some doc you turn out to be."

She grinned feebly, her stomach in her throat. “I found it.”

Using the longest, thinnest pair of pincers from Papa’s bag, she decided to see if she could extract the bullet that way, rather than chance cutting into Jim Tom’s back. But a few attempts proved futile and brought beads of perspiration to her forehead.

“I can’t get a good hold on it,” she said.

“Cut it out,” Quint told her.

She felt Jim Tom’s cold, clammy face, then his pulse “He’s in bad shape.”

“Go ahead,” Quint said. “It’s his only chance.”

She nodded, knowing what he said was right, yet desperate now that this patient could very well die if she cut into the wrong area.

But she didn’t. She made the incision without incident, extracted the bullet, stitched the wound, and bandaged Jim Tom in clean flannel.

Calling to Rosie to bring blankets, she wrapped the patient head to foot, then tried to rub some life back into his hands and arms.

Finally Quint pulled her to him. “Come on, Holly Mavis has a bed ready for him upstairs. You’ve done enough.”

She breathed deeply, watching the men carry Jim Tom to the hotel. A tiredness swept over her such as she had never felt before, yet so much remained to be done

Before she let Mavis move her instruments, she made Quint remove his shirt and sit in a chair while she cleaned and dressed his shoulder.

“Satisfied?” he grinned, when she finished.

Upstairs she found Tom Farrell sitting on the bed holding his son’s hand.

“It isn’t over yet, Mr. Farrell,” she told him. “You’ll notice his shallow breathing. Even if he makes it through the next few days, the danger of infection is great. He may not live."

Tom Farrell gave Holly an abrupt look, and she continued. "I'll remain with him throughout the night."

He stared at her absently, still not speaking, turning his full attention to his restlessly sleeping son. After a while he crossed the room to a straight-backed chair, where he had a full view of the bed.

Holly started to tell him to leave, to go downstairs with Mavis who stood in the doorway, but she thought better of it, and she herself took a chair beside the bed.

Quint touched her shoulder. "Come let Rosie fix you something to eat."

She shook her head, and he left, speaking quietly to Mavis, then returned with two steaming cups of coffee, which he handed to Tom Farrell and Holly. "I've got things to tend to now," he told her. "I'll be back later."

She watched him look down at Jim Tom and purse his lips before leaving the room a second time.

Tom Farrell neither moved nor spoke, and Holly sat transfixed by Jim Tom's irregular breathing, her mind in a jumble.

Once Mavis rustled in with a shawl for Holly and whispered words for Tom. She seemed to be coaxing him to come away from the patient, but after hearing her out, he shook his head wordlessly, and she left the room.

Through the ensuing hours, the happenings of this day took on a timeless quality for Holly. She reviewed each moment, as though it had happened in ages past, her emotions dampened by sheer physical exhaustion.

All she could think of with any measure of clarity was this patient's life, and all the death she had witnessed—today, during the war—death which she had hoped to put behind her long since.

Death which she was forced still to face. Today she

had killed and almost been killed, witnessed and participated in murder and mayhem, and now she sat preoccupied with saving a life.

A life which, of all those involved in the day's events, deserved least to continue.

A life whose very existence had caused untold pain and suffering to the people she loved most.

A life, nevertheless, which by reason of being deserved to be saved.

The incongruity of sitting in the room with the man she had come to Silver Creek to find and see punished for Papa's murder, of watching with him as his son struggled for life, of playing an active part in that struggle herself . . . this incongruity faded.

As it had been easy for her to judge them as Tom Farrell and Jim Tom, she now found them as father and patient beyond her judgment, and, as during the war she had performed live-saving service to captured Yankee soldiers, so now she knew her only concern must be—was—to save the life of Jim Tom Farrell.

Whatever came afterward for him was up to the courts, and she would come forward with her evidence against them both in a court of law. Here, in this room, however, his life was sacred to her. And with that thought, her anger subsided.

She dozed off and on, and once upon waking, found Davy Westfield standing beside her chair, staring at her through the darkness.

When he saw her eyes open, his own lighted up, and he grasped her hand. "Sancho said they hurt you."

She hugged him to her, shaking her head. "I'm fine, Davy."

In his eager way he leaned forward and whispered in her ear. "Remember those men I told you about? The ones who said they'd eat my ears for supper?"

She nodded.

"The sheriff has 'em in jail, now."

She smiled. "I think I met up with them earlier today. Did one of them have a wounded leg?"

He nodded.

"I'm glad they're in jail," she told him. "They won't bother any of us again."

Quint returned near daybreak. She had gotten up to check Jim Tom's breathing and he stepped up beside her.

"How's he doing?"

She sighed, feeling a shiver of anticipation course her body at his rich, full voice. "It's still too early to tell. He's awfully restless. But that's normal."

Quint waited until she finished checking Jim Tom, then guided her into the hallway.

He leaned against the wall just outside the door and pulled her to him. She rested her head on his chest. "I brought you something," he whispered, handing her a packet of letters tied in pink watered silk.

She pulled back and gasped at the sight of Papa's letters. "Where . . . ?"

"In Tom's desk." He ran a coarse finger over the scratches on her face. "I rode out to the TF to see if we'd rounded up the lot of them, and caught Banker Norton going through the desk. He was all packed and ready to pull stakes, leaving behind everything he couldn't fit in his saddlebags."

Tears brimmed in her eyes as she clasped the letters to her bosom. Suddenly she was very, very tired.

Quint pushed her head back to his shoulder and kissed the top of her head. "Time for you to get some shut-eye. Mavis can take care of Jim Tom for a spell."

She nodded.

Still speaking into her hair, he continued. "I'm taking these fellers down to San Antone—all except Jim Tom. I've deputized Woody to take him over to the jail when he's well enough." Then he released her and motioned into the dimly lit room for Tom Farrell to come out.

"It's time to go, Tom."

Farrell glanced from Quint's face to Holly, then with a final look at Jim Tom, he headed down the stairs.

Quint studied her face. "I'll be back in a few days, Holly, so don't you be going off anywhere till then." He kissed her lips once, a solid, strong kiss that left her head spinning. "We've got some mighty hard talking to do when I get back."

The hall lamps were too dim for her to see the look in his eyes, but she knew it by heart now. Tears trickled down her cheeks when he squeezed her neck and turned toward the stairs.

Quint left with heavy steps, the light in the hallway too dim for him to see the tears in her eyes.

Chapter Twenty

When Quint rode back into Silver Creek two weeks later, red, white, and blue bunting adorned the Hotel O'Keefe, the Woodcock, and Herman Crump's Mercantile, and the town was abustle with people and commotion.

He headed for the livery stable, but drew up sharply when he saw Holly swinging on the porch of the hotel with Jed Varner's wife.

She had not seen him yet, and his heart stuck in his throat as he stared at her, seeing her as she had appeared through the stagecoach window so long ago. Her hair glistened like ebony in the early afternoon sun and her face was relaxed, alive, a deeper tan now than when she arrived in Silver Creek. As she slowly rocked back and forth, he recalled when they first rocked in that very swing, when they walked by the river, loved in . . .

The two weeks had passed slowly for Holly. At first she busied herself tending to Jim Tom and sorting out her own emotions. As her body caught up on its much needed rest, her mind began to put the events which had swept her to this point in her life into perspective.

And when at last she awoke on a clear summer

morning to familiar activity outside her bedroom window, she knew she was eager for Quint's return and ready for the hard talking he suggested they had in store.

For a week she and Mavis had argued over this Independence Day celebration.

"I cannot honor a country which attacked and destroyed my own," she insisted.

"Don't be foolish, Holly," Mavis had argued. "The war's over, and the Confederacy doesn't exist anymore. Besides, we're all Texans now, and this is as good an excuse as any for a party."

Ranchers and their families had begun arriving in Silver Creek last evening, and as the smell of roasting meat and the sounds of chattering men and women wafted through her bedroom window, Holly found herself anxious to join the visiting downstairs.

Jed and Anne Varner would be here, and Maggie Sperry sent word that the parson was on his way to town. If he came today, they could baptize little Miracle.

Dressing quickly, she dropped her blue plaid silk dress over her five petticoats and twirled in front of the looking glass. The festive costume with its trim of white floss fringe lifted her spirits even further, but when she smoothed the trim about her tiny waist, she breathed in a deep draught of loneliness. Oh, to have Quint home again!

The first person she saw downstairs was Soly Wiseman, rolling himself around on a contraption that Mr. Crump and Slim Samples put together for him. It had a wooden bed long and strong enough for him to sit on with his broken leg supported straight out, and four wheels which Soly could push to roll himself along. Mrs. Wiseman walked behind him, guiding his way.

"Mr. Wiseman," Holly greeted him. "I'm proud of you for staying off that leg."

He looked at her with an open, frank expression. "I'll tell you, Doc, it ain't been no picnic, but I've knowed a passel of men who lost their legs, and none of 'em lived over it. I figure if you got a different way, I'll sure enough give it a go."

Mrs. Wiseman smiled at Holly. "When do you reckon it'll be safe to try out the leg?"

"Very soon, I should think," Holly answered. "I'll talk to Mr. Crump about making some crutches."

Holly was engulfed then by the ranchers' wives, and after a while, Anne Varner drew her to the front porch, where they sat visiting about little Miracle's progress and the successful capture of the rustlers.

Mavis's voice interrupted their conversation. "Why, Sheriff, you look like a trail-worn doggie if ever I saw one."

Quint jerked around at the sound, blood warming his face.

"I told Holly you'd make it back for the Fourth of July festivities," Mavis continued, but Quint barely heard her. He stared at Holly as she turned toward him in surprise.

A smile lit her eyes, and she jumped up from the swing. "Welcome home."

He stepped down from the saddle awkwardly, cautioning himself not to trip over his own two feet. With deliberate motions, he hitched his horse at the rail and approached the steps. Her eyes spoke the sincerity of her welcome, but he hadn't forgotten her cold rejection of him—her insistence that they would have no life together.

Of course, he reminded himself, she had warmed to him just before he left town, but he was afraid that had more to do with the troubles she was having than with any change of heart on her part.

These last two weeks away from her had convinced him of one thing—Holly Campbell was his woman and he intended to make that clear to her.

Trouble was, he didn't quite know what to expect from her at this moment. It wasn't that he was afraid to play the game, he told himself. But he sort of dreaded throwing out the first card.

Quint removed his hat and ran a hand through his hair. "I'd plumb forgot about it being Independence Day," he said. "Reckon that explains all the company in town." He nodded to Anne Varner. "Ma'am."

"Come, Anne, darling." Mavis took Anne by the arm. "Shall we see if Aggie's finished with little Miracle's christening gown?" Her green eyes twinkled mischievously at Quint. "Word is the parson's headed this way."

Quint and Holly stood staring at each other as the two women left them alone on the porch. Quint shuffled his hat from one hand to the other and cleared his throat.

Holly found her voice first. Then suddenly they were both talking at once.

"Jim Tom has recovered," she told him, drinking in the thrill of seeing him again. "Woody has him over at the jail, and he's as ornery as ever. Elena won't even walk on that side of the street, and I wouldn't either, if I didn't have to. What will you do with him?"

He stood mesmerized by her loveliness. "He'll go to San Antone to stand trial with the others. The judge indicted them, and Sheriff Bales and I were mighty glad to get them locked behind bars."

"When will you take Jim Tom?" she asked, fearing he would leave town again too soon . . . ever . . .

He shrugged, then saw the stagecoach in the wagonyard. "I might send Woody down with him on the stage. It depends on who's . . ." Suddenly he stopped speaking, struck with the thought that this was the stagecoach Holly had been waiting for. His heart quickened in his chest, and his eyes searched hers. "Are you . . . ?"

She diverted her gaze, sensing his question. It was too soon, she thought. Too soon to talk about leaving and staying and . . . Quickly taking him by the arm, she steered him up the street. "Come, I want to show you what Jed Varner made."

As they climbed the hill to the cemetery, she told him about the happenings in Silver Creek during the past two weeks, ending with Sancho.

"Aggie has even let Davy go out to the canyon with him a few times. They're sure they've located the treasure, except . . ."

He laughed easily, covering her hand as it draped through the crook in his elbow with his other hand. "Except they don't actually have it in sight yet."

She laughed with him, shaking her head. "Not yet. But you should see Davy. What a difference having his friend back has made for him."

They stopped before her father's grave, and Holly pointed to the granite marker which was carved in the shape of a cross with the simple statistics of Doc Holly's life etched in bold Gothic letters.

"Jed did a mighty fine job," Quint said.

Standing at the summit, they looked out over the river and pastureland below.

Suddenly she took a deep breath, pursed her lips together, then blurted out. "Now it's done."

He glanced at her abruptly, alarmed at the words she spoke, at the tone of her voice. "What's done?"

She felt her chin tremble and quickly looked away. "Everything I came to Silver Creek to do," she answered. "I came to apprehend Papa's killers, and to put a marker on his grave." She studied the serene valley below them, a scene which had brought her a great deal of comfort lately, but which now lay in stark contrast to the upheaval inside her stomach.

Quint hesitated, then draped an arm almost casually across her shoulders. He tried to calm the uneasiness building inside him, to restrain the frantic urge he felt to smother her in his arms and *tell* her how their life was going to be from here on out. He wanted to give her a chance to say it first, to hear it from her. He wanted her to want it as badly as he did. "What'd you figure on doing now?"

After a long while, she answered. "Mavis wants me to petition Tulane University in New Orleans for admission to their medical school."

His thoughts . . . and fears . . . spun to a stop. "Mavis wants what?"

She laughed then, an amused challenge to his reaction.

"I mean, you'd make a fine doctor, no doubt about it, but . . ."

She turned back to the river, serious again. "I know enough about a doctor's life to know for sure that it isn't for me, even if they would let me in. Besides, I'm not a trail blazer." She thought a moment. "Not in that sense, anyway."

With his hands on her shoulders, he turned her to face him and looked long into the depths of her velvet eyes—his thirsty soul drinking in her beauty, her freshness, thinking that this was only one of the reasons he loved her so much, that he could not lose her. She was forever fresh and exciting and often made no sense to him at all.

"You told me how Davy looks," he said, his voice low and rich and a bit tremulous, "but . . . what about me?"

Her body quaked at the need she heard in his voice and saw in his golden eyes. "Why, Quint," she answered, surprised at such a question, "you look wonderful."

"Because I have my friend back, too," he said. "You would see a terrible difference if I lost you."

They came together then, fiercely, their bodies, their arms, their lips . . . expressing physically in heated flesh their innermost fears . . . longings . . . love.

Finally he held her at arm's length, knowing he had to speak honestly with her. "Things haven't changed, Holly. You must know that. I'm going to keep this job as long as they'll have me, and sometimes things will crop up that I can't tell you. That's part of the job; it won't ever change."

She smiled. "I've changed, though. I understand your job now, and I accept it." She grinned at him. "I'm not saying that it won't make me mad on occasion, but . . . but I won't stop trusting you, or being proud of what you do."

He kissed her again, and when they turned to go, she looked down at her father's grave. "Papa's buried now, Quint. You don't have to try to be like him . . . or to make up for anything he did."

Later, as they returned to town hand in hand, she told him, "I didn't tell you the whole truth back there. There was another reason I came to Silver Creek."

He frowned.

"I came to find you."

"Me?" he asked with raised eyebrows.

She laughed. "That first day when I arrived on the stagecoach," she said. "When I saw you through the window with that silly hat, I knew you were all I ever wanted in my whole life."

He stopped in the middle of the road and kissed her with a commanding, promising kiss. "I knew then, too," he said, then kissed each of her eyelids softly. "But we sure had some trying times in between."

A rider approached from behind, and they stepped off the road to let him pass. Quint tipped his hat. "Howdy, Parson. Fine day for a christening, wouldn't you say?" He looked down at Holly and winked. "And maybe a wedding?"

Holly gasped and held her breath practically all the way down the hill. It wasn't what she had expected, yet out here months passed between the parson's visits.

The next few hours passed in a whirlwind of activity which, even later when she looked back on this day, left Holly breathless.

As soon as they returned to the hotel, Mavis took over, shooing Quint away and ushering Holly through the crowd which was gathering for the Fourth of July festivities and straight upstairs to her room.

In a stupor brought on by suddenly finding herself in the middle of her own wedding day, Holly had followed Mavis on numb limbs. But once inside her room, her heart rate quickly accelerated at the sight of the glorious white dress which hung like a shimmering cloud beside her dressing table.

"It was my wedding dress, darling," Mavis said, "but Aggie has restyled it for you."

While Holly stared at the dress transfixed, recalling Caroline's slashed wedding dress and the veil that had become little Miracle's christening gown, Mavis bustled around, mumbled something about more preparations to attend to, and left the room, saying, "Aggie will come in to help you dress, Holly. Now don't be long."

At Mavis's familiar commands, Holly snapped out of her trance, and excitement and anticipation began to pound through her veins. She was marrying Quint today! Truly, she was! And Mavis, like an honest-togoodness fairy godmother, had seen to all her earthly desires.

Quickly discarding her blue dress, she sponged off in the delicately scented rose water she found in her basin, and slipped into Mavis's petticoats, unable to take her eyes off the heavenly dress she would wear to marry her prince.

The skirt was of white silk faille, embroidered with white silk thread in an intricate paisley pattern. Seven ruffles of the same material trimmed each side of the skirt, descending from waist to hem. Each ruffle was edged on top with embroidered ribbon and at the bottom with scallops of real Valenciennes lace. Two broad ribbons extended from beneath the ruffles at the side and tied across the back of the skirt, forming an elaborate puff above and an extended train of embroidered faille below.

After adjusting her bustle and the skirt over the ruffled petticoats, she picked up the Pompadour basque which fit just above the skirt's pouff in the back, but fell to peplum length in front. The bottom of the basque, the flowing embroidered sleeves, and the square neckline were all edged in dripping ruffles of the pure white lace.

Just as she finished buttoning the last of the tiny pearl buttons, Aggie arrived to help pin her hair in black ringlets to the crown of her head.

Oohing and aahing, Aggie stood back from the looking glass and handed Holly a delicate wreath of waxed orange blossoms, onto which had been gathered yards and yards of the sheerest blond veiling.

The wreath shook in her hands, and she realized with horror that a sure case of the jitters was taking hold of her. Willing her body to relax, she attached the wreath to her crown of curls with its strong ivory comb, telling herself all the while to enjoy every precious moment of this most happy day.

Satisfied at last with her radiant image in the looking glass, she twisted around to straighten the train, and a knock came at the door.

Aggie opened it to Quint, then quickly tried to send him away. "Don't you know it's bad luck to see your bride before the ceremony?" she fussed.

Quint caught his breath at the sight of Holly's beauty, and when she looked at him with smiling eyes, he suddenly felt intimidated by such loveliness. Never had he imagined himself with a woman like this—walking through throngs of people with her on his arm—pledging his love, and she hers, before God and man. Damn, if he wasn't one lucky man! Swallowing the lump in his throat, he held out his hand, silently beckoning her to him.

In her addled state, she didn't recognize him for an instant after Aggie opened the door. She'd never seen him dressed in anything but denims, and here he stood tall and handsome in a black broadcloth suit with white shirt and all the trimmings.

Aggie's words registered then, and she hesitated, but Quint spoke without taking his glittering eyes from her face. "Don't you believe it, Aggie. Holly and I make our own luck, and from here on out, it's uphill all the way."

Holly smiled at that, a glowing smile that set his heart on fire, and somehow together they maneuvered her skirts and train through the doorway, where his hand in hers sent shivers up her very gussied-up spine. His grasp was firm, and by the time they reached the parlor, her jitters began to calm.

Entering the empty parlor, she turned to him with curiosity. "Where is everyone?"

He bowed formally. "Your wedding, ma'am, will be under the trees by the river." Then he winked at her.

"But first, I want you alone." With that he led her in all her finery straight to the swing on the front porch, where he helped her arrange her skirts so she could sit beside him.

With gentle hands, he lifted her face to his and looked deep into her eyes. "I've wanted to do this since that first night in this swing when we were so rudely interrupted," he said quietly, claiming her lips with such tender passion that her senses spun. She responded with eager desire.

Then suddenly he pulled back and drew a small box from his pocket, handing it to her.

"For my bride," he said, grinning. "I got it in San Antone, along with this dandified suit."

She felt all thumbs as she fumbled to open the unexpected gift, and when at last the box fell open, she gasped in delight at the gleaming golden heart-shaped locket that lay on a bed of blue velvet.

Holding it up to better see the delicate etching, she snapped it open and found the place for a photograph empty, but across from it, inscribed in fine script, were the words, "Sweet Holly."

Tears sprung to her eyes. She blinked furiously to hold them back, whispering, "It's beautiful," while he took the locket from her hands and fastened it around her creamy white neck, his touch sending shivers along her senses once again.

"Hold your horses a minute," he told her. "I'll be right back." Leaving her alone in the swing, he soon returned followed by a man laden with a tripod and camera, and as Holly and Quint sat in the swing, talking, smiling, almost relaxed, the itinerate photographer took their wedding portrait, here in the swing where they had first sat not so very long ago, she thought. Not so very long ago.

"Now we'll have a special photograph of our own,"

he told her, and she knew how important that was to him.

Barely had the photographer completed his work, when Mavis appeared and bustled them around back, where an altar had been set up by the river. The parson waited in front of it. Fifty or so people of all ages sat on benches placed so that a grassy aisle cut between them.

At their approach, Monk tuned up his fiddle and began a halfway decent rendition of "Here Comes the Bride," and the crowd turned to greet them with more oohs and aahs.

Holly suddenly stopped short. "I forgot to ask someone to give me away!"

Tightening her arm in the crook of his elbow, he looked at her solemnly. "You're your own woman, Holly. You give yourself to me . . . and I give myself to you."

She stared at him then, thinking how fortunate she was to have found such an extraordinary man . . . such an understanding man. And he loved her . . . she knew he did. Even if he never said the words, she would always know.

She straightened her shoulders, and with two broad smiles, they began their untraditional walk down the aisle, at the end of which they pledged the traditional vows of the ancient church—he to worship her, she to obey him—and when the parson blessed their union and they sealed it with a passionate kiss, the congregation applauded and cheered in a quite untraditional manner.

Afterward they sat straight-backed on the wooden benches for an hour or more of preaching, before the parson called them to the river where he baptized Holly's Miracle, signing her with the sign of the cross on her forehead. Then, at the parson's instructions Holly carried the baby through the gathering, symbol ically introducing her goddaughter to the congregation, again in a most traditional way.

But from the crowd good-natured and slightly ribald comments reached her—comments like "We'll be abaptizing your babe next year," and "After tonight you'll need to come again, Parson," causing Holly's ears to burn and her face to flame.

Next came the barbecue and dancing, and toward the end of the evening, Mavis produced champagne—from only heaven and Mavis knew where—and they toasted the bride and groom.

Finally, after Monk played "Home Sweet Home," the crowd gathered around the newlyweds, and Mavis called for silence.

"The infare dinner will be held here at the hotel beginning at noon tomorrow. Now let's usher the bride and groom to their chamber."

Apprehension raced through Holly's brain. She'd had hardly any time to speculate on the sleeping arrangements. Now, looking to Quint for help, his satisfied grin told her that everyone must know but her.

Suddenly she felt herself hoisted on high, and both she and Quint were then being carried from the parlor into the street on the shoulders of the crowd.

Beneath them the crowd laughed and sang to the accompaniment of Monk, who followed behind. They carried the pair across the street, and Quint's eyes met hers in merriment. She knew he wouldn't go along with anything that would truly embarrass her, so she nervously joined in the laughter.

At the jailhouse door, Quint's voice rose above the din. "Your trail ends here, boys. Set us down." He winked at Holly. "The rest is private."

Her face burned so hot she was sure she glowed like a lantern on a dark night. Inside, however, her emotions were a jumble of embarrassment and anticipation and longing.

The crowd grumbled, but set them down to the tune of an off-colored ditty about a man's first sexual encounter. As soon as her feet touched the boardwalk, Quint gathered her up in his arms.

Turning to the crowd, he said firmly. "Good night, fellers. See you tomorrow . . . late."

Laughter erupted and Quint quickly carried her inside, through the office, past the cells, and to the back, where he kicked open the door to his room and carried her over the threshold.

Suddenly her eyes were filled with glistening candlelight, her senses with the sweet fragrance of roses. Everywhere she looked she saw clouds of white and gleaming brass and candles, candles, candles.

The walls were draped from ceiling to floor with sheer white muslin, pale rugs adorned the floor, and a white hinged screen stood across one corner for dressing. The only color in the room came from the gleaming brass bedstead. On a white marble table beside the bed, she saw a white porcelain lamp, its glistening light shining through roses etched on its shade. And in every corner, on every flat surface, flickering candles burned gaily, turning the small room into a sensuous wonderland.

Quint set her on her feet slowly, pleased with Mavis's handiwork. Holly crossed the room as in a glorious trance. Removing the ivory comb from her hair, she hooked the orange blossom wreath and trailing veil over one of the brass spindles on the bed. Then, her senses spinning, she fluffed the thick white counterpane and lace-edged pillows and looked to Quint quizzically.

He let a slow whistle escape through a mischievous grin. "Ol' Mavis sure came through this time."

Suddenly recalling his oft-repeated desire to have a

perfect place for their lovemaking, Holly gasped. He wouldn't have . . . she thought. He just wouldn't have. "What did you tell her?"

His glittering eyes narrowed to a twinkle. "What did I tell her?" He stepped toward her. "Only that I wanted a fancier . . ."

Her eyes flared wider, as embarrassment heated the roots of her hair. "Not about the other times . . . ?"

He reached down and clasped her face in his hands. "About the wanton woman I took for a bride?" he teased. "About the other times the naughty Holly Campbell gave herself so shamelessly in any old shack that was available?"

She laughed, knowing he was teasing. "You didn't, Quint?" she pleaded. "Say you didn't."

Still his eyes glistened as they bore into her soul. His hands dropped to her shoulders, and he pushed her back to the soft feather bed, then fell on top of her. "You know Mavis," he whispered, their lips almost touching. "I didn't have to tell her a thing."

Their lips met in a deep, passionate kiss and her arms circled his neck eagerly; her fingers played through his hair and massaged his back through his broadcloth jacket.

He kissed her hungrily, his body reminding him how long he had been without her, his mind telling him that by some unheard-of stroke of good fortune, he would never be without her again.

Drawing back, he gazed longingly into her deep brown eyes. "We don't have to hurry anymore, sweet Holly. Now we have forever."

Lazily she traced the outline of his lips with the tip of her tongue while the candles flickered in celebration around them. "Then we can get out of these dastardly clothes and do it properly," she said laughing.

"You're damned right," he answered, surprised and

very pleased at her response.

But when he reached for the buttons on her dress, she pushed his hands away. "You stay here," she commanded, rising and crossing to the screen. "We'll see what other surprises Mavis has in store for us."

While she curiously examined the lacy garments she found draped over the dressing screen, he discarded his jacket and opened the bottle of champagne that stood cooling in a brass bucket filled with spring water.

"I talked to Jed Varner today," he called over the screen. "He's going to get started on our house as soon as he finishes his. He would've started ours first, but I told him you would want some time to get your plans together."

She almost squealed with delight as she struggled to get out of the cumbersome garments. "Then we can start out living at the cabin?"

"I'm afraid we'll have to," he told her apologetically, pouring the fizzing amber liquid into two crystal goblets he found on the tray with the champagne.

"Oh, I want to live there, for a while at least." She giggled. "But I never imagined spending my wedding night in jail!" Then, as she dressed, she suddenly shivered at the thought of who their houseguest was. "Where's . . . Jim Tom?" she asked, chilled at the idea of undressing in the same building with that demon, even with Quint here beside her.

"Woody took him over to our first jail," he called to her, settling himself back with his glass of champagne.

"Where's that?" She couldn't recall seeing another building in town that resembled a jail.

"Out behind Mavis's smokehouse. Before we built this jail, we used to handcuff prisoners to that skinny pecan tree behind the smokehouse. That's where Jim Tom is tonight. Safely out of our house . . . and out of our minds."

She emerged shyly from behind the screen then, and he handed her a stemmed goblet of the bubbling liquid, almost spilling it as he stared unabashedly at the flimsy garment cascading over her slim frame.

Holly blushed at his reaction, and every nerve ending in her body tingled with anticipation. Delightedly, she twirled in front of him in the gown which was made of something closely resembling the sheer material of her bridal veil. Lace ruffles formed the straps and draped in a sensuous spiral down the length of the gown, covering only the most strategic spots, and those only sparsely. "Where in the world do you suppose Mavis found such a costume?" she asked. Then, coloring deeper, she said, "Surely Aggie didn't make it."

Feeling his need for her grow stronger by the minute, Quint took the glass from her hand and set it on the marble-topped table. Then with the gentlest of motions, he slipped the ruffled straps from her shoulders and watched the filmy garment drift to a rumpled heap around her delicate ankles. "From a whorehouse, I reckon," he said with a husky voice. "We have no need for such things. You would set my soul on fire clothed from head to toe in a washerwoman's getup." Seized then by how very much he loved her, he crushed her body to him with an almost painful force, assuring himself that tonight was not some scene from a dime novel. Holly had really married him today. She was his now . . . to love forever.

Picking her up in his arms, he carried her to the bed, where he deposited her admist the flurry of pillows, and all the time he undressed himself, he never took his eyes from her face.

Holly watched Quint undress in the golden candlelight thinking of that night in the cabin when they loved in the glow of the single lantern. By contrast, tonight was like being inside a mansion full of crystal chandeliers, for light danced from every corner, from every conceivable surface, filling the room with undulating brilliance.

When he joined her on the bed, it was to lie close beside her, arms entwined, bodies lightly touching, each becoming more aroused, more impassioned, simply by the nearness of the other.

"I can still hardly believe it's true," she said softly, nipping at his nose with her teeth, gently kissing his eyelids.

He tightened his grip around her. "I'm going to make you happy, sweet Holly. I promise you that."

The intensity in his voice sent a shiver up her back, and she arched toward him, raising her lips to his fevered kisses. Suddenly their bodies joined, rolled, and tumbled in the soft, yielding bed of feathers. This was what they had each longed for all day, Holly thought, and after all the activities and ceremonies, after coming together quietly, they found themselves once again entangled in the fierceness of their passion.

It was like coming home, she thought, her senses reeling with his kisses, his lips, his tongue, his roaming hands that moved so tantalizingly over her yearning body.

Leaving her lips, his tongue tasted her chin, traced her jawline, lingered on the throbbing pulse at the base of her neck, then hungrily suckled at first one swollen breast, then the other. Calming his racing heart, he slowed his motions, until his tongue lazily circled a small, taut nipple, setting her whole body on fire with frantic desire for what she knew would come.

Replacing his lips with a caressing hand, Quint raised his passion-glazed eyes to her soft, velvet ones. "Sweet, sweet Holly. I was wrong. I thought we would slow down."

"No, Quint," she whispered. "You were right.

Remember? You said it would get better and better?"

His senses shattered at the softness of her voice, the sweetness of her words, and his lips once again lavished her body with kisses, this time following his hand as it traveled her curves and recesses, leaving a trail of flaming wetness from her breasts down her midriff, circling her navel, coming at last to the soft protective curls, then the smooth inside of her thighs.

The path left by Quint's loving tongue suddenly flared like a trail of lighted kerosene as he teased her sensitive flesh. Spurred on by the conflagration raging within her, she raised her hips to meet him, her hands finding his head, pulling him nearer with fevered ecstasy.

At her frenzied response to his lovemaking, Quint felt his enflamed body quicken with impending release, and when Holly's body quivered with the same emotion, he lifted his head and retraced his path to her aching nipples. His hands found her tousled tresses, and he caressed her head in rhythm to his suckling at her heaving breasts.

Then suddenly her hands moved between them, guiding him into her silken flesh, and their eyes met at the moment of their joining.

Gazing desperately into the depths of velvet eyes that were so full of wonder and desire, Quint was gripped by such an overwhelming urgency that he cried out. "I love you, Holly Campbell Jarvis.. God, how I love you!"

At his words, words she had given up hope of ever hearing, Holly clenched her eyes tightly closed, fearing the sweetness of this moment might escape. Then she opened her eyes to his passion-racked golden gaze and whispered softly. "Say it again. Please, Quint."

He began to move within her slowly, meeting her undulating hips with increasingly wild thrusts. "What?"

he murmured into her mass of hair.

"All of it," she breathed in rhythm with his fiery assault. "My new name . . . and the rest."

His breathing ragged with the heightening force of their lovemaking, he rasped. "Holly . . . Louise . . . Campbell . . . Jarvis. I love you . . . I love you . . . I love you . . ."

At that moment she shuddered convulsively in his arms, and a second later, he joined her in a violent, sweet release. Afterward, through a haze of dizziness, he felt her arms tighten around him fiercely.

"And I love you, Quintan Jarvis. My husband. My husband. I love you."

Later, recovered, but still lingering in a languid bliss, Quint stroked the love-dampened tendrils of black curls away from her face and gazed lovingly into her eyes. "Do you know what's the best part?" he asked.

"What?" she questioned softly, mesmerized by the golden light playing in the fine hairs of his mustache.

"That this is just the beginning," he whispered.

"Mmmm," she sighed. The fragrance of roses filled her senses, bringing contentment and joy and thoughts of long ago, of a lady Papa had called Tomorrow . . . and the promise she held. "So many wonderful tomorrows," she murmured.